SUMMER VISITORS

Susan Sallis

severn
House

This first hardcover edition published in Great Britain 2002 by
SEVERN HOUSE PUBLISHERS LTD of
9–15 High Street, Sutton, Surrey SM1 1DF.
Originally published 1988 in paperback format only
by Corgi Books.
This title first published in the USA 2003 by
SEVERN HOUSE PUBLISHERS INC of
595 Madison Avenue, New York, N.Y. 10022.

British Library Cataloguing in Publication Data

Sallis,   Susan
    Summer visitors
    1.   Mothers and daughters - Fiction
    2.   Cornwall (England) - Social life and customs - 20th century - Fiction
    I.   Title
    823.9'14 [F]

    ISBN 0-7278-5904-8

Printed and bound in Great Britain by
MPG Books Ltd., Bodmin, Cornwall.

TO
MY FAMILY

CHAPTER ONE

1964

Madge had never imagined St Ives could be so cold. Of course it was January, and they'd never been down later than October, but sometimes even in the summer the wind and rain had been such that they'd yelled into it: 'Like November, isn't it?'

But at its worst it had been exhilarating, never depressing. Once, just before war was declared, when she was expecting Rosemary, the skies above Clodgy had split open in a spectacular thunderstorm that had been intoxicating in its Wagnerian magnificence. Madge recalled standing on Old Man's Head, mouth open, trying to drink the rain, and shrieking, 'It's warm! It's lovely, warm, sky-water!' And they had laughed together because water at St Ives, whether it were sea or rain, had a special unifying effect on them.

Now, twenty-five years later, she did not smile at that particular recollection. Her grimace – or so she told herself – was in response to the biting wind that shrivelled – not exhilarated – and scoured the tiny cobbled streets and sandblasted the granite cottages. No wonder St Ives looked so clean if all winter long it was subjected to this brand of sterilisation. Suddenly St Ives itself felt very old. And so did she.

She turned from Rose's window and went to the one-bar electric fire in the immaculate hearth. She could not remember feeling so cold. Even in the war when there had been no coal to speak of, she'd kept warm by working or piling on clothes. Now, dressed in her respectable camel coat, there was no room beneath for more than a twin-set and silk scarf. She looked at the borrowed black hat waiting for her on the corner of the dining table. She wore scarves or knitted caps at home during the winter. That hat was going to offer no protection at all.

Rose came in from the kitchen across the hall and caught her expression of misery before she could wipe it off with a smile. Rose did not feel the cold any more than she felt the heat. Her nature, physical and mental, was not so much hard as completely resilient.

'Have they opened up yet?' she asked. She went to the window which afforded a perfect view of the chapel. She answered her own question. 'No. Well, they'll hang on to the last minute this weather I suppose.' She had no time for funerals and Etta Nolla – even Philip – had been shocked that she did not attend her husband's. But she never missed watching one from her front room window, just to see who was there and what they were wearing.

She glanced over her shoulder at Madge and gave her the same open smile she'd given her forty years ago.

'So. You've come all this way for old Philip Nolla's send-off. Seems daft to me. But you've got some guts, I'll give you that.'

Madge raised her brows, surprised. Guts had not been needed, though resolution had. To come to Cornwall in January on her own entailed making complicated domestic arrangements, and organising her own travel arrangements too. But there had never been any doubt in her mind that she would come.

She spread her hands to the pale glow in the hearth and said, 'I had to come. I've known Philip and Etta all my life.'

There was a funny little pause, then Rose coughed and said, 'Yes. Well . . .' and rubbed at an imagined smear on the pristine window. 'I really meant coming here to stop. To me. Folks who knew me when I was Rose Care, still don't have nothing to do with me now I'm Rose Foster!'

'Oh, Rose.' Madge could still feel embarrassed by Rose's determined frankness. 'Where else would I go?'

'There's plenty of room in the town at this time of year, young Madge. And what will Etta Nolla say when she knows you're here?'

They both knew that Etta's comments would probably be condemning, but Madge said quickly, 'I should think she'd be pleased. Philip always spoke very highly of you.'

'Aye. He would.' Rose rested her hands on the sash and stared through the window. 'He would that. He was a good man. And there's going to be a good turn-out for him, too.'

Madge stood up and turned her back to the fire, hoping that some of its feeble heat might find its way inside her coat and struggle past skirt and petticoat to where there was a gap between stocking-tops and knickers. She looked at the ramrod back at the window and remembered the young woman Rose had been; supple and carelessly beautiful. The town's scarlet woman.

Madge said carefully, 'I wish you'd come. Philip told me how well you looked after Martin Foster when he was dying. And I could see – that day you introduced us – that you made him very happy.'

Rose turned and smiled and for a moment was the old Rose Care, thumbing her nose at her world.

'I expect Philip told you too that I didn't go to Martin's funeral. My own 'usband.' She laughed. 'They all wanted me to go so they could cold-shoulder me. But when I didn't . . . oh my dear Lord, you should 'a seen the faces that day when they went into the chapel!'

'You watched? From the window?'

'Aye, I watched.' She turned back. 'Like now. I'm an outsider, Madge. Always 'ave been. An' certainly where Martin was concerned . . . dear Lord, I was married to him just over a twelve-month. He married me to look after him when he was dying. And I did that. And this house is his, thanks to me. I'm a lot of things, Madge, but I'm no hypocrite.'

There was a long silence while both women thought about times they had shared and could not talk about.

Then Rose said, 'Here they come. Nearly time.'

9

Madge joined her at the window. Two men were unlocking the chapel doors and latching them back with great difficulty. The wind ballooned their sober overcoats and they held their hats beneath their arms.

Madge murmured, 'Poor Etta.'

'She'll enjoy it,' Rose assured her hardily. 'She's Cornish from the year dot and they all enjoy a good funeral.'

Madge was silent. Rose had called herself an outsider. That was certainly what Madge was. A summer visitor, like the swallows. Not used to this scouring wind and freezing cold. Would Etta resent her presence?

Rose darted her a look, then almost as if she'd picked up Madge's thought, she said, 'Philip Nolla will be glad you've come, at any rate. And looking so nice too. That hat . . . and the coat. The sort of thing they wear at Mennion House. County. You've done him proud.'

Madge swallowed sudden tears and both women stared out of the window stolidly, waiting for the embarrassment to pass.

People began to arrive. The Trevorrows in identical black overcoats, she with a veiled hat, he with a bowler. They tried to enter the chapel with dignity and were routed by the wind turning them inside-out.

'Black boots *and* stockings,' Rose commented. Then, as the bowler was only just saved, 'Such a mortal pity men can't use hat-pins.'

She was rewarded by a laugh from Madge. She turned briskly. 'Well. If you're going, I reckon it's time to go.' She surveyed Madge critically. 'Bring the hat forward a bit so that your bun is outside. That's better. Funny, there's a bit of you that hasn't aged at all. I can still see you with that long plait hanging down your back. And now you're knocking on fifty.'

I'm forty-five,' Madge protested humorously because she could have wept at Rose's words.

'Aye. I can give you a few years. Fifty-two next birthday. Ah well.' She went ahead and opened the front door just wide enough for Madge to slip through. 'Don't you take no notice if they're funny with you," she said into the wind. 'Come straight back 'ere and we'll 'ave a cup of tea or something stronger!'

Madge held her hat and turned to smile up into those bold black eyes that hadn't changed in forty years. Strange, this feeling she had that Rose had always been there in her background. Yet she'd never seen her more than half a dozen times in all those years.

She went down Bunkers Hill bent almost double into the wind. Her own personal grief for Philip was just below the surface of her thoughts and was very deep; she dared not try to imagine how Etta must be feeling. Deep emotion always had made Etta tetchy; if she was short with Madge today, if that strange all-seeing stare was cold, then Madge must understand. Whether anyone minded or not, she'd had to come. She represented so many people whose lives had touched Philip's briefly and had been changed by the contact. She had to forget herself. She had to be . . . thankful.

The chapel was packed, literally to the ceiling. The gallery was tiered so that the congregation in the back row had to wear flat hats to fit beneath the planked roof. Those in front hooked umbrellas over the balustrade and arranged veils and skirts. Madge wished she'd gone upstairs where her camel coat wouldn't have stood out quite so much. Thank God Rosemary had lent her the black hat. She had refused it at first. 'I'll wear my brown felt. It's warmer and just as suitable.' But Mark, who understood the Cornish like a native, had said, 'Don't be daft, Ro. Mum can't go to Philip's funeral in a brown felt hat.' And Rosemary had gone upstairs to fetch the hat she had bought for herself only five years before.

How right Mark had been. And, in spite of Rose's approval, what an idiot she had been not to borrow a black coat from somewhere too. Camel might be respectable but it was a glaring contrast to the all-pervading black. She tried to sit lower in her seat, caught Mrs Trevorrow's eye and was treated to a strange kind of smile. Pitying? Surely the

11

Trevorrows could have no idea what Philip's death meant to her? However, any kind of smile was better than the frozen stare she was getting from everyone else, and she returned it warmly. Immediately, like a light, it was switched off. Madge shrank into herself. So Rose was right; they were going to be 'funny' with her. Philip was a local hero and they were jealous of him, possessive, resentful of 'outsiders' like herself who might try to claim something of his memory. Yet she and all her family had been closer to Philip and Etta Nolla than anyone else. It was an acknowledged fact. They might be just summer visitors, but they'd been the Nollas' only visitors and there had always been a special bond between them. And she, Madge, was representing all of them. She mustn't forget that. And she mustn't forget what else Rose had said: Philip would be pleased to see her, camel coat or no camel coat. He'd glint up at her and say slyly, 'Fancy up-country 'at for fancy up-country woman!'

She straightened her back and smiled as she conjured up a picture of him. If he were sitting by her side now he'd reach to her shoulder and she'd catch his expressions in fleeting glimpses when he chose to lift his head and show her what he was thinking. He did not do that with anyone else; she'd realised that a long time ago. He was a very closed-in man. But he had opened for her. He teased her and let her know that she was special.

Someone stopped by her side and looked at the empty pew next to hers. It was Jim Maddern. It was years since they'd exchanged a word, but she knew him. He had been on the periphery of their group when they were children; a link between them and Rose Care. Now his dark eyes met hers without recognition and he walked on to the front pews reserved for the close mourners, though he had little to do with the Nollas. She felt a flush break through the crust of cold over her face. She had been deliberately cut and by Jim Maddern of all people! This was what Rose had meant. As soon as the service was over she'd get back to the safety of Bunkers

Hill and wait till this evening for a quiet word with Etta.

Then the harmonium squeaked to a stop and everyone began to stand up. The wind gusted into the chapel and the minister's voice began. 'I am the resurrection and the life saith the Lord. Those who believe . . .' Madge dropped her chin and held her breath. She no longer thought of Philip alone; the words dealt with the whole of humanity, the quick as well as the dead. As the procession came slowly up the aisle it was as if she could see them all . . . more than a dozen of them, all caught and held in Philip's net.

The coffin went past her. Cheap elm because Etta would have no money to spare. The lifeboat crew bore it on their shoulders. Then came Etta who was older than her husband, so must be nearly eighty. She was walking alone and leaning hard on her stick. Surely there was someone to walk with her, childless though she was?

She drew level with Madge and stopped. The mourners following, neighbours mostly, shuffled to a halt and exchanged glances. Etta lifted her stick and tapped Madge sharply on the arm. Alarmed, Madge looked up and saw that familiar, toothless grin.

'I thought as 'ow you'd come,' she said in a voice audible above the minister's incantations. 'I saved you your place.' And she transferred her stick to her other hand and held out her arm for Madge. As in a dream Madge stepped sideways out of the pew and took the arm. Etta gave a grunt of relief and surrendered her weight to Madge. Together they walked up the aisle and took their places in the front row, and watched in silence as Philip's unwanted physical body was lowered gently on to the coffin rests in front of the minister. There was Etta's wreath in the obligatory shape of an anchor, lying the length of the wood; and above it, as if holding it in place, was a circlet of Christmas roses which Madge had chosen on her arrival yesterday when she had walked down Tregenna Hill from the station.

The last time she'd seen him was five months ago; last

13

summer. She should have known then. Perhaps she had known and not been able to face it.

She'd been sitting with her back to the harbour wall, dreaming. The tide was coming in and Maddern's pony and trap waited patiently on the shore for the first of the boats to bring in its catch. Madge wondered idly about mackerel for tea. Etta would pickle them in vinegar and they could have salad, and a mountain of bread and butter. Then, if the weather held, they could drive to Marazion and watch the sun go down behind St Michael's Mount. It was so hot. So gloriously hot. She closed her eyes against the healing sun and could still see the white sand and the glass-green of the sea; but not exactly where the sea became translucent blue and merged with the sky.

She opened her eyes to check on this, and there was Philip signalling to her from the Fisherman's Lodge. She moved, getting to her feet with some difficulty, gathering up handbag and book and shuffling through the sand barefoot to meet him. He opened the gate for her. Strangers were not allowed in the Lodge but she had gone there with Philip as a small girl and was reluctantly accepted.

They sat outside, backs to the wooden shack with its leaning chimney, the milling crowds shut away behind them. They could still see Maddern's pony and trap waiting patiently by the glinting sea.

'Here they come,' Philip said quietly. And around Smeaton's Pier came the first of the diminished fishing fleet, a big tub-like boat, broad in beam with a wide stern, like a child's toy boat bobbing down a bath of water.

'Good catch by the looks of 'en.'

The boat was wallowing under its load of fish. It berthed alongside Smeaton's Pier with much shouting and leaping about from its crew. A boat put off from the harbour beach and the business of unloading began. Madge was reminded of an oil painting by Sargent in one of the galleries. Painted over a hundred years ago, it bridged time to the present.

Philip said, 'Broodin' over young Mark, are you, woman?'

'No. Thinking of time. Some things never change.' She

14

smiled down on the ancient trilby. 'I don't think of Mark all the time, Philip.'

'But most of it, I reckon.'

She was silent, remembering the heartache for Rosemary not long ago.

His hand came out and rested for an instant on the skirt of her sun dress. It was gnarled as the twisted ropes tethering the boats to the shore. Then he leaned forward, elbows on knees, fingers hanging loosely. 'I think o' young Mark as my own son. You know that, dun't you?'

She swallowed. There were things between them that were never said.

He did not wait for a reply. 'You dun't need to worry about 'im, woman. Like I said . . . my own son.'

He did not look up and she stared down at the crinkled neck above the blue kerchief, realising how much of her anxiety for Mark Philip had carried over the years.

She cleared her throat. 'I wish there was some way I could tell you how grateful . . . you've always been *there* . . .'

'The shoe is on the other foot, woman. Entirely.'

But he did not look up to reassure her and she felt a pang of concern.

She said, 'Are you all right, Philip?'

At last he flicked her one of his quick smiles.

'Course I'm all right, little woman. Etta and me, we've allus been all right.' He looked at the sea again. Jim was bucketing fish into his cart. Mackerel, silver and blue and fluid as mercury. 'Our needs are small, d'you see. Our bodies thrive on sameness. Fish and tea.'

It wasn't what she had meant but she was glad that the conversation was back to everyday things. 'You should have fruit and vegetables, Philip.'

He laughed with genuine amusement. 'Woman . . . woman. We're both nearly eighty years old. Whatever we've ett, whatever we've done . . . must be right, mustn't it?'

She laughed too, ruefully. Neither of them wore glasses, neither of them had ever been to a hospital; they were bent with rheumatism, but they still walked the beaches daily.

15

Their silence was companionable from then on. They watched people gather around Jim's cart to buy the mackerel; he pocketed the money eagerly. His father still paid him pre-war wages for his part in the fishing business. Another boat came around the jut of Smeaton's Pier and the whole business of berthing began again. The heat soaked into them like balm and Madge closed her eyes, reliving the total security of childhood when there had always been someone else to plan tomorrow.

The cemetery, clinging to the cliff above Porthmeor beach, was a nightmare of freezing wind, but it was exactly the place Philip would have chosen; within sight of the sea but far above its clawing fingers. Madge supported Etta at the graveside, unable to slip away, physically held by those black-gloved fingers.

Afterwards they gathered in the house: the Trevorrows; the Gurnards and the Madderns; old Mrs Peters and Miss Lowe who delivered pamphlets and tracts. Mrs Fosdick from next door had pushed chairs in anywhere, and they sat back to back, cheek by jowl, while cups of hot sweet tea were passed over their heads and potted meat sandwiches put on their laps. When Etta saw a free hand or knee she would place a photograph in or on it. 'That's Philip when he was with Jem in the ole lugger.' 'There's Philip there, behind that easel thing. One of they artists was always painting him.' She handed a bundle to Madge. 'Take them. They're mostly your brother and your pa. Used to make my life a mis'ry they did.' But she drew her mouth inside-out as she spoke, in silent, reminiscent mirth.

Mrs Fosdick passed Jem Gurnard a plate of sandwiches and ignored Madge. Etta immediately took the plate from her and sat down on the slippery sofa, sharing the sandwiches solely with Madge and talking to her alone.

'I well remember they cricket matches on Porthkidney sands. Your pa. 'E liked bowling best. Yonkers didn't 'e call it?'

'Yorkers,' Madge said faintly, wishing she was in the

16

kitchen at home, cutting up vegetables for the casserole they always had on a Thursday. For the first time in her life the cottage's smell of fish made her feel queasy.

'Ah. That were it. Yorkers. 'E bowled 'em sort of lovingly, didn't 'e? D'you remember that, my girl? 'E'd put us all over the beach, jus where 'e wanted us, then 'e'd run up ever so careful-like an'—'

Mrs Trevorrow said, 'Well, if everyone is ready, I think Mr Trevorrow had better begin. We have an engagement this evening.'

Madge would have made her excuses then, she had no wish to hear Philip's last Will and Testament. She half rose, but Etta pushed her back down and put photographs and sandwich plate firmly on her lap.

She said, 'Let's hear it then. Though I reckon there's not many 'ere what doesn't know it already.'

Mrs Trevorrow addressed the chandelier which hung so incongruously above the table.

'If you are imputing that my husband discusses the business of his clients—'

'Oh be silent, woman. Philp wrote his wishes on a piece of paper in this room with the help of Mr Fosdick for a scribe, and with two witnesses who could 'ave told anyone. The paper was put in your man's safe. That's not being a client!' She hunched an irritable shoulder. 'Get on with it. Get it over.'

Whether or not Philip had been a client, Mr Trevorrow was determined to do him justice. With much shoving, he ousted Jim Maddern from his place at the plush-covered table, made enough elbow room for himself to scatter a few papers around, picked out the relevant one, adjusted his pince-nez, and proceeded to read.

'I, Philip John Sebastian Nolla, being of sound mind, do hearby bequeath all my wordly goods to Mark Briscoe, on the understanding that my wife, Etta Margaret Nolla, may continue to live in Zion Cottage until her death.' He paused until the various muttered exclamations had died down, then went on without expression. 'I know this will disappoint

17

my partners in the *Forty-niner*, and I ask them to understand. I am going to make it all legal-like with Mr Trevorrow, but I want them to know that this is my real true wish and they would oblige me by not questioning it.' Mr Trevorrow looked up, avoiding Madge's gaze, and commented, 'It was indeed witnessed by two friends, and again by my two clerks. Although it is not couched in legal terms, it is, nonetheless perfectly valid.'

There was a long silence in Etta's parlour. Madge understood now why she had been ostracised during the funeral and since her arrival in the house. She could understand their resentment; Philip was giving away a slice of St Ives, and to an outsider; a summer person.

And then Mrs Fosdick said cuttingly, 'Well. Well, now we know, I suppose. We often wondered whether young Mark's trouble was anything to do with the St Ives hip. Now we know.'

Madge's stomach heaved against the fish smell. It was dying out now, but in the old days many St Ives people had been born with dislocated hips and, untreated, had swayed their way through life accepting their disability without question. Philip had been one of them. But how on earth could anyone, however evilly inclined, associate Mark's 'trouble' with the St Ives hip? She choked and put a hand to her mouth.

Etta said loudly, 'Now listen to me. This is Philip's last wish. I knowed about it and I agreed to it. Philip an' me, we 'ad no fam'ly as you all know. *They* was our family – ' she put a hand on Madge's shoulder, 'an' better than most real fam'lies they was too. All we've bin able to give 'em is their 'olidays. An' they've 'elped us over all our 'ard times agin and agin. We couldn't do nothin' in return. Till now. They're summer people and that's the way they will allus be. But young Mark is summat different. 'E en't a summer visitor. We can give 'm summat. An' that's what we want to do. An' if I 'ear anything more about it, I'll start a spate of gossip myself. Oh yes. I know a bit about most of you. We all know a bit about each other I reckon, and we keeps

18

our counsel. But counsels can be unkept. If necessary.'

Madge sat with bent head. But Etta did not actually deny what Mrs Fosdick had implied. And Philip himself had said that Mark was like his own son. Had Philip twisted the truth until he deluded himself that that was true? Did Etta believe it?

Madge concentrated on controlling herself while the mourners filed out. The very air was full of their resentment and anger. Some of them managed a civil farewell to Etta; no-one spoke to Madge. She might not have been there.

When she and Etta were alone at last she still could not look up. She put one hand over her eyes.

'I don't know what to say, Etta. Your home. The *Forty-niner*. *We* can provide for Mark. You must know that. He won't be able to accept this – he *can't* accept it. It will confirm . . . people will think . . . he *can't* accept it!'

'Don't you be too sure, my girl. Philip knew what he was doing.'

'If *only* he hadn't done this, Etta. Don't you see – don't you realise what Mrs Fosdick meant? We can't ever come here again!' Her voice rose to a wail of despair, but Etta, as always when confronted with anguish, chose to ignore it.

'Don't talk rubbish, girl. And help me put these chairs back in the passage. Ernest Fosdick will come and take them tonight. I think Philip would have been pleased with it all, don't you?'

'Yes. I'm sure. But Etta—'

'I'm not talking about it no more, Madge, and that is that. My strength is all gone somewhere, and I want a proper cup of tea and my kitchen fire.'

She led the way into the back quarters where the range glowed comfortingly, shoved the kettle on to the trivet and sank into the chair that had always been Philip's. Madge saw that her face was a network of deeply etched lines and her eyes were red-rimmed with weariness.

'Etta, I understand how you feel . . .' She stood miserably in the doorway. 'But you do realise what people are thinking? They're not just angry because Philip willed his property to an outsider. They think he's done it for a reason. They think . . .'

'That young Mark is Philip's son?' Etta laughed grimly. 'No, they don't. They want to think it, yes. It makes it more int'restin'. But if they think that, they've got to take Philip off that pedestal they put 'im on. An' they wun't do that!'

The kettle began to spit into the coals. She hauled herself up.

'Dun't be 'ard on them, Madge. Folks is only 'uman. There's allus bin a bit o' gossip round Philip an'me. It never worried us, you know that. An' Mark will revel in it − all of it. Philip knew that. That's why 'e did it. It will give Mark a *place* 'ere, like 'e's allus wanted. A place to live and a right to live in it.' She made the tea and sat back down with an audible gasp. 'Now. Are you 'avin' this pot with me, my girl? Or 'ave you got to be packin' up your traps to get back 'ome tomorrow?'

It was crystal clear which reply she wanted, and Madge knew that any further discussion would be dismissed as 'useless talk'.

She said in a small voice, 'I suppose I must go and pack. I'll write to you. I'm only round at Rose Foster's if you . . .'

'Rose Foster? What possessed you to go there?'

'She's respectable now,' Madge said defensively. 'Philip thought a lot of her too.'

'Aye. He did. He thought a lot of most people. He valued people. Even the bad ones. Even . . . even himself.' She glanced up. 'That's something you could learn from 'im, Madge.'

'I . . .' Madge wondered how much Etta knew. 'Yes. But Philip was good. Through and through.'

Etta smiled into the fire. 'Aye. Perhaps he was.' She sighed sharply. 'Now get off to Bristol, Madge, and tell 'em what's 'appened. I want young Mark to come 'ere afore I joins Philip. I can do for'im till then. An' after . . . well, after will take care of itself.'

20

'Mark is working, Etta. He can't give up a perfectly good job and just come here like that.'

'Why not? This is 'is 'ome now. An' 'is share o' the *Forty-niner* will bring in enough for 'im to live on, if you'll 'elp 'im out now and then.' She sipped gratefully. 'Goodbye, Madge. Close that door as you go out, there's a draught like a knife coming down the passage.'

Madge did as she was bid and walked for what she knew would be the last time down the long passage to the front door. In spite of the funeral, it was as cluttered as ever. Sheets, probably Philip's sheets, hung over the line to air, and the borrowed chairs took up most of the floor space. The tears, which she had held in check all day, started to flow. She walked into the centre of the cobbled court, and tipped her head to stare blindly up at the dormer window which had been a lookout in the days when the cottage was first built, and Philip's bedroom every summer when 'the family' had come to stay.

'Philip,' she whispered. 'What have you done?'

She swallowed her tears, afraid that Mrs Fosdick would see her in the gloom, then she walked slowly to the harbour wall to gaze across the wind-chopped water to where the *Forty-niner* tossed on her anchor. She understood why he had left everything to Mark, she understood only too well. But what would happen now? Was this the end of her summers here? And was that perhaps what Philip wanted too?

CHAPTER TWO

1924

The train journey from Bristol was endless. Eight hours of sulphur-tasting salmon sandwiches and bitter Thermos tea, itchy liberty bodice and pencil-and-paper games with Neville which she never won and never expected to win. Her role as baby of the family and a girl at that, was clearly defined.

She was dazed when they reached the tiny junction of St Erth; she had almost forgotten that there was a world outside the railway carriage. But as she tumbled on to the platform conscious only of the elastic on her hat biting into her chin, the enchantment started to work. There were trees lining the station; they did not have leaves, they sprouted sabres. There were enormous pebbles bordering the burgeoning flower beds – obviously they were magic pebbles because they glinted crystal and blue in the fast-setting sun and the flowers were laying their heads on them as if they were pillows. And the air was different. She'd never considered air as an entity before, not in the whole four years of her life. It was part of the world; she breathed it; there could be lots of it, especially in Park Street in the winter; or there could be not much of it, in which case a feather filched from one of the sofa cushions would float up to the ceiling and bob around like a paper boat on the River Avon. This air was completely different. It did not only smell different, it actually tasted. The awful aftermath of sandwiches caking up her mouth began to dissolve; her hair, stiff and tight under her panama, loosened and lifted; her soot-lined nostrils were soothed, and her ears heard it.

'Oh . . . oh . . . oh,' she sighed. 'It's like Fairy Twinkle Land.'

Neville scoffed loudly, and her father smiled in his lofty indulgent way, but her mother, who read nightly from the big book about Fairy Twinkle and who had sewed a sampler for her daughter which read 'Be good sweet maid and let who will be clever', hugged her and said, 'You've been such a good little girl all day long. Such a good, good little girl.'

They climbed wooden steps, crossed a bridge, and found what Mother called 'the little train' waiting for them. People sat with picnic baskets and dogs and shouted to each other. Not because they were angry, but because that was how Cornish people conversed. Father's colleague at the office who had recommended St Ives had warned them about this. And he had also said they wouldn't understand a word that was said. Marjorie understood everything and found it fascinating. They shouted about the weather and the pilchards and the luggers up north. Marjorie knelt on the seat so that her mouth was close to her mother's ear, and whispered, 'It's a shame the poor buggers won't be here to see the pictures, isn't it Mama? They must be such pretty pictures.'

Mother glanced apprehensively at Father who did not always appreciate Madge's mis-hearings.

'Little girls shouldn't listen to grown-up conversations. But luggers are boats, my darling, fishing boats. And they won't miss seeing pictures. It's the pilchard catch they're talking about. Now, no more listening.'

But Marjorie loved listening, and it was irritating that many of the grown-ups she knew, talked in whispers or spelled out words as if deliberately trying to shut her out. The Cornish people weren't like that. They shared what they said; she didn't have to listen, not really.

Mother turned her towards the window. 'Look, darling.

23

There's St Ives. Isn't it beautiful?' And Madge looked, and listened, and breathed, and fell in love.

They had booked in at Zion Cottage with some trepidation. The Nollas had never taken summer visitors before and the Bridges had only stayed at boarding-houses in Weston-super-Mare and Rhyl. Father's colleague had told them that 'rooms and service' was the best way to do it in Cornwall. You got the full flavour of the place without having to put up with their fish diet. The rooms came at seven and six each per week, and you bought your own food for the landlady to cook. She also cleaned, made beds and put up with buckets, spades and sandshoes in her hall. He had given them the address where he and his family had 'gone native' last summer; but Mrs Warner had decided that foreigners weren't worth the money and had passed Alfred Bridges' letter on to the Nollas. They had had two bad pilchard years and although Philip Nolla took his lugger up to the North Sea each summer, the income was always uncertain. Etta Nolla decided to supplement it with summer letting. But they would have to take her as they found her.

The hall which would accommodate their holiday impedimenta was a passage boarded with ship's timbers and strung with washing lines. The sitting-room, suspended above the fish cellar, creaked like a boat's cabin and wasn't much bigger. Above the circular plush-hung table a delicate chandelier swayed and tinkled when anyone breathed, and curios of a lifetime spent by the Atlantic were packed on shelves, window-ledges and fireplace. Shells, driftwood carvings, ships in bottles, sepia photographs, lace antimacassars, polished crab claws, ships' bells . . . all jostled for place. Mother breathed something about the amount of dusting, but it soon became apparent that Mrs Nolla did not dust. Madge knew that it was the original Aladdin's cave.

Phillip Nolla was still 'taking herring' off the Northumberland coast; with the slackening of the pilchard harvests most of the St Ives luggers went north for the summer months. He might well be home in time to look

24

over the foreign family who were paying so handsomely to share his home. It became obvious very quickly to the Bridges that they were on approval. If they gave satisfaction they would be welcome next year. If not, no amount of rent would secure their rooms again.

Etta lived in the back in conditions so primitive that at first Marie Bridges was shocked, and then full of admiration. The 'back' was built right into the living rock and had no window. Light came from the open door into the passage-way, and from the trap in the floor which led via a ladder to the old fish cellar. One wall contained a cooking range, another a long table and storage shelves. Dry goods were kept in an airless little pantry beneath the stairs, perishables down in the fish cellar. Water and toilet arrangements were also down there. In the bedrooms above were elegant chamber pots, china basins and ewers. Etta was won over immediately by Alfred Bridges' first edict. 'Neville, you will take down the slops each morning and bring up fresh water for Mrs Nolla.'

She showed her gratitude plainly when she told him, 'There are a litter of Nollas in St Ives. My name is Etta and my man is Philip.'

She was a small, wiry woman, all bone and sinew. Her hair was already turning grey and screwed painfully into a bun on the top of her head. She wore black; high necks and long sleeves; a shawl for outdoors. She was one of nature's stoics. And she preferred men to women; Neville and Alfred got smiles from her, however grim. Marie and Madge were usually treated to a tight-lipped approach which could soften into indulgence or explode into exasperation as the situation demanded. That first evening it was the latter.

Madge, as a reward for being such a good, good little girl, was kept up late and allowed to join in the family walk to Porthmeor. Directed by Etta, they strolled up Virgin Street to Barnoon and walked along the top of the cemetery. The view was breathtaking; the sun just drowning in the sea. They lifted Madge on to the wall to get her first glimpse of the Atlantic.

25

'America is over *there* – ' Alfred told her, jabbing a finger at the horizon.

But as she peered, a fly, drunk with sun and summer evening, zoomed straight into her eye.

'Oh it hurts,' she sobbed. 'Oh it does so hurt!'

'That's because it's come all the way from America!' Neville joked.

'Do be quiet Neville,' Marie begged. 'Oh my darling!' She appealed to her husband. 'What can we *do*, Alfred?'

'Her own tears will wash it out,' he said sensibly. 'Home to bed. That's the answer.'

As they entered the cottage, Etta emerged from her back room at all the commotion. She screwed up one corner of a not-too-clean handkerchief and poked at Madge's eye. The commotion increased.

'She should have gone straight to bed,' Etta declared, giving up. 'No good ever came of keeping a child out of bed after six o'clock!'

Madge wept anew at this lack of sympathy and Marie said, 'Oh Etta, she's been such a good little girl all day long – such a shame—'

Etta was mollified by the use of her name. She said, 'Come and sleep in the little truckle bed I've made up for you, my maid. 'Tis like a canoe.'

Suddenly, just as Alfred had said, the fly was washed out on a wave of salt tears, and the pain went away. Madge gave her wide, painful smile, and held out her arms to this new friend.

'Come with me. Please come with me, Etta. You're a real proper Cornishwoman.'

The words were filched from her father, but Etta did not know that.

'From the mouths of babes . . .' she murmured, herding Madge up the stairs. They knew they would be welcome next year.

Alfred Bridges was a strange mixture of modern and Edwardian. He revered, even worshipped, his wife, but his

26

treatment of Etta Nolla was as one man to another. Etta – and later Philip – became his henchmen, and as such came with them on most of their expeditions. Etta baulked at sitting on the beach; she was averse to sand. But she was soon taught how to hold a bat and how to field a cricket ball. When her advice was sought about good picnic sites, she would smile her grim smile and say, 'It do depend on whether you're taking the bat and stumps. If not, there's a little rocky cove just beyond Zennor there.'

'Caves?' asked Neville, wide-eyed.

'I reckon. They caught smugglers there when I were a girl.'

'Golly!'

'But if you want a proper cricket match, you can't beat Porthkidney. Just b'low the golf links.'

Alfred considered. 'Not really enough of us for a proper match, Etta. We'll go and look at the smugglers' cave.'

Neville whooped his delight and Etta said seriously, 'Reckon we can make up a team when Philip gets 'ome, Mr Bridges. There'll be six of us then. And we could get little Jim Maddern along, an' p'raps Jem Gurnard. Dependin' o' course.'

Everyone knew that meant depending on whether the Bridges were considered acceptable or not. Meanwhile the picnic hamper was lugged along the cliff path and for the last mile Madge was carried on her father's shoulders. She could see Neville's dark brown head bobbing among the fern in front, closely followed by Etta's topknot, while behind, her mother's old-fashioned boater floated genteelly over the top of the foliage like one of the many gliding gulls, and her voice emerged from it in ecstatic exclamations at the view.

Since that first night when Madge had been adjured to admire the view and had succeeded only in collecting a fly in her eye, she had been suspicious of views. But now, quite suddenly, the sheer magnificence of the meeting of land and sea hit her in the eye with far more force than the fly had done. She rode her father's shoulders as if they were the wings of a bird; she saw the cliffs and the ocean as her true environment. She was four years old but already she knew

27

that the beginning of human life had happened here, on the edge of the water. She felt it in the bones of hands and feet, in the bellows inside her chest. She was conscious for the first time of her physical being, its wonderful intricacies, its oneness with everything else. At that moment she thought she could have taken flight from her father, dived into the sea with the seals, dug her fingers into the ferny earth and grown roots. Instead she cradled her father's skull in her plump arms, lowered her cheek to the bald spot on his crown, and wept.

Her parents were concerned.

'Madge, what is it?' Father lifted her down and held her away from him commandingly. 'Tell me why you are crying, child. Come along now.'

'I don't know . . .'

'Alfred dear – let me hold her. My poor baby—'

'Marie, she must explain properly. She is quite old enough to identify a problem causing her such distress. Now, stop crying, Madge, and think. No, I'm not cross with you, dear, I merely wish to discover the trouble so that I may alleviate it.'

'Alfred. She cannot possibly understand—'

But Madge understood that her parents were disagreeing, and she was the cause of it. She swallowed her tears, gulped, then gasped, 'I was so sorry for everything. The world. It's so beautiful, you see.'

For a moment Alfred stared at this child of his who, please God, would never know war, then he clasped her to his shoulder, rested his chin on her ordinary brown hair and closed his eyes. Somehow she had inherited the things he knew; the shadow behind the sunlight.

He said firmly, 'No need to feel sorry, Madge. It will always be here. However much we try to muck it about it will always be here.'

Marie put her arms around them both.

'She is so senstive,' she murmured, deeply thankful that Alfred understood.

Madge had already lost her moment of epiphany. She dried her face briefly on her father's linen jacket and lifted her head.

'Don't tell Etta,' she begged. 'Please don't tell Etta that I cried again.'

They smiled and assured her they would do no such thing. Marie took her hand and began to lead her through the shoulder-high fern.

'I think you and I will have to work hard to gain Etta's respect,' she said.

It was the first time she had acknowledged that she and Madge were equal females. Father often referred to Neville and himself as 'We men', but to Mother, Madge had always been a very precious, very little, girl.

The picnic was a great success.

There was a great deal of driftwood on the enormous pebbles at the shoreline, and Madge scurried about with Neville, slipping and sliding on the rocks unheedingly, to build a huge pyre. Neville tried to shock her by asking her to look for a dead gull – 'Give it a proper funeral, Sis,' – but she shook her head and said inspirationally, 'It's a signal fire, Nev. Like in your comic. We're shipwrecked, see, and we have to keep a fire going day an' night—'

'I know about signal fires, Madge! It's my comic!' But Neville was just as keen as she was and he prevailed on Etta to feed the fire while he and Madge climbed a finger of rock and waved the picnic tablecloth.

Marie would have ordered them away from such dangers, but Alfred restrained her smilingly.

'They won't try to do more than their capabilities,' he murmured. 'Neville must be permitted to chance his arm. And this is an important step forward for Madge. She's coming out of her chrysalis.'

'Yes. Well. I want them to be good friends in spite of the age difference,' Marie conceded.

'When he's twenty-four and she's twenty, there will *be* no age difference,' he said strongly. And she smiled, believing him.

By the time Philip Nolla returned from the north, Madge had established a reputation as a budding tomboy. Neville, sensing competition as well as companionship, tested her to the limit. She could climb cliffs, scramble around rock pools and walk the cliff paths as well as he could himself. Neither of the children were allowed out of their depths in the sea, but Madge was not scared of the giant rollers and would either bob over them like a cork, or sit on the sandy floor of the ocean and let them guggle harmlessly over her head. She did not realise as yet that Neville removed himself hastily when a wave built itself up above his head; so far he had managed to cover his retreat with war whoops, but Madge's courage – which obviously came from stupidity – annoyed him greatly.

One afternoon towards the end of the holiday, they were on Porthmeor beach as usual, the children in the sea, Alfred and Marie in deckchairs outside the canvas bathing tent which they had hired for the fortnight. The picnic hamper, covered with a damp towel to keep the contents cool, served as a footstool for Marie, who if the truth were known, partially shared Etta's dislike of the all-encroaching sand. Etta was not with them; she rarely joined them for their afternoon bathes and that day was awaiting Philip's arrival from his three months at sea.

A wave broke beyond the children. It looked enormous but Madge knew it would flatten out by the time it reached them. Neville never quite believed that and began to retreat. 'Come *on* Madge – it's coming!'

'It's only little, don't run away, Neville.'

He said furiously, 'I'm not running away, stupid! It's a game. Don't you know that? You have to see who can go the fastest. The wave always catches you. You always lose!'

But he stood his ground and sure enough the wave surged around his waist harmlessly. The next one began to pile up inexorably. Madge paddled legs and arms like fins and watched it coming. Neville said nervously, 'It's the seventh. The seventh wave. I've been counting. We ought to race this one, Madge. Come on.'

Against all instincts Madge put her feet down and tried to stride back to the shore. Neville, much taller than she was, lifted his legs crazily clear of the water and lept ahead of the wave like an ungainly ostrich.

That was how Philip Nolla first saw them all. The boy leaping clear of the clawing sea; the girl suddenly and horrifically disappearing beneath it; the parents, either indifferent or totally ignorant, sitting placidly high up the beach drinking tea from Bakelite cups.

Like many others who get their living from the sea, Philip could not swim. And his respect for the moods and vagaries of the ocean was akin to fear. But his instinct to save the small girl surmounted all that. He struggled through the dry sand frantically, then tore along the firm wet shoreline and plunged fully clothed into the next wave. His heavy boots filled with water and his trouser legs pressed coldly against knees and thighs. He shuddered convulsively and pushed on. Then, just to his left, a white bathing helmet suddenly bobbed to the surface, and beneath it a small face, curved and dimpled like a sprite's, smiled beatifically at him.

'Isn't it bootiful?' Madge asked. 'All bubbly like lemonade sherbet!'

He hardly heard her words. He grabbed her and lifted her to shoulder height; her knitted costume provided a good grip; he turned and struggled out of the water and there were the parents and Neville, wide-eyed and alert at last.

Philip put Madge down carefully.

'You all right, my girl?' he asked.

'Yes.' Madge thought it was all a game. She surveyed this small, soaking new arrival with delight. 'Are you Philip?'

'I am.' He looked at Alfred with a mixture of pity and censure. 'You did not see the maid go under. Good job I were coming down the path just at that moment.' Then he turned to Neville. 'Never leave your sister like that again, young man. It is your job to look after her.'

Marie spoke. 'But Mr Nolla — there was no need — Madge always goes under the big waves—'

And Alfred said quickly, 'It was damned good of you, Philip — mind if we call you Philip? You deserve a medal!'

31

Neville, red-faced, said, 'I told her to run. She's silly. I told her. I did. Honestly.'

'Then you must listen to your brother, my girl. Listen and pay heed.'

Madge nodded, wide-eyed, realising now that she had been rescued from drowning. She remembered some words from her Fairy Twinkle book.

'I am eternally grateful to you,' she said.

Everyone laughed except Philip, who smiled gravely. Neville, vindicated and won over completely, said manfully, 'I say. You're a good egg, Philip. A really good egg.'

He shook Philip's hand, so did Alfred, then so did Marie. When it was offered to Madge she took it and did not let go. They all walked back to the bathing tent together.

'Etta sent me to tell you that she is putting tea on the table in half an hour,' Philip told them.

Marie said, 'But we've had our picnic. We can't eat any more.'

Philip said seriously, 'This is my first meal in my house since the beginning of the summer. I would be honoured if you would eat with me.'

They all loved him. He was so different from Etta; Alfred recognised all the qualities of a top-rate sergeant – reliability, initiative, loyalty; Marie thought he was biblical; Neville reiterated at intervals that he was a good egg; and Madge knew he was her rescuer.

They got to know him well during their last three days. He took them around the *Forty-niner* and showed them how to rig her two big sails. They watched as he spread the drift nets and mended them with a fat-packed bobbin, throwing it back and forth, knotting the line, snipping with the knife kept inside his boot. They listened avidly to his tales of old St Ives. He could remember the hurricane of '93 when four steamers had been wrecked in the bay and he had gone over in a bosun's chair on one of the rocket lines to help with the injured. The following year there had been the flood, and just before the war a winter blizzard that had buried

32

the little town and cut it off from all its neighbours.

'What about the war, Philip?' clamoured Neville. 'Tell us about St Ives in the war!'

'Same as everyone. Short of food and too much talk. There was a German woman over to Zennor way – trouble there. But then she went away and we settled down to sit it out. Or was it the other wars you was meaning, young Neville?'

'Other wars?' Neville was round-eyed.

'The Turks landed 'ere y' know. And them Spaniards, and that Mr Warbeck who called himself Richard the Fourth or somesuch. And there's always bin the smugglers.'

He entertained Neville; he never tried to entertain Madge. They were quiet companions, perfectly at ease in each other's company, sometimes talking, sometimes happily silent.

They sat together like that beneath Old Man's Head on the last day of their holiday. Neville, fired by Philip's stories, was trying to climb the big square rock that sat high on the headland, so like a human skull. Philip made no attempt to call him down as his parents would have done. Neville expended all his energy on the hopeless attempt, and was content.

Madge was nevertheless anxious.

'Is he all right, Philip? Etta says only grown-ups can climb Old Man's Head.'

''E won't get nowhere, my maid. But 'e's enjoyin' the attempt I reckon. An' when 'e's a bit bigger, Philip will show 'im the proper way to go up the Old Man. There's a way at the back.' He looked down at her beneath the brim of his trilby. 'I could show you too, little maid. Anyone can do it.'

She smiled at him. 'Neville first,' she said.

And he touched her shoulder as if congratulating her. 'Aye. Neville first.'

They were silent; behind them Neville dropped to the ground and surveyed the rock face for concealed toeholds. He had seen people atop the Old Man and wanted quite desperately to climb it.

Madge said, 'We've got to go home tomorrow, Philip.'

'I know that, my girl.'

'Will you miss us?'

'Will you miss me?'

'Oh I shall, Philip – I shall.'

'Then that is a question you don't have to ask of me. But that doesn't mean either of us must be sad for very long. A bit of you will stay here in St Ives and next year you'll come back and it will be just the same.' He looked round to check on Neville. 'Next year Philip will take you out in the *Forty-niner*. We'll go and look at the seals.' He raised his voice. 'And next year I'll teach you to climb that there rock, Neville! But not now. Come on, the pair of you. Mackerel for tea!'

He did not wait for any discussion but plodded off towards the wishing well at the top of Porthmeor. Madge watched him for a moment, then took out her handkerchief and ran after him.

'Here you are, Philip. Put it in your sleeve.'

He looked at the scrap of cambric in puzzlement.

'What's this, my maid? 'Tis not big enough for me to use!'

She said very solemnly, 'That is the bit of me that will stay in St Ives with you, Philip. And I'll come back for it when I'm a big girl. I shall be five years old when I see you again.'

He folded the handkerchief carefully and put it into his pocket. Then he took her hand and they walked sedately together. After a few more fruitless moments of token defiance, Neville gave up rock-climbing for a year and galloped along the sandy path to join them.

CHAPTER THREE

1932

The fact that the National Government was in did not console Alfred Bridges for the fact that Ramsay MacDonald was still Prime Minister.

'How can it be a National Government with a Labour chappie at the top?' he harangued his family as he flapped the *Daily Mail* over the breakfast table, making the chandelier tinkle madly and causing his wife to replace the cover over the bacon and eggs before the children had helped themselves.

Neville could not resist picking up the challenge and riposted with: 'Well, what's the alternative, Dad? If Mr Baldwin took it on, it would be no more nationalistic than it is now.' He looked at his mother for support and received an admonitory shake of the head. 'Would it, Tagger?' he asked of his schoolfriend Clem Briscoe who had no father and had come with them on this holiday.

Clem was torn between loyalty to his friend and diplomacy towards the man who was paying for the holiday. He made noises in his throat.

Twelve-year-old Madge, sentient beyond her years and overflowing still with a compassion that frequently annoyed Neville with its solemn piety, said quickly, 'Does it really matter, Daddy? You said last week that so long as MacDonald has proved beyond doubt that a Labour government cannot possibly work in this country . . .'

Her memory was a little too accurate for Alfred and he flapped the paper again, this time across the marmalade jar.

'We'll see. We'll see how long he can stay at the helm. A year at the most. I'll give him a year at the most.'

Neville lifted the cover from the eggs and shovelled two very slippery ones on to his plate. Over the years Marie had introduced her own cutlery and crockery to supplement Etta's basic supply and – with enormous tact – insisted on laying the meal tables herself. But she could do nothing about Etta's cooking and the eggs were always floating on a bed of liquid dripping.

'I doubt that, Dad.' Neville wasn't going to give way in front of Tagger Briscoe. 'I'd give him four. Wouldn't you, Tagger?'

Clem made more sounds which Neville chose to interpret as total agreement.

'Right. Then he'll have proved he can do it and the country will send in another Labour government, and *this* time—'

Clem glanced at his host and said quickly, 'Steady on, old man. Remember the vote of confidence before . . . remember the plus-four boys and all that.'

'Thank you, Clement,' Alfred said, smiling jovially over the newspaper. 'Thank you for saving us all from Communism. Yours is the voice of reason and I am glad to hear it these days!'

Neville dropped his knife and seized Clem's free hand. Beneath the level of the table-top he began to exert vengeful pressure on Clem's little finger. Clem laughed, so did Alfred and Etta appeared from the back kitchen to enquire whether the teapot should be 'drownded' yet again.

Alfred folded his paper and turned in his chair. He was, in his own words, a pre-war man, and at breakfast he always wore his iron-hard collar and his waistcoat. But he was also a jocular man, and this morning he was in a particularly good mood.

'Etta, the teapot is full and the leaves are by no means drowned. Please sit and have a cup with us.'

Etta favoured them all with her grim smile. This was the eighth holiday the Bridges had spent at Zion Cottage, and they were her only summer visitors. Alfred insisted on increasing the rent each year, and he was always giving her presents. She would have accepted them from no-one else, and she looked on all of them – even Neville's friend – as her own.

'I 'ope you'll excuse me from that, Mr Bridges.' She took the paper away from him and put it on the window seat. 'I like my tea to taste like tea.'

Madge looked at Neville, half-hoping he might make a jokey reference to what he called Etta's 'cup of black treacle'. But he was concentrating on something else. She saw that beneath Clem Briscoe's unfolded napkin, the boys had linked their little fingers and appeared to be trying to tear them out by the roots. Her eyes watered sympathetically. Neville often recounted the trials of strength undergone by new boys at his school, and she knew that this was one of them. There had been a harrowing story about an important old boy who had come to Speech Day and proudly displayed a crooked little finger; legacy of his first day at the school when it had been broken during this frightful initiation.

Etta went on, 'I might as well ask you now, Mrs Bridges. What is it to be today? Hot or cold?'

Marie Bridges knew that this was no reference to possible weather conditions. It was misty outside the small parlour window, but it was a heat mist and would probably disperse by the time breakfast had been cleared. She in turn raised her brows at her husband.

'Well, dear? What are our plans today?'

Alfred was the one who made the plans.

He looked at the two straight-faced boys, his daughter – solemn as usual but with her eyes suddenly enormously blue in her round brown face – his wife smiling and beautiful, Etta at his right shoulder, a ready henchman. He smiled, letting his love for them shine through like the sun through the mist.

'We'll have a cricket match,' he pronounced. 'We'll take a big hamper on to the dunes at Porthkidney and we'll make camp there. And after lunch we'll have a cricket match.'

'Two-a-side?' queried Neville, relaxing his hold on Clem for a moment.

'Etta will come, won't you, Etta? And we'll ask Jim Maddern. Is there anyone else to make up the numbers?'

'Rose Care,' Neville suggested quickly. 'She's home again and was helping Jim with the donkeys yesterday.'

Alfred looked repressively at his son. Rose Care's name was bandied around the Sloop sometimes; she was purported to be short on underwear. Alfred wondered how much Neville might know. He was sixteen after all, and boys talked a lot at boarding school.

Etta picked up the paper again. 'Ah. She's home again because she's bin dismissed from the big house at Hayle.' She brought the folded paper down smartly on the napkin between the two boys. 'Stop that silly finger-wrestling this minute, you two. There's a chap over Helston lost both his little fingers that way. You should know better, eddycated lads like you!' She replaced the paper on the window seat. 'No need to worry about numbers. Philip bin sighted just off Five Points. 'E'll be 'ere in an 'our or two. 'E'll be wicketkeeper just like usual.'

Neville and Madge both cheered, Neville to take his father's attention away from finger-wrestling, and Madge because her St Ives was never complete without Philip Nolla.

In spite of losing the toss that afternoon, Alfred settled back among the picnic paraphernalia, knowing that he was probably the luckiest man on earth. Some of that luck he had made for himself, that was certain. He had gone against family wishes by joining the Engineering department of the Great Western Railway straight from school instead of going to a respectable redbrick university. And now he was the Assistant Divisional Engineer with a good salary and enough first class rail passes each year to enable him to bring his family here, go up to Scotland, or even across to France. He'd made that luck himself. And marrying his beautiful Marie – that had gone against the family grain too – but that had been the best thing he had ever done. She had been a pupil in the girls' school opposite his own, unnoticed in her uniform among two hundred others. But she had come to his Sixth Form Leavers' Dance and floored him – quite literally – by dropping her lemon ice in his path. When she had picked him up, her beautiful dark eyes full of apology, he had known he must marry her and be with her for the rest of his life. But her father was a jeweller from Amsterdam and she was destined to work in his shop. The Bridges did not consider it a suitable match at all.

That was in 1908; he was eighteen, she was sixteen. By 1912, established at the Engineering Office in Bristol, he was seeing her every day, although his father believed they met only on Sundays. And in September 1914 when he went to be measured for his uniform, he arranged a registry office wedding and married her before he went to France. His parents had flung up their hands, but when her father died, they had had her to live with them and had learned to love her before they too died. He thought of how he had bludgeoned his way through those years, and smiled.

But his luck in getting through the war was not self-made. He had not thought he would make it and on his leave before the battle of the Somme he had ceased to be 'careful', wanting a child quite desperately to be his immortality when he was gone. And he had got a child. And he had survived against all odds. There was the gas of course, but he had still survived. And Madge was no armistice conception; they had considered the advisability of another baby and decided for it coolly. Madge was not luck, she was judgement, but she was a privilege too.

That day it seemed to Alfred that the privileges rained thick and fast. It was good to see Philip Nolla. Short and wiry, his beaky face hardly visible beneath the brim of his ancient trilby, Philip had become over the years like a family retainer. Etta cared for their bodily needs as best she could, but there was always an element of grim reluctance about her fondness for them. They were foreigners and always would be. Philip's feeling went deeper and was very near to devotion. He treated Marie like a

39

goddess, and probably thought of Madge as the child he'd never had. Now, as he crouched behind the makeshift wicket, he glanced sideways to check on her.

'Keep your eye on that ball, my maid!' he called. 'It might be a tennis ball, but it'll 'urt ee 'ard if it catches you.'

And Madge smiled blindly into the sun and called back, 'You keep your eyes peeled too!'

Alfred smiled again as he leaned against the hamper and watched young Clem Briscoe taking his run-up to the crease. Etta waited for the ball, bat held casually at knee height, voluminous skirts kilted into her belt revealing black stockings and men's boots. What a character. She and Philip were individuals down to their toenails. Typically Cornish.

Neville and Clem took their cricket very seriously, and Neville, waiting to bat with his father, felt bound to yell 'Well bowled sir!' in spite of the fact that Etta hit an easy six with one hand behind her back. Mrs Bridges fielded the ball from below the tide-line and returned it to a flushed Clem.

Alfred said, 'Seems a nice young chap, Briscoe. Glad you brought him along, Neville.'

But Neville would not permit himself to be conciliatory with his father. He grunted.

Alfred persevered. 'Mother a widow, I believe?' He narrowed his eyes to watch his wife lope back to her out-field position. She was still startlingly beautiful with her jet-black hair and dark eyes. Unexpectedly he saw her in a different perspective: as a widow. His heart thumped with a terror he hadn't experienced since the trenches.

'Don't think so.' Neville almost grinned at the chance to shock his father quite legitimately. 'Husband couldn't take any more. Tagger doesn't say much but she does nag him. And if she did that to her old man, it's not surprising he did a bunk.'

Alfred frowned but decided to make allowances for his son. After all, sixteen was a tricky age.

'Why do you call him Tagger?' he asked mildly instead.

'Don't know. He said something about tagging along on

40

his first day at school and that was that. He calls me Bridal Chamber sometimes.'

'What?'

'Bridges. Bridal. You know.'

Alfred let it go. He could imagine the two boys sniggering about it.

'Yes. Well. Have you thought any more about your future, Neville? If engineering doesn't appeal, I could get you into the office, you know.'

'Pen-pushing.' Neville made a face.

'You'd start *off* as a clerk, of course. But the promotion would be good. Especially if you'd get some qualifications first.'

Neville was almost overwhelmed at the impossibility of explaining anything to the older generation, but he made a gigantic effort.

'I want to *do* something first, Dad!'

'Give me a clue, old man. I'm fogged at the moment.'

'Well. Like *you* did! The war!'

'My God. I put up with that so that no-one else – especially you – would never have to go through anything like it!'

It was a hopeless task. He'd never make his father understand that he was suffocating already; if he went into the Great Western offices at Temple Meads, it would be the end of him. He became argumentative again.

'The war to end wars. Well, we know what happened to that ideal, don't we?'

Alfred looked at his son with resignation. Why was there never a way to pass on experience? He said, 'There's not been another war so far.'

'What about China's appeal to the League? I don't expect they think much of our kind of *peace*.' Neville made it sound like a dirty word. But Alfred refused to lose his temper.

'That's on the other side of the world, Neville. They have a different set of rules. Everything is quite different in the East.'

'And Spain?'

41

'There's no war in Spain.'

'This new republic isn't going to work! Surely that's *obvious?*'

'Not to me I'm afraid, old man. In any case, Spain and China are none of our business. You're sixteen, Neville. Full of romantic ideas. Which is fine. But until you can make up your mind properly, I want you to get a good matric result and start working towards a university entrance. You can do it.'

Neville flushed darkly. It all came down to the same old pep talk in the end, however reasonable his father might sound. He felt rebellion bubble and simmer in his chest like bile.

'I'm no Einstein – I don't think I *can* do it.'

'Look here, Neville—'

'Okay, okay. I didn't say I wouldn't try. It's just that I'm an outdoor man. Swotting . . . all that stuff . . .' He saw his father's chin begin to jut and tried to turn the subject slightly. 'Taggers now, he's a different kettle of fish. In fact if you want to do him a good turn, Dad, take him into the Engineer's office with you. He's forever drawing plans for this and that, and maths is his favourite thing. I do believe if he had the choice between cricket and maths he'd choose . . .' Etta caught the tennis ball on the edge of her bat and it soared into the air. Neville held his breath. Philip wasn't quite underneath it and he never ran on the sand; Etta was going to get away with it. Then Philip reached out and took the ball from the air as if it had been sitting on a shelf. Etta began to walk back to the 'pavilion'. Neville was forced to say, 'Oh well *caught*, sir!' And the subjects of his matriculation and Clem Briscoe's mathematical mind were dropped.

Alfred leaned back, determined to remain unruffled. So far Neville was a disappointment to him, he had to admit it. But there were so many other privileges, they kept coming. And Neville was still so young. As for Clem Briscoe, yes, he would mention him to the powers that be. It might go towards paying some of his debt to a strangely benevolent fate.

Tiny, bow-legged Jim Maddern was bowling to Clem who had put himself in as first man to boost morale. It was an easy ball but he stonewalled it anyway. Neville was standing ankle-deep in water, waiting for the mighty swipes he was certain would come his way. He booed loudly. Clem grinned. He wanted to give Mrs Bridges, young Madge and Philip time to recover.

Philip puffed some more air in the deflating cushions and put them against the hamper to make a back rest for Marie Bridges.

'Jest you close your eyes for a few minutes, m' 'ansome,' he said, holding her paper Japanese sunshade while she settled herself in the shifting sand. 'You can go in as last man which will give you 'aff an hour at the very least.'

'So kind . . .'

'Philip is like a courtier, Mummy, isn't he?' Madge's single plait fell over her shoulder as she crawled around gathering up books and knitting and a stray Thermos cup. 'D'you remember that book we were reading called *Queen Bess and her men*?'

'Really, Madge dear. Philip is just a natural gentleman. Courtier indeed!' Marie Bridges fussed with the parasol, embarrassed on Philip's behalf.

But he was delighted.

'I've allus looked on your ma as a sort of a queen – you're right there, my girl. Funny thing, this summer I took a coupla days off the lugger and went along to this 'ere 'Adrian's Wall. 'Ave you 'eard of 'Adrian's Wall, my girl?'

'No. And I wish you wouldn't keep calling me a girl, Philip. I'm as tall as you now, you know.'

He said solemnly, 'Then I shall call you woman from now on. Is that all right?'

Madge dimpled, then ducked her head and laughed.

Marie Bridges said automatically, 'Don't giggle, dear. And you *should* know about Hadrian's Wall. It was built by the Romans when they lived in Britain. It was to keep the Scots out of northern England.'

43

Philip nodded. 'Goes right across the country, coast to coast. And parts of it is still there.'

Madge flipped her plait back and sat down.

'Tell us about it, Phillip. And what has it got to do with Mummy being a queen?'

'Ah . . .' Philip removed his pipe from his top pocket and knocked it experimentally on to the palm of his hand. 'Well, it were just one o' they trains of thought, little . . . woman. See, there's bin a lot of – what d'you call 'em – groups of people—'

'Societies?' supplied Mrs Bridges.

'Umm . . .'

'Civilisations? Clubs?'

'Civilisations. That's it. An' some of them 'ave looked after their women. Which they should do because . . . well, you'll understand about that later, woman. An' others 'aven't. They've treated them like workhorses.'

'Slaves?' Madge looked eager. 'There was a bit in the *Windsor* magazine about white slavery. It was really exciting—'

Her mother said, 'You're too young to be reading the *Windsor*, Madge. I've told you before—'

'Oh, it was ages ago. I haven't since you said not to. Go on, Philip.'

'Well. The civilisations what 'ave looked after their womenfolk 'ave prospered. Them Romans. And the Cornish King Arthur. And them Elizabethans in the 'istory books—'

'Only for a time, Philip. The Roman Empire collapsed, remember. And King Arthur isn't true. And—'

''E certainly is, woman! If your pa will allow, I'll take you along to Tintagel in the lugger and you can judge for yourself whether King Arthur were true or not!' Philip made this point emphatically, the stem of his pipe held towards her like a small pistol. Madge was remorseful.

'I'm sorry, Philip. I do believe in King Arthur, of course. And it would be marlovely to see Tintagel. I'm sure Daddy will permit it, won't he, Mummy?'

'Madge, don't pester. And kindly use decent King's English.'

Philip said, 'Let me tell you about this 'ere 'Adrian's Wall, woman. Our port up there is Seahouses as I've often told you before. Different from the harbours round 'ere, but just as inter-esting. Just as . . .' he hesitated, then chose an unusual description. 'Just as businesslike.'

Madge understood very well. A port was always a business, a form of co-operative. She buried her bare feet in sand, keeping a weather eye on Clem at the wicket, and listened to Philip's impression of Hadrian's Wall. Years later when she viewed it for herself, she was able to see it through his eyes; not as an archeological treasure, but, like Arthur's Tintagel, a clever piece of tactical engineering.

After the cricket match there was the bonfire.

Alfred was in his element.

'Children, we need kindling. Search up in the dunes, it will be really dry there. Neville, keep an eye on your sister. Etta, can you take young Jim here and find us some decent logs to keep the whole thing going?' He turned to his wife. 'Dearest, I need your expertise with building the fireplace again. Did you bring the grid? We need something long enough to take the frying pan and the kettle . . .'

He deployed them well. Etta needed someone to command, and Jim needed to be commanded. Madge and the two boys wanted to be on the move, running up the dunes and sliding down, looking for basking snakes on the golf course, hiding in the thickets of coarse grass, and wrestling more or less amiably. And Philip, the real power behind making fireplace and fire, was more than willing to give all the credit to smiling Marie as she passed him flat stones and the old footscraper they always used as a hob.

Distant shouts from the shore reminded the wood-gatherers of their task. Neville piled hastily snatched twigs and stalks into Madge's arms.

'Off you go, Sis – keep the old man happy!'

She tightened her face at him to show her disapproval of

45

this remark in front of Clem Briscoe, but launched herself heels first down the next dune towards the fire-makers. When she got back Neville and Clem were trying to suppress furtive laughter and kept their backs to her as they bent to pick up more kindling.

'Daddy says that's not half enough and we are to hurry,' Madge informed them. 'What's the matter? Why are you making those grunting noises?'

'Nothing,' Clem managed in the face of Neville's red-faced inarticulateness. 'Just couldn't help laughing at something.'

Neville exploded and knelt in the sand with lowered head and watering eyes.

'Nothing is right,' he gasped. 'Clem was right first time. We were laughing at nothing. Honestly, Sis. Nothing.'

Madge said primly, 'It was something rude, I know. It's always something rude when you look like that.'

Clem turned bright red. 'I'll just get some of that dry bracken,' he said quickly and giant-strode up the dune and out of earshot.

'Now look what you've done,' Neville snapped resentfully. 'Honestly, Sis. You and Dad between you can put a blight on anything!'

'I wish you wouldn't talk about Daddy so disloyally in front of Clem,' Madge said even more prudishly. 'And I know exactly what you were laughing about. And it's horrid. Unkind and horrid.'

Neville looked wary. 'What was it then, sister dear?'

'It was because Rose Care doesn't wear any knickers! You shouldn't laugh at people's misfortunes, Neville! If she hasn't got enough money to—'

'Who told you *that*?'

'Jim Maddern. That's why she was dismissed from Mennion House. And it's not fair.'

Neville was shocked into silence. He was furious with young Jim Maddern for talking to his sister in that way. She was twelve years old and didn't know a thing. And he was angry with her for not knowing a thing; it made her vulnerable and unprotected and . . . *stupid*!

46

He said roughly, 'You little idiot. Rose Care was sacked because she's pregnant.' He saw her incomprehension and said succinctly, 'She is going to have a baby.'

Madge didn't turn a hair. 'I know what pregnant means Neville! I know that babies grow inside their mothers' tummies!'

'And who told you *that*? Jim Maddern?' Neville knew he would kill Jim if he had acquainted Madge with the facts of life.

'No, he didn't. I wouldn't listen if he did.' Madge turned her back and began to fill her held skirt with twiglets. 'As a matter of fact, Rose Care told me that.'

Neville said tightly, 'You have talked to Rose Care? You have actually talked to her?' He took a deep and ragged breath. 'What else did she tell you?'

'Nothing. Just that babies grow in their mothers' tummies. I knew she was right because of Timbo.' Timbo their cat, had been hastily spayed when it was discovered she was female.

Neville felt all his dissatisfaction and frustration come to boiling point. His carnal knowledge was one of the few things that gave him any pleasure recently and he and Clem – but mostly he – had been very preoccupied with the plight of Rose Care and how it had come about. Somehow, Madge, as usual, had got in first. Madge had talked to her, in all innocence, doubtless had all the facts at her fingertips and did not even know it.

He probed roughly. 'Didn't she tell you how they get in their . . .' he raised his tone to falsetto . . . 'mothers' tummies?'

'Oh, Neville.' Madge looked round, indulgently amused. 'They *grow* there. I just told you.'

'Hmm. You have to plant a seed to grow things, don't you? Who planted Rose Care's seed, d'you think? And . . . *how*?'

She was still completely assured. 'God, of course.' She tucked the hem of her skirt into her belt to hold the sticks and dusted her hands. Far away now, Clem began to run down his dune towards the fire-makers, his arms full of brushwood. She waved to him, then turned to her brother and held out a friendly hand. 'Come on, Nev. Let's get back to the others.'

He knew he should leave it there, but he couldn't. Initiating Madge gave him a certain satisfaction. He did it as kindly and gently as he knew how, but to watch her disbelief change to horror made him feel slightly less . . . lonely. Her primness had been an adjunct of her innocence, and they had gone for ever. But he felt guilty too as he watched her face turn jaundice-yellow beneath its tan.

'I have to tell you, Sis,' he said earnestly. 'I have to tell you in order to protect you. You understand that, don't you? I mean, Mother should have said something. You'll be starting your monthlies any minute now – or have you started?'

'Mummy said it was all right. Nothing to worry about.'

'Well, it isn't. It's when it stops you have to worry!' He tried to laugh and couldn't. 'Look if anyone – if that Jim Maddern – ever asks you to show your knickers . . . you'll know what they're after and you just run a mile. Okay?'

'I don't believe you. God wouldn't have invented anything so horrible to make his little children. God's gifts they're called. So how could they be made like . . . you say?'

Neville stared at her. With her bulging skirt she herself looked eight months pregnant. It could be her. That bloody Jim Maddern . . . it could be her. Neville hardened his heart.

'Look, Madge. Think. You've seen dogs do it. You've studied birds and bees in your silly nature lessons.'

'But people are people, not animals!' She sobbed suddenly, not able to meet his eyes, so that he had a view of her long brown lashes pearled with teardrops. But he had gone too far to draw back now.

He said very gently, 'Listen, Madge. How do you think the parents had us? You? And me?'

She was deeply shocked all over again. Her sobs checked and she looked at him with appalled eyes.

'Mummy and Daddy?' Her voice was a thread of incredulity. 'Mummy and *Daddy* doing . . . what you said?'

'Yes. Doing what I said. So that first of all I grew. Then

you grew.' Neville pulled a dirty handkerchief from his pocket and touched her cheek inexpertly. 'There. That makes it all right, doesn't it?'

She shrank away from him.

'Mummy would never . . . Daddy would never . . . Daddy *loves* Mummy!'

'Of course he does. That's what I'm trying to explain. It's love. It's called *love!*' He whistled with exasperation. 'Listen, idiot. You sleep in the same room with them. Haven't you seen them jumping about on the bed at night?'

She said faintly, 'It's dark . . .'

'Oh I *know!* But you must have heard something. Bedsprings or something.' Her silence confirmed this. He said encouragingly, 'What did you think they were doing?'

'I thought . . .' Her voice was a whisper. 'I thought . . . they were . . . bouncing.'

Suddenly the tension was too much for Neville. He began to laugh almost hysterically.

'Yes. Of course. That's what they were doing. Bouncing!' He bent double, eyes streaming. 'Oh that's a good 'un. Bouncing. Oh I like that. Oh Madge, that's rich!'

She did not laugh or speak. She stared down at the sand.

Neville controlled himself with difficulty. 'Anyway. You know now. And if anyone tries anything – just shout for your big brother. Promise?'

She ducked her head in what might have been a nod of assent.

'Come on then.'

'In a minute. You go on.'

He went, glad it was over. When he was halfway down the dune he thought he could hear her retching and half turned. Then he shrugged. Best to leave her alone. Get over it in her own good time. It was too bad though. Really, Mother should have said something to her before now. It just wasn't fair to leave it all to him.

The sausages tasted wonderful and no-one seemed to notice that Madge ate nothing. After the food had been partially digested, Alfred suggested to the boys that they should have a swim. They had brought no costumes or towels, but the weather was halcyon and Jim Maddern, grinning like a monkey, ran into the sea in his shirt and trousers while the discussion was still going strong. Neville followed suit, ignoring the female protestations, longing to feel clean again. Alfred and Clem retired behind a rock, stripped to their underwear and entered the water more discreetly. Marie Bridges began to shake the sand off the rugs so that they might be used as towels. Madge sat very close to Philip.

'You not going in?' he asked with a measure of relief.

'No. I don't feel like it.' Madge darted him a swift look and said in a low voice, 'Philip, why did you never have children?'

'Hey?' Philip darted a look back. 'May patience guide me, woman – that's not for me to say. That's the Lord's work as you should know.'

'Is it? Is it really, Philip?' She gave him another more searching look, saw the honesty in his face and moved closer to his side. 'Did you not ask Him for children, Philip? Did you not want any?'

Philip squinted at the horizon.

'No. I don't reckon I did, woman. I reckon I left that in the hands of the Lord and din't ask nor want.'

'You're a very godly man, Philip, aren't you?'

He lowered his head so that the brim of his hat hid his face.

Then he said in a steady voice, 'I dun't know about that, my little woman. But I reckon 'E's allus around somewhere. An' I reckon 'E knew I wouldn't be much of a full-time fayther, because of the fishing d'you see. So 'E let me 'ave a share in you. An' 'E made sartain sure that your dear ma and pa would *let* me 'ave a share in you.' He lowered his head still further but she could hear laughter in his voice. 'I 'ope that meets with your approval, woman?'

For the first time in two hours she smiled. She was going to tell him not to tease her, then she pursed her lips to seriousness and said sedately, 'If it meets with His approval, that is all that matters.'

Alfred swam strongly out to the rocks at Carrick Gladden and hauled himself up. He was out of breath and there was a sharp pain across his chest which he thought must be indigestion.

'Serve you right for swimming after a meal, my lad,' he addressed himself, forcing a grin to his face. He puffed the breath right out of his lungs like the army doctor had told him to do after the gas exposure, and the pain blessedly subsided. He watched the three lads cavorting in the shallows and felt deep thankfulness for the day, the hour, the minute . . .

Neville waited for a roller to pass, then he dived and grabbed Clem's feet. They spluttered beneath the surface, grinning hideously into each other's faces, their hair floating above their heads like weed. They surfaced, shouting.

'Rotter!' Clem was enormously relieved, knowing that everything was now most definitely all right again.

'Rotter yourself!' Neville fell on to his back and splashed with his legs. Clem flung himself on to his friend and they both went down again. Another roller tossed them about like flotsam, and Jim Maddern grabbed them by the hair and hauled them up.

'Don't mess about with the sea!' he admonished them. 'You should know better after all this time.'

Neville threw him off furiously. It was all his fault that poor old Madge had had to throw up in the marram grass.

'Clear off!' he yelled. 'And keep away from my sister too – d'you hear?'

Clem looked surprised and Jim staggered into another wave and got a ducking. He came up spluttering.

'No need for that. No need at all. I thought you young gentlemen wanted me to take you to see Rose Care.' He sounded belligerent; the implication was that if they didn't play their cards right, there would be no such meeting.

Neville turned his back.

'I never want to hear her name again!'

'Neither do I,' Clem backed him up staunchly.

51

Jim said philosophically, 'You'll change your tune,' and swam off.

Neville floated over an unbroken wave. 'We'll show 'em. We'll join the Foreign Legion. We'll see the world.' But even as Clem applauded this enterprise, Neville was thinking of Rose Care and wondering what he would say to her when he saw her.

That night Alfred and Marie went candle-less to bed as usual so as not to disturb Madge. On the other side of the stairwell, Clem and Neville could be heard sniggering and moving about.

Marie whispered, 'I do hope those boys are safe with their candles. I don't know what we'd do if there were a fire.'

Alfred whispered back, 'We'd evacuate very quickly, my darling. But I think we can trust the boys with their candles.'

Marie, sentient to near-telepathy where Alfred was concerned, breathed, 'Meaning we cannot trust them in other ways?'

Alfred might have laughed if it hadn't been for waking Madge, and if there had been light enough he would have smiled reassuringly at his wife. As it was he said softly, 'Dearest, I love you very much.' He reached for her in the darkness and kissed her tenderly, then with greater intensity.

'Darling, wait. I'm not undressed and I cannot find my nightgown.'

'You won't need your nightgown,' he murmured automatically. But he released her and completed his own undressing, putting his pyjamas carefully on the ladder-back chair by the bed ready for afterwards. Most nights one of them had to get up to use the various china chamber pots under the two beds, and after her first exhausted sleep Madge might easily wake. He peered in the direction of the truckle bed. His eyes were becoming accustomed to the darkness and he could see the humped silhouette of his daughter beneath one of Etta's patchwork quilts. He smiled. She was truly a manifestation of his love for Marie; a perfect combination of his nondescript fairness and

Marie's vivid dark colouring, of his practical nature and Marie's saintliness.

He whispered, 'Madge overdid it today, I felt. She was so quiet this evening and she couldn't wait to get to bed.'

He saw his wife's teeth flash whitely.

'After one of your cricket matches we are all tired out, Alfred!'

'But not too tired, dearest?'

She whispered submissively, 'Not too tired if you are not, my darling.'

He lifted the unbleached calico and slid in beside her. Her breasts were heavy in his hands and after a very little while her submission gave way to a compliance that he knew from delightful experience would quickly mount to passion. He was a lucky man; there had been many anecdotes in the army of wives who lay rigidly beneath their spouses, eyes tightly shut in horror, putting up with the frightful indignity by 'thinking of England'. Those wives had been unwittingly responsible for much of the popularity enjoyed by the French prostitutes, and Alfred was grateful too that because of Marie he had been spared that.

He waited until her breathing quickened to desperation, then carefully clambered between her legs. The brass bed creaked a protest but the hump that was Madge did not stir. Gently he impregnated his wife and stifled her gasp with his mouth. And then, with no warning at all, the pain was back. It was like the point of a bayonet sliding between his ribs. For a split second he reviewed his supper: simple cheese and lettuce, it could not be that. Then he succumbed to the pain, collapsing over his wife and muffling his groans to a kind of wheeze.

Marie was terrified but competent. She rolled him away, knelt above him lifting his body and ramming pillows behind him until she had propped him up.

She panted, 'Alfred . . . darling. Just nod. Is it your heart? Just nod.'

He shook his head. His grip on her wrist was strong but not frantic.

She was reassured and leaned closer.

'Show me where the pain is. Here? Here?' She moved her hand across his bare chest. He grunted. 'Does that help? If I massage gently?'

'Indigestion,' he managed after a while. 'Stupid of me to eat cheese before bed.'

She left him and went to her handbag.

'I could make you up some bicarb, but these are just as good and less horrid. Suck one gently, darling.'

She put a minty sweet in his mouth and continued her massaging. He closed his eyes as the pain receded.

'Dearest, I'm sorry . . . sorry . . . so very sorry . . .'

'Don't you ever apologise to me, Alfred Bridges,' Marie said fiercely. 'Just get better. That is all I ask of you and all I shall ever ask.'

'My darling girl.' He was ashamed to feel tears behind his eyes; he was weaker than he'd imagined.

At last he could murmur, 'It's gone now, Marie. Absolutely gone.'

She was still. 'Are you sure? Perhaps it was indigestion after all.'

'I told you that's what it was, darling.'

She said soberly, 'It was more than that. We both know it.'

He sighed. 'Maybe the gas, my dear.'

'Oh Alfred.'

He breathed a laugh. 'Hooray for the Hun, eh?'

'Darling—'

'It's a small price to pay, Marie. A small price.'

They were quiet; there was nothing to be done about it, after all.

At last he said, 'Our night clothes . . . Madge.' They both looked over at the truckle bed. 'She's slept through it all. A quiet mind.'

Marie reached for their things and helped Alfred with his pyjama jacket before she slid into her nightdress. Then they lay side by side, holding hands beneath the rough calico sheets.

When their breathing became loud and even, Madge moved at last. She ungummed her eyes with spitty fingers and stared at the grey outline of the window where she had seen her mother's breasts, pendulous and bell-like against the curtains. She had tried to take Neville's advice and not to listen, but she had not been able to miss her father's agony.

Slowly and carefully she turned on to her side and faced the wall. Once, many years ago, Etta had described the truckle bed as a canoe. Tonight it seemed storm-tossed. She closed her eyes tightly and thought of Philip. Her rescuer.

CHAPTER FOUR

1936

Madge had borrowed the beach pyjamas from her friend at school. Her father did not really approve of them, but had to admit that sixteen-year-old Madge looked like someone in one of the magazines Marie loved – not even an English magazine; *Vogue* or *Harper's Weekly* from America. But of course Madge wasn't like that really, and she knew it. She still wore her hair in a single pigtail and her blue eyes, though no longer full of wonder, could widen with bewilderment that was almost innocence.

She said, 'Don't worry, Daddy. I'm wearing them to go rock-climbing with Philip, that's all. You have to admit they're very practical.'

'Hmm,' was all Alfred could manage, but Marie smiled. 'It is amazing how such practical clothing can look so chic,' she commented. 'How long before women realise that, I wonder, and take to wearing workmen's overalls?'

'Oh Mummy,' chided Madge.

Neville had no wish to go rock-climbing. He had been initiated into the Old Man's Head route two years before, and such childish feats no longer interested him. He had failed his matriculation and gone into the sooty offices just outside Temple Meads station, where he felt sometimes he could smell his own soul gently rotting away.

'Have you seen the latest from Spain, Dad?' He flapped the *Mail* before his father. 'The army is still in a state of mutiny. It's civil war, no less.'

Alfred shook his head. 'I thought they wouldn't take to

a republic. And that President Zamora was too weak.'

'Weak? What about when he put down the uprisings in Madrid? I told you then there would be trouble.'

'Well, they can't bring back the king. What else is there?'

'I don't know.' Neville looked through the parlour window. 'But if the army takes over it will be a dictatorship. They won't like that.'

Alfred shook his head again. He wasn't that interested. He was busy putting his own affairs in order, making certain that Marie would be all right if the pain in his chest finally got him.

Neville said with a kind of yearning, 'The Ruskies ought to help. If they really believe that a country belongs to its workers, then they ought to do something.'

'D'you mean the Bolshies?' Alfred was roused from self-absorption. 'Don't talk about them to me. Murdering devils. There was a chap – white Russian – talked to us at the annual luncheon last year about the trans-Siberian Railway and its maintenance. He could tell you about the Bolshies, my lad!'

'There's rot in all idealisms, Dad. But the Communists are *right*. Dammitall, you're supposed to be a good churchgoer. Surely Christianity is based on the same principles as Communism! Or t'other way round!'

But Alfred had learned that this kind of heated discussion was not good for him and he shook his head yet again and went into 'the back' to consult Etta about the catch of mackerel he had brought in that morning. Philip had brought the *Forty-niner* home early that summer and he took Alfred out regularly on local fishing trips. Marie had asked him to do so. It relaxed Alfred and made him sit still. She hoped very much to avoid a cricket match that year.

Madge trailed self-consciously along Porthmeor beach, her black jersey trousers whispering oddly against her calves. Neville had accused her of fancying herself these days, and perhaps she did. She tilted her chin in the way Hedy Lamarr did when she was provoking Charles Boyer, and lowered her eyelashes until they brushed her cheek.

'Ello there Madge! Coo. Looking proper growed-up this year, en't we?'

It was Jim yelling halfway across the beach as he led the two donkeys towards the customers outside the beach tents. Madge flushed with annoyance and assumed her normal expression as she walked towards him. There were plenty of people in family groups at the top of the beach, but nobody Madge recognised from previous years. She was thankful; she had no wish to be told by anyone else how growed-up she looked now she was sixteen.

'Good morning Jim,' she said formally. 'How are you?

'Okey-doke.' He waited hopefully while she untied the strings of the Bridges' tent, but it was early in the day for parents to be spending money on donkey rides.

''Oo wants a go on Brownie? Best donkey this side o' Newquay sands. Can gallop as fast as an 'orse but twice as safe.' Children's voices were raised in frantic pleas, and Jim, encouraged, continued his patter. 'Or 'is mum 'ere. Jennifer. Quiet. Docile as a kitten.'

Two small girls prevailed on their parents to pay for a ride. Jim left, and Madge breathed a sigh of relief and erected two chairs just to show she was expecting company. She rummaged in her beach bag and extracted dark glasses, then settled herself down with her book. After the prescribed literature of the last year at school, it was bliss to open the pages of an Ethel M. Dell.

Ten very short minutes later, Jim was back.

'Neville with you this year?'

Madge lifted her glasses reluctantly.

'Oh. Hello Jim. Yes, he is. I think he might have gone fishing with my father.'

'What about that other one. Came once with Neville. Clem wotsit.'

'He's not with us. I believe he is very well.'

'Both of 'em working now I suppose?'

Madge sighed and closed her book.

'Neville works with Father . . . well, he works for the Great Western Railway. In the office in Bristol. And

Clem is a trainee draughtsman at the Aircraft Corporation.'

'Suit 'im. Bet Neville 'ates and loathes bein' in an office, don't 'e?'

Madge was surprised that Jim knew so much about her brother, but she was admitting nothing.

Jim tried again.

'What about you then? You left school too?'

'Not yet.' Madge glanced around. 'Isn't that little boy interested in a ride, Jim?'

'Naw. 'E 'ad one yesty an' they're mean as mice. So what you gunna do then, Madge? Nurse, I bet.'

Madge was surprised again. 'What makes you say that?'

'Dunno. You'm always lookin' after folks.'

Madge, who felt useless and knew she must be a great burden to all her loved ones, opened her face in complete astonishment.

'Me? Who – whom – do I look after, Jim?'

'Well, nigh everyone it seems. Ole Philip Nolla for a start—'

'Philip?' Madge's embarrassment and surprise began to merge into irritation. 'Philip? I can assure you, Jim, that the shoe is on the other foot entirely!'

But Jim was not going to give up.

'Well then, your Neville.'

'My Neville as you call him, would have a lot to say about that! Neville is as independent as Philip. I wish I *could* look after them. Neither of them would permit it.'

'I din't mean look *after* zackly.' Jim at last realised he was putting his foot in things. 'I meant . . . oh it don't matter.' He hit Jennifer's coat and sand rained from it. 'I just wunnered . . . See, I knows your Neville thinks the world o' you—'

It would have been laughable if it hadn't been so annoying. Madge interrupted stiffly, 'I'm his sister.'

'Ah. But I reckon 'e'd do a lot for ee, which en't the case with all brothers and sisters as I know very well.'

Madge recognised Jim's typically diplomatic turn, which usually heralded the end of a conversation. She began to polish her sunglasses on a scrap of handkerchief preparatory to resuming her novel.

'So I wunnered . . . that is *she* wunnered . . . whether you'd 'ave a word with 'im about meeting up.'

Madge looked up in utter incomprehension.

'Your sister? She wants to meet my brother?'

'*Naw* . . .' he laughed. 'Not my *sister*. Rose Care. You know Rose Care – you used to chat with 'er at times when she 'elped me with the donkeys. She thought the world o' you, Madge.'

'Well, yes. I liked Rose. I haven't seen her for a long time. I thought she must have left St Ives.'

'She got a cottage out Zennor way. Makes enough out o' it to keep 'er goin' nicely.'

'She lets rooms?'

'In a manner of speaking 'er does. 'Er's a good girl is Rose.' He laughed again. 'In a manner of speaking that is.'

Madge vaguely remembered old gossip. She frowned. 'And she wants to meet my brother?' She put her glasses on top of her book again. 'In that case why does she not call at the cottage and state her business?'

''Er's done that. 'E weren't in at the time. Philip Nolla did say 'e'd pass on a message, but Neville en't been up to see 'er yet. She'd be mortal grateful, Madge, if you'd press 'im into goin' along one day. She don't want to make no trouble. Tell 'im she don't want to make no trouble at all. She wants to see 'im for 'aff an hour of 'is time. Dun't seem much to ask now, do it?'

She looked up at him. He was silhouetted against the sun so she could not read his expression, but he did not sound underhand or sly, which was unusual for Jim Maddern.

She said slowly, 'No. No, it doesn't. I had no idea . . .' She picked up her glasses and put them on. 'All right, Jim, I'll tell Neville that Rose would like to see him. Then it will be up to him, won't it?'

'I reckon so.' Jim shoved Brownie and he meandered over to the small boy who was still pestering his parents for a ride. 'Be sure and tell 'im she don't want to make no trouble. Dun't forget that, will you Madge?'

Madge pretended she was deep in her book.

Jim said, 'All right then. Come on, youngster. 'Aff price 'cos you're a good customer. 'Ow's that?'

The parents had little choice, Jim was already lifting their offspring into the saddle. As they wandered down to the firm sand, Madge hurriedly moved her two deckchairs back to the flaps of the beach tent where Jim would be unable to bring the donkeys. She was hot and uncomfortable now in the pyjamas and wished she'd stuck to her usual cotton frock until she actually went rock climbing with Philip. She made herself think about clothes and rock climbing and Ethel M. Dell so that she would have no room for puzzling thoughts about Neville and Rose Care.

That afternoon Philip led her carefully over the tumbled rocks to the very edge of the cliff itself. Fifty feet below, the sea snarled and waited.

'Looks dangerous, woman, but t'ain't at all – leastways, not yet. Ketch 'old o' the finger rocks and feel with your foot. Got it? That ledge runs right along to the back of Man's Head and the finger rocks follow it if you look for 'em.'

It was like the running board of a car. hidden by sea grass, but wide and firm. The tumbled rocks above it presented handholds here and there. She shuffled along in Philip's wake, glad at last of her trousers. The weather was as warm as this morning but there was a breeze now and then which would have lifted a skirt to waist level.

'Is this a secret way, Philip?' she asked.

'Aye. We tells it to the children when they gets old enough. Saves 'em breakin' a leg or an arm that way.'

'They could break their necks if they fell from here,' Madge commented, taking an unwary glance into the depths.

'That's why they mustn't know about it till they got a bit o' sense!'

Philip paused. He was beneath the looming mass of rock that sat apparently casually on a thin neck of stone. It did

61

not move like many such monoliths, but it looked as unsafe as Pisa or the Chesterfield spire.

Madge eyed it apprehensively.

'Why do people – nearly everyone really – want to climb Old Man's Head, Philip?'

'Not everyone do, my woman. But them as do, does. So they might as well learn 'ow and save some cracked bones, I reckon.' And he began to climb.

Madge had watched him often as he climbed the iron ladders along Smeaton's Pier; she had seen him scale the side of a boat and go aloft to fix a damaged sail. He was not a graceful man, he climbed like a monkey, bow-legged and claw-fingered, but he always made it look easy. He paused now, halfway up, and instructed her as to hand and foot holds. Then he went on to the top, turned and came down again. This time she went first and he waited. It was an easy climb and would have been simple if it weren't for the dizzying drop beneath.

'If you feels giddy, woman, just spread your arms and lean into the rock. Looks plumb vertical, but 't en't. If your foot slips, do the same. You'll slide down and skin yourself, but you'll land right 'ere on the ledge, no bones broken.'

So she reached the top and waited for him, grinning and triumphant.

'I've always wanted to do it. And it *looks* just terrible, Philip! How clever of you to find such an easy way.'

'Not me, woman, not Philip Nolla. All these ole ways was found by the smugglers long time since. That ledge do go on round to one of they ole mine adits. An' comes up in a cellar in Ayr.'

'Oh Philip. I shall come and sit up here and sketch. I don't know whether to be an artist or a nurse, Philip. What do you think?'

'Whatever you wants. Don't matter what you do s'long as you're 'appy.'

They were silent, sitting in the natural eyrie, feeling one with the gulls. Far below them the beach was crowded with tea-time deckchairs. Madge thought of Jim Maddern.

'Philip, did Rose Care come asking for Neville?' she asked.
'Aye, she did. I told 'im.'

'Well, it seems he took no notice. Jim asked me to have a word with him. What d'you suppose Rose wants with Neville?'

Philip's hat brim hid his face as always. He said in a flat voice, 'The usual I s'ppose.'

Madge felt her face becoming warm. She swallowed and said nothing.

Philip sighed. 'Well. Time we weren't 'ere, Madge. I'll go first. But just remember, unless you push yourself back'ards, there's no way you can fall down the cliff. Ready?'

'Yes.' Madge's voice was small. She cleared her throat and said over-loudly, 'Philip, when I was a little girl . . . ages ago . . . you said something about you and Etta not having children.'

He replied without embarrassment, 'I remember it well.'

'Do you? I just wondered . . . it's such a cheek, I know, to ask you this, but I just wondered if there was a reason. For you not having children.'

'You asted me that before, woman. Dun't you remember what I answered?'

'You said it was the Lord's Will.'

'So I did. And so it was.'

She said desperately, 'Yes but . . . I was a little girl then and now I'm grown up. I mean I understand things. And I wanted to know if there was a – a clinical reason.'

'You mean is Etta barren? Or me likewise?' He rolled round on to his hands and knees and felt with his right boot for the first foothold. 'I dun't know about that, woman. I'm not really a medical man, y'see.' He began to descend and when his eyes were on a level with her plimsolls he looked up for a moment into her red face. 'We knew it weren't the Lord's Will for us to 'ave children. So we didn't try.' His hat brim disappeared from view and she turned and backed towards the edge herself. She began to follow him down. Her feet found the toeholds, her fingers the niches. The thought of Neville and Rose Care was frightening. It was comforting to know that some people . . . didn't.

Madge did not have to broach the subject of a meeting after all. Neville, furious with Rose for actually coming to Zion Cottage, backed out of the afternoon on the beach and went to Prynn's in Tregenna Hill to hire a bicycle. He knew he could be as late as he wished; his father had approved of his cycling trips last year and was pleased to hear Neville was proposing to take some similar exercise this holiday.

As Neville strained the ancient cycle up Trevalgan Hill he changed the word exercise to hard labour. Unless it was something really vital, he'd murder Rose for getting him out to Zennor on a day like this. He was hot, sticky and fed up. If Rose thought they could go on with the affair year after year, she'd got another think coming. At the moment all he wanted to do was get out of the office and go to fight in Spain. He wished to God the Ruskies would organise some kind of foreign intervention. He couldn't simply land at Bilbao or wherever, and ask for a gun. When he got back he'd write off to the London Comintern and see what they were going to do about it all. Or better still he'd get Clem Briscoe to write. Clem could put a letter together better than anyone he knew.

He dismounted and pushed his bicycle up the slopes of Boscubben to Eagle's Nest. There he wedged his buttocks against the crossbar and rested, looking over the enormous expanse of land falling into the sea beyond Wicca's Pool. Last year the excitement of this trek, the feeling of becoming a real man at last, had filled his head completely. He had shown Rose an illegal copy of one of Lawrence's books and told her that they would live in poverty here, just as Lawrence had with his German wife in the Great War.

It had seemed wonderfully romantic at the time. Now he saw it as just another trap. Everything in this country – even St Ives – conspired to hold him down, to stop him doing anything exciting. Clem had said wistfully last week, 'God, I'd love to be coming down with you and your family, old man. Mother has booked a holiday for us in Yarmouth, of all places.' He'd grinned with some affection. 'She's always hunting for the Peggottys' boat, y'know. Security, warmth, that kind of thing.' Poor old Tagger, having to explain his awful mother.

Neville had said to him glumly, 'Glad you're not coming, actually. We'd probably have a row, then I'd have no friends at all.'

'Rubbish.' Clem had looked uncomfortable. 'Why should we have a row?'

'You'd take over with Rose where I left off. And I'd have to challenge you or something. Oh God, I don't know, Tagger. I'm at odds with everyone and everything. We should have done what we planned and joined the Foreign Legion.'

'We were silly kids, weren't we? When I remember some of the things we said and did . . .'

Neville straightened and swung his leg over the bicycle. That was the trouble. Clem had put all that behind him and settled for the humdrum. And Neville hadn't.

He freewheeled down the hill to the village, and the scented air blew away some of his ennui so that he could begin to anticipate the pleasure of seeing Rose again. She must be desperate for him if she'd come knocking at Zion Cottage. Good job Philip had answered the door. Etta would have told her where to get off, and his parents would have been bewildered by her enquiry, then horribly suspicious.

He smiled, remembering last year and the year before that. Jim Maddern must have reported to her ages ago that Nevill Bridges was 'h'intrigued and h'interested' as he put it. And Rose had lost no time in accosting him and inviting him to see her cottage. Her brazenness was such that it was almost innocent; the master at Mennion House had told her she was beautiful, and she knew he would not lie about things like that. Her confidence as she undressed was enormous. She pointed out violet threads around her abdomen. 'Them's stretch marks from the master's babby. Oh 'e were a lovely babby. 'E went to someone out 'Elston

way and the master do pay 'ansome an' 'e's bein' brought
up like a li'll gentleman.' She had laughed unaffectedly.
'Think o' that! Rose Care's babby – a gentleman!' Then
she had sobered and said, 'I 'aven't 'ad no more babbies.
Nor I shan't. It do 'urt 'aving of 'em, and it do 'urt givin'
'em away. I got some stuff to put up inside me what stops
anything 'appening.'

Neville had been horrified at first and then she had kissed
him and said, 'You can do it for me if you like.' And it
hadn't been sordid any longer. Nothing was sordid with
Rose. Everything was 'natural'. Morals and ethics were
words in the dictionary; if you wanted to do something, then
it must be 'natural'.

He walked his bike around the back of Skinner's Cottage
and propped it on the dry stone wall which kept the
encroaching thistles and fern of the clifftop from the tiny
neat garden that Rose tended so expertly. A clothes line ran
from the privy roof to this wall, and the laundry on it was
still dripping. Rose must be in.

He knocked on the back door. Nothing happened. He
knocked again. She could have popped to the Tinners' Arms
for bread. Or . . . she could have someone with her. Neville
was under no illusions as to how she paid the rent of the
cottage. This could be damned embarrassing.

There was a click from above and the scraping of the sash
being lifted. He stepped back and looked up at the window.
Rose was framed there, her shoulders bare, hair down. She
did have someone with her.

'Sorry', he began. 'Was just passing and thought—'

'Neville Bridges! I thought you'd never bloody well come!
Wait!' She stood up to pull the window down and he saw
she was naked at least from the waist up. He felt hot, then
cold. Supposing whoever it was came down with her and
chose to be aggressive? Neville was spoiling for a fight, but
not in these circumstances.

Bolts were pulled at the back door, and Rose opened it.
She wore one of her usual unsuitable dresses, bright red
silk, much too short, but at least she was clothed and

66

buttoned. Her normal high colour was hectic, her dark eyes flashing all kinds of messages, her glorious mass of black hair all over the place as always. She gave off a smell; not Roses of Attar, or Evening in Paris. Slightly sour.

'Where the hell have you *been*? I told Jim to tell you and I thought you'd be up the next day! Christ, I began to wonder if you were trying to get out of it or something!' She stood aside. 'Get in for God's sake. You look 'alf gormless.'

He'd heard Rose had a temper and could be sharp, but he'd never seen her like this. He stepped meekly past her into the dark scullery. The smell wasn't here; she'd been scrubbing, and everything was damp. The smell came from her. He wondered if she was ill.

'Have you got someone with you?' He resisted her prodding hand, looking at the door of the room with some trepidation. 'I mean, I don't want to make things awkward for you, Rose.'

''Course I ain't got no-one with me! 'Ow can I 'ave anyone 'ere *now*?' She shoved him impatiently and he went through the door with a rush and stood blinking in the lighter room.

It was as he remembered. Rose was a good housekeeper, properly trained at Mennion House; the grate was black-leaded, the rag rug shaken and the window diamond bright. On the big round table which took up most of the space, she had plonked her laundry basket; that wasn't like her.

She flounced past him impatiently, and he saw with something of a shock that she was unbuttoning the bodice of her dress; this was carrying naturalness a bit too far, surely? Then she leaned into the basket, scooped out a baby and sat herself in a chair.

'I was feedin' 'im. 'E'll go mad if I don't finish off. You'd better sit down, 'adn't you? Stop gawping as if you'd never seen my titty before too!'

He drew out a chair and sat down very slowly while she poked one of her nipples into the baby's avid mouth. She flinched as the small lips began to suck, then sighed and

67

settled herself more comfortably with elbow on the table.

Neville said, 'What on earth – I thought you said – what happened?'

''E's yours, you great lummock! You couldn't 'ave put that stuff in proper! All that messin' about instead of getting on with the job – I told you at the time—' the child came up for air and she waited until he was feeding again. 'I nearly bloody died when nothin' 'appened that next month. If you'd bin 'ere, you'd 'a got the rough edge o' my tongue, I'm tellin' you!'

Neville realised his jaw had dropped and he put his teeth together with an audible click. The scene before him was incredible. He could not take in that he was responsible for it. Quite simply, he had never seen a woman breastfeeding before and the sensuality of it took his breath away. He cleared his throat to speak, then said nothing.

Rose gave him another look.

'Well? You gunna pretend it can't be yours, I s'ppose? That's what Mr Trewyn said before.' She put on a mincing voice. 'Oh it can't be nothin' to do with me, my dear, and as you go with anyone 'ow you goin' to prove it's mine?' She removed the baby from her breast forcibly and held him forward. 'Look at 'im, Neville Bridges. Look at 'im and tell me 'e's not yours!'

The baby opened its mouth and let out a piercing yell of frustration. It was practically bald and with its eyes screwed tight there was no gauging the colour of them. But Neville could see that this mewling infant was his. There was nothing of Rose in the furious face; but there was a ludicrous look of Alfred, and both Marie and Madge had that dark line of down following the jawbone.

He muttered, 'Oh my God . . . my God . . .'

She was satisfied. 'Ah. I've called on 'Im too. 'E don't do nuthin' about it, Neville. This is something we done, and that's that.' She turned the baby and put him over her shoulder; he burped a mouthful of milk on to her bare neck and his cry reduced to a grizzle. She rubbed his back.

Still he watched, horrified yet fascinated. The discarded

breast hung flaccidly, the nipple wet and shining. She saw him looking and said sharply, 'There's none there for you so you can stop that!' And he turned, revolted by his own thoughts, and stared at the rag rug with burning eyes.

She went on doing things; he heard her murmuring to the baby, fiddling with it's clothes, then standing up to put him back in the basket. The chair creaked as she sat down again and he realised she was buttoning her dress. He looked up.

'Oh lor' . . .' she was still sharply impatient. 'Dun't look like that, man – like a beaten dog. What's done is done. What we got to think about, is what we do next!' She laughed suddenly with a flash of her old provocative sensuality. 'Aye, we can do *that* o' course – though I'll see to the jelly this time if you dun't mind! But what we gunna do about the babby? I can't keep 'im. My callers dun't like it, y'see.'

'Oh God. Rose. Why didn't you tell me? Going through all that on your own! Why didn't you let me know?'

Her face softened again.

''Ow could I? I cain't write, Neville, surely you knows that? An' if I'd 'a got someone to do it for me – what could you 'a done? Eh? Left your job and come down 'ere to be another mouth for me to feed?' She laughed. 'My lover . . . all that talk about living in a cottage on cabbages . . . that were talk. Nuthin' more.' She touched the back of his hand. 'I got my ways and you got yours, my lovely.'

He muttered, 'I can't bear it.'

'That's laughable, that is!' She showed him that it was, throwing back her head, exposing the magnificent throat and white teeth. 'You din't 'ave to bear nuthin', m' 'ansome. I dun all that.' Her mood changed again and she left her chair and sat on his lap. 'We'll think o' somethin', never fear. 'E's 'ealthy and 'appy enough. Someone 'll 'ave 'im for us. What about your mam?'

He was appalled, and she laughed again, pressing him against the chair back, covering his face with her hair, enveloping him in the smell of sour milk.

'I were just 'avin you on, my lovely. Give us a kiss now.'

'But Rose – how did you – where did you go – who looked after—'

'Jim Maddern.'

He was appalled again. 'But Rose – darling – stop it – Jim Maddern is a kid! He's younger than Madge!'

That made her almost helpless with laughter and she did indeed stop doing what she had been doing and lifted her face to look at him.

'Oh Neville Bridges! You're younger than any of 'em and you dun't even know it!' She controlled her laughter with difficulty, then cupped his face in her capable hands. 'Don't worry, my 'andsome. Jim and me managed very well, no 'arm to either of us. And the babby's lovely. Nuthin' wrong with 'im at all. I do swear I never tried to get rid of 'im. I wanted 'im to be good.' She lowered her mouth on to his very gently. The front of her dress was open again and he felt her warmth and a dampness against his shirt front. He put his arms around her and held on as if he were drowning. When she let him, he cried out, 'Oh Rose . . . Rose . . .' and she crooned, 'There there, my lovely boy, there there.' Just as if *he* were the baby in the laundry basket.

This holiday Madge had Neville's old room and Neville slept on the sofa in the parlour window. It gave Alfred and Marie a privacy they needed more and more as his chest pains worsened.

That night he lay gasping for breath, the pills easing the burning in his lungs only slightly. Marie lay quietly by his side, trying to control the thumping of her heart. Since that awful attack four years ago, he had definitely deteriorated. But it was twenty years since he had been gassed; surely he should have got over it by now.

She whispered, 'Is it getting any better, Alfred?'

'Yes,' he breathed, so that she knew it wasn't.

'Let me get you a drink. Cocoa. Something soothing.' She was halfway out of bed as she spoke. He put a restraining hand on her arm.

'No. It's going. Really. Don't leave me, Marie.'

Terror knifed her. 'Oh my darling. Never. Never.'

'Talk to me, Marie. Talk to me about . . . us.'

Her eyes filled but she would not let them spill over. This might be the end. It really might be the end. He had always treated her like a queen, and like a queen she would be.

She murmured, 'We've always loved each other, my darling, haven't we? Since we met that night at the school dance. You were so handsome, like the old king, blue eyes, and always smiling. And you danced beautifully. Beautifully my darling. It was one of the reasons my papa thought so highly of you. He was a good dancer. Many Dutchmen are. Not that he thought of himself as Dutch. Always British.'

Alfred squeezed her hand gratefully. She took three breaths in time with his. They were very shallow.

'It was the war that made us marry so quickly, wasn't it, Alfred? And it was the war that made us decide to have dear Neville. And then Madge was a thanksgiving for – for – survival. She still is. All her life she will be . . .' The tears were there but she forced herself on. 'Every time we look at Madge we remember the years we have had together. Which others did not have.' She stopped and swallowed hard, then went on quickly, 'And coming here . . . how lucky we've been, Alfred. Always. So lucky. So much more than a holiday here with Etta and Philip. A sort of renewal each year. A summer tryst.' She measured her breathing to his again; it was deeper. Her low whisper grew stronger. 'You'll get better here, Alfred. I know it. The air is soft and will soothe your chest. You must give it a chance to work, dearest. No more fishing trips, I beg of you. Let us sit quietly and allow St Ives to do its work.'

His grip on her hand was firm now. She waited, straining her eyes through the darkness to read an expression on the grey-white face.

At last he said very quietly, 'Marie. Darling. You are right. You are always right. We have borrowed so much time together. We are so very, very lucky.' He held her hand hard as if she would protest. 'It is always borrowed, Marie. Always. We had an overdraft!' He tried to laugh and

71

stopped. 'Marie, listen. If it should . . . if the bank will not extend the overdraft . . . it is important not to cavil. Not to become bitter. To keep the sweetness. Can you do that, sweetheart? For the children's sake? For my sake?'

She took a breath and held it for a long moment until the tears subsided once more. He lifted her hand and put it to his face. His skin felt chill and clammy.

'I think . . . this will be my last time in St Ives,' he said simply.

Her body jerked involuntarily but she said nothing. After a while he went on, almost musingly. 'Neville is a man and will protect you. I have no need for anxiety on that score. And I would like to think . . . it would be a triumph for our years together, if the happiness could go on. Especially here. Especially in St Ives.'

She hardly heard his words, she was concentrating so hard on his breathing. It was better. His words emerged in two's and three's instead of singly.

She whispered, 'I think it's going. I think you're getting better, Alfred.'

He gave a shallow sigh. 'Yes. I am better, Marie. Lie down now. We are together at this moment and nothing can change that.'

'And we will be together tomorrow too,' she said stubbornly. 'It is eighteen years since . . . nothing is going to happen now. Not after eighteen years.'

She lay by his side and let the tears slide silently down her face and into her pillow. She had been brought up to believe that a woman was never complete without a husband and though she had faced widowhood during those four terrible years of war, the thought now was unbearable.

In the end it was Philip who 'sorted it out' for Neville.

The next day Alfred did not go out with the *Forty-niner*, and Neville had Philip to himself. He did not enjoy confessing his sins to the old man, but at least he wasn't completely Bible-bound like Etta. And Neville had to tell someone.

'God, Philip. When I think of her all alone in that cottage

– just Jim Maddern, would you believe it – couldn't let me know!' Neville dropped his head in his hands and remembered again the utter deliciousness of Rose Care. It gave him the strength to go on. After all, that deliciousness was known by many others beside himself.

'She still . . . I mean there are plenty of *friends* . . . they'd have taken the child. But she wasn't sure . . . and anyway she wanted me to see him and have some sort of say in where he should go.' He darted a look up and was comforted to see that Philip's shaded face was not expressing anything but listening silence. He put his hands on his knees and said earnestly, 'What I'd like, Philip, is to come down here and marry Rose and keep the baby. But she won't. Can you *believe* it–' he asked for the second time. 'She won't hear of marrying me or keeping the baby!'

There was a silence and Neville wondered whether Philip was going to react at all to his shattering disclosures.

Then the old man took his pipe from his mouth and said unexpectedly, 'She's a good girl is Rose Care. Stupid in that way. But in other ways, very sensible. You shouldna gone with 'er, Neville, but if you 'ad to go with someone you coulda done worse. There's lots 'ud 'ave made trouble for ee, boy. You know that, dun't you?'

'Yes. That's what I've been saying! I love her, Philip! I want to marry her!'

'Well, she d'know that's impossible even if you dun't. An' a good job too. 'Ow long d'you think it would be afore you were fed up with our way o' life? Then you would leave a lot o' misery be'ind you. Whereas now . . .' Philip put the pipe back between his teeth and drew experimentally. It had gone out. 'Now I think we can do something for the littl'un. Cos that's 'oo we got to thing about. Nemmind you, young Neville. Nemmind Rose Care – she'll be all right whatever do 'appen. It's that young 'un we got to look out for. 'E's your son so 'sno good puttin' 'im where 'e'll end up in the mines or even on the sea. 'E's got to 'ave a good chance in life. Some'ow. Somewhere.'

It occurred to Neville that Philip was making the problem more complicated.

He said, 'He's Rose's child as well, remember, Philip. Wasn't her father a miner?'

'Aye, and killed afore he could look after Rose properly. She won't want that for her son any more than you.'

'Yes but . . . what's the alternative?'

Philip said quietly. 'Mr Trewyn. That's the alternative. 'E's done it for Rose before and 'e'll do it again. I'll 'ave a word with 'im this very afternoon.'

'Mr Trewyn? Mennion House? Never! I'm not going cap in hand to that . . . lecher! If it weren't for him Rose wouldn't be . . .' Neville's voice faded. Rose was born to be a jezebel. Her first employer had merely discovered as much. He cleared his throat. 'No, Philip. Not the Trewyn man. I can't face him. Sorry.'

Philip made no comment on Neville's lack of courage. He simply repeated. 'I'll 'ave a word with 'im.'

'But—' Neville searched for tact. 'Look. Philip, old man. He won't *listen* to you. Or if you manage to tell him your errand, he'll think – he might even think – you're the father! Either way he'll throw you out. Sorry, but he will.'

Philip sucked on his empty pipe and grinned.

'He might at that. But I shall convince him in the end. Make him see that in the circumstances he ought to help Rose again.' He glanced at Neville. 'His young wife is expecting their first child. He wun't want 'er to be upset like.'

Neville looked at the man of whom his mother had once said, 'He's never done a bad thing in his life.' He swallowed. 'That's a kind of blackmail, surely, Philip?'

'Aye. I reckon it is.' Philip pulled his hat down over his eyes. 'I'm not doing this for you. Understand that, boy. I'm doin' it for your ma and your pa. And for young Madge.'

'Madge. I'd forgotten Madge. Oh God, I'd die if ever Madge found out.'

'Well, she won't. So stop calling on God unnecessary-like.' Philip removed his pipe once more and knocked it

74

out on the gunnel. 'That's another reason for me goin' alone this afternoon.'

Neville put his face back in his hands. 'I think I'm going mad, Philip.'

'You're certainly not doin' that neither, boy. Once we got this arranged you can put it be'ind you and get on with your plans. Next year you'll 'ardly remember it.'

Neville said with sudden assurance, 'I'll never come back to St Ives, Philip. This is the last time.' He lifted his head. Philip was already clambering over the wide stern into the dinghy and probably hadn't heard him. Neville stared out at the glassy sea and wondered at his own words. Were they true? Surely he would come back next year and the year after, ad infinitum? Yet he had spoken with a kind of prescience not easily dismissed.

He stood up to follow Philip and the thought suddenly struck him forcibly: whatever happened to him, wherever he went, he would leave part of himself in this corner of England. His son would be a Cornishman. It was the one good thing to come out of this mess.

CHAPTER FIVE

1938

Marie Bridges maintained she never wanted to go to St Ives again. She insisted that the memories would be simply unbearable. If Alfred had been spared to her, they might have gone without Neville and found comfort in the familiarity of the place; if Neville had lived she would have gone for his sake. With both of them dead it seemed the last place on earth for a holiday.

But Madge felt differently; and surprisingly, so did young Clem Briscoe. Madge set great store by the physical and mental doctoring of Etta and Philip Nolla. She and her mother had tried a very good private hotel in Bournemouth last year and had both been miserable and rather frightened. They might well feel sad in St Ives, but they would not be miserable nor frightened. Especially if Clem Briscoe was with them.

Clem was quite simply desperate to go. He had been standing next to Neville when he had been killed at the siege of Madrid and he felt a mixture of guilt and bewilderment at the whole 'Spanish interlude' as his mother now called it. The happiest two weeks of his life had been spent at St Ives with Neville Bridges and his sister and parents and he had some obscure idea of recapturing that holiday; if possible recapturing it for ever. Besides his doctor had told him that if he could get away for a while and completely relax, the dreams would cease and he would be able to start work again. He owed it to Mr Bridges to start work again; it had been Neville's father who got him into the drawing office at the aeroplane factory.

He broached the subject himself on one of his many visits to the Bridges' tall house in Clifton.

'Neville would be so disappointed to hear you say you'll never go to St Ives again.'

Since he had returned home, wounded, he had an occasional stammer which came on him when he was anxious. He stared at Mrs Bridges hard, willing his tongue to command speech.

'You know how he kept on about the place. On-and-on-and-on—' he clamped his mouth shut and looked away, flushing.

Marie Bridges pushed her constant grief aside for a moment and concentrated on feeling protective towards this old friend of Neville's. His hair was already thinning and now that he could not meet her eyes his gaze flicked everywhere, at the floor one moment, then, with a nervous flick, at the ceiling. On his last visit to London to see the army doctors at Woolwich, he had collapsed in the Mall. Nerves. They did frightful things to people apparently, a bit like shell shock after the war. Alfred had not had shell shock, that was one good thing. He had just had gas.

She turned to the empty summer fireplace with its arrangement of fir cones.

'We all love St Ives, Clem. You did too, didn't you? We've had such happy, happy times there.'

Clem looked at young Marjorie Bridges, then quickly away. But not before he had registered every last detail of her. She was four years younger than he was, and with her newly bobbed hair held back on one side with a tortoiseshell slide and her fashionable sleeveless dress, she looked all of her eighteen years. But with his inner eye he still saw the twelve-year-old innocent.

He stared at a point between the two women and saw that they were both looking at him with identical expressions of sadness and understanding.

He stammered, 'That's why I'd like . . . that's why I want . . . the chappie in London says a fortnight's rest and change before I go back to work.'

He saw Marjorie turn and look at her mother pleadingly and his heart leapt. She wanted to go to St Ives with him. She wanted to be with him as much as he wanted to be with her. It was going to be all right. At last something was going to be all right. She knew all about unhappiness, but it had not dimmed her own joy and youth. She could give him some of her assurance, some of her . . . essence. He had to have her; he had to.

She said softly, 'It would do you good, Mother. It would do all of us good.'

Mrs Bridges murmured, 'I thought I'd never go back there.'

Marjorie seized her mother's hands and held them tightly. Sometimes she could hardly bear the sheer weight of the pain borne by Marie; now this feeling was extended towards Neville's friend. She wanted to put her arms around both of them and physically lift them away from their burdens.

She said gently, 'You *thought* you'd never go back, Mother? And what are you thinking now?'

Marie sighed very deeply.

'I daresay it is what your poor father would like us to do.'

Marjorie said rallyingly, 'Neville would like it too, darling. They would both want us to carry on, you know that.' She stood up and came to Clem's side and held his arm. 'And they'd certainly like Clem to come with us. It will set him up for the winter.'

She used a phrase spoken often by her father and was rewarded by a rueful smile from her mother.

'I suppose it will set us all up for the winter,' she said.

They caught the Cornishman from Temple Meads and got a first class compartment to themselves. Marie liked to travel with her back to the engine and Madge settled by her side. Clem sat in the corner seat opposite the two women, at first grateful for their silence, then sweating at his own thoughts. As the train pulled out of Taunton he had reached the usual impasse: Mr Bridges had talked his mother into allowing him to take the Technical College course, and then had got

78

him the job with National Aeroplanes. He had repaid him by letting Neville persuade him to throw it all up and join the Comintern army in Spain. Perhaps he had been the cause of that final and fatal attack, perhaps Mrs Bridges actually held him responsible for the death of her husband.

The train drew in to Exeter and Madge went down the corridor and bought some fruit from a trolley on the platform. He jumped up to follow her and the pain in his leg made him gasp. Mrs Bridges said, 'Do sit down, Clement dear. Madge promised me she wouldn't actually get off the train, so she'll be all right.' He collapsed again, feeling stupid and ineffectual. He wished he could ask her whether she realised that it had been Neville who had wanted to go to Spain; perhaps she thought it was the other way round?

He darted one of his surreptitious glances at her. Her black hair was turning dramatically white in places; two wings of ermine swept away from the centre parting and beneath her Queen Mary toque. How old would she be – mid forties? Younger than his own mother, that was certain. And so different. No bitterness here, no inversion of mouth, nostrils, eyes, cheeks. Rather, a late flowering. He couldn't bear it if she thought ill of him.

Madge came back in and offered him an enormous Comice pear. A whistle blew and the train started forward, then paused while the locomotive tried to grip the rails a little better. Madge smiled. 'The rule of necessary friction,' she quoted at him. He smiled back; they were her father's words. She was including him in the family. He bit into his pear and did not panic when juice ran down his chin.

They went into the corridor as the train ran along the coast to Teignmouth. Madge's enthusiasm was boundless.

'I remember that heron from the last time we were here! No honestly Mother, it's the same one. Of course they don't all look the same. You might as well say we . . .'

Mrs Bridges said apologetically, 'Take no notice of Madge, Clement. She sometimes forgets she is eighteen and not eight years old!'

He had heard that phrase before too; Madge had used

79

it to Neville once. He smiled and said without a trace of stammer, 'I hope she can always forget her age and be like you are, Mrs Bridges. Herself.'

Nobody knew quite what he meant, but it was an obvious compliment and Madge dimpled delightedly while Mrs Bridges inclined her head and murmured, 'Dear Clement . . .'

His confidence grew. At Plymouth he undertook to fetch tea. At St Erth he found a porter and shepherded the luggage across the line to the branch train while the women used the footbridge. When he joined them Madge was already stationed at an open window.

'Come on Clem, you can get your head above mine. This is the best bit. D'you remember? We shall go right past the place where we had the bonfire.'

The train moved off and almost immediately they were running alongside the Hayle estuary where Madge claimed to see cormorants, kittiwakes and sandpipers within the first five seconds. Her hat had long been discarded and she now pulled out her slide so that her short hair blew up into his face. He closed his eyes against the rushing air and breathed the scent of Cuticura soap. The train slowed a second time.

'Carbis Bay,' Madge announced. Two sedate ladies in spotted voile and carrying parasols, embarked. Madge turned her head. 'Very see-lect here,' she whispered conspiratorially. He opened his eyes and looked at her. She was so close he could see each individual freckle on her nose. He closed his eyes again.

Mrs Bridges said sharply, 'Sit down Madge! Clement's leg must be aching by now!'

Clem sat down abruptly and Madge withdrew her head and looked at him, all concern.

'Clem, I'm so sorry. I didn't think. Is it very bad?'

He couldn't very well tell them why he had closed his eyes. He forced a smile. 'No. I'd forgotten it. Honestly.'

'Are you sure?'

'Absolutely.'

The train jolted carefully against the buffer stops and Mrs

Bridges announced, 'We're here. Are you all right to get to the taxi rank, dear boy?'

Madge said, 'Look at the boats. I can see S.S.48 but not the *Forty-niner*.'

'You know very well Philip and the lugger will be in the North Sea grounds now.' Mrs Bridges gathered her handbag, umbrella and picnic basket close to her. The porter appeared at the open door and drew out the cases. 'Has the trunk arrived yet?' she went on anxiously.

Madge said, 'I thought he might have been here to meet us. That's all.'

The porter looked at the label on the cases.

'Bridges,' he recited. ''Tis 'ere already. Bin delivered this morning.'

Madge said, 'Don't forget your mack, Clem. And where are the books and maps?'

'In the picnic basket.' Mrs Bridges tried to adjust her hat and knocked her glasses askew with her handbag. Clem picked up the picnic basket, his mack, Madge's mack, his umbrella and a roll of newspapers, and followed the two women on to the platform. There were flowers everywhere. The air seemed to tingle in his nose and chest. Above him the cliff rose perpendicularly, shelved by a road and villas and a sumptuous hotel. It was a different world here; everything would become all right again here; he was certain of it.

They struggled to a taxi and he loaded the cases methodically.

'Oh it is so nice to have you with us, Clement.' Mrs Bridges settled herself comfortably. 'You are so reliable.'

Clem thought he had never received such a wonderful compliment in his life.

They walked a great deal. Etta Nolla and Mrs Bridges would ensconce themselves on the seat by the harbour wall and talk about Neville and Alfred and do some knitting, and the young people were expected to amuse themselves. Madge would have been happy to lie on the beach all day and take a dip in the surf of Porthmeor just before they went

81

in for their high tea. But Clem was restless and eager to explore.

'You've had so many summers to get to know this place,' he told her. 'I've only been here once before, remember. I want to see it through your eyes.'

Madge smiled instant reassurance. She knew he was shy about swimming because of his leg. When he had reluctantly come in with her on their second day, she had seen that he had hardly any calf on his left leg. The skin had been stitched tightly around his shinbone, giving the appearance of a peg-leg. It did not stop him doing most things; he could clamber around the rocks and he was a very good walker. He used a stick with which he slashed at encroaching nettles on the footpaths.

Madge said, 'Actually I've never explored around here either, Clem. Father liked the walks up-country better and Philip always warned us about the old mine-shafts along here. So you're opening up new territories for me.'

He flushed with pleasure. 'Well, you were rather young for walking much when you were here before.'

'I don't know about that. I was expected to keep up with whatever was happening. But Father was such an organiser. And walking didn't satisfy his urge to organise!' She laughed. 'He loved a good picnic. We all had to carry something – I managed the cushions and sunshades.' She paused for a moment to look over the Atlantic. 'And of course there were the cricket matches. You must remember the cricket matches.'

'Yes. Whenever I think of Neville, it is always playing cricket.'

She turned to him, her eyes very bright, but happy. 'How lovely! How perfectly lovely! I know just what you mean. And I think of him here too. Always here.'

He nodded, mesmerised again by her eyes. She was so like Neville in a feminine way. She kept Neville alive. Somehow.

Impulsively she took his arm and led him to an outcrop of rock which made a natural seat.

'D'you know, that's the first time you've mentioned Neville. I think if you could talk about him more, you'd begin to feel better.' She glowed at him, her eagerness to help flushing her face. 'How much do you remember of that cricket match, Clem? Tell me – talk to me!'

He said hypnotically, 'I remember bowling Mrs Nolla and Neville congratulating me even though she whacked it to the boundary. I remember Neville saying he didn't want to join the G.W.R. with his father. I remember him suggesting we try to get into the French Foreign Legion.'

'Did he really? Even then . . . sorry. Go on, Clem. Keep going.'

'I remember Neville talking about some girl and you telling him that this girl did not wear knickers and then—'

Madge said quickly, 'No, not that bit. Just the bits about Neville.'

He realised with a start what he had said to this eight-year-old girl . . . no, eighteen. His stammer came back with a rush.

'I – I – I – I—'

She looked away from him but kept his arm between her hands. 'Not if it hurts you, Clem. I shouldn't have asked you.'

'It's not . . .' He wanted so desperately to explain to her that it wasn't enough to talk about dead people. Somehow you had to link them into the present and the future. But he couldn't find words. Maths had been his subject at school; it had been Neville who had been good at English. They were so different in every way. Thrown together for alphabetical reasons – Bridges and Briscoe sat together, ate together, prayed together – Neville had called him Tagger Briscoe because he always tagged along. Now, somehow . . . however impossible . . . he had to make certain that Neville could tag along with him.

'It's not that it hurts. But I – I – I – I want to do more than just talk. I want to *do* something to make them remembered always.'

83

There was a silence which both thought was one of complete mutual understanding.

Madge said quietly at last, 'Is that why you wanted to come to St Ives?'

'With – with – with – with *you*,' he blurted.

She tried to ignore a stab of unease; she had always felt awkward with the opposite sex. But not with Clem Briscoe; she must not feel awkward with her brother's friend.

She said slowly, 'I don't think we can suggest another cricket match, Clem. There aren't enough of us. And it would hurt Mother unbearably. Perhaps a cooking fire though?'

'It's all right. You don't have to . . . it's too soon. Just to be here together, you and m-m-me. That's enough for now. Isn't it?'

'Oh it is, Clem. It is!' She clasped his arm and through the thicknesses of his shirt and jacket he could feel faintly the thump of her heart. Then she released him and gave him a sisterly pat. 'Come on, let's move off. Mother is trying to teach poor Etta how to cook mutton chops. I really should help. It's an uphill task!'

He was disappointed; he wanted that moment of complete understanding to go on for ever. But as he followed her back along the cliff path to Clodgy and Old Man's Head, he accepted that he mustn't hurry her. The pat had been a promise as well as a caution. They both knew that their salvation lay in each other.

That evening Mrs Nolla told them that she'd had a message from Seahouses in Northumberland. Philip would be home before the end of their holiday and was looking forward to seeing them. Madge's joy was obvious; Clem remembered that Philip Nolla had been her special friend. For some reason Clem felt a foreboding that with Philip's arrival the wonderful easy solution to everything would go wrong. He bit his lip and shifted his leg to an easier position. He must settle things with Madge. He must settle things quickly before this other permanent figure from the past returned.

Marie Bridges and Madge took their candle up to the front

room at nine-thirty and got ready for bed back to back. If either of them felt distaste at sharing the big feather bed, they said nothing.

Marie blew out the candle immediately they climbed between the sheets, then said anxiously into the darkness, 'Darling, did you make sure you'd brushed all the sand off your feet?'

'Yes Mother. In fact I washed them under the cellar tap before supper.'

'Good girl. It's just that the bed felt slightly gritty when I put my legs down. It's this unbleached calico. Honestly, Etta and Philip do not move with the times.'

Madge said comfortably, 'That is what is so absolutely marlovely about them.'

'Oh that silly word again . . . You're looking forward to seeing Philip?'

'Oh yes. It doesn't seem right without him.'

The words fell deadly into the darkness and the women thought of the other two men who would never be with them again.

Mrs Bridges sighed. 'No. Not right at all.' She heaved her shoulder over so that she was facing Madge. 'You know, darling, Philip made a specific point of being home when we were here. He never had before we began to come in August. Most of the luggers stay away till mid-September.'

'Yes, I know.'

'I sometimes think that as he and Etta had no children they thought of you and Neville as their own family.'

This seemed so obvious to Madge she did not reply.

Marie went on musingly. 'Etta must have written to him about Clement. He'll be coming back to meet him again, I expect.'

'Why on earth should you think that, Mother? Philip is coming to see us, surely – not Clem.'

'Well . . . oh I know you're still very young, my darling, but you must know why Clement was so insistent on this holiday. And actually you are older than I was when I met your father first of all.'

Madge went hot then immediately stone-cold.

'I'm sure you're wrong, Mother. Clem wants to be with us down here because of Neville. Nothing to do with me. In that way.' She flushed hotly again.

Marie said soothingly, 'I expect you're right, my dearest. Please don't let it worry you. It's just that . . . it would be so suitable. And your father liked him.'

'I'm never going to get married, Mother. When you . . . when we . . . feel strong again, I wondered whether I would go to a teachers' training college. I know I'm not good enough to be a real artist, but I think I could teach art.'

Marie gave a low laugh. 'We'll think about that later, Madge dear. Meanwhile, don't set your face against marriage. It's a natural state and you are a very natural person.'

In the darkness Madge set her lips hard.

Marie said suddenly, 'What's that?'

They both listened. Above the sound of the waves came a sudden scrabble on the roof.

'Gulls,' whispered Madge.

'Yes.' Marie Bridges settled her pillows beneath her head. 'Turn over and sit in my lap, Madge. We really should go to sleep. Those blessed birds will wake us at the crack of dawn!'

Madge turned over gratefully and closed her eyes. Once Philip came home everything would be all right. Anyway, Clem Briscoe was ill and looked on her as his nurse. That was what she was: his nurse. And if she could persuade him to talk about Neville, she would have done a good job.

Clem was in the room he had shared before with Neville. He lay on his back, staring at the candle shadows which leaned and leered across the planked ceiling as if they were reaching for something. He felt very tired, but sleep meant nightmares and he always fought it for as long as he could. He concentrated on thoughts of Madge Bridges and forced a smile at the candle flame. She wasn't really beautiful but

86

in her way she was so . . . perfect. Her hair was abundant though its mouse-brownness meant it was not sensational. Her blue eyes were clear and untroubled, yet at the same time full of sympathy and understanding; they were never provocative and they rarely 'sparkled'. Her nose was small but it had a definite bump in the middle, and her mouth was too big for beauty. She had the sort of attraction that he was certain he alone could see; only he could see that the sum total of all her slightly imperfect parts, was perfect. He could make that full mouth tremble, those eyes fill with tears. He wished her hair was still uncut so that he might remove the pins and let it tumble around her shoulders.

He must tell her the truth about Neville and himself. He nearly had today, then his tongue had stuck to the roof of his mouth and prevented proper speech. But if he could be completely honest with her she would understand about the necessity of bringing Neville into the present and carrying him with them into the future. They could do it together. Between them they knew everything about Neville; good and bad. They could cherish it all, nourish it, make it possible for Neville to live through them so that his terrible, stupid, unheroic death wasn't wasted.

His muscles were knotted rigidly beneath the sheets and agonising cramp sheathed his left shin. He tore his thoughts away from Neville with a physical wrench of his body, closed his eyes on the candle flame and muttered aloud, 'Madge . . . Madge . . .' And as if she had heard him and was coming immediately to his summons, the bedroom door opened.

He felt his eyelids snap open and then real terror gripped him. The figure who stood in the doorway was not Madge. In its long gown and with its veined hands outstretched and its hair a wispy halo, it reminded Clem of a picture in one of his mother's books: Marley's ghost from *A Christmas Carol*. He moved at last, clutching the sheet up to his chin and crooking his legs, ready to leave the bed at a moment's notice.

Then Etta Nolla advanced into the room, went straight

to the candle and snuffed it between thumb and forefinger. He shrank further into the bed and waited for the next horror.

'You've laid awake quite long enough, my 'ansome.' Her voice was low and unexpectedly gentle. 'I 'ad to come and put out your candle before – d'you remember?' She put a rough, fish-smelling hand on his forehead, forcing him to close his eyes again. The bed dipped as she sat on the edge of it.

'Now. Just you listen to me and pay attention. You 'aven't got no need to take everything on your shoulders. No-one else thinks it's your fault and you musn't neither. ''Tweren't your fault that the ole Kaiser decided to go into Belgium and start the war, were it? You was only a twinkle in your daddy's eye then, I reckon.' She gave her horrible cackle. 'So it certainly weren't your fault that poor Mr Bridges got that gas poisoning. An' it weren't your fault that young Neville was headstrong neither. If 'e 'ad to find a war to fight in, then I reckon it was best you should go with 'im. Try to 'old 'im back a bit.' The hand cupped his cheek and Clem turned his head slightly so that he could smell the fish. It was a clean, good smell.

She paused and he could tell from her held breath that she was fighting tears. When she spoke again her voice was lower still.

'I'm chapel. You know that, my 'ansome. I believe what they believe. An' a bit extra too.' She tried to laugh again and failed. She leaned closer. 'Oh I know they're in 'eaven. I know that. But where did they think 'eaven was? Right 'ere. In St Ives. Every summer.' She paused, cleared her throat and went on, 'We can't see 'em, I knows that. But they're there. On Porthkidney. 'Long the 'arbour. Porthmeor beach. Everywhere.' This time she managed half a cackle. 'So you keep coming, my 'ansome, an' you'll never lose 'em. Marry young Madge – and do it quick before someone else gets her – and spend your summers down 'ere. You'll be all right. Etta Nolla's telling you. You'll be all right.'

88

It sounded like a gypsy's promise, and Clem's mother hated gypsies almost as much as she hated her absent husband and the Hun. But when Etta stood up to go, he whispered hoarsely, 'D-d-d-don't go. Don't leave me.'

She cackled properly this time.

'Not many men said that to me, young Clem.' Then she moved her hand from his face and gripped his shoulder. 'Your stick be hard by the bed. I'm right above you. If you need aught, just jab the stick on the ceiling and I'll be down. But you ain't goin' to 'ave no more marbid thoughts.'

She tightened her fingers, then released him and padded out of the room. She must have left her own candle on the attic stairs and he watched her silhouette bend and pick it up before she shut his door.

Suddenly and inexplicably his limbs creaked loose and peace was with him. He thought of the tall thin house built into the rock, with its fish cellar below and its loft above; the simplicity of it engulfed him. It would be like this always; if Madge would marry him.

The next day some old friends from ten years before were discovered during the morning shopping trip. The McGoverns had spent two months in Penzance in 1928. Mr McGovern had inherited a cotton mill from an uncle in Lancashire and though he had moved his family down to Todmorden from Stirlingshire, he had no aptitude for business and left a manager in charge while he indulged his hobby of 'taking pictures'. He found the ideal light for photography in Cornwall and during one of his expeditions in search of the perfect composition, he and his wife had met the Bridges. Mrs McGovern had been so attracted by them all that they had made a point of meeting up with them each day during their two weeks' stay. Now, suddenly, they were walking down Fore Street, Mr McGovern shouldering his tripod, naturally more stooped than before, but otherwise amazingly unchanged.

There was a great commotion. Mrs McGovern fell on Mrs Bridges, and Mr McGovern pumped Clem's hand under the impression he was a grown-up Neville. Madge stood back smiling anxiously; they did not recognise her and she had time to wonder about the explanations that must follow and how they would affect her mother and Clem. Like any good nurse she was doubtful about having too many visitors around the bedside.

However Marie Bridges had no reservations about the meeting. She and Etta talked all the time about the past. It never hurt. It cocooned it and made it all the more precious. The McGoverns suggested a picnic on the beach as soon as they learned the tragic news about Alfred and Neville, just like the good old days. It couldn't be the same of course. Alfred was no longer there to organise things: decide where the chairs should be placed, what time the food would be unpacked, who would swim and when. There were no games. No small tête-à-têtes between the women. Clem was much too embarrassed to swim with such an audience, and Madge would not get into the sea without him. The five of them sat in a large semi-circle facing the incoming tide and conversation soon flagged.

Mr McGovern gestured towards the Island where the enormous stretch of Porthmeor sands deteriorated into the town's rubbish dump.

'Proper mess. It wasn't like that ten years ago.'

Marie peered short-sightedly. 'Etta tells me that the beach has been leased to a local builder. He might tidy it up.'

'He's making a pretty penny out of the tents.' Mr McGovern gestured again, this time towards the canvas swimming tents behind them. 'Half-a-crown a week he wants for one of those. Can you credit it? How much were they when we were here before?'

'A shilling,' said his wife. 'The bathing machines at Porthminster were more expensive, of course. But this beach has never been developed for bathers.' She smiled at Mrs Bridges. 'That's why we liked it so much.'

Everyone smiled. They waited for Mr McGovern's next lead, but he was squinting at Old Man's Head trying to see it as a print.

Mrs Bridges said desperately, 'Why don't you young people look for cockles? The tide is only just coming in. You should be able to find buckets of them.'

Clem jumped out of his deckchair as if shot.

'S-s-splendid idea. How about it, Madge?'

'Yes of course. Will you be all right, Mother?'

Mrs Bridges laughed with relief. 'I've got plenty of company. Most congenial company.'

Everyone laughed with her, and Mrs McGovern murmured, 'Compliments, compliments.' And Madge suddenly took to her heels in the sand, calling, 'Race you to the sea!' Then halfway down the beach remembered Clem's leg and stopped abruptly.

'Is there going to be a match there?' Mrs McGovern murmured archly.

'I rather think so. As I told you, he was a friend of Neville's. They were the same age. He was actually with him when . . . he can't talk about it properly but . . .'

'My dear, don't upset yourself. Let's have a cup of tea, shall we? Angus, why don't you stroll over to the Head and see if there are any likely camera shots the other side?'

Clem took off his shoes and socks and rolled his trouser legs to his knees. The hem of Madge's shantung dress was already dripping, but she did not seem to care. Her bobbed hair hung over her face, and her hat dangled down her back on its elastic. He thought how good it would be to look after her. To tell her she might catch cold or get sunburn.

He opened his mouth and blurted suddenly, 'It was a day like this. It had been raining and we waited for fine weather. And it was a day like this.'

She was suddenly still. She had been bending over a rock, pushing experimentally at the covering of shellfish. She stayed where she was, not looking at him; waiting. He wondered whether to tell her what they had carried. Her hat, lying on her shoulders, was an odd reminder of his own gas mask that day. But how to convey the sheer weight of his 220 rounds of ammo, the Mills bombs, the water bottle

91

and extra rations, the three empty sandbags and his rifle and bayonet? She could not possibly imagine such encumbrances; and he did not want her to.

'It was jolly hot in boots and uniform,' he said heartily. 'The sweat dripped from under our tin hats. And then when we got to the outer defences, it started to rain!' He tried to smile, then she looked up at him and he tried no more. Her eyes were enormous and very serious. 'But then it was hot again. Like this,' he repeated lamely.

She did not speak or take her eyes off his face. When he paused she sank slowly to her knees in the wet sand, and waited. A tiny rivulet of sea washed around her skirt, obviously soaking her to the thighs; she ignored it. He bent laboriously and squatted on a low rock, then, unable to meet that gaze any longer, he stared down at his submerged toes. They still bore the marks of his army boots.

'There was a village. It was called . . . I don't know . . . something like Tarantella. But that's a dance, isn't it? The church had been shelled and one of those statue things was hanging out of it. Some of the other chaps said it was blessing us. They crossed themselves and sort of bowed . . . it seemed to me it was cursing us.'

He remembered the Madonna and Child far above their heads. Neville had wanted to know if anyone could spot her knickers. But he couldn't tell Madge that. Typical of Neville.

He said, 'There were barrage balloons all around the city. They were supposed to stop the dive bombers, but they didn't. The Condors were a crack Fascist squadron. Nothing could stop them. They shot up the balloons first, then came in.' He stopped and closed his eyes.

Madge said, 'You don't have to—'

'I want to.' The words started pouring out of him, running into each other but overcoming the stammer. 'You should have heard your Neville. He started cheering at the top of his voice and he turned to me and said, this is it old man, we're as good as out. And he was right of course . . . oh God he was right. The whistles went but Nev and I, we

92

had to wait because of the wire. We had a roll of it on a stake – he had one end and I had the other. It made us slow and clumsy. Perfect targets.' He opened his eyes wide. 'It was like a fairground. Those ducks that swim along in formation at all the rifle ranges. Making it so easy to pick them off.'

Yet no-one had faltered except himself. Some Russian captain had strode between them all, waving encouragingly, and Neville had glanced sideways and grinned mockingly and Clem knew exactly what he would say when he got the chance. 'The dusky Rusky is somewhat husky' or words to that effect. But Neville would never utter those words or any others. Because there had been a sodden smacking sound then and his end of the wired stake went down. There were bits flying. Earth. Clothing. Flesh. Neville's tin hat spun back down into the trench they'd just left. Amazingly, his smile, like the Cheshire Cat's, hung for a moment in the air. Then someone else picked up the wire and went on walking.

Clem thought he'd dreamed it. He thought when the face looked round at him it would be Neville's. When it wasn't, he knew he had to look for Neville. There must be something left, and he had to find it.

'That is why I was shot in the calf of my leg,' he said in the same gabbling voice. 'Because I'd turned around and was heading back to the trench. The bullet caught me behind the knee and I fell down. No-one seemed to realise I was facing the wrong way. The chap who picked up the wire – perhaps he knew, but he was probably killed anyway. I didn't tell anyone I was running away.'

Madge interrupted him. Her voice was hoarse, but she did not pause to clear her throat.

'You weren't running away, Clem. You were looking for your friend!'

'Our orders were not to stop to help the wounded. And certainly never to go back for the dead.'

'What do you think Neville would have done if it had been him? He'd have gone back to look for you!'

93

He said morosely, 'It's what I've tried to tell myself ever since. Every day. And every night. Especially nights.' He looked again at his toes. 'If anyone had twigged, I would have been shot for cowardice.'

'Oh Clem – no! You were helping a friend.'

'I knew Neville had gone. I was running away.'

She said stubbornly, 'I don't believe that.'

He was silent, staring at his feet, letting her words soak in and comfort him like the water. She must be right. She was young and saw things properly.

She said in a thin voice, 'You never found . . . anything? You said his tin hat . . . did you pick it up?'

He thought of the number of tin hats that day and laughed. Then he checked himself and shook his head.

'Someone picked *me* up and dragged me back to the trench. Then there was a dressing station. Morphia there. We were laid on straw in the sun and someone put a newspaper over my eyes . . . No, I didn't find Neville's tin hat.'

He took off his panama suddenly. 'Can you see the cross? They put a cross on your head when you'd been pumped up with morphia. An indelible pencil. It wouldn't come off.'

He thrust his head towards her and she looked at his forehead as he pushed back his hair. There was nothing.

'It's still there!' He heard his voice rising. 'It won't go away. My mother saw it and thought I'd got the plague or something! You must see it, Madge!'

She peered. 'No . . . No, I can't.'

'Here. Put your fingers just here . . .' he grabbed her hand and put it to his head. 'Feel the imprint – go on, feel it!'

Obediently she made a sign of the cross on his forehead, kneeling upright, looking scared. She would have sat back on her heels but he held on to her wrist.

She said quickly, 'Yes, I think I can feel something, Clem. But it will fade. Gradually.'

'No, it won't! Not unless you—' He tightened his grip, feeling her pulse thump beneath his fingers. 'Madge, listen to me. I love you. I love you, Madge.' He kissed the back

94

of her hand frantically as she tried to pull away. 'Madge, you must have guessed . . . why do you think I wanted to come here?'

'Well, I thought . . . Neville's favourite—'

'To be with you. I want to be with you all the time. When I'm with you it doesn't happen.'

What? Clem, I don't understand.'

'The nightmares. Delusions they call them. I don't get the delusions. Of course the people who call them that, weren't there.' He laughed wildly and when she pulled away again he dropped his forehead to her wrist, feeling tears flooding out. And worse than tears; his nose was running. She stopped pulling and leaned over him protectively.

'Oh Clem.'

'It's all right. Don't worry.'

'It's just so awful that you . . . I mean, I feel so safe with you. Mother and I – we've been *leaning* on you instead of – we've been burdens!'

He screwed his eyes tight to wring out the tears and said gruffly, 'You could never be burdens, either of you. You make me feel . . . I don't know – like your father. Whole.'

'Oh Clem.'

'That's what I want to do for the rest of my life. Look after you. Protect you.'

'Clem, you're wonderful. You talk about cowardice but you're a hero. That's what you are. A hero.'

He looked up at last and saw her face ablaze with exaltation. He wanted to grovel at her feet, but heroes did not grovel. He stood up, pulling her with him, and water poured from his trousers. They both watched as the rolled flannel at his knee unfurled heavily.

His voice full of consternation, he said, 'My lord, just look at my flannels. What a mess.'

But nothing could dim Madge now.

'Clem, don't bother about that! Look at my dress! And shantung is much worse than flannel when it's wet – it sort of shrivels like liver in a frying pan!'

'Liver?' Under cover of his flopping hair he knew his face was beginning to look slightly more heroic.

'Yes. Haven't you noticed how liver sort of cringes when it goes into hot fat? No, I suppose you haven't. Men don't cook, do they?'

He started to laugh, and after a second so did she. Once started they couldn't stop. Their laughter was near hysteria, but it unified them. Clem had a jumbled vision of frying liver, crumpled shantung, waterlogged trousers; images which obliterated the other unspeakable sights of his mind. He gasped, 'Oh Madge, I do love you. I really do love you.'

She was eighteen, had lost all the men in her life, and was being offered so much. All she could say was 'Oh Clem.' But it was enough for him; it was acceptance.

He said, 'What can we *do*? We ought to do something special so that we'll never forget this moment even when we're old and grey!'

She held out her hands. 'Come on. We're wet already. Let's do the job properly!'

Clem had no time for the bright young things cavorting in fountains in London; but this was no drunken splash. This was in the nature of a baptism. He and Madge leapt over the small waves and then strode strongly into the deeper water. Clem felt his flannels cloyingly heavy around his calves and had a momentary misgiving: what would Mrs Bridges say? But Madge still held one of his hands and she looked up at him with that brilliant smile of hers and led him deeper. A roller was creaming towards them.

They cast a look up the beach and saw Mrs McGovern and Marie Bridges on their feet, staring anxiously. Jim Maddern had led a single donkey down the cliff path in another effort to make some pocket money. Silhouetted against Old Man's Head, Angus McGovern framed his hands around possible photographs. Madge started to laugh just as the roller engulfed them.

Mrs Bridges was cross but not angry. She had also read about the bright young things in London and had hidden a smile even while agreeing with Clem's censorious mother that it was a crying disgrace.

'You need not keep pretending it was an accident,' she said, pushing one of the towelling robes over Madge's cumbersome wet dress. 'I saw you go in quite deliberately. No, I don't blame you, Clement, whatever you say. I saw – we both saw – Madge dragging you further and further – it's not funny, Madge, so just stop that silly giggling.' But she did not dare meet Mrs McGovern's eye and that lady was forced to hold the day's newspaper over her mouth at the sight of Clem, miserable and stuttering again, trying to give some cogent explanation.

'I'll run for dry clothes if you'll keep an eye out for donkey riders,' offered Jim Maddern, his eyes as bright as two threepenny joeys.

'We'll go ourselves, thanks all the same, Jim.' Madge treated him to a smile as well. 'We won't be long, Mother darling. And sea water never hurt anyone. Don't you remember Father saying that?'

'I do. And if you think you're going to swan off like that . . . excuse me, my dear. I won't be long.'

Mrs Bridges swept ahead of them up the cliff path, parasol like a banner. There was nothing for it but to follow her back to Zion Cottage like two naughty childern. But Clem recognised this as yet another bond. He could not take Madge's hand again because Mrs Bridges, like all mothers, had eyes in the back of her head, but he knew they were still joined. When they reached the cottage and he struggled out of his ruined flannels, he thought suddenly, 'My God, we're engaged. *That* is what has happened this afternoon. Marjorie Bridges and Clem Briscoe are engaged to be married!'

He was so happy he forgot to worry that his spare trousers were rather too short.

Madge was delighted that somehow she had comforted Clem. The word 'comfort' was used a great deal when it came to soldiers, wounded or otherwise. Comfort for the troops consisted of anything from smokes to socks. Words, looks, hand-holding were all used by nurses. But underneath her pleasure, she knew very well that the comfort had gone much deeper than that. When he had told her he loved her, she had almost told him that she loved him too. And she did. At that moment. He had been dear companion, hero, a substitute for her father and her brother, and she had wanted to fling her arms around his neck and hug him desperately. But after her mother's words she saw only too clearly what would then be expected of her. It seemed suddenly as if everyone was standing around waiting for her to marry Clem: her mother, Etta, even Mrs McGovern. And she could never marry, not ever. She shuddered, not allowing herself to remember Neville's words, not allowing herself to recall that night when her father had collapsed on top of her mother. All she knew consciously was that marriage was not for her.

When Philip arrived the next day, she felt happier. It was wonderful to see him again anyway; she had been sixteen when they'd come to St Ives last, now she was an adult. It made no difference. He seemed shorter than before but he'd always had to peer up at her from beneath the brim of his trilby, so that was the same as ever. There was a slight change of roles; he was no longer the family retainer, right-hand man to Alfred Bridges. In many ways he stepped into Alfred's shoes. He was no organiser and he still went about his own business most of the day, but subtly he was the final authority now, just as Alfred had been.

The day after his arrival, Madge got up very early, took her wrap and costume behind Smeaton's Pier where the ebb tide had left a tiny private beach, and swam quietly in the tingling water until Philip appeared above her to spread his nets. Then she got out, dried roughly and slipped her still-crumpled shantung over her head. In the old days Father had encouraged a before-breakfast swim; it would not be remarked upon. She climbed the slippery weed-covered steps to the pier head and greeted Philip as if the meeting were a happy coincidence.

'Hello, woman,' he returned, giving her one of his quick

upward smiles before going back to the nets. 'Mad as ever, I see.' He had never come to terms with the family's habit of immersing themselves. 'Do you do it as early as this every morning?'

She was going to lie, then knew she would be easily discovered. 'No. The tide hasn't been right just here and I don't like going to Porthmeor on my own.'

'Sensible.' He held up an enormous hole for her inspection. 'Etta and me'll be busy for a week or two, I reckon.'

'What did that, Philip?'

'Wrasse.'

He began to tell her about the summer in the north-east and about the people of Shields and Seahouses and Berwick. She sat on the wall while the sun gained strength and her hair dried. The first train of the day arrived from St Erth, crawling along the side of the cliff above Carbis Bay, its plume of smoke spreading among the trees and rocks. In the harbour the boats lay on their sides as if resting and the town cats prowled and chased the gulls.

'D'you remember telling me about Hadrian's Wall?' She smiled at him. 'I must have been nine or ten. I went home and read and read about it. The Roman Legions. The sort of country around it. I'm sure that's why I got a place at the Girls' College. When I had my interview they were terribly impressed by my history and geography!'

She laughed and Phillip glinted a grin at her.

'Thought as how you were at a paid-for school, woman. Was it a scholarship you got?'

'No. It was paid for. But they wanted to make certain their standards would be kept up. So there was a sort of exam and the interview at the end.'

'You did well?'

'At school? I matriculated. It doesn't mean much. I need to get some more training. Office stuff. Or . . .' she sat on a bollard so that she could look into his face, '. . . what I'd like to do, Philip, is to train to be a teacher. I'd like to teach art. There's someone called Dalcroze – a German I think – and he says that all art is good for people.

99

Therapeutic is the word he uses. So if I taught art to people who . . . weren't well . . . I don't know . . . I thought I might do some good.'

He grinned. 'Saint Madge', he said but without mockery. He shook his head. 'People do not always want all that sympathy you've got, my little woman. Go steady with it.'

She was stung into replying, 'Clem does. Clem *appreciates* my sympathy – he – he's grateful for it.'

'Ah. So it's Clem we're going to talk about.' He kept looking at her quizzically until she was forced to give him a brief rueful smile.

'It's not funny, Philip.'

'No, it isn't.' He looked at the toe of his boot. 'That young man needs help. But afterwards, when he is whole, he will need something more. Have you got anything more for him, Madge?'

'I don't know what you mean.'

'I mean friendship. Love. The sort of feeling your mother had for your father. Can you give him that?'

She blurted, 'No.'

'Then be careful, woman. Don't let your sympathy run away with you. You understand what I am saying?'

She swallowed. 'Yes.' It was what she felt herself, and she knew he was right.

He sighed sharply. 'Right. That's good. Come along then, back to breakfast.' He picked up his bag and threw it down to the harbour beach, turned and began to clamber down the iron-runged ladder.

She waited until he was at the bottom and then called, 'You think I should train as a teacher then, Philip?'

He picked up his bag and looked up at her.

'I wouldn't presoom to say any such thing, woman!' He looked quite shocked at the thought, then he added, 'Madge, don't you know that whatever you do you can give . . . what you have to give . . . to people.' He shook his head impatiently. 'I ain't got the words, but you are one of life's givers. You don't have to look for your work. It will always be there.' Then he quickly negated what he'd

100

said with an even more vigorous shake of his head. 'Take no notice of me, woman. I'm getting old and I was never much good . . . take no notice of me.'

He tramped away from her and she stared after him, puzzled and a little hurt. Only much latter did she recall that he had talked of her mother's love for her father. Not of his for Etta.

Clem too got up early and almost joined Philip when he saw him going down Smeaton's Pier to begin the interminable task of net-mending. Then Madge's head appeared above the wall, her hair damp and clinging to her scalp like a cap. He should have joined her immediately and talked openly about their adventure two days ago, but he hovered uncertainly for too long. The two of them looked more and more private, more and more intimate. He did not want to share Madge and their wonderful experience with anyone. First he must cement it permanently in both of their minds. Eventually he walked along the wharf in the other direction and threaded the narrow streets of the town until he reached the Malakoff where the telescope turned its eye over the Bay, and the buses took on passengers.

Again he was caught in the trap of his own indecision. It was rather like his sudden and unexpected stammering; he knew what he wanted to do but the action would not somehow materialise. A bus to Land's End was waiting, engine running. Its long bonnet was hooked up at one side and the driver, with a man in greasy overalls, was surveying the hiss of steam which threatened to lift off its radiator cap. But half a dozen passengers were already seated inside. Clem stood four yards off, one eye on the bus, the other gazing unseeingly at the opalescent sea with Godrevy lighthouse sitting so gracefully in its midst. He wanted to get on the bus. He wanted to do something on his own, something worthwhile, something especially his, not even to share with Madge. Yet if he got on the bus he would be gone at least all the morning; a whole morning away from Madge. The weather was perfect, they might go swimming.

101

The man in the overalls leaned over the engine with a long screwdriver and did something. Steam came from another source for about three seconds, then the whole bus ceased to fume and settled down to a rythmical bumping. There were congratulatory shouts from within. The driver put down the bonnet and fastened it with two leather straps. The mechanic kicked the wheels affectionately. Clem thought, it's now or never. And into his head came Neville's impatient voice: 'For Pete's sake, old man! Don't wait for me any more – you're out in front!' There was a moment of terror when he thought he was having another delusion, immediately followed by enormous relief because even if he was he was in full control of it.

He got on the bus.

It climbed up the Stennack with difficulty, Trevalgan hill with more difficulty. At Boscubben the passengers got out and let it groan on alone to the Eagle's Nest. It cooled down a little while, waiting for them, and free-wheeled down to Zennor like a cumbersome bird. Clem alighted at the Tinner's Arms and looked around him with more misgivings.

There was nothing to Zennor. The pub, the ancient church next door, half a dozen cottages and a Methodist chapel. The pub was closed and there wasn't a soul about. A few hens strutted around his legs as the bus snorted away and on the churchyard steps a cat surveyed him lazily. He went towards it and it stood up, stretched mightily, pushed against his proffered hand then dissolved beneath the gates and disappeared among the overgrown tombstones.

Clem sat on the steps in the cat's place and checked his watch against the sundial on the church tower. He couldn't think whether to add or subtract an hour, but anyway it was ten o'clock and the bus wouldn't be back till gone twelve. He couldn't think why he'd come, it was another wrong decision. He tried to summon up another Neville-delusion. Nothing happened. But if it were Neville here, he'd certainly not be sitting on the churchyard steps waiting for time to pass. However, he knew where to go in Zennor

102

and what to do! For a moment a smile flickered on Clem's face at that very Neville-like thought. Then it died. He wasn't Neville. He did not know where to go, nor what to do.

After another timeless span had been bridged, he got up and opened the gates and walked along the path to the church. The doors stood wide and he walked through them into the cool darkness of the interior and stood still, waiting for his eyes to see again. When they did he gazed around with pleasure, his draughtsman's eye revelling in the ingenuity of design and material, his nose consciously enjoying the smell of ancient wood. Suddenly filled with purpose, he walked up the centre aisle searching for the pew-end which was supposed to be carved with the figure of a mermaid. Not just any mermaid; the one who actually came out of the sea at Zennor and bewitched one of the choir. He found her and traced the rough-hewn outline with his finger. She was not beautiful; she was squat and utterly determined and she reminded him of someone. Etta Nolla. Yes, she had magical properties all right! He smiled again. He must remember that Etta was on his side.

A sound came from the sun-filled doorway and two women came in carrying trugs of flowers. They were talking in low voices and did not see him; he stood up from the mermaid and coughed discreetly. They both squeaked in unison, then began to laugh. He went towards them, smiling apologetically. They were easy and pleasant with him; he felt his confidence growing.

'You must 'a thought it was a village o' the dead!' one of them said jovially. 'All the men out on the fields and the women indoors. If it's the footpath to the headland you want, you can walk back with us in a few minutes.'

'We're doin' the church up for a weddin'.' They displayed their trugs and, in case he hadn't followed them, 'There's a weddin' 'ere this Satty.'

He had a sudden feeling. 'Would that be Miss Care?' he asked. 'Miss Rose Care?'

The pleasantness vanished, wiped from their faces in an instant. One of them said, 'Rose Care married? Who'd 'ave 'er? I ask you – who'd 'ave 'er?' Then the other said expressionlessly, 'You know Rose Care?'

'Not personally. I was looking for her as a matter of fact.'

'Ah.' They exchanged glances. 'Ah. Yes. 'Course. You should 'a got off the bus last stop. Skinner's Cottage. That's where Rose Care keeps 'erself. Or is kept.' They brushed past him to the altar. That was that. It hadn't occurred to him that Rose's reputation would still be bad. Neville had thought such a lot of her that Clem had assumed she must have reformed. He did not like the idea that these two village women assumed he was one of Rose's 'paying guests' either. He turned as if to follow them, then realised he could not. He left the church feeling as unsatisfactory as when he had entered.

It was not difficult to find Skinner's Cottage; there was only one road in and out of Zennor, and he walked back the way the bus had brought him until he came to the gate of a tiny hovel set in a neat garden hedged around with encroaching thistles and weeds of all descriptions. It was so appropriate he did not even bother to read the name on the gate; like Neville before he followed the path to the back of the house; like Neville before him he was nervous – not only that someone might already be with Rose, but that his stammer would put an end to what he had to say to her.

She was gardening. The sight of her bent back above a row of broad beans was reassuring; his mother was a keen gardener and there was something universal, almost sexless about people who dealt with the earth. She was picking the beans and hoeing at the same time and as he paused, about to give his introductory cough, she stabbed at a particularly recalcitrant dandelion and said loudly, 'Come on, you little bugger!'

It made him laugh, it was so unusual to hear a woman swear, though he would have been shocked to the core if it had been any of the women he actually knew. Rose Care still had the amazing frankness Neville had spoken of so often. Though Neville had called it 'basic innocence'.

She twitched a little with surprise, but turned to look at

him with a twist of her supple waist that had little to do with innocence. She was wearing an old stained cotton skirt and an unsuitable satin blouse 'gone' under the arms. Good enough for gardening and, he suddenly realised, anything but sexless. He started to stammer apologies for startling her, but she ignored him and studied him carefully from head to toe. When he stopped speaking, she said slowly, 'You're Tagger. Neville's friend. I can't remember your other name. He spoke about you.'

Her voice was almost free of accent, which was not how Neville had described her. And that name, Tagger, wrung his heart. He said clearly, 'Yes. I am Neville's friend. My real name is Clem Briscoe. You are Rose. He spoke about you. Often.'

She seemed to sag. 'Oh my dear lord. Oh my dear, dear lord. Philip told me he'd gone. I thought he would have forgot me entirely. Oh my dear, sweet lord.'

'Miss Care – I'm sorry – old wounds – I do understand—'

She said automatically, 'Rose. Call me Rose. No-one . . . oh my lord. Let us go inside. Please.' She dropped her hoe on to the path with a clatter and went through an open door. He had to follow. He was conscious of a dark, damp-smelling scullery, then there was a lighter room. Small; a typical cottage parlour, not unlike the Nollas' but much less cluttered, and sparkling with what his mother called 'elbow grease'. Rose stood by a table, supporting herself with her knuckled hands, head down, mass of dark hair falling about her face. She said, 'He asked me to marry him. Did he tell you that?'

'No.' Clem cleared his throat, not from nerves this time but because it was clogged with tears. 'He told me nothing personal, Miss . . . Rose. Before we went to Spain I knew that you and he . . . he told me that. But then, nothing until the siege.' The satin blouse was ancient, but it was beautifully pressed and he knew that satin was difficult to iron. He could understand why Neville had found this girl so attractive. He said inspirationally, 'I think you were too private, too precious, to be . . . talked about.'

'But you said he spoke of me often.' She turned and faced him defiantly. Bland words were not enough for her.

'I meant, before Spain. When we were . . . younger.'

'Children. That's what you were. Schoolboys.' She was angry. 'So why have you come here today? You want a bit of what Neville talked about? Is that it?'

He was suddenly so hot he thought he might faint.

'I'm no good at words. I'm sorry. Neville . . . he was like a brother . . .' he cleared his throat again. 'It's just that – just before we broke out of the siege – he said if anything happened, would I try to find you and tell you. That's all.' He turned. 'I'd better go. I'm so sorry if I've . . . I'm so sorry . . .'

She said sternly, 'Philip Nolla told me. Neville would know that Philip Nolla would tell me.'

'Not that he was *gone*! Not that.' Clem felt desperate. 'He wanted me to tell you that he loved you. Really loved you. That's all. He wanted you to know, you see. That it wasn't just . . . he wanted you to know that he *loved* you!'

She let him stumble back through the scullery and into the open air. He paused at the corner of the cottage, clung to the granite and took deep breaths. She was by his side, earthy hand beneath his elbow. Her voice was different, no longer her best and carefully tutored accent.

'Come on back inside, m'dear. Or better still, sit 'ere on the stones while I make you a cup o' tea.' She piloted him backwards and pressed him down on to the wall. Her hair brushed his face. It smelled like hay. She smiled right into his face and he saw that her dark eyes were no longer angry and certainly not sad. She looked happy.

He waited there while thistledown from the fields floated about his head. He wondered what would have happened if Neville hadn't been killed. Would he have come back here and made Rose Care a respectable married woman? Already Clem suspected that was impossible.

She came back with strong sweet tea in a decent china cup with a saucer and a silver spoon. There was a crest on the spoon – he felt it with his thumb when he stirred the tea. She waited while he drank it, pulling up a weed within arms' length, already eyeing up the bean-row again.

When he said, 'I'd better go,' she did not try to delay him. She took the cup and smiled knowingly.

'It's Madge Bridges, isn't it?'

He was shocked by her prescience and began stammering again.

'I could 'a tole you that six year ago. She and me used to 'ave a little chat now an' then.' She drooped very slightly. 'She 'asn't 'ad nothin' to do with me since she got to know about Neville an' me. Still . . . I know a lot about most people.' She laughed. 'The ole biddies 'oo talk so much about me 'ud be surprised if they knew 'ow often my visitors come for a chat and a cup o' tea.' She opened the gate and stood behind it. 'You an' Madge, you're right for each other. Me an' Neville weren't, nor never would 'a been.' She sighed sharply and transferred his tea-cup to the other hand to enable her to scratch her shoulder. The satin blouse fell back to reveal no shoulder straps, just bare brown flesh. Clem averted his eyes.

She said, 'You need 'er. That's for certain. An' I reckon she needs you too. But she prob'ly don't know it, so you better do something quick afore she sets off on another course.'

She closed the gate. He moved off down the road, wondering where he heard those words before. Then he remembered. Etta Nolla knew that he and Madge were 'right' too. He propped himself against the stone hedge by the bus stop, feeling heartened. He must start looking on the positive side of things. He was as good as engaged to Madge. Etta Nolla approved. Rose Care approved. He did not think Mrs Bridges disapproved. He had spoken of Neville's death; he had *faced* Neville, stopped him being a delusion, made him into a thought, a memory, which he could himself recall or banish at any time. And he had carried out Neville's wish: he had been to see Rose Care.

In due course the bus came along, snorting and steaming like a dragon. He hadn't looked at his watch; it could be late or early, it didn't matter. The flowers thrusting from the drystone walling left their pollen over his jacket and trousers. He didn't worry about that either. As they began the descent into St Ives, he made another decision. He wouldn't walk back to the cottage through the Warren this time, he'd go down Tregenna Hill where all the shops were, and he'd buy a ring. A proper, diamond engagement ring. And as soon as he could get Madge to himself again, he'd put it on her finger. And all would be well.

But it was difficult for Clem to get Madge to himself any longer. Etta Nolla, presumably secure now that her husband was home again, succumbed to Mrs Bridges' pleas, and joined them for their beach picnic each day. Philip had his business to see to, but he too usually appeared about mid-afternoon and then Madge pestered him to 'show Clem the old mine', 'show Clem the secret cove'. He was not an obtrusive companion, he did or said nothing to come between Madge and Clem, but more often than not, he was just there. It was like the comic song – and Mother came too. Except that the presence of a chaperone would have made the situation more definite; Philip was just one more valued companion.

Clem tried referring to their 'baptism'.

'It was marvellous of you to listen to me the other day, Madge dear.'

'Don't be silly. It wasn't marvellous at all. It was a privilege.'

'D'you know, when we went into the sea together like that, it was as if we were starting a new life.'

'That's St Ives for you.'

'Yes. But together. A new life together.'

'Philip says we're all intertwined. Like the fishing nets. We make a pattern. If the pattern gets torn we have to mend it as quickly as we can.'

'He's right. I was in a hundred pieces. You're mending me, Madge. Mending me.'

'No. That would make me too important. Self-important.'

She scrambled ahead of him through a mat of rhododendron bushes which met overhead. 'Come on. Here's the monument I was telling you about. There's a terrific view from up here.'

He told himself it was all right, nothing had changed since that day in the sea; but he felt his nerves beginning to stretch again, and at nights he would wake sweating and think for a terrible moment that he was in that field hospital again, believing his leg had been shot off.

On their last day the weather was not so good. A vicious little wind had sprung up overnight and whipped the sand everywhere. The McGoverns came to say goodbye, Mrs Nolla declined to go to the beach, and Philip and the Gurnards were repairing the *Forty-niner*. Clem knew this was his opportunity.

They walked along the farm footpath at the top of Ayr, picking blackberries as they went and tying them in Clem's handkerchief. Then they dropped down over the cliff fields to the first of Five Points. The wind flapped Clem's trousers against his legs and threatened to take his hat altogether. Looking at Madge bracing herself against it, her hat hanging down her back as usual, he had a miserable sense of doom. She was enjoying the change in the weather, he was not. He felt as if he were in a pit, looking up at her playing in the sunshine miles away.

He said abruptly, 'Madge, let's sit over there out of this blasted wind. And watch that blackberry juice. I don't want your mother blaming me for another ruined dress!'

She looked round, surprised, but followed him to the overhanging rock and crouched there obediently, holding the stained and dripping handkerchief away from her flapping frock.

He said tensely, 'Look Madge, I know you're quite happy with things the way they are. But I'm not. I don't like secrecy. Not for long. It begins to smack of underhandedness.'

Her sheer bewilderment increased the distance between them. Was he sinking deeper into his pit or was she being

109

elevated towards the stars? Whichever it was he was forced to raise his voice to be heard.

'Well?'

She flinched. 'I don't know what you mean, Clem – have I done something?'

We've done something, Madge. As you very well know. And I want it made public. Official.'

Her eyes became enormous and the blueness of them darkened with anxiety. He would have liked to have put his finger on the bump in the middle of her nose but she was too far away.

'Clem, I honestly don't know what you mean.'

'Stop pretending, girl! Or woman, as *he* says! Have you told him? Does he know about our engagement?'

'*Engagement?* Clem, how can we be engaged? You've said nothing. And I'm only eighteen!' She took a step away from him and the wind came round the corner and fluttered her dress frantically. He thought she might take flight at any moment.

He said furiously, 'I – I declared myself, Madge. And you let me think . . . we agreed on it. We got baptised together, didn't we? We started a new life together, didn't we? I want to announce it. I've been patient, waiting for you to say something. But before we leave I want to go up Tregenna Hill and buy a ring. I want it to happen at St Ives. It's our special place now. We'll come here every year until we're quite old and it will be like a celebration each time. Neville and your father and you and me and—'

'Clem, stop it!' She had her hands splayed on the rock behind her as if he were attacking her. 'It wasn't like that. I wanted to hear about Neville, but he's dead! I thought if you told me – got it out of your system, you would be able to realise that – accept it. We could talk about them like Mother and Etta talk about them, lovingly and without pain—'

'Never mind all that!' He shook his head to clear it. 'You're prevaricating again. You keep doing it. Holding me off as if I were a mad animal or something! Let's go

110

back and get a ring and tell everyone . . . come *on*, Madge. Come down. Come here. Don't keep going away.'

'I am here. Right here. I'm not going away.' She took a step back towards him. 'Listen, Clem, you've got it wrong. I'm honoured – yes I am honoured – that you want to marry me. When you told me you loved me the other day I was so honoured I wanted to make everything all right for you. Immediately. And no-one can do that. I takes time and patience—'

'We've got time. We've got our lives. And when we're together I can be patient. Is that what's worrying you, Madge? My dear, I can be so patient . . . you've no idea. I'll look after you. I'll protect you and be your friend—' He put his arm high in the air, reaching for her, and she stepped back.

'Clem, *please*. I can't get married yet. I haven't *done* anything. I want to train to be an art teacher—'

'You're not saying you don't love me?'

'Clem, I just don't know.'

'You like me?'

'I like you more that anyone I know.'

'That's what it is. That's what love is. Liking someone very very much. You do love me, you see. I knew you did – I could tell. Don't worry, I'll help you to train. I'll—'

'They don't *have* married teachers!' She took a deep breath and said loudly, 'No. I'm sorry, Clem, but no.'

It was like a death knell. Her voice was sonorous and her eyes were black with pupil beneath the short mane of brown hair. If she were wearing a tin hat she would look like a feminised Neville. And she was leaving him, just as Neville had.

He said with great conviction, 'I can't manage this. Not again.' And he turned and began to walk towards the edge of the cliff.

He heard her gasp a scream and knew she was coming after him. It was the same as before. When he'd turned to flee.

'Clem – what are you doing? You can't—' Her fingers

111

tore ineffectually at his sleeve. They left stains like blood.
'Clem – please come back with me now.'

He marched on. She got in front of him and he pushed
her aside. She hung on to him physically untill he stumbled
to a stop, then she wept and said she was sorry she had
misled him but . . . He disengaged himself and began to
run. As he reached the long finger of rock pointing out into
the Atlantic, her voice came to him on the wind, screaming
like a gull's.

'All right! All right, Clem. We'll make it official! Come
back. I do love you. I can't live if you do this, Clem! I can't
live without you!'

He fell in a heap on the hard limpet-encrusted rock and
she came to him and took his head in her lap. She was
weeping as if she'd never stop.

'Oh Clem, I'm sorry. Sorry. Oh my dear . . . I do love
you. Really I do. Honestly. Oh Clem . . . Clem.'

His jacket was covered in blackberry juice, and so was
she. First baptism and now blood. She had come down into
the pit to be with him. A sacrifice. They held each other,
and the sea, green and angry, rushed along the rock as if
it would engulf them; then fell back, hissing.

CHAPTER SIX

1944

It was almost September and already the sun was autumn-warm after what Etta called 'the invasion summer'. With the D-day landings, they had all assumed that the war was as good as over. It was a shock to hear of the doodlebugs arriving over London and to realise that the German snake was scotched but not yet killed.

Madge sat on the harbour beach, her back to the warm wall, her writing things on her lap. She was supposed to be writing to Clem; she had been trying to write to him each day since she arrived here. She knew exactly what she had to say; she had to find the words for telling him that she forgave him and that it was all because of this rotten war and he could come home at the end of the month and everything would be just as it had been before. The first two items were perfectly true, of course. If it hadn't been for the war, Clem would not be on 'important war work' in Canada, so he could not have met this Other Woman. Madge looked again at his letter. The Other Woman's name was Julie, apparently. Madge wondered why she could never remember it. She'd come down here with Rosemary especially to think about what Clem had told her, to write to him telling him that she forgave him. The least she could do was remember the name of the woman who had . . . what did he say? The woman who had 'captured his heart'.

Madge looked up to check on Rosemary whose white sun-bonnet seemed to flutter along the distant shoreline like a cabbage butterfly. Of course she must forgive him and of course he must come home when they sent him back next month – for Rosemary's sake. But she hoped very much that things would not be as they'd been before. She remembered all those nights before Rosemary's conception and her eyes widened behind her pre-war sunglasses. He had said he would be patient . . . he would be her friend. But his patience had been short-lived and his friendship had taken on an aggressive quality when she failed to respond to his engulfing ardour.

She simply hadn't understood. After all, she had made no protest. She had lain beneath him, rigid with horror, letting him do unspeakable things to her, and when he accused her of 'not responding', she had wondered whether he actually wanted her to scream and fight.

She remembered with deep shame the underlying relief she had felt when they had listened together to Mr Chamberlain's speech on the wireless nearly five years before. 'A state of war now exists . . .' War was terrible. Her mother had told her so often enough and even gone so far as to say that Daddy had been a 'delayed war casualty'. But she could do nothing about it, it had happened and she would have to bear it as Mother had borne it. Clem would go away to fight just as Daddy had. And there would be no more bedtimes.

But Clem had not gone away. His Spanish war wound had seen to that. So bedtimes had gone on until she knew she was pregnant. Then Clem himself had called them off.

'This is our dream come true, Madge. We must do nothing to put it at risk . . .'

She wondered as she sat on the sand that mellow misty morning, whether Clem had been glad of the excuse to give up on her. She knew more now. The Americans had joined in the war and there had been many girls willing to risk disgrace for what they called 'love'. She knew now what Clem meant when he accused her of being unresponsive. She knew there was something wrong with her.

She picked up his letter once more and skimmed through it, feeling again the terrible drag of pity she had always felt

114

for Clem. It was so easy to forgive him; and where else would he go except to her and Rosemary – they were his home now. But to go back to how it had been before . . . Madge bit her lip. She loved Clem. But if she loved him in her way then she couldn't 'love' him in *that* way. The two simply did not add up. She did understand now about the pleasures of the flesh, but they had nothing to do with friendship or pity. They might perhaps be indulged in with a complete stranger whom one would never see again after-wards, otherwise it was simply impossible.

She lifted her sunglasses and rubbed one eye. If only Clem hadn't written 'You and Ro are everything. Without you life is simply unbearable'. If he'd said 'I still love Julia but I'm willing to come back to support you' she could have told him to stay. She could have been warm and understanding then. And if he wanted to come back so much, why had he told her about Julia in the first place? She sighed for the umpteenth time and looked up to check on Rosemary's sunbonnet again. It was all worth it for Rosemary. It had to be.

At nearly four years old Rosemary was beginning to 'take shape' as Mrs Bridges put it. She was in fact very shapely; her nose, chin, eyebrows and mouth were all dimpled or tip-tilted or delicately arched; her shoulders were little apricot-coloured pads of fat above rounded arms, her belly was thrust out like the belly of an African child; her buttocks and thighs were strong and thick, and her pudgy little feet made Madge laugh.

She was old enough to want to make her mother laugh. She pouted and lifted her wonderful brows and lowered her lashes. She wriggled her bottom and looked at Madge, waiting for the smile. Then she would come and lay her head in Madge's lap and wait for all the grown-ups present to say, 'What a little darling!'

Neither Etta nor Philip said that, and consequently Rosemary was behaving impeccably in an attempt to win approval. It meant that the holiday was going really well; there were no tantrums and so far she had not declined any

115

of Etta's eccentric meals. Yesterday Madge had had over an hour to herself while Rosemary helped Etta to shake the sand out of the mats. And when the child came down to the beach with her bucket and spade, she would play happily with the local toddlers and never attempt to bite them or snatch their toys away. When she did that sort of thing at home, Mrs Bridges said she needed a father's strong hand. Maybe Rosemary knew that if she played up at Zion Cottage, Philip – or Etta – were quite capable of administering that strong hand.

The sunbonnet was bobbing up the beach now. Madge smiled, glad to be able to forget her letter to Clem yet again. She had written, 'Of course I shall say nothing to my mother nor to yours. Your mother called last week to wish us a happy holiday. I think she might have come with us if she'd realised that my mother was not coming. However this did not crop up in the conversation until it was time for her to leave and then it was rather late to change our arrangements. Father's old colleague had secured me a seat on the West Country Express . . .' Madge's smile deepened guiltily as she remembered her mother's adjurations. 'Now darling, don't say a word when Mrs Briscoe arrives. Wait until she is leaving and then mention it as if we'd already told her. I think you and Rosemary should have time alone. Without me. And without Clem's mother. We both spoil her. She needs Etta's firm hand!'

Dear Mother. She always said to her friends 'How I'd manage without Madge, I do not know. She is a tower of strength . . . an absolute tower.' And the boot was on the other foot entirely.

Rosemary arrived, lugging a bucket of sea water. She poured it carefully into a prepared hole. It disappeared.

'Oh damn!' she said vexedly.

Madge protested automatically, then explained. 'The sand up here is too dry, Ro, it soaks up the water. When I've finished Daddy's letter I'll come and dig a hole in the wet sand and you'll be able to fill that up and make a lovely lake!'

116

'Come *now* Mummy. I want you to come *now*! You're always writing to Daddy!'

The truth of the last statement overrode the petulance of Rosemary's voice and Madge began to put everything away in the beach bag while Rosemary goose-stepped on the spot.

'Come on then. Back to the sea. Don't forget your bucket. Left right, left right . . .'

'Sojers, Mummy. Like the sojers.' Rosemary pointed and Madge paused to look over her shoulder.

A platoon of the Marine Commandoes appeared on the wharf behind them, shouldering a life raft. It was a familiar but still exciting sight. Eight men, four to each side of the raft, ran in perfect synchronisation down the slipway and along the sand to the water. Without any audible order being given they then slowed to a loping wade through the water until they were waist deep. The boat was lowered from shoulder height to the surface, and the men hoisted themselves aboard with hardly a ripple disturbing the sea. They knelt and leaned over the side, paddling smoothly with their hands. In less than three minutes from their first appearance, they had disappeared silently into the mist.

'Bye-bye,' sang Rosemary sweetly. 'Bye-bye sojers.'

Madge smiled sentimentally, and the two of them went to the water's edge where Madge began digging and Rosemary filling. The 'lake' was taking shape nicely when Rosemary looked up and commented, 'A nunny sojer, Mummy,' and Madge glanced over her shoulder and saw another camouflaged giant pounding down the beach. He was making straight for them, but Madge, with complete faith in the trained reactions of all the Mountain Warfare regiment, watched smilingly until almost the last minute. As the booted foot was lifted above the water-filled hole, she gasped a warning. It was too late. The marine, his eyes on the invisible horizon, had seen neither them nor their lake. At the sound of a voice from beneath his raised boot, he managed to gather himself in a kind of writhing knot in mid-air for a split second. Then he crashed into the hole, emptying it of water instantly and soaking the two females on its edge. Rosemary screamed piercingly and began to wail. Madge dashed water from her eyes and picked her up to jiggle her against her shoulder. The marine scrambled to his feet without so much as an exclamation and climbed out of the hole. He marked time experimentally.

'Okay,' he said of himself. Then to Madge, 'You okay?' She nodded above Rosemary's head. 'What about the kid?' She nodded again. 'Sorry.' He stopped marking time and looked out to where the sea merged with the mist. 'Where are the others? Did you see them?'

'Yes. They launched about five minutes ago. You'll never catch them.'

Rosemary lifted a head to protest furiously at her mother's wandering attention. The man ignored her.

'I'll have to try.' He leaned down and ripped at the laces of his boot. 'Look. Can I leave these with you? And this?' He tugged off his flat hat and battledress top. 'Where are you staying?'

'Zion Cottage.'

'Right.'

He ran into the water, staggered, plunged, and was gone.

'There, there, darling. Everything is all right. No need to cry.'

'I'se all wet Mummy!' Rosemary, who got wet regularly of her own volition, decided to object this time. 'That nasty sojer wetted me!'

'Well, I'm wet too. It's our part in commando training I suppose!'

Rosemary stopped crying, intrigued. Madge followed up quickly, 'Let's take the soldier's things back to the cottage and have a drink. It's time for your rest.'

'No rest Mummy – I don't want a rest!'

Madge put down her daughter and gathered up the enormous boots and clothing. She said with unusual severity, 'You will have a rest, Ro. Remember, there's a war on!'

Rosemary wrestled with the logic of this all the way up the beach and was still frowning when Madge picked up the beach bag.

'Is having a rest doing my bit, Mummy?' she queried then.
'Yes.'

'Orright then. And shall I carry the sojer's hat? That would be doing my bit too, wouldn't it?'

'It would.'

Madge tucked her letter to Clem at the back of the bag and capped her fountain pen. Maybe the encounter with 'the sojer' was going to be another bonus about this holiday. She smiled as she watched Rosemary gallop across the cobbles towards Philip. Whatever was happening, it was terribly difficult not to be happy in this place.

Normally they would have spent the afternoon on Porthmeor beach with a picnic. Etta ate well at midday and liked to rest afterwards. Philip and Jem might take the lugger into the bay to fish sometimes, but they were both over sixty now and officially retired. This afternoon, Madge was strangely unwilling to move out of sight of the cottage.

Etta said, 'Get you off, my maid. I'll give that commando 'is stuff when 'e comes for en.'

'It's rather hot, Etta. I think I'll stay near the house if you don't mind. Then if Ro needs a drink or anything I'm handy!'

'Not got an eye on that there commando, 'ave you, my maid?' Etta said sharply. 'You'm a married woman, remember!'

'Oh Etta. Don't be silly.' Madge looked at the silent Philip. 'Are you going out with Jem today, Philip?'

'No.'

Etta was on to him instantly. 'What d'you mean, no? You tole me you was trawlin' all af'noon and ev'nin' – I dun't know where I be to with you these days, Philip Nolla.'

'I'm staying ashore.' Philip looked at her with his clear blue stare. 'I kin please myself now, wife. An' I'm stayin' ashore this afternoon.'

Etta was silent. Madge felt her neck warm with resentment. It was as if she were an unmarried girl again having to be chaperoned. She recalled how Etta had snuffed

Neville's candle in the old days; she had wondered at his annoyance then; now she did not.

She took up her position near the harbour wall again and looked at her letter to Clem. Rosemary, sensing her mother's uncooperativeness, joined a little knot of local children who were playing a complicated game among the beached boats. She toddled after them, crouching obediently when they screamed that Jerry was coming. She was beginning to feel part of the big world.

Philip came slowly down the slipway from the Fisherman's Lodge. His trilby hat was looking too big for him, which Madge saw as a sign of age. This and his diffidence forced an unwilling smile from her.

He said, 'That's better. How did I offend you, woman?'

'Oh . . . sometimes you still treat me as if I'm a child. Come and sit down here.' She made room on the rug. 'Where's Etta?'

'Feet up, snoring away. Minister's calling later. Can't abide him so I'll have to stay out.'

'That's why you were going trawling with Jem.'

He nodded and gave her one of his upward grins.
'True. True.'

'So you did cancel it to keep an eye on me?' She was cross again. 'Honestly Philip, it's too bad. I'm twenty-four, you know. And there's Ro to chaperone me if I should go berserk!'

'Ah . . . it's not that, woman. Did you think I didn't trust you?'

'Then why?'

He was silent, getting out his old clay pipe, then his oilskin tobacco pouch. He looked inside. Tobacco was scarce and after a moment he closed it again and put everything away.

'I can't find words, woman. Once before I din't keep you close and you was pushed into something . . . maybe not right for you. I don't know. I en't aimin' to interfere . . . only . . . only to be at hand if you need someone.'

She was silent for a long time, trying to remember all the tiny events that had led up to her marriage to Clem.

At last she said in a low voice, 'Philip, tell me honestly. Do you think I shouldn't have married Clem?'

He did not lift his head again. The rim of his trilby was ridiculously wide, almost like a cowboy hat.

'That's what I don't know. I know you're not 'appy. But you've got your little girl and there's much more to life than bein' 'appy. But . . . I shoulda liked you to be 'appy too, my maid. I shoulda liked that.'

'Dear Philip. I'm happy enough. Really. And if I weren't . . . you must never feel responsible.'

'Responsible, aye.' He seized on the word. 'That's what we are, woman. Responsible for one another. Your pa, and now you and your ma . . . you feels responsible for Etta and me. You – you *keeps* us.'

'Rubbish, Philip!' Madge laughed uncomfortably. 'We remember you at Christmas and—'

'I don't mean keeps. Not like that. Not pays us. I mean you keeps us, like a keeper keeps sheep.' He lifted his head. 'Isn't that right, woman? Don't we keep one another?'

'Oh Philip. Yes.' His flattened vowel sounds gave the word even more meaning. She remembered how he had dived into the sea twenty years before to pull her out. He had indeed become her 'kipper' then.

He patted her hand quickly and looked back to where Rosemary was playing. 'Ah. Well then. Kin I sit 'ere for a bit and talk to you?'

'Of course. And I'm sorry I was touchy about it.' She too patted his hand. 'Tell me one of your stories, Philip. Tell me about the flood of '94.'

'That weren't no story, woman, not in the sense o' fairy tales.' He got out his tobacco pouch for the second time and looked into it. 'Great rocks a-'urtling down the Stennack. In the front doors, through the walls, out the back. Terrible it was.'

She said, 'I used to pretend I was sitting in the train when the Malakoff walls broke. And I had to get up steam and get the train out of the station before it was washed over on to Porthminster.' She paused. 'What is Rosemary up to now?'

They both squinted into the bright mist. Rosemary was talking to one of the soldiers.

Philip said, 'Is that your commando? The one who gave you his boots?'

'I don't remember.'

Philip turned and gave her a level stare quite unlike his usual glinting looks. Then he faced front again.

''E's a-pickin' 'er up. I'd better go and see.'

'No. Stay here, Philip. He's bringing her up. She's telling him that we're here. It must be the same man.'

'Aye. Must be.' Philip's voice was as dry as the sand.

The soldier, with Rosemary on his shoulders, approached them. All the commandoes were hefty, muscular young men, but this one seemed especially so. His dark red hair was stiff with salt and sprang out from his beret like wire wool, his brown eyes were not large but very round and shiny, like boot buttons. His nose might have been broken at some time, it took a sharp turn to the right halfway down and seemed to pull his top lip up towards it. When he smiled, as he was then, it showed his two front teeth and made him look like a schoolboy.

Rosemary yelled, 'Shoes, Mummy! Sojer wants his shoes!'

Madge said, 'They're at the cottage with the other things. I'll get them.'

The man knelt and bent his head forward and Rosemary stepped off his neck on to the rug. He looked up.

'Don't go yet. I must thank you. For this morning. I was supposed to go in uniform but I'd never have caught the others with my boots on!' His grin made him look about fifteen. 'I'm the sort of cox.'

'Cox?'

'Coxswain. Of the raft. Four a side and one directing ops. The blighters pulled a fast one on me.' He did not move from his position on all fours in front of her. 'My name is Edward Nicholls. Everyone in St Ives calls me Ned.'

Rosemary was goose-stepping again and Philip reached for her hand.

'Pull me up, young lady. Come on. Heave-ho.' He got

to his feet. 'This is Mrs Clement Briscoe who is staying with my wife and me. An' 'er daughter, Rosemary. I am Philip Nolla.'

Madge looked up in surprise at Philip's dignified formality. She had expected him to discourage the young marine, in his efforts to 'kip' her. Here he was lifting the whole chance encounter into something more . . . important.

Ned Nicholls straightened his back but stayed on his knees. He was almost as tall as Philip who was on his feet by now.

'I've heard of you, sir. You went to Dunkirk, didn't you? And they talk about you at the Clipper – you went over on a rocket line to one of the steamers in the hurricane when you were just a kid.'

Philip avoided Madge's gaze.

'I'll take Rosemary up for her tea,' he said instead. 'You two come on later. Give me time find a cloth for the table.'

'Oh Philip—' Madge began, and Ned Nicholls said at the same time, 'Really, sir, there's no need . . .' Then they both stopped speaking and looked at each other.

Philip started up the slipway. ''Alf an 'our,' he stipulated. Then he bent his head to listen to something Rosemary was saying and they crossed the cobbles together.

Ned Nicholls sat back on his heels and said, 'He wants us to get to know each other. Is he a relative of yours?'

'No. But more than a relative.' Madge felt herself flushing at Philip's obviousness. She said, He's has always . . . well . . . kept an eye on me when I'm here.'

'You come regularly?'

'Yes. Since I was four.'

The boot-button eyes were full of questions, but he must have decided that they could wait. He unfolded his legs and sat on the edge of the rug.

'I'd never been until I came on this training course. A week in Weymouth each year when I was a kid. That was as much as they could manage.'

'Your parents?'

'Barnado's. I'm a Banana Boy.' He grinned. 'Isn't

123

that why your Mr Philip Nolla is being kind to me?'

'No. I'm sure . . . I don't know.' It made Philip's actions much more acceptable, though it couldn't be true. Even so she relaxed slightly. 'What did you think of St Ives when you arrived?'

'Beautiful. Wonderful. I couldn't believe such a place existed. What about you?'

'The same. Quite literally I thought it was fairyland.' She smiled into the sun. 'When I'm here it's as if it's the only reality. Everything else seems like a dream.'

'Perhaps it is. A dream. Or a nightmare.' He laughed to take the seriousness out of the exchange, then went on, 'I gather from your daughter's remarks to me that you were both thoroughly wetted this morning when I emptied your pool of water.'

Madge laughed too. 'It was so funny. The whole thing was like a Marx Brothers farce. Did you catch the others?'

'Yes. They knew I would. I'm fairly fast in the water.' The dark eyes were laughing right at her. 'I'm glad no harm came to you. Do you swim, Mrs Briscoe?'

'Yes. Philip doesn't approve. He worries about the sea claiming all of us back. But I love swimming. Mostly I mess about in the surf round at Porthmeor beach.'

He looked at her covertly. Her hair was brown with lighter bands of colour from the sun. There was a lot of it and she had it tied on her neck with a blue ribbon. There was nothing remarkable about her, yet he had a job not to stare rudely. She was the sort of girl who would never get boring. Her face was so mobile, laughing one minute, solemn the next. And the way her neck went down between the clavicles, leaving little shallows each side . . . it was so endearing. He wanted to tell her she must eat more because she was too thin.

He said, 'The sea is treacherous round there. Safer at Porthminster.'

'But tame.' She smiled. 'That's what makes St Ives so special. It seems civilised, but only just under the surface it's dangerous and exciting.'

He laughed aloud. 'That is what the artists see, of course. I know someone. A painter. She would agree with you. She says she has seen one of the standing stones marching over Trencrom hill!'

'Are you an artist, Mr Nicholls?'

'Ned. Please call me Ned.'

'Oh. Well. Ned, then. And you had better call me Madge. Mrs Clement Briscoe is rather a mouthful.' She smiled and he wondered why he had thought her unremarkable.

'Thank you . . . Madge.' It was such a stupid, ordinary name. What sort of parents named their child Madge? 'Well then, no, I don't paint. I mean I don't earn a living by painting. I was hopeless at school. But these people – Mr and Mrs Scaife – they say I could paint if I tried.' He laughed. 'They don't realise I am trying my utmost!' He sifted sand through his fingers and Madge noticed the bluntness of the nails. 'Do you paint, Madge?' he asked.

'I draw. I used to have an easel at the cottage and set it up like a real artist. I played at being one, I suppose. Mother encouraged me but Father thought I made a much better wicketkeeper!'

She began to tell him about the cricket matches. He listened, his eyes going from her hand to her face. He noticed the blue veins along the back of her hand, the small bump in her nose, the way her mouth curved, her rather long chin.

'I wish I'd known all of you. It sounds great fun. We played lots of cricket, but it wasn't like yours. We were in teams and if we didn't win, we'd let our team down.'

'Oh crikey, it was the same for us. Father was livid if anyone on his side dropped a catch or got a duck.'

'Did your husband play cricket with you?'

'Yes. He came down here with my brother once when we were all much younger. He was at school with Neville and then in Spain. Neville was killed out there. And the cricket matches finished.'

There was a small silence. Madge began to gather her things together. Ned got to his knees again.

125

'It's rather marvellous that you draw. Would you like to meet the Scaifes? They hold classes, you know. Half a dozen of us go along. Keeps us out of mischief.'

'Well . . . I . . . yes. Thank you.' She stood up. 'That is if Etta will stay with Rosemary. Sometimes she won't go to sleep until I go to bed. I suppose the air raids have made her nervous.'

He picked up the rug, shook it and folded it.

'She's so pretty. It's hard to think that she will miss so many things if this war goes on much longer.'

Madge thought of Clem coming home next month. She shouldered her bag. 'I think we'd better go up to the house. Philip obviously wants to do the honours. Do you mind? Can you spare the time?'

'I'm off duty now until three, and I don't mind one bit. It's good to get out of the mess.'

'Three? In the morning?'

'It's the best time for our sort of training.'

'I suppose so.' She glanced at him. 'I should have thought . . . with the war nearly over . . . the commando training wasn't quite so necessary.'

He shrugged. 'If we can hurry this last bit it will be worthwhile.'

She knew better than to ask more, but she wondered if the training could have anything to do with the new doodlebugs. Strange . . . Clem's important war work had something to do with a different kind of bomb, and this young commando was trained to destroy a different kind of bomb. It was all so . . . unnecessary.

He followed her to the cottage, the rug over one arm. It was the usual fisherman's dwelling, built on and into the rock; a fish cellar at one level, a flight of steps to the living area, bedrooms above and the attic like a lookout perched on top. There were no ceilings – the floorboards above occasionally snowed flakes of whitewash on to the plush-covered table. A crystal chandelier incongruously tinkled from one of the heavy timbers, and every nook and cranny was filled with bits and pieces. Rosemary was ensconced in the window seat among cushions, two pieces of driftwood on her short lap. Etta and the Methodist Minister were at the table, an open bible between them. Philip cut bread at the sideboard.

Rosemary greeted her mother vociferously.

'We bin singing, Mummy. A woodin cross, Mummy.'

The minister said sonorously, ' "The Old Wooden Cross", my child.' He looked at Madge. 'A hymn, Mrs Briscoe. We cannot start too early with hymns.' He nodded at Ned. 'One of our brave men. May God be with you, my son.'

Ned nodded too. 'Thank you, sir.'

Etta said, 'Sit down then. Making the place look a muddle. Don't let the child put that in her mouth, Marjorie. It will splinter.' She gathered cups around her and began to pour tea. 'Help yourself to jam, minister.' She pushed his cup towards him and smiled dourly as he shovelled the bible hastily away. 'And you're Private Ned Nicholls, then? Where you from, young man?'

'Wiltshire, Mrs Nolla.' Ned sensed animosity in the lizard-like stare. He smiled frankly. 'I haven't got a family, ma'am. I was found in a railway waiting-room twenty-two years ago. Doctor Barnardo took me on.'

The wind had been taken from Etta's sails, but she managed a broadside even though becalmed. 'Mrs Briscoe's 'usband is doin' very important war work in Canada. He's always been a friend of the family. A great friend.'

Ned nodded gently and bent his head to look at Rosemary's driftwood. He was intrigued. They hadn't known he was an orphan, so Philip Nolla's invitation had not been given from pity. He wanted Madge to have a . . . friend? Was that because her marriage to Clement Briscoe wasn't happy? Etta Nolla's aggression might bear that out. And Etta had called Madge Marjorie. That was much more like it; there was something satisfying about three equi-syllable names. He repeated it in his head: Mar . . . jor . . . ie. On the wild country between Zennor and St Ives there was a bank of purple flowers, tall and strong, yet unbroken by

127

the wind, so very supple. He thought they might be marjoram. Perhaps he could take her there.

He glanced up at her and discovered she was looking at him. Her eyes were navy blue with a kind of intense sympathy. He realised she was sorry for him because he had been abandoned as a baby and he grinned at her, trying to reassure her. Without conscious thought his blunt fingers reached out and touched hers.

Philip plonked the jam pot in front of him.

'Better take some jam, Mr Nicholls. Before the littl'un 'as the lot.'

Ned sat up straight with a jerk and was thankful to see that Etta was still attending to the chapel wallah. He met Philip's stare for a brief moment, then mumbled, 'Oh . . . thanks,' and applied himself to spreading jam on his bread.

A week later he took her to see the flowers, and she agreed they were marjoram.

They were into September and the mist on the high cliffs above Zennor had deteriorated into a sea fret and was cold and wet. But the weather proved an ally to Ned. Rosemary's halcyon existence on the beach was suddenly interrupted. Limited to twice daily walks in wellingtons, she became obstreperous. The Mountain Warfare Group came to the rescue and held a party for all the children they could muster. Their mess, high above Bamaluz Point, was transformed from its grim bareness to an Aladdin's cave. The bar looked like a Wild West frontier saloon, the billiard and ping-pong tables covered with hardboard and cloths and laid as one enormous banquet-cum-buffet, the girdered roof was hung with fishing nets, shells and pre-war balloons. Rosemary, escorted by Philip, was entranced. She dismissed her mother instantly. Ned seized his opportunity, and one of the jeeps.

Madge, walking behind Ned through the shoulder-high fern, the sea either side, the mist pearling her hair, knew one of those moments of conscious happiness. The excitement of St Ives, which she had thought gone for ever with

128

the terrible deaths of her father and brother, was tangible again. She smelled it, felt it vibrating through the soles of her feet as they contacted the springy turf, heard it in the scream of the gulls, saw it in the looming shape of the enormous headland pushing into the Atlantic.

When Ned Nicholls paused and quested about in the fern for the flowers in which he seemed so interested, she began to laugh.

'What's up?' he asked, looking at her with brows raised ridiculously above his round eyes.

She couldn't explain. 'I was remembering you landing in our lake,' she improvised lamely. 'You're almost as wet again.'

'So are you,' he came back promptly, grinning like a schoolboy. 'It's rather good, isn't it?'

She recalled Clem's unwillingness to get himself wet, and nodded. It was something to do with becoming part of the earth, a one-ness with the elements that was completely delightful at this moment.

'Here they are.' Ned disappeared among the sodden fern and she followed somewhat cautiously. Philip had warned her frequently about the many old mine shafts on the cliffs. But Ned was only a few feet from the path. And there, almost buried by the burgeoning fern, was a clump of purple flowers growing strongly and independently.

'Well!' She was genuinely surprised. 'Yes, I think they are marjoram plants. Why here? I suppose a bird must have dropped the seed.' She held the heads between her fingers and sniffed experimentally. 'This is wild marjoram. The other is much smaller. Called sweet marjoram.'

Ned took a lethal-looking knife from his belt and crouched by the flowers.

'What are you doing?' Madge asked.

'I'm going to dig a root. That bit of land behind the mess – I'm going to try to get it going there.'

'But why? It's not the kind used as a herb. It's really a weed.'

He looked up. 'I wouldn't dream of using it as a herb.

129

And it's certainly not a weed in that sense. It's your flower. Marjoram. Marjorie. Wild marjoram too.'

Suddenly Madge understood. She felt the dangerous heat tiding up her face and felt a sudden pang of anger with Philip. Surely he must have realised what he was risking when he so carefully began this friendship? Ned Nicholls was a young man – a boy practically – with no family; he was in imminent danger of idealising Madge, Rosemary and the Nollas and even feeling a kind of romantic attachment to Madge herself. And in a few days or weeks he was going off to God knew what . . .

She said flatly, 'I'm always called Madge. People never use my full name unless they're annoyed with me.'

He was struggling with the matted roots, determined not to tear them.

'I heard Mrs Nolla call you Marjorie that first day,' he panted. 'It seems so right for you. Natural, liking seclusion. Yet . . . a little wild.' He grinned. 'Wouldn't you agree with that character assessment? That's what they call it in the Marines – character assessment. If there's no wildness there, they won't look at you!'

She was forced to laugh with him, though already she was wondering what to do next. How to get away from this lonely place and back to the safety of Ro.

Ned gave up with the knife and knelt in front of the tottering flowers, easing them out of the ground with his hands. She stared at the top of his head; it was the colour of dark rust; why on earth should it remind her suddenly of Neville's head? Neville had been older than her and this boy was younger. But Neville had been the same age as Ned was now; Neville would always be twenty-two.

She said hoarsely, 'Ned. Is this . . . is your next mission very dangerous?'

The roots came away from the shallow earth with several snapping sounds and Ned fell back into the fern, buried in flowers and scattered soil. He kicked his heels in the air clownishly until she laughed again.

'Come and get me up!' he spluttered, pretending complete

helplessness. 'Your contribution to this exercise has been . . .' he struggled to his feet with her help and met her eyes through the enormous bush of flowers. '. . . Oh Madge. I haven't had such fun since I was about ten years old. Thanks. Thanks so much.'

She didn't risk looking at him for too long, but as she turned back to the path, still laughing, she was reassured. After all, that's what it had been for him: fun. No more than that. And it had been fun for her too. More than fun; a marvellous experience. She was reminded of a time way back in the past . . . hadn't it been on this same path? Then she had been allowed a glimpse of the rightness of things, their intricate simplicity, her own place in such an amazing scheme. She smiled. Of course, it was the place. It had always been the place. Nothing at all to do with Ned Nicholls.

Yet that night as she listened to an unsleeping Rosemary discoursing on the glories of the party, she recalled that Ned had not answered her question. She had known he wouldn't even as she asked it; but then he had thanked her in the way people thank you when they are leaving a party.

'I thanked that nice captain-man. Mummy. I said "thank you for having me". Was that good?'

'Very good, my darling.'

Madge kissed the top of her daughter's head and told herself she was a fool.

Ned continued to spend all his off-duty time with them. Madge, well chaperoned by Rosemary at all times, subtly changed their relationship to avoid any sudden awareness. She referred to him humorously as 'Uncle Ned' and would scold him in a Auntly fashion – 'dry off after those night exercises' and 'keep your sweet ration for yourself' as if he were in the Boy Scouts and she were indeed an anxious aunt. She did not mention the marjoram plants again, and neither did he. Presumably they had withered and died on the thin soil behind the Commando Post. He called her Madge, never Marjorie.

She did not mention her departure date either, and the day before it he took her to meet the Scaifes.

They had a studio on the neck of the Island, overlooking Porthgwidden cove. It had been a small boat store and the smell of tar had soaked into its wooden walls and still wafted about in the high room. Gerald Scaife was very avant-garde and painted enormous abstracts. They caught him halfway up a pair of paint-spattered steps with a huge paste brush, looking for all the world like someone sticking an advertisement to a hoarding. He did not hear their arrival, owing in part to his concentration, but mostly to the fact that the wind-up gramophone in the corner was going full-blast with an Offenbach piece. Madge, who had 'done' Paris for a month when she was seventeen, was transported to the area around Sacre Coeur. She put her fingers on Ned's sleeve as if she expected to be whirled into a mazurka.

Then a small figure on the other side of the studio turned and saw them and darted for the gramophone, brush still in hand.

'Ned! How delightful. Gerald dear, it's Ned Nicholls come for tea. Get down and put the kettle on.' This small figure advanced and became obviously female in spite of trousers, shirt and a man's cap. 'You must be Madge. Ned said he'd bring you along. And Rosemary – where is Rosemary?'

'I didn't think it was safe to bring her. With all your stuff about.' Ned glanced down, saw Madge's hand on his sleeve and covered it with his own. She shook hands with her spare hand, then laughed as Mrs Scaife remembered the condition of her own fingers and apologised. Ned said, 'Don't worry, Barbara. Madge is used to sand, jam – whatever comes.'

Madge said, 'Rosemary is just at that age.'

'Oh, I wish we could have seen her. Ned says she is so sweet. Gerald and I were going to have a baby last year but then we didn't and we're getting rather old anyway.'

By this time Gerald was on the level and encircled his tiny wife with an enormous arm.

'We're all right as we are,' he said. 'Let's all sit down

132

in the window and look at the rain and drink tea. Shall we?'

The two of them led the way to the large windows beneath the skylight. There were steamer chairs and a card table, and Gerald settled everyone with great care. Ned linked Madge's hand in his between the arms of their chairs. Gerald shifted her a little nearer to Ned. 'It's all right, we don't want to split you up,' he chuckled as if it were the most natural thing in the world for two comparative strangers, one married and much older than the other, to hold hands. Madge did not want to make a fuss about releasing her hand, but a blush started at the neckline of her cotton dress and began to work its way up.

'Tea à la Scaife,' announced Barbara, staggering from behind Gerald's canvas with a loaded metal tray. 'Very strong and very Indian. With rock cakes practically from the beach.' She plonked the tray on the table and picked up one of the cakes in question to tap it in the edge of the teapot. It did indeed have a geological sound to it.

In spite of that initial embarrassment, Madge began to enjoy herself. It was one of the happiest tea parties she could remember. And it was bliss to be away from Ro and talking with adults; the Scaifes were very adult and very interesting. They were trying hard to bridge the gap between the slightly Bohemian arts and crafts set in St Ives and the rest of the population. Like many outsiders they were more aware of the town's traditions and history than its natives, certainly more determined to preserve and respect both.

'We want to start something. A society or something – to stop developers coming in and changing the place,' Barbara explained. 'Once the war is over there will be a building boom. It's always the same. They'll ruin St Ives.'

'That's why we started art classes for the commandoes,' Gerald put in. 'It was our bit of war work of course, but we hoped some of the locals would come too and join us.'

'And did they?' Madge asked.

'Yes. A chap from Zennor, invalided out of the Navy, he cycles over twice weekly. And of course we've got Alfred Wallace to prove that it's never too late to start painting.'

They told Madge about Alfred Wallace the fisherman and his curiously childlike paintings on bits of wood and card.

'Philip has told me about him,' she said, dipping her rock cake in the tea as Ned was doing. 'Philip said that one day when they were mending nets on Smeaton's Pier, Mr Wallace stopped work and just stared and stared at the net for ages. Then at last he said – I don't know – something about everything being there, the whole world, intertwined like a net.'

Barbara Scaife smiled. 'I suppose one always feels that where one lives is the centre of the universe, but I'm sure that a place like this, bringing people from all corners of the globe together, gives them a common denominator if you like. They have time in their busy lives to look and appreciate.'

Gerald said, 'It's a microcosm as all communities are. This microcosm reflects man's purpose and fulfilment in a special way perhaps.'

Ned nodded. I'll go for that. Even in wartime I've never been happier in my whole life.'

Gerald said, 'Yes, well old chap, you've had a fairly grim time of it up to now, haven't you? Barnardo offers bread and butter, but not much jam I imagine.'

Ned shrugged. 'It wasn't that bad actually. Just a feeling of marking time until real life began. I thought real life was the war. But no. It didn't make sense until I came here.' He leaned forward and let go Madge's hand. She brought it surreptitiously on to her lap and put it under her plate. He said raptly, 'I remember when we arrived the lorry spilled us out at the top of the Stennack, and we had to come down in full kit. I was dreading it. It had been a long haul and one of the chaps had been sick in the lorry – God it was awful. But as we started down I looked over the tops of all those funny old roofs and saw Godrevy sitting in the middle of the sky, and I breathed the air . . . it must have been a Monday because all the washing was out on the Island, bleaching in the sun. And it was January!' He laughed. 'By the time we got to the mess we were sweating like pigs. We chucked our stuff into the corner and went straight into the sea. It was like being born again.'

Everyone laughed. Madge thought that she was glad his happiness did not depend on her. She'd been right. It was the place.

'A baptism,' she murmured, remembering Clem.

'That's it exactly!' He turned to her joyously. 'A baptism!'

Later Gerald took them the length of his enormous painting.

'It's to do with the relationship between land and sea,' he explained to a mystified Madge and Ned. 'The way the Island pierces the ocean. Then Old Man's Head. Then the Five Points . . . all those lovely headlands pushing back the rollers. Next time you walk along the coast, look at them. The way the sea tries – it throws itself on each of the rocks. Then slips back.'

Madge said soberly, 'Philip says it will win in the end.'

'Perhaps he's right. But not in our lifetime.' Gerald took his brush and drew another line. The effect was of a comb with one tooth much longer than the others. He said, 'There. That concedes his point.' He put down the brush and turned to Madge. 'Remember – when you see this picture in the Tate one day – remember that line is agreeing with Philip Nolla. The sea has won.'

Madge shook her head and Ned said, 'No, it hasn't surely? If the lines are the land then surely that bit of land going farther than any of the others means that the land has won?'

Barbara appeared, drying her hands on a piece of rag. 'I think it means that we've surrendered. Like we do when we bathe. We surrender to the sea.' She opened the door and looked out. 'Still raining. And you've no umbrellas. You're definitely surrendering to the general wetness!' She danced outside, holding her face upwards and opening her mouth to the downpour. Gerald reached out and grabbed her back.

'You've got to look after yourself,' he grumbled, holding her tightly to him. Her cap caught on his arm and was pulled off. Unexpectedly her head was revealed covered in grey stubble. It was a shocking sight and Madge looked quickly away, understanding the reason for the endearingly ridiculous man's cap. When she looked back, it was in place again and Barbara grinning her gamine grin.

'Fare thee well, children,' she said. 'Come next week and have some more rock cakes.'

Madge did not look at Ned. 'I'm afraid I am going home tomorrow,' she said.

Ned did not tighten his hold on her arm. 'And my posting is the next day,' he said levelly.

'Never mind!' Gerald held out his free hand and pumped theirs in turn. 'We'll meet again. I know it. I feel it in my bones.' He smiled at Madge. 'Like Alfred Wallace's net, you know, Madge. We're going to be entwined.'

Barbara kissed her paint-stained fingers at them as they moved into the rain and Madge gave a final wave before they were enclosed in the high wall of Teetotal Street. She saw them silhouetted in the strange grey light of the studio door: a big, bear-like man, holding his tiny wife as if he would never let her go.

He said, 'Why didn't you tell me today was your last day?'

'I thought it might spoil it. I hate last days.' They turned into Back Road West and were met by gale-force winds. 'You didn't tell me about your posting date either.'

'I'm not supposed to.' The words sounded cold and he grabbed her upper arm and held it to his side. 'It wasn't that, of course. I hate last days too. Let's abolish them.'

She laughed with relief, thinking they were back to their bantering footing. 'All right, Uncle Ned. How do we do that?'

'Well, we make next week happen now.'

'Sounds interesting.' Her laugh became indulgent. She was terribly conscious of his hands above her elbow, pulling her to him. His strength was there, manifest. She could not resist it. She said breathlessly, 'And what are we going to do next week, d'you think, Uncle Ned?'

'The weather will be okay again. So we'll have a swim at Porthmeor. The wild beach.'

'Lovely.' Rain trickled inside her mack and she moved her neck to block it, then gave up. She remembered something Barbara had said about surrendering. Surrender. It need not mean defeat. She saw suddenly that it could mean more than victory itself. She was breathing very quickly now, though they were not walking fast. 'Yes. Lovely. We'll ask Philip to come with us so that he can mind Ro. And we'll swim right out past the old wreck and look at St Ives as if we're seals.'

He stopped and turned to face her. Rain streamed down his face like tears.

'Madge. Marjoram. My marjoram. We haven't got next week. We haven't got much time left. Only now. And Ro will be in bed. Philip will look after her. He understands.'

She was aghast. This was the moment she had tried to avoid, knowing, beneath her superficiality, that it was unavoidable.

Nevertheless she panted, 'What are you saying, Ned?'

'Come swimming with me, Madge. Please. Now.'

'I can't! Rosemary. And the weather! It'll be like a seething pot at Porthmeor in this wind! And Philip hates me going into the sea.'

'Just tell him. Get your things. And come.' He shifted his grip and pulled her up so that their eyes were level. 'A last swim, Madge.'

But she knew it would be more than that. Total immersion in water had always had a special significance for her ever since Philip had 'rescued' her.

She said on an upward note, 'We're *friends*, Ned.'

'Oh, we are.' He grinned unexpectedly. 'I've never had a proper girlfriend before. I didn't know what it was like.'

She did not know whether to be reassured or not, but when he put her down and turned back the way they had come, she walked slowly down the court, certain she had no choice in the matter.

Philip and Etta were in the kitchen and Etta had put Ro to bed and announced with grim triumph that there had been no fuss, nor bother, and the child was already fast asleep.

When she said she was going for a swim, they both looked up at her, startled and disbelieving.

'Oh no, you're not,' said Etta. And Philip said, 'In this weather?'

'I have to. Ned is being posted somewhere tomorrow. I think it must be dangerous.' She sobbed suddenly. 'I have to, Philip. I have to.'

Etta said furiously, 'Yes. This is all your doing, Philip Nolla, and don't you ferget it!' She rounded on Madge. 'You'll be drownded and worse!'

But Philip said, 'Do you really have to? You're married to Clem Briscoe.'

How could she tell Philip that her marriage was for Rosemary's sake only? How could she explain to Philip that Ned was her best friend? And he was also the stranger in the night that she would never see again.

She sobbed, 'It will be all right. I will make it all right.' And she turned and grabbed her costume and towel from the passage lines and shovelled them into the beach bag of American cloth. Then she was out in the rain again and running for the deserted expanse of Porthmeor beach.

They changed in adjacent canvas tents which creaked and groaned around them in the wind. He made no attempt to come into her tent and when she emerged he was waiting outside for her, staring at the incoming tide as if calculating their chances of survival. The surf was creaming in perfectly but mountainously. Not a living soul was in sight. If they got into difficulties no-one would know. Madge wondered if that was to be the end of it: she and Ned lost in the sea for eternity. Her calf and thigh muscles shook momentarily and then were still. Surrender. To the sea. To events. To fate itself.

Ned turned and smiled. 'Ready?'

'Ready.'

'He took her hand and they lowered their heads and

138

walked into the wind and rain. There was one moment of caution; as the sea rushed up to her knees, she gasped and pulled back and would have run ahead of the next breaking wave as Neville did in the old days. But Ned leaned down and picked her up bodily and ran forward before it could lay them flat. They were both lifted high to its crest as it gathered itself into a crescendo of water, then it was past them and they were both swimming for the next one.

For ten glorious minutes they were one with the ocean. Occasionally a wave would threaten to break right upon them and Ned would shout a warning and they would both sit on the sea bed. It was the usual immediate and strange translation; sound became something felt and not heard through the ears. They were rocked where they sat and above them was a turbulent madness. Then they would bob to the surface like corks, hold hands, laugh crazily, all tension and fear gone. She felt part of this different element, as if she could live like this for always. All too soon Ned was pulling her into the white water again, making her body-surf for the shore. A roller took them to the edge of the dry sand and left them slowly, almost with regret.

Madge rolled on to her back and sat up in the shallows.

'It's over,' she gasped, but not sadly. She was warm now, invigorated, her blood coursing fast through her veins.

'No. That was the beginning,' Ned gasped back at her. And she knew what he meant and at that precise moment was not afraid or even reluctant. But that couldn't last. By the time they had dragged themselves back to the tents, she was beginning to shiver again.

She stammered, 'Ned. I have to explain. There is something wrong with me. I'm sorry. I should have told you sooner. Oh Ned, I'm so sorry.'

He came inside her tent and fastened the fly-sheet with great care. After the wind it was warm and in spite of the flapping canvas there was a sort of cosiness in the small space.

He misunderstood. 'It's all right, Madge. Don't worry.' He put his arms around her and held her tightly. 'I'm just thankful you came swimming. I know some girls won't when they're that way.'

She almost laughed. 'Oh Ned. It's not that.' She pushed her face into his shoulder, then put her arms around him and held him to her. She explained.

'Madge. Darling. I can't hear. Did you say . . . what *did* you say, my dearest?' She said it again and he shouted, 'Frigid? You? Oh Marjorie-marjoram.' He laughed very tenderly. 'You're not frigid, my love. My only love.' He began to kiss her.

She could respond to kisses; friends kissed. Her hands slid from his waist to his neck. There were cords there going from his scalp into his back. She was reminded again of his strength, yet knew that he would never exert it on her. She moved her fingers into his wiry, rust-coloured hair.

He lifted his head and she could see the white of his smile. 'Oh Madge. I wouldn't care if you were made of ice. I do love you so.' And then, incredibly, she heard her own voice say very steadily, 'I love you too, Ned. You are my friend, and a stranger. And I love you.'

This time she cupped his face and kissed him herself, then dropped her hands long enough to slide off the shoulder straps of her costume. They came together naturally; it was all so easy, so uncomplicated. Madge recalled the twanging bedsprings of long ago and smiled blindly over Ned's shoulder. She had been right in the first place, before Neville had enlightened her. It might be serious, but it was fun too. And it was the ultimate giving; the ultimate surrender; the ultimate triumph.

She kissed his neck and lay within his arms, calming her own breathing while his calmed too. She wanted to rejoice with him that she was not frigid, but she waited for him to speak first.

At last he said in a low voice, 'You have given me my whole life in this past hour, Marjorie. Do you know that?'

She held him more tightly. 'No. That cannot be. You will live and know love often. Often.'

140

'Perhaps. But if I don't, it won't matter.' He stroked her hair back from her face. She had let it grow again because Clem had asked her. It was out of its knot and everywhere. He whispered into it, 'You have made me immortal.'

'Oh Ned. You must not talk like this. Please.' Tears ran down her face and he felt them with his own and kissed them with a kind of reverence.

'Listen, my darling. We both know that you would never leave Rosemary. And that is what it would mean if you came to me, wouldn't it? Your husband would be the injured one . . . he would be given the child . . .' She was sobbing now and he soothed her with shushing sounds as if she were a child herself. After a while he went on. 'That is what I meant, my Marjorie. We have done all the living we can do. Like Barbara Scaife.'

'Barbara Scaife? I don't understand.'

'Couldn't you tell from the way Gerald looked at her? She had a brain tumour, Madge. It will probably recur.'

She cried out at that, understanding now the shaved head, the crazy cavorting in the rain.

He whispered, 'Don't be sad, Marjorie. They've had more than most people have in their three score years and ten. Just as we have.'

'Ned, I'm frightened. I feel now as if I cannot live without you. And tomorrow . . .'

He kissed her silent.

'There are no tomorrows. I am just with you from now on. Whether it's one day or ten thousand. And because of us, everything will be better. Believe that.'

'I'll try.'

Suddenly he laughed again. 'You don't have to try. You know it! You thought you were frigid—' his laugh became a shout. 'And now you know you are not! You thought you were frightened, and you are one of the bravest people in the world!' He got to his knees, drawing her with him. His hands moved over her like a sculptor's making

141

a new creation. He whispered, 'Be proud, Madge. Be proud because of me.'

And she knew as she kissed him that in spite of her own innate humility, she would always be proud because of Ned. And at last she would understand. She would understand her father. And . . . Clem.

CHAPTER SEVEN

1945

Clem had never been so happy. His special war work entitled
him to one of the new Mayflower cars and he drove the
whole family to St Ives as if he were leading a triumphal
procession.

It was September again and he'd been home almost a year.
He couldn't believe it; time had telescoped for him. The
long years of his depression, his constant striving for the
sunshine, had seemed endless. The last year, so full of joy
and incident, had gone before he'd been able to savour it.
Now, here they were, back at Zion Cottage with a whole
month in front of them. He could gather up all the scattered
pictures in his mind and assemble them; gloat over them.
Even Julia; he could even think about Julia again and feel
no guilt.

His mother said grudgingly, 'Well it's certainly quaint,
I'll give you that.'

Rosemary, tired and peevish after six hours on the road,
whined, 'Where's Philip? I want to see Philip!'

'Do be quiet, darling.' Madge sounded edgy too. 'Here,
hold Mark for me while I take his things up to the house.'

Clem would have liked to hold Mark himself, but it gave
him even more pleasure to see Ro with her baby brother.
Ro was so like her Uncle Neville, discontented, always
chasing rainbows; but her love for Mark could make her
forget all imagined tribulations. She smiled now, cooing
down at the tiny round face, smoothing back the pale,
gingery quiff.

Mrs Bridges said, 'I do hope you like it. The quaintness includes candles, I'm afraid. And no bathroom.'

'I expect I'll survive. As a girl we had an outside toilet. In fact we considered it unhygienic to have such things inside the house!' Mrs Briscoe actually laughed. 'It'll be like putting the clock back forty years!'

Clem felt another surge of pleasure. He had thought it impossible to make his mother happy again. He took the heavy case from the boot and staggered up the courtyard to the house. Etta was already on the steps to welcome them. Clem heard her say straightly to Madge, 'You all right, my maid?' then before Madge could reply, she put her arms around her – Mark's basket and all – and held her for a moment. It was an unprecedented action from Etta. Clem put the case down on the steps and stared.

'Don't I get a hug too, Etta?' he asked with mock plaintiveness. 'I'm the one who's home from the war, doncha know!'

Etta opened her eyes and looked over Madge's shoulder for a long moment. She seemed to come to some conclusion and went from Madge to Clem.

'Oh I'm that glad – that glad I am!' She was almost in tears. 'Philip said it would be all right! The old fool – 'e's never wrong, is 'e? Oh my boy, my boy—'

Clem said, 'It's all right, Etta. I wasn't in any fighting. Safer than you, I expect.'

'Ah. There's fightin' and there's fightin',' she came back cryptically. 'An' where's the rest o' you then? Where's your ma and Madge's ma? An' where's this new babby oo's so good no-one knows 'e's around? And that young flibbertigibbet of a Rosemary!'

Madge said, 'She was asking where Philip was just now, Etta. Is he inside?'

'Naw. 'E's a-gone down to 'elp Jem tar the *Forty-niner*. Couldn't face ee, I daresay.'

Clem wondered what on earth Etta meant. He dumped the case and looked at Madge with raised brows. She was still deathly pale. Worse than usual, if anything. She'd had a rough time with Mark, but everything would be all right now.

'I'll get everyone inside, darling,' he said reassuringly. 'Go on upstairs and lie down until the rush is over.'

He expected her to turn down that suggestion on the spot. She would want to find Philip, or take Ro down for a paddle, or make sure her mother was all right. But she said, 'Yes all right, Clem. I'll do that.'

He was disappointed, but then told himself he couldn't expect St Ives to work its miracle immediately. Madge had changed anyway; she had grown up and matured in those two years he was in Ottawa. The way she had forgiven him; there had been none of the old sentimental pity; she had wept, certainly, but with understanding. She had kissed him repeatedly and when he'd made love to her – so diffidently – her kisses had become fiercely possessive and she had cried out, 'Darling I do love you – is it too late?'

He remembered again his joy in trying to reassure her. He was still trying to reassure her. It was part of his happiness – to protect her, to enfold her in his love, to make her realise that now, with Mark's birth, they had everything – everything on earth it was possible to have.

He helped the older women out of the car and passed them their handbags and scarves and magazines. Then he reached inside again for Rosemary and Mark.

'I can carry him, Daddy – I can *do* it!' Rosemary insisted, emerging rear first, her small body arched protectively over the baby. Already, at three months, Mark was too big for her to hold properly and his head hung awkwardly over her elbow. Clem hovered anxiously.

'Go 'way Daddy! I want him to see the sea an' you're in the way!'

'Well he can't see a thing if you hold him like that, honey.' Clem supported the heavy, gingery head on his palm. 'There. Now tell him all about it.'

Rosemary rattled off in a strange cooing voice, 'That's Smeaton's over *there*. And that's Westcott's. And there's the train just coming into the station. And back there

145

again is the commando's big house where we had the party.'

Clem had heard about the commando's party ad nauseam and he said hastily, 'See the boats, Mark? And the little waves splashing up on the sand?'

'Oooh! There's the *Forty-niner*! An' I think it's Philip! Daddy, hold Mark for me—' she thrust the baby at him and went flying along the wharf. Clem watched her indulgently. She'd been two and a baby when he'd gone to Canada; now she was almost five and a proper little girl. He'd pictured her as another small Madge while he was away, but she wasn't a bit like Madge. She was wayward and often very selfish; but she was lovable too. Very lovable. He held Mark above him and looked at the round placid face. 'You're going to have to understand your sister, young man,' he said, grinning, one male to another. 'Women are the very deuce and she's going to be particularly difficult.' He lowered him and kissed the tiny nose. 'But if you remember that she loves you, then you'll manage.'

The dark eyes, changing from blue to brown crinkled in real smile and Clem felt his heart lift with the brand of proud happiness which was still so new for him.

He turned and went quickly towards the house.

'Hey Mother – Hey Marie! Guess what? He just laughed at me! No, it wasn't wind. It was a real laugh!'

The two grandmothers exchanged glances. Baby Mark had bound them together in a way none of them would have believed possible. He looked around the tiny parlour now, as if he'd seen it before and was checking on its furnishings. Etta, coming in with a big pot of tea, paused to look at him with an approval she had never given Rosemary.

''E's at 'ome already,' she said, well pleased. 'Look at 'im staring around! Oh 'e's just like 'is father.'

Clem was delighted. 'No-one's seen that before, Etta! You always were a dab hand with the compliments!'

Everyone laughed except Etta. But they were used to her dourness.

It was dusk when Madge walked down Teetotal Street and

146

into Porthgwidden Place. There were no lights in the studio. The gaunt old tarred-wood building rose stark against the evening sky, its windows reflecting the nearby street lamp emptily. Madge felt every muscle in her body tensed against incipient shaking; she kept swallowing though her mouth was without saliva. She had rested until tea-time, then fed Mark while her mother put Rosemary to bed and sang her to sleep. At the familiar strains of 'Golden Slumbers' Madge's eyes had filled with tears, and Clem, coming upstairs to check on all the family, was concerned all over again.

'Darling, I won't go out. Philip is no drinker and we were going along to the Clipper simply to get to know each other again.'

'Of course you must go. You'll enjoy it, Clem. And Philip wants to re-introduce you to everyone . . . please go.'

'If I do, will you promise not to do a thing? Let the grandmothers cope with the children?'

'Of course. Now go. There's nothing wrong with me. A touch of the nostalgia!'

Her mother's head appeared around the door.

'Neuralgia? I knew something was wrong. Get into bed, my girl, and I'll bring you some warm milk.'

Madge exchanged a smile with Clem but she accepted the milk and lay on top of the bed for half an hour while the house settled around her and Clem and Philip finally went for their glass of stout. Then she got up very quietly, leaned over Mark's carrycot for a long time and eventually fetched a cardigan and left the house. She mustn't be long. She hardly knew why she was here, but she knew she mustn't be long. No-one had seen her leave and no-one must know where she was. She put a hand to her throat and knocked on the door of the studio.

It was all of a piece with her foolish behaviour over the past year – it was quite obvious no-one was in the studio. Just as it had been obvious that Mark couldn't be Clem's baby; she had known herself she was a month ahead of her doctor's diagnosis and that the baby was not premature. Yet she had refused to face facts until she had looked at

Mark's round, honest face, and fingered the dusting of rust-coloured hair.

Hopelessly she waited, then knocked again without urgency, like any polite visitor making an unscheduled call. Then she turned the handle and pushed, and the door swung inwards on to impenetrable blackness.

She called shakily, 'Hello! Is anyone there? Mrs Scaife? It's me. Marjorie Briscoe.'

There was complete silence for a long half-minute. In that time her eyes could make out the dark shapes of several small gigs up-ended for tarring. The studio was back to being a boat store. She began to close the door.

'Madge Bridges that was?'

The voice was female and as politely formal as her own, yet her bunched muscles tightened further then collapsed into uncontrollable spasms. She could hear her teeth chattering and she made a small involuntary whimpering sound.

'Oh my dear God. I made you jump, din't I? 'Tis on'y me. Rose Care. You d'remember me, don't you? We used to 'ave many a word on the beach when I helped Jim Maddern with them there donkeys.' The laugh was rich and untroubled. 'Then I went to live in Zennor, and I don't think I've seen you since . . .' the voice paused fractionally '. . . since then.'

A shape detached itself from the gigs, and came to the door. Madge was conscious of a great deal of very black hair and very white teeth. She was perilously close to tears.

'I was looking for—' she drew a long breath that got hitched on a sob. 'Barbara Scaife. She and her husband used to . . . they were artists . . .'

'Oh my 'ansome. I'm sorry. That Mrs Scaife, she died. Oh my dear Lord, you en't goin' to faint are you? Come on in now and sit on one of these boats. Come on now. Put your 'ead down. That's it. I'll get you some water. 'Tis all there is, but . . .' the voice went away for a while, then a cup was held to Madge's mouth. She drank. The water had the indefinable St Ives taste, straight from the mine where Madame Curie had procured her radium samples. Madge sat up straight.

'I'm sorry. Just a little weakness. The shock, I expect.'

Rose squatted in front of her. The place seemed full of silvery light now; Madge could see that Rose's garish red dress was covered in dust and her bare feet were dirty.

'I really do apologise.' Her voice was steady now. 'Barging in like this. You must be living here.' It wasn't a question, Rose would only be dressed like this in her own home.

But the older girl gave her careless laugh again.

'Here? In this boat store? Not likely. I've still got my cottage up Zennor way. Nice it is.' She paused, then said with a mixture of defiance and frankness, 'Jim and me meet 'ere sometimes. 'E won't come up to the cottage – dun't like most o' my callers.' She hugged her knees. 'I'm fond o' Jim. 'E's been a good friend to me.'

Madge felt colour flood her face. She made inarticulate noises.

Rose said, 'That's 'ow I am. You've always known it, so dun't pretend you 'aven't.' She turned so that she was looking out of the window. Below them the small waves lapped up the sand on Porthgwidden beach. The arms of the cove seemed to embrace and welcome the moving water. Madge was reminded of Gerald Scaife's enormous abstract canvas. Rose said very quietly, 'It din't stop me lovin' your brother in my own way. An' 'e loved me too. 'E was the only one who asked me to marry 'im. Did you know that?'

Madge cleared her throat. Rose waited. Madge said hoarsely, 'No.'

'He would have told you one day.' Suddenly the rough voice was soft and the consonants clear. 'You were still a schoolgirl, but he would have told you when you were grown-up. He thought you were pretty well perfect.'

Madge drew another shuddering breath and the tears began to run down her face.

Rose went on in her different voice, 'I sometimes think . . . if I'd said yes, he wouldn't have gone to Spain and got himself killed. He was such a boy. A stupid, headstrong, wilful boy. But he would have been a lovely man.'

Madge forced herself to speak through her closed throat.

149

'If he'd not gone to Spain there was the war.'

'Yes. Yes, there was that.' She glanced up at Madge. 'And you got married to Neville's friend, didn't you?' Her teeth flashed whitely again, nostalgia over. 'See? There's not much Rose Care dun't 'ear about!' She laughed. 'Cheer up, little Madge Bridges! That Mrs Scaife did what she wanted to do in life – that's the main thing, in't it?'

'How do you mean?' Madge could hardly speak for the tears. The way Rose ignored them, let her weep freely, was a wonderful relief. She thought she might cry aloud any moment: 'Daddy's dead! Neville's dead! Now Barbara Scaife is dead! And I love two men and my baby belongs to the wrong one!'

Rose said matter-of-factly, 'Well. She 'ad a babby. She left 'er man with a bit of 'erself as you might say. To be goin' on with. An' she were lucky I reckon. She knew that babby would be loved and looked after always. That's the trouble for a woman left on 'er own. Tidn't easy earnin' a livin' and bringing up a strappin' boy.' She hesitated then added, 'Nor a girl, neither.'

Madge took in half of this and stammered, 'She died having a baby, d'you mean? But I saw her just a year ago! I'm sure she wasn't . . . Ned said she had a brain tumour!'

Rose's eyes flashed blackly at her for an instant, then she said, 'The baby was born two months ago. The brain tumour grew again, you see. An' I s'ppose she wanted . . . well, like I said, she got what she wanted.' She paused again, then went on slowly as if Madge might be deaf, 'She knew she 'ad got the tumour. She knew she 'ad to leave 'im anyway. An' she wanted to leave 'im something of 'erself like.' She stared directly into Madge's face. 'I don't think that is anything to grieve over, Madge Bridges. If it 'appened to me – if it 'ad 'appened to me – I reckon I'd be thankful.' She waited while the tears dried stiffly on Madge's face, then she asked very quietly, 'Wouldn't you?'

Madge whispered, 'I don't know.'

Rose said, 'People thinks I haven't got deep feelings, and mebbe they're right. How should I know? I only know the

150

feelings I got, not the ones I ain't got!' Her laugh rolled out again. Then she said seriously, 'What I do know is, you can go on making other folks 'appy, even when you ain't *that* 'appy yourself. An' that sort of . . . makes the wrong all right. In a way. Surely?'

Her voice on that last word was a plea for reassurance and Madge responded instantly.

'Yes. Oh yes, Rose. I'm sure you're right. Up to a point.'

'An' another thing.' Rose was crouching forward now, very earnest, 'You dun't tell no-one. You keep it to yourself. So that no-one else 'as to carry any burdens. See? It's like a lightning conductor. Takes it straight into yourself like.'

'Barbara Scaife was so open—'

'You dun't know that. She might 'a bin lonely and frightened and in a lot of pain, and kept it to 'erself.' Rose unhooked her arms and stood up lithely. 'But we weren't talking about Mrs Scaife then. We were talking . . .' She brushed her skirt vigorously and began to feel around the floor. 'We were talking *generally*.' She found what she was looking for and began to fit ridiculous high-heeled shoes on to her bare feet. 'I reckon you should be getting back to your family, Madge Bridges. Before they start wondering where you are an' feeling worried about you.' She put a firm hand on Madge's shoulder and through the wool of her cardigan and the cotton of her frock, Madge could feel the warmth of that palm. 'I should thank God for a husband who loves you. An' who you love too. Put everything else to one side. That is what is important.'

Madge smiled ruefully. 'Live for today,' she murmured.

'What's wrong with that?' Rose teetered to the door and opened it, and the cool air of the evening swept through the boat store. ''Tis all we got when all's said an' done!' Her laugh rang out. 'It's not been a bad day for me. An' it's brought you back to S'nives, so it can't be a bad one for you! I reckon you've prob'ly made that young Clem Briscoe a 'appy man. An' . . .' her laugh became a gurgle of innuendo. 'An' I know I've made Jim Maddern very 'appy indeed! So sit you there a minute and think about

151

that. Then go back to your fam'ly.' She half closed the door then pushed her face back through the opening. 'If you need anyone, you know where I am. Skinners' Cottage. After all—' a final laugh echoed around the upturned boats. 'Things bin a bit diff'rent and we might 'a bin sisters!' And she was gone.

Clem had been almost too gentle with Madge since the birth of Mark and her unaccountable depression, but that night she clung to him as if she could not bear to let him go and he made love to her with a deep and tender passion that transcended even their reunion last autumn. Then he was frightened.

'Darling. Did I hurt you? Oh Madge, I do love you.'

'And I love you, Clem. Oh I do. I really do. And I am glad and thankful you persuaded me to come to St Ives again.'

'Are you sure? You needed a holiday and if we'd gone anywhere else we weren't certain we'd be all right with such a tiny baby.'

'I'm fine, Clem. Please don't worry about me.'

He was silent for a long time, staring at the outline of the window and listening to Mark's steady breathing from the basket. From the room next door a strange humming sound started up.

'What the dickens—?'

Madge said with a smile in her voice, 'It's Mother. Ro must have roused when they went to bed and Mother is singing to her. "Golden Slumbers".'

'Sounds like a vacuum cleaner.'

Madge actually laughed and Clem was so delighted that he laughed too at his own feeble joke. They clung to each other giggling foolishly until Etta – or Philip – thumped irritably on the floorboards above them. Then for a moment they were silent before pulling the sheet over their head in an effort to suppress incipient hysteria.

Clem did begin to wonder whether he might explode with his own happiness. As he held his wife through each muffled paroxysm of mirth, there was a part of him that was quietly, deeply thankful. At last he had done the right thing and the fates had smiled on him. He had confessed his brief affair with Julia so that Madge could get out of their marriage if she wished, and incredibly, that confession, which could so easily have been another barrier between them, had somehow melted Madge's inhibitions at last. And that all-pervading, confounded pity of hers had gone, too.

He held her close now, his mouth full of her hair, and remembered his arrival at Temple Meads station. His own loneliness had seemed to hold him in a vacuum; post-war Bristol had been unutterably bleak and hopeless. And then, through the grim-faced crowds, he had seen Madge and she had seen him and there had been no hesitation. She had started to run towards him, arms outstretched. He hadn't moved from his pile of luggage; even then he had thought she would weep over him, tears of forgiveness. But her face had been shining. She had thrown herself on him, laughing, kissing him with little excited pecks. Then she had said, 'Darling. It's all right. I understand – at last I understand. Can we start again?'

And they had done that; they had made a new world together. Slightly dimmed since Mark's premature birth, but still there, waiting for them while Madge regained her strength. And she would do that down here. A whole month down here. It was wonderful.

She stilled her laughter long enough to whisper, 'D'you think Ro will be all right in there?'

'With two grandmothers? One a singing vacuum cleaner?'

He wanted to make her laugh again, but she did not. Instead her free hand came up and cupped his face and her thumb moved down the channel from eye to nose and so to the corner of his mouth.

She murmered, 'You are such a good man, Clem. I loved you all the time and did not know it until . . . the war, I suppose.'

He did not reply. She knew he wasn't that good a man, but that she loved him in spite of it was wonderful.

She left her thumb on his lips and kissed him.

'Oh Clem, I wish . . . I wish . . .'

'What do you wish, my darling?'

'I wish I hadn't wasted so much time. Time is all we've got, darling. We must never waste it again.'

Her hand slipped to the back of his head and her kisses became urgent, almost desperate.

For an instant he held back. A sudden terror seized him that she was warning him her time was limited. He thought of the two lonely women across the landing and felt a new compassion for them both.

'Madge – Madge, you'd never leave me?' he panted, even as he returned her kisses.

'No, Clem. We must stay together. Whatever happens. We must.'

Then they were lost in the maelstrom of their own passion again. And afterwards they slept.

The days fell into an unplanned pattern as they always did. The mornings were short; there was shopping to be done, Mark to be bathed, fed and 'settled'. They tended to stay on the harbour beach within easy reach of the house while Etta cooked a lunch for them. Afterwards the two grandmothers packed a picnic and joined the younger generations on Porthmeor beach for a long afternoon in the sun. They were lucky with the weather; one day it was grey and overcast and they left their deckchairs and strolled along the cliff to Old Man's Head. Another day a sudden squall blew up and they piled into the beach tent with much laughter and ate their sandwiches while they watched gigantic waves pound the beach unmercifully.

Mark accepted whatever happened to him with equanimity and absolute trust in his family. Clem was amazed – and delighted – that he was so different from Rosemary. She had been a difficult and discontented baby, and even now caused more trouble than her brother. With two grandmothers at her beck and call, she could still have spells of stubborn boredom so that no diversion on earth could please her. After one such day, Clem was forced to come the heavy

154

father and send her to bed as soon as they got back to the cottage. Mrs Briscoe and Etta nodded their approval; Marie and Madge did not meet Rosemary's outraged face and fussed around Mark's cradle; Clem hated himself. As soon as Madge took the baby upstairs and the two older women settled down with their knitting in Etta's small back quarters, Clem went up to make his peace with his daughter.

The truckle bed, which Madge had occupied for so long, had been shifted into the back room and the bedroom door opened right against it. Rosemary, against her will, had sunk almost immediately into a deep sleep, exhausted after a day of exercising her contrary will against the lesser ones of her family. She woke with a jerk as the door knocked against her bed and immediately began to cry bitterly. Clem, under the impression that she had wept continuously since being sent upstairs, crouched by the bed and took her in his arms.

'Darling. Daddy's sorry. There . . . it's not as bad as all that, surely?'

Rosemary clung to him thankfully.

'Oh Daddy, I'se all right. I'se really all right. Is Mummy all right?'

'Of course Mummy is all right, baby. She's just across the landing putting Mark to bed.'

'She's not drownded?'

Clem smoothed the ash blonde hair away from the small hot face. 'Mummy hasn't even had a paddle today, Ro. Have you been having a nasty dream?'

The sobs slowed to sporadic hiccoughs.

'Was it a dream? I thought Mummy and Uncle Ned were drownded in that great big sea. Etta said they shouldn't ought to go swimmng when it was so rough, but Philip said they ought to be young once. An' I dreamt they were both drownded, Daddy!' She started to cry again and Clem soothed her automatically, frowning slightly above her head.

'Listen, Ro,' he said at last, settling her on to her pillow again. 'I want you to have a nice dream now. I want you to pretend this little bed is a boat, and you're bobbing over the harbour with Daddy and Mummy and Mark—'

'And Philip?'

'And Philip. You know Philip wouldn't let you do anything dangerous. So your last dream was very silly, wasn't it?'

'Yes Daddy.' Rosemary's voice was sleepy again. 'I only dreamt I heard him let Mummy and Uncle Ned go swimming. 'Cos I was only a little girl last year, see.'

'I know. I know . . .' Clem made his voice into a drone. 'And now you're a big girl, so you won't have any more nasty dreams.' Next door Madge was crooning some Bing Crosby tune at Mark, and Clem took it up quietly. Rosemary's hold on his finger began to loosen. Downstairs Jem Gurnard tramped through the front door and he and Philip held a rumbled conversation in the passage. Clem wondered whether to mention Rosemary's dream to Madge . . . or Philip. No. It was too ridiculous for words. As if Philip would permit Madge to do anything even slightly dangerous. Though of course, years ago he had shown her the way to climb Old Man's Head, and she had continued to do so until she was expecting Rosemary.

Still singing quietly, Madge crossed the landing and put her head around the open door. It was just light and he could see her conspiratorial smile. For a moment he did not move. Then he rose and crept outside with her. They stood at the top of the stairs; she struck an attitude and sang, '. . . Someone, waits for . . . me.' He hesitated another moment then, when her outflung arms collapsed to her side, he forced a smile, put a hand to his heart and warbled softly, 'Where the blue, of the night . . .' She put her face against his shoulder, laughing silently, and he held her there, while above her head his smile slowly died.

For some reason he did not understand, Clem stuck close to Rosemary the next day. She was delighted. She had accepted that her parents stayed with Mark and her grandmothers took it in turns to play with her. But there were very many limitations to grandmothers. She enjoyed her father's exclusive company and was a biddable and charming companion. Together they clambered over the more inaccessible rocks with bucket and shrimping net. He did not scream when she managed to shovel a tiny crab from beneath a stone, and when a wave splashed her shorts there was no suggestion of an immediate return to the beach tent for a change of clothes. He just laughed.

When Madge signalled to them from the beach that tea was ready, he picked Rosemary up and said, 'Shall we have a quick dip before our picnic, Ro? I'll show you how Mummy and I had our first swim here, shall I?'

'What do you mean, Daddy?' She leaned back to reveal a huge wet patch on his shirt. 'I'm making you all soggy, Daddy – look!'

He laughed again. 'That makes it even easier. Come on, let's do the job properly.' And he began to advance into the sea.

Rosemary screamed pleasurably.

'We haven't got our costumes on! Daddy – your trousers are *soaking*! Grandma Briscoe will be so *cross*!'

For answer he advanced into a wave and jumped up and down until his leg ached. Then he waded out and put Rosemary on to the firm sand.

'Off you go then. Run and tell Grandma Briscoe what we've done so that she can be cross.'

Rosemary was thrilled that her careful, conservative father could behave so outrageously. She laughed and capered about, one pudgy hand over her mouth, the other swinging her bucket madly. Only when she discovered that her crab had disappeared did she sober slightly.

'All that time, and we've lost the one thing we catched,' she mourned.

'But what an adventure we've had!' Clem reminded her.

'Yes. Oh just look at your trousers, Daddy. Why don't you roll them up?'

He wouldn't do that and expose his wasted calf.

'Run! Go on – before you start to feel cold!'

He chased her half-heartedly up the beach. He was already feeling idiotic. Madge would understand of course, though

157

she would wonder why. But his mother would nag and nag about the kind of example he was setting, et cetera. He slowed and let Ro go on ahead. Why on earth had he repeated that 'baptism' business? Was he trying to remind Madge of something? Or remind himself? He mustn't be possessive. There had been Julia . . . Madge had been so marvellous about Julia. Only when she had been so marvellous had he realised that Julia had meant nothing. Nothing at all. Madge – and now the children – were at the very core of his being.

A ball landed at his feet and he kicked it automatically, his heavy wet flannels spoiling his aim so that the gaily coloured ball rolled just a few yards away.

'Well done, old man!'

The voice was slurred and as its owner broke into a shambling trot, Clem could see a wine bottle dangling from one hand. The man gave a mighty kick, even more unsuccessful than Clem's. It landed him flat on his back, wine bottle held safely high and away from the sand.

'Christ almighty!'

The expletive was humorous and was greeted by a great deal of feminine laughter. Other players converged and looked down at the supine man, who made no attempt to get up.

'Come on, Gerald!'

One of the women leaned above him and removed the bottle from his hand. He yelled a protest but did not move.

'Gerald, get up and behave yourself.' The woman sounded severe. 'You can't play football when you're sober, let alone when you've been drinking this filthy plonk all afternoon.'

'Slander!' bawled the man at the top of his voice. 'You witnessed what my tyrant-sister just said! I've been on this bloody beach for exactly one hour! Is that all afternoon? Is it? I demand an answer! And you're all sworn to tell the truth, the whole truth and nothing—'

'Gerald. I am going to take the baby back to the car and feed it.' The woman was not seeing the joke at all now, though the others still laughed. 'If you are not there when

I have finished, I shall drive back to Penzance and you can walk it for all I care!'

Clem did not hear his answer but the tone was conciliatory. He obviously took his sister's threat seriously. Clem smiled, remembering Madge and Neville. And then stopped smiling because the memory snowballed into something painful. For an instant he wished he'd stayed in Canada, sent for Madge, made a new life away from all the old entanglements. Then he saw his mother and Marie Bridges fussing over Rosemary and knew that there was really no escape.

'Daddy's wetter 'n me!'

Rosemary was thoroughly enjoying being on the carpet with her father. She was wrapped in a towel and he was despatched into the beach tent to manage as best he could. Madge, knowing how he felt about wearing his costume and exposing his leg, poked her head through the tent flap.

'Darling. I'm going back to the cottage for some fresh milk. Etta has scalded this lot and you know Ro won't drink it. I'll bring your linen trousers, shall I? Or would you rather the other flannels?'

'Oh . . . linen please.' He grinned at her gratefully. 'It seemed the thing to do at the time.'

'Of course.' She smiled back. 'There are times when you have to go into the sea. It's unfortunate if you're fully clothed, but really there's not much choice!'

They both laughed. Clem felt ridiculously reassured and no longer foolish. Madge disappeared and his mother's nagging voice fell silent as she and Marie moved away with Ro to dig a sandcastle. And into the sudden silence came another voice; that of the erstwhile footballer. It seemed he too was being nagged.

'Di. If you don't shut up I'll let you go back to Penzance without me and stay without me! Got it? Christ, if the bloody baby wasn't part of Barbara, you could have it for good and all and bring it up how the hell you liked!'

The voice passed close to the tent; shuffling steps began to climb the sandy path to the top of the beach. Di began, reluctantly, to apologise. 'I'm sorry I get on your nerves,

Gerald, but I think even you must realise I do it for your own good. All this drinking – would Barbara approve? Of course she wouldn't!'

Gerald's voice changed to utter weariness.

'She'd understand. That's what Barbara would do. She'd understand.' And on the last word it changed again and lifted. 'By all that's holy! Is that – hey! You! Turn around!'

Clem was curious enough to push up the roof awning and make a peephole. Through it he saw 'Gerald' and 'Di' sitting on the grass of the cliff, struggling to put shoes over salty feet. They were surrounded by the usual beach paraphernalia plus a basket – presumably containing the baby. Gerald was waving to someone at the top of the path. Someone who obviously obeyed his summons and turned round.

'Good God, it *is* you! Marjorie, wasn't it? Young Ned Nicholls' girl, at any rate!' Gerald struggled to his feet half shod and hobbled out of sight. Clem dropped the canvas and stared blindly at Rosemary's spare sunbonnet dangling from a cup hook by its strings. In spite of the tent, in spite of the distant roar of the surf, in spite of them meeting halfway up the cliff, he had no difficulty in recognising Madge's voice.

'Mr Scaife? I thought you'd gone! I went round to your studio the first evening we were here—' Clem closed his eyes tightly. She had gone to lie down that first evening. She couldn't have walked down the stairs and along the passage without him knowing. Except . . . after Ro went to bed he'd taken Philip down to the Clipper for a glass of stout. He tightened his eye muscles until he could see stars.

The man was speaking again and he couldn't catch everything he said.

'. . . had a baby – did you know?'

Madge's voice, familiar in its cadences, was clearer. I heard . . .'

Gerald's voice was suddenly high and forced.

'She went into premature labour and died.'

'I'm so sorry. So terribly sorry.' Clem could imagine that

terrible pity of Madge's; her eyes filling, her hands reaching out.

'I'm glad you know. After Ned was killed I always felt . . . Barbara wanted to see you.'

There was a pause then Madge's voice, slightly breathless, said, 'Ned? Killed?'

'Christ, didn't you know? He was off to Arnhem that following week. His name was in *The Times*.'

'I didn't see . . .'

'Are you all right? You're not going to faint, are you? Hey – Di—'

'No, I'm fine.' Madge's voice did indeed sound much stronger. 'Look, I have to go.' Now she sounded formal. 'It was . . . good . . . to see you, Mr Scaife. I'm terribly sorry about your wife. But you have the baby. That is what is important – she was right there, you know.'

The voices receded. He must be walking up the path with her. 'Di' was not long starting up again. 'Gerald! How long have I got to sit here waiting for you? Gerald!' And then he must have returned because there was a muttering, mumbling period, and they scuffed off. He heard 'Di's' voice say, 'You sound better, my dear.' And the man answered with a kind of surprise, 'Yes, by God. I feel better. I feel . . . my perspective coming back. I might paint tomorrow.'

'Good.'

They were gone. Clem found he was crouching on his haunches, both hands clutching his wasted calf as if it were paining him. He lowered his forehead to his knee and tried physically to blot out the thoughts cascading through his brain. After some time he stood up slowly. His muscles were shaking after the enormous tension, but he had in fact succeeded in pushing the whole peculiar incident out of his head. He began to roll his wet clothes into a bundle, changed his mind and hung them over the hooks next to Rosemary's sunbonnet. Outside he heard the three females return from their labours and his own mother commented, 'He's still in there – it always took him an age to change his clothes.'

He pushed his head through the flap.

'Just waiting for Madge to bring me some trousers,' he explained. 'Start on the picnic – she won't be long now.'

They all looked at him and smiled. Rosemary still with collusion; Marie Bridges with affection; his mother with a kind of exasperation.

'Honestly, Clem. You're not tanning at all, are you? You look as white as a ghost still!' She stooped and peered into the cot, where Mark, so placid, so unlike Rosemary, gave her one of his now-famous gurgles. 'Even the baby is a better colour than you are.'

Unbidden, Madge's words came into his head. 'You have the baby. That is what is important.'

Madge said nothing about her meeting with the man Gerald Scaife. Clem found himself watching her like a hawk. He remembered the sister had mentioned Penzance, and he waited for Madge to suggest a shopping trip there. She did not. At times he found this even more suspect than her clandestine walk around to the Scaife studio that first night. After all, she liked shopping in Penzance; they always had a day there; why was she avoiding the place this year? The answer was that her sole connection with the Scaife man was through . . . he had to force himself to think of the overheard name . . . this Ned Nicholls.

In quite a separate way, Clem also watched Mark. There was no doubt about it, Mark was a model baby. He slept all through the night, and during his waking hours he would wave fists and legs occasionally with a kind of joyous abandon that was utterly endearing. When he cried, it wasn't as Ro had cried, in anger or frustration; it was a wail of despair because no familiar face was in sight, no bottle of milk was available, no comforting hands were reaching for him. Once these needs were supplied, the tears dried instantly and the magical smile reappeared. Marie Bridges said he was like Madge. Maybe he had her nature, but he didn't look like her. His hair had a coppery tinge and his eyes were small and round and his ears were big and flappy.

162

He didn't look like Clem either.

The twin mysteries of Madge and Mark seemed insoluble. Mark did not even know there was a mystery, and Madge suddenly and inexplicably 'went down' with a kind of flu which kept her in bed for a whole day and then forced her to rest frequently until almost the end of the holiday. Not that Clem could have cross-questioned her anyway; more than half of him did not want to know precise details. But he might well have asked casually, 'Who is this Ned Nicholls that Rosemary keeps talking about?' and seen what kind of reaction she would register.

And with that thought came an idea. He would ask Rosemary some questions. Obviously Rosemary would not know exactly what had happened last year – which was good because of course he must remember he didn't want to know – but she might be able to slake partially the terrible thirst he had for a picture – a knowledge – of this man.

Utterly confused, he began a careful pattern of questions the day after Madge's illness began. He decided to limit himself to one question per day so that Ro did not become suspicious. He even listed them in the back of his diary.
1. Was Uncle Ned a soldier?
2. Did he take you swimming every day?
3. Did Mummy mind you having a grown-up friend?
4. Depending on the answer to 3, did you stay with Etta and Philip when Mummy and Uncle Ned went out?

He wasn't certain about 4. It might have to be changed or omitted altogether. He did not want to put ideas into Rosemary's head for later years.

Responses to 1, 2 and 3 revealed a lot. Rosemary was still enjoying her fathers' company and wanted to keep his interest, but allowing for this, it was obvious that Ned Nicholls, soldier and great swimmer, had not been Rosemary's friend. She had liked him and admired his physical prowess, but had been conscious even at four years old that he was her mother's special property.

'But he arranged the party, Daddy,' she said as they

163

paddled around the harbour to Porthminster at low tide. 'Oh it was a lovely party, with real b'loons and presents. Philip took me and I held his arm like a grown-up lady and made him play musical chairs an'—'

'Didn't Mummy come with you?' interrupted Clem, bending down to roll up his trousers. He had no wish to get a second pair wet.

'No. She went for a walk along the cliff. They found some flowers what had got the same name as hers.'

'Oh.' He did not need to ask who 'they' were. 'I've never heard of Madge flowers, have you?' He laughed loudly and Rosemary joined in. 'Race you to the raft!' he suggested, not wanting to talk about Ned Nicholls any more.

'Okey-dicky-dokey,' spluttered Rosemary, knowing that he would let her win.

He watched her climb up to the beached diving raft and caper about on it before he broke into a loping run. They'd been after marjoram. It told him everything he hadn't wanted to know and it linked the mysteries of Madge and Mark for evermore.

They went for a sedate walk along the Carbis Bay footpath. It was the first time Madge had been far from the cottage since her rather odd illness, and she leaned heavily on the hired pram and let her mother take over when the footpath became narrow or overgrown. Clem and his mother walked behind with Rosemary, who had suddenly decided she wanted to collect wild flowers. She darted about like a gadfly, ignoring Grandma Briscoe's requests to look for blackberries, running on to put a bunch of cow parsley on the pram, then hanging right back so that they all had to wait for her.

Clem wasn't sorry. He did not want to be with Madge or Mark. Somehow he was behaving normally, but he had no idea how he was managing it. At night he lay by Madge's side not daring to move until she was asleep, then he tossed and turned for hours while his brain chugged monotonously around getting nowhere, like the old Hornby steam engine he still had from his boyhood. Eventually he would fall into an uneasy sleep, conscious all the time of a headache. Each morning he woke late after Madge had crept downstairs, taking Mark with her. He welcomed his new pairing with his daughter because it avoided the former arrangement of him and Madge sitting in deckchairs with Mark between them. Now his mother was an added barrier. When Rosemary galloped ahead again and demanded to push the pram, he talked quite animatedly to Mrs Briscoe in an effort to keep her with him. She, sharp as ever, was quick to notice his unusual enthusiasm for her company.

'You never talk about your proper job like this, Clem,' she commented, lifting her gaze from the ground for a moment; she believed in looking to see where her feet were going. 'Anyone would think you preferred war work – my God, anyone would think you were sorry it's all over!'

The remark was so absolutely typical of his mother, he ignored the criticism. 'My job at the factory is interesting, of course. But this atom bomb is going to open up new fields entirely. There will have to be some kind of international control. It'll be centred in America, of course. As a matter of fact I've been approached—'

Mrs Briscoe looked up again and stumbled on a pebble. 'Teach me to look where I'm going,' she grumbled. 'And are you trying to tell your mother you're going off to America – deserting her just like your father did?'

He said impatiently, 'Oh for goodness' sake, Mother!'

'I mean it, Clem!' She paused and her voice suddenly lost its sharpness. 'You don't know what it means to me – coming here with all of you, being part of a family again. If you all go and live on the other side of the world, I'll never see Rosemary and Mark again!'

'Don't be silly, Mother. I wouldn't try to transplant the children like that. It would be a temporary thing anyway. There will have to be some kind of commission. It'll be like a committee. We shall meet – discuss certain aspects – then permanent staff will carry out recommendations—'

Mrs Briscoe stopped short in order to survey him properly and with amazement.

165

'You would leave Madge and the children behind? You would go off and leave them here?'

He wanted to throttle her. 'Mother. I've already explained that it would be for short periods only!'

'You men have always got excuses for what you want to do, Clem.' Her face seemed to shrivel with obstinacy. 'If you accept this – offer – whatever you like to call it, you will be deserting Madge. Just as your father deserted me!'

He looked at her helplessly, seeing all the years of bitterness in her as she stood there. He wondered if Madge could go the same way, then knew she couldn't. It wasn't in her nature. And immediately followed a thought worthy of his own mother: she consoled herself when I was away before, presumably she'd do it again.

He said aloud, 'Come on, Mother. You know damned well I'm not going to be deserting anyone. Take my arm over this rough bit and let's talk about something else. Did I ever tell you that Ginger Rogers came to entertain the troops when I was in Toronto?'

'Yes. Several times,' she said, but she took his proffered arm grudgingly and got under way. And he changed the topic of conversation yet again and told her about the work at the Aircraft Corporation, which always pleased her. But the back of his mind still dealt with the conversation he'd had with his contact in the Admiralty, a man called Bill Penney, who foresaw enormous peacetime possibilities for atomic energy. If he *was* offered some kind of place on a commission, it might well mean protracted absences from home; protracted absences from the intolerable situation he had discovered.

As if she could read his thoughts, Madge finally surrendered the pram handle to Rosemary and came back to him and his mother.

'Are you all right?' She spoke to both of them but she looked at Clem. 'Is it too rough for you, Mother?'

'Not a bit.' Mrs Briscoe let go of Clem's arm and straightened her shoulders. 'My goodness, I used to walk almost into Keynsham when I was a girl – along the river bank!' She put a hand in the small of her back. It's not far now, is it?'

'No. We shall be at Carbis Bay station in a few minutes now. I was just saying to Ro that we could catch the train back if you were tired.'

'I'm not tired. But of course she is only five and I daresay . . .' Mrs Briscoe listed reasons for returning by train while Madge continued to look at Clem. He smiled vaguely over the top of her head and quite suddenly could bear it no longer. He left the two of them in the middle of the footpath and went on to join Rosemary. That wasn't much better. Mark was propped on a pillow so that he could see over the edge of the pram, and his contented round face looked foreign now. Clem remembered his own bursting pride in the child and wanted to groan aloud. There was another week of the holiday to go. How could he stand it? As soon as they got back he would ring the Admiralty and let it be known he was willing and eager to go to San Francisco . . .

Marie Bridges said, 'Clem, you're a million miles away. I just asked you if you'd got a handkerchief I could put these blackberries in.'

'Sorry . . . yes. Sorry.'

He fished out a clean handkerchief and they bound up the blackberries Marie had collected. She went on chattering.

'D'you remember that awful windy day you proposed to Madge and she accepted?' She laughed. 'You came back to the cottage covered in blackberry juice, and so happy you were incandescent!'

'Yes. I remember.'

'And before that you'd gone into the sea, the two of you, and got soaking wet. And you've done the same this holiday with Ro! Talk about history repeating itself!'

'Yes. Yes I suppose, in a way . . .' Madge hadn't really wanted to marry him. He had known that and not faced it till now.

Marie smiled at him fondly. 'Dear Clem. You were made for each other, you and Madge. Etta could see it – I think

167

she knew it the very first time you came with us on holiday. That year you came with Neville.'

'Did she?'

'And it would have pleased Neville, of course.' Marie was waxing thoroughly sentimental now. Her smile was faraway. 'You were such a good influence on Neville, Clem. Don't think we didn't realise it and appreciate it. He was a madcap and you kept an eye on him . . . I was always so grateful you went to Spain with him. So grateful.'

It was as if she was spinning a cocoon around him and holding him down. It hadn't been like that anyway. He had followed where Neville led, always. Tagged along. Tagger Briscoe he had been.

He heard Madge scream his name and looked back at her in amazement, convinced she really had read his thoughts this time. She and his mother were clutching each other; she was pointing. 'Clem! Look!'

He turned his head. Rosemary had wheeled the pram on to the footbridge which spanned the railway line. It was very high up. At its other end a flight of steps led down to Carbis Bay bridge and from its parapet there was a magnificent view of the perfect cove, the Hayle estuary, and the dunes of Hayle itself. Rosemary was lugging Mark out of the pram. It was quite obvious what her intention was. She was going to sit him on the parapet to admire the view.

Clem did nothing. He could not remember afterwards whether he was paralysed with terror, or whether, quite cold-bloodedly, he decided to leave it all to fate. Whatever the reason, he stood still while Rosemary lifted the heavy baby and got its flaccid legs the other side of the parapet high above the burnished railway lines. Madge screamed again, and still he did nothing. Then Rosemary held the child into her shoulder with one hand and pointed with the other. She must have heard her mother and with Briscoe obstinacy she ignored her. They all heard her as she said in her baby-voice, 'See the pretty boats, darling? See the pretty red sails?'

Clem was conscious that Madge was running; he could

168

feel the thud of her sandals on the footpath like a heartbeat. Twenty yards in front on him Mark responded as always to Rosemary's cooing voice; he stiffened his plump legs and threw out his arms. Madge stopped and choked out another cry: 'Clem – Clem, please!' And at last he moved.

It was too late. Mark's sudden spasm had jerked him free of Rosemary's restraining arm. He pushed himself forward slightly to look at her pointing finger, and he had gone. Rosemary started to scream, she grabbed, her small fingers grasped Mark's matinée jacket and clung on, the matinée jacket slid off the plump shoulders and dangled in her hand. She went on screaming and screaming so that nobody heard the sickening thump of the body hitting the rails beneath.

Now Clem could not stop moving. He crossed the bridge without pausing by Rosemary, without looking over the parapet. He took the steps half a dozen at a time and leapt over railing and barbed wire on to the ballast. Mark lay, a small globule of humanity, on one of the sleepers, neatly between the two metal lines. Amazingly he was upright, his head undamaged, resting on his chest. Clem thought fleetingly that he looked like a small buddha.

He crouched and peered. There was a great deal of noise; he had no idea whether it was inside his own body or sounds of distress from the bridge above. Mark was breathing. It was shallow, a kind of panting snort, but air was going in and out of his lungs. There was no blood as yet. The snorting was horribly loud; Clem put his hands on the tiny body and a voice said, 'Don' ee touch 'im, m'boy. Someone be gettin' th' ambulance. Leave 'im be till they gets 'ere.'

Clem looked up. Standing in the station was the small train which served the branch line. The man speaking to him was the guard, navy blue uniform, gold braided cap, whistle, carnation . . . and the snorting came from the square-boilered locomotive.

'Oh God – oh no – it's not Mark—' Clem flung himself full length and put his ear to the soft body. He could hear nothing. He looked up and could no longer see the railwayman through his tears. 'I thought he was breathing and it was the bloody engine all the time!'

The man got down on his knees. From his waistcoat pocket he produced a silver half-hunter and turned it shiny-side to Mark's mouth.

''E's breathin' all right my 'ansome, never fear. 'E landed feet first like a kitten. We was just drawin' in an' I saw 'im fall. 'Tis 'is back we got to be careful of. I'm an ambulance man myself an' I know that's the danger.' He straightened. 'I'll go an' tell your wife an' by the time I gets back, the men will be 'ere and they'll take 'im straight to Camborne General. Best 'ospital in Cornwall. They'll take care o' the babby there, never fear.'

He went and Clem put his head as close to Mark's as possible. The pudgy cheeks were pushed up into an unconscious smile and the round eyes closed; there was a passing resemblance to Neville . . . or rather a universality about his babyhood.

Clem whispered, 'I'm sorry. Oh God I'm so sorry. It doesn't matter . . . after all, it just doesn't matter. I love her. And you belong to her. Oh dear God . . . dear God . . . what have I done? What have I done?'

Someone lifted Madge over the barbed wire and she crouched by him. She looked terrible. He thought of what she had had to bear this last year. She had been down in that pit and he had been wandering about in the sunlight on top, never realising she was down there.

He said, 'Madge, can you forgive me?'

She stopped looking at Mark and turned her gaze on him. She must have seen that he was down there in the darkness with her, and she lifted a hand and touched his cheek with a kind of gratitude. From the top road there came the familiar clanging of an ambulance bell. Marie's voice came down to them from the bridge: 'Go with him, my dears! We'll look after Rosemary.' And the blessed bustle of the experts took over.

They never saw the ambulance men take the crumpled body up the station approach to the ambulance. They were ushered ahead, and in any case Mark was swathed in a sheet before he was lifted. But at two o'clock the next morning, when the surgeon, grey-faced and weary, saw them, they were allowed to look into the incubator where Mark lay on his stomach, stark naked. He had no recognisable legs. They had been quite literally concertinaed into his trunk and the surgeon had removed them. Whether the child could survive the twin shocks of fall and operation was doubtful. They could stay in the hospital with him but he would not know they were there, and no-one would think badly of them if they preferred to return to their other child.

They stayed. They sat by the incubator and watched. And Mark did not die.

CHAPTER EIGHT

1948

That year they went down in July. Grandma Briscoe was not well, but they took Grandma Bridges with them to help with Mark. He was still small enough to be carried upstairs, but he was fascinated when Philip outlined plans to make a bed for him in the window seat.

'For next year that'll be,' Philip said, holding the truncated body tenderly on his knee. 'When you're a big boy.'

Mark looked into the sea-blue eyes close to his own and gave his contented smile.

'Like a bunk in a boat, Philip?' he asked.

'Just like a bunk in a boat!' Philip agreed. 'And it'll be your boat too. Your very own boat. You can come and sleep in your bunk whenever you want to. Not just in the summer. Any time.'

Mark said in his clear, precise voice, 'That will make me very happy.' And, as usual, everyone in the room smiled at him.

At three years old Mark was surprisingly mature. Sometimes, when the pain in his stumps was bad, he would cry, otherwise nothing seemed to upset his sunny disposition. He found his circumscribed life full of interest; already he could read and write, but mostly he communicated through his drawing. His father brought him home unlimited supplies of paper from the drawing office at the factory, and he used charcoal, pencils, even ancient stubs of wax crayons to record what he saw around him. The world through Mark's eyes was invariably optimistic. This had been made

172

plain to the whole family about three weeks previously when Rosemary had come home from school with a face as long as a fiddle. She had borrowed her best friend's fountain pen, crossed the gold nib, and now the best friend wouldn't speak to her.

Mark had drawn her with fiendish accuracy: the stubborn set of the mouth, the flaxen, day-long plaits fraying at the ends, the angry eyes. And then when his mother said, 'Oh dear, yes. I'm afraid that's how you are looking, Ro,' and Ro herself was protesting furiously that it wasn't in the least like her, he had gently stroked one of her eyelids down so that she was winking. Immediately the whole thing became a joke. Rosemary was duping the world; making everyone think she was cross and hard-done-by when really she was laughing at her own performance. He looked surprised when she hugged him, and pleased when she laughed and relaxed in front of his chair, combing out her hair with her fingers. He wasn't old enough to work things out logically, but his instinct often led him unerringly to the right action. More than anything he wanted his sister and his parents to be happy. Already he knew that sometimes when they looked at him, they weren't.

Marie Bridges clambered the last few steps to Saint Nicholas' chapel and leaned on its retaining wall, recovering her breath with some difficulty. Etta Nolla, older than her friend, but as spry as she had ever been, grinned smugly.

'Might look like an old crone, but I've got more puff in me than you, my 'ansome.' She commented as she shoved stray hairs beneath her trilby hat. 'Now just raise your eyes and look at the view for a spell and you'll feel like a young woman again.'

Marie did as she was bid. The long line of Porthmeor beach soared away beneath her, the black promontory of Old Man's Head a silhouette against the grey morning sky. She drew a deep breath and thought of Alfred. Was he out there somewhere, hovering between land and sea perhaps? She believed implicitly in an afterlife and was certain she

would see him again, but where *exactly* was he? Supposing
he wasn't? She shivered. Mark's terrible accident had put
her off St Ives, and for two years now Granny Briscoe had
accompanied the young people. This year, when she had
been ill, Marie had come with them reluctantly. There was
something about that huge sweep that made her think that
Alfred might not . . . was not.

'Well?' prompted Etta.

'It's very beautiful,' Marie temporised prosaically.

'Dun't it take the years off your back?' Etta straightened
her own back as if to prove the point.

Marie said apologetically, 'Not really. But it's different
for you. You and Philip. You . . . you're indestructible. And
this is your place – it belongs to you. We're just summer
visitors.' She attempted to laugh. 'Like the swallows.'

'We've 'ad to fight to stay 'ere – oh not Philip mebbe.
'E's allus bin a bit of an 'ero, 'as Philip. But I were a
stranger from Menheniot, an' I din't give 'im no children.
There's bin times they'd 'a stoned me out.'

Marie was aghast. 'Surely not? This is the twentieth
century, Etta!'

Etta tugged at her hat brim and cackled. 'Not then it
weren't. When I kem to Snives first, there were plenty o'
folks 'oo still believed in witches.'

'Oh no! Etta – no.'

'An' why not?' Etta stared up from beneath the trilby with
a kind of defiance. 'I looked after young Clem Briscoe din't
I? I fixed it so that 'im and your Madge would get 'itched.'
She turned and gazed across to the headland. 'Couldn't do
nothing about the other. Philip wouldn't let me.'

'The other?' Marie made the query wildly; she wished
Madge were here so that they could laugh about it afterwards. Hearing it tête-à-tête with Etta gave it a certain
horrific credibility.

Etta dived another glance around, then looked down at
the tumbling rocks and said quietly, 'Mark. I couldn't do
nothing about Mark.'

Marie put her hand on the ancient black shawl. 'He lived,

174

my dear. Maybe your prayers tipped the balance there.'

'Oh aye. 'E 'ad to live.' Etta covered Marie's hand with her horny one. ''E 'ad to live so 'e could bring you all down 'ere.' She grinned again. 'You bin swallows long enough, my 'ansome. Mark en't no swallow. Mark is a native Cornishman. 'E'll bring you all down 'ere one o' these days. You'll see.'

Marie smiled back. What else could she do? One of the many aspects of Mark's tragedy was that he was never going to be independent. He would never be able to decide his own destiny. Dear Etta, full of folklore and barren of children. No wonder she took such an interest in all of them, especially Mark. She looked back at the enormous view and it was as if loneliness, cold and tangible, entered her very soul.

Etta said briskly, 'Best be gettin' back now. They'll want their dinner early if they're going up to Knill's to see the dancin'.' She began to clamber down the steep slope of the Island, then looked back up at Marie. 'Don't you get tryin' to find 'im out there, my 'ansome. 'E's right with you, lookin' at all that from 'ere. 'E'd 'ardly be out there lookin' at *us*, would 'e?'

But as Marie followed the black-shawled figure through the tumble of rocks, she wondered whether she wanted Alfred to be as close as that. He would grieve so for Mark, and for Clem and Madge who were just as much victims as the child. And as for Rosemary, naughty one minute, angelic the next . . . she had never spoken of the frightful accident since she had said to her two grandmothers, 'I know Mark will get better because I've prayed to Jesus.'

Marie caught up with Etta and they strolled through the town together.

'I hope it's not going to rain,' Marie said as they came down to the harbour. 'Hayle looks awfully near today.'

'They'll 'ave the dancin', rain or no rain, never fear.'

'I do hope so. Ro is looking forward to it so much.'

The rain started when they were in the middle of their mutton stew. Rosemary pretended to choke on one of the

175

small bones. Etta, coming in with another dish of potatoes, thumped her on the back with unnecessary force.

'Best end o' neck is that,' she announced. '*And* I took all the bones out after I'd boiled 'en. Just like your ma asked me to!'

'There was a bone!' Rosemary whimpered, looking at the rain lashing the window.

'Where is it then? Show it to me – go on!'

'I've swallowed it.'

Clem said quickly, 'That's all right then. No harm done. This is delicious, Etta.'

'Duff afterwards. You'll want somethin' to stick to your chest this weather. Take your brollies and wear some good thick boots. It gets muddy up at Knill's.'

'I don't want to wear boots! Mummy, you said I could wear my rosebud dress – how can I wear boots with my rosebud dress?'

'I don't know about the dress either this weather, Ro.' Madge retrieved a piece of carrot from Mark's shirt front and returned his smile. Rosemary, infuriated by her mother's lack of real interest, said loudly, 'I'm not going then! If I can't wear my dress I'm not going!'

Philip had come in behind Etta to clear the empty dishes and he said peaceably, 'You can wear your dress, my maid. I'll get a donkey and jingle down to take you up there – 'ow's that?'

Happiness was restored instantly. Rosemary demanded to be told the old story of John Knill yet again and Philip obliged.

'I know about the ten maidens and two widows dancing around his monument,' Rosemary chipped in. 'But what do they ackcherly *sing*?'

'The Old Hundredth. And some kind of rhyme.'

'What are the *words*, Philip?'

'Strange they are. Dun't know 'em for sure.'

Etta chipped in. 'If you've finished messin' with that good food, you'd best go and change into this 'ere dress, my girl.' She watched her scrabble down from the table. 'Anythin'

176

for a bit o' peace and quiet,' she commented. Marie glanced at Madge and tried to look reassuring. She really must explain some time about Etta's 'magical powers'. They might be something anyone could learn!

It was Jim Maddern who arrived with the donkey cart. Jim had gone through the war as a submariner, but it had not changed him. Even when he shook hands it was with palm upward as if hoping for a tip.

They piled into the jingle, Rosemary between her parents, Mark on Madge's knee. Marie had asked to be left out of this trip and was thankful as she watched them move off along the harbour, Jim leading the donkey. The four of them positively bulged out of the tiny cart and with umbrellas held above them they looked like a bursting flower pot of petunias. But there was a snugness inside the little cart and a sense of adventure which they could all share. Mark sang 'Jingle bells, jingle bells . . .' and Rosemary shivered in her thin frock and her father put his arm around her and held her into his hairy jacket.

Disaster threatened when they had to pile out at Skidden hill and walk ahead of the donkey until they reached the Catholic church. They sat on the bench where John Payne had been hung four hundred years before and waited damply for Jim's arrival – the donkey took mincing, three-inch steps – and then everything was redeemed by a most enormous rainbow which materialised out of the mist over the Malakoff. They climbed back into the jingle and folded their umbrellas. Jim yelled, 'Told ya, din't I?' Rosemary said, 'He didn't tell us at all!' And her father whispered, 'Don't spoil it for him. He wants another tip for being a weather forecaster!' And Rosemary giggled helplessly.

It was the first of the Knill's Dancings since the war, and in spite of the weather hundreds of people turned up and stood among the rhododendrons at the base of the tall spire. Rosemary could easily have been mistaken for one of the maidens had it not been for the pink rose sprigs on her white dress. As it was she stood in the front, smiling and

177

curtseying when they did, very aware of being the object of much admiration. When the 100th psalm was sung she made a great to-do of inclining her head every time the Lord was mentioned, just as Grandma Bridges had taught her. And she joined in the Gloria with great aplomb. Clem whispered, 'I don't know where she gets it from. Neither you nor I, that's for sure.' It was by pointing out Rosemary's uniqueness that Clem somehow avoided even noticing Mark's.

Then it was over, and the mayor was distributing the monies and conducting his little band back through the rhododendron grove. The rest followed more slowly, and Clem and Madge lingered to climb on to the plinth of the monument and show Mark the tiny huddle of houses that was St Ives. Rosemary, uninterested in views, held her skirts wide and circled the monument, reciting a parody of the little rhyme she had just heard.

'Give a bun to your daughter today . . . hum, hum, hum . . . Give a bun to your daughter today . . . hum, hum—'

'Give a *what*?'

She looked up, startled. A big boy – but still in short trousers – stood behind her. His question was asked of another boy, smaller, in shorter shorts. Both boys were grinning widely, but the big boy's grin was full of confidence, the other's more diffident.

The big boy looked back at her.

'Yes. You,' he said. 'Give a *what* to your daughter?'

'A bun. They were just singing – give a bun to your daughter—'

Her words were lost beneath the big boy's guffaws and the smaller boy's whinnies.

'I thought you said *bum*! It sounded like *bum*!'

Rosemary primmed her mouth. 'I don't say rude things. You're horrid.'

The big boy controlled his mirth with difficulty.

'A bun, is it? To your daughter? Is that it?'

'Yes,' Rosemary came back with dignity. 'It's what they've been singing this afternoon.'

The big boy doubled up again and Rosemary seized her

umbrella from the steps of the monument and whacked him hard across *his* bum. He yelped and rounded on her furiously, wresting the umbrella from her and hurling it into the rhododendrons.

'You . . . you little termagant! If you weren't a girl I'd give you a good hiding!'

'Steady on, Rory,' said the smaller boy, 'her mother and father are up there.'

It was that fact which was giving Rosemary her sang-froid. She smiled at the furious face above her and said, 'I gave *you* a good hiding – and you deserved it. You're a very rude boy. And if I can't find my brolly, I shall tell the police about you.'

The smaller boy said quickly, 'I'll go and find it.'

'Let her find it herself, Jan,' ordered the bigger boy who had the fascinating name Rory. But 'Jan' was already leaping into the undergrowth like an eager puppy.

Rosemary, enjoying her unexpected victory, smiled pityingly at Rory.

'All because you were poking fun at the dancing maidens. You really are a silly boy as well as a rude one.'

Rory looked as if he might explode on the spot. After a boiling, inarticulate few seconds, he swallowed and said with tight calm, 'You little idiot. For your information, the words are ''Shun the barter of the day, Hasten upward, come away''. You can't be expected to understand what that means, I suppose, at your age. But you could at least listen and get the proper *words*! Or are you deaf as well as daft?'

It was Rosemary's turn to boil. Jan, arriving with the retrieved umbrella, took the situation in at a glance and spoke in his clipped precise voice. 'Here it is. And no damage done. And I think you look pretty in that dress. Were you one of the dancing maidens?'

'No,' was all Rosemary could manage.

'How could she be? She didn't know the proper words.' Rory forced another scornful laugh. 'Give a bun to your daughter indeed! I've never heard anything so stupid in my whole life!'

179

'Well, the real words aren't much better, Rory,' Jan said pacifically, smiling from one to the other.

'Well not to you, of course. You're a foreigner. You can't be expected to understand. That man, John Knill – ' he gestured towards the monument, 'was a customs officer or something. I suppose he's telling us to give up trading and arguing and money and things, and think about heaven. And she thought he was telling us to give buns to our daughters!'

Rosemary raised her umbrella again. And her father's voice came sonorously from above.

'Ro! What on earth d'you think you're doing?'

Rosemary shouted with devastating honesty, 'I'm going to hit this boy!'

Her mother's voice from much nearer said, 'Hang on, darling. I'm coming.' And there she was, not trying to take the umbrella away, stooping down to Rosemary's level and looking at the boy with mild surprise. 'You can't hit people, darling—'

Rory burst out. 'She already has! She walloped me and I took the umbrella away and threw it into the bushes and Jan found it and gave it back and she thinks she's going to do it again!'

'He's rude, Mummy. He said bum. And he called me an idiot—'

Jan, red-faced and worried, intervened, 'We were teasing. That was all. We must say sorry with great sincerity—'

Rory yelled, 'Stop being so – so – *Polish*!'

And Madge picked up smoothly, 'Ah, you are Polish? I thought I recognised a slight accent, though your English is perfect. Please let us dispense with apologies on both sides, shall we? Misunderstandings often happen and should be ignored, I think.' She stood up and held out a hand to Jan. 'My name is Madge Briscoe. This is my daughter Rosemary. And here is my husband with our son Mark.' She indicated Clem coming down the steps, then shook Jan's hand and turned to Rory. 'And you are?'

Rory allowed his hand to be taken but said nothing. Jan

said, 'This is . . . I mean, allow me to present . . . Rory Trewyn. My father and Rory's father were together in Lancaster bombers, and now I live with Rory because my father is dead. My name is Jan Frederic Grodno. I am delighted to make your . . .' his voice petered out and Rory supplied gruffly. 'Acquaintance.'

Madge and Clem exchanged a glance. Mark said happily, 'Hello.' Clem said, 'How about an icecream? To – er – heal the breach.' And Mark said, 'Yes please.'

Everyone laughed except Rosemary and Rory, but Rosemary couldn't resist a smile up at her brother and Rory saw it and fell in beside Jan as they began to walk back down the hill. But by the time they reached the lane Rosemary had skipped and flounced too much for his taste.

He said stiffly, 'Well . . . we'd better get back, Jan. The parents will be expecting us.'

Madge glanced at her daughter and smiled right at Rory's dark face. 'I think Rosemary would like to apologise first, Rory. Wouldn't you darling?'

Rosemary's face was a picture. She wanted the boys to stay very much. She did not want to apologise. Eventually she addressed the rhododendrons. 'I'm sorry I hit you with my umbrella.'

Jan said enthusiastically, 'I say. That's so very English. Yes, Rory? I think your parents will not mind if we are a little late.'

Rory said nothing but he shrugged a kind of resignation and fell into step with Jan as he escorted Rosemary down the lane. Behind them, Mark looked deeply into the faces of Clem and Madge in turn and smiled. Madge suddenly hugged her son and husband, then they all three laughed.

Marie Bridges walked with her granddaughter along the harbour shoreline.

'Just how do you mean, darling? Surely it's rather difficult for a small boy to look like a pirate?'

'He wasn't *small*, Grandma! He was very tall. And he was very strong. And he was really, really dark. Black hair, black eyes – they flashed!' Rosemary stooped and picked up an empty crab shell. 'He is one of the Trewyns from Mennion House and Philip used to say that back – back – back years ago, they were famous smugglers.'

'I don't know whether a smuggler ought to be famous exactly, Ro. Surely nobody should know about them? They're very secret people.' Marie could smell the crab shell. She took it from Rosemary's sandy fingers, cast it away and scrubbed with a handkerchief. 'And you *did* say they were small boys. You said they were in short trousers.'

'Well they *were*! But they weren't *small*. They go to a school in Truro and after the summer hols they go into longs.'

Marie felt her brows go up into her hairline. Rosemary must have listened hard to glean all this information; and Rosemary was no listener.

She finished – or gave up – the task of cleaning Rosemarys hands and they resumed their walk. 'Tell me something about the Polish boy, darling. He sounds far more interesting.'

'Jan? He's very fair. His hair is like wet straw – he's a real Brylcreem Boy.'

'His father was an airman, I believe. He is doubtless copying him. So sad that he is alone in the world. The Trewyns must be good people to give him a home and a family.'

'Yes. Phililp says they're philanderers.'

'Phil – ? I expect he said philanthropists, darling.'

'I don't know, Grandma. Rory's father and Jan's father were in the same aeroplane and when it was shot down Jan's father was killed.'

'What about his mother?'

'She died in Poland, I think. Anyway he's English now and not all that interesting really. He keeps saying yes sir and being polite. Rory is really *rude*!' She giggled.

Marie had heard the tale of the bun already and had a definite feeling Rory Trewyn might prove to be a bad influence. She said, 'So you enjoyed the Knill's celebration?'

'Oooh yes. Rather.' Another new expression. 'When

I'm old enough I'm going to be one of the maidens.'

'I think you have to be born in . . .' Marie's voice died away as a motor boat came creaming around Smeaton's Pier and began to zigzag perilously between the moored craft. 'Goodness, look at that idiot – showing off I suppose.'

Rosemary looked up and screamed ecstatically.

'It's Rory! Look Grandma – it's the S.S. *Lancaster*! The Trewyns' boat! He said he was 'llowed . . . oooh he's going to . . .'

The boat was heading right for them. Marie clutched Rosemary to her and closed her eyes. The next moment they were sprayed with water, the engine cut, the shallow keel planed over the last six inches of water, and the boat came to rest within arm's length of the two females.

Marie opened her eyes and released the wriggling Rosemary. Two grinning boys were sitting in the boat, one dark, one fair. The dark one tried to get his grin under control as Rosemary cavorted excitedly. The fair one called, 'It's all right, we know Rosemary. We met yesterday.'

Marie had lost her voice which perhaps was as well because irate boat owners and fishermen were converging from all directions and their voices were loud and clear. Phrases ranging from 'damn young idiots' to 'bluggy fools' surrounded Marie. She hated it. She wanted to grab Rosemary and rush away, but that was very much easier to think than to do; Rosemary was loving every searing minute.

She experienced again the feeling of Alfred's complete absence. Last night, as Ro slept beside her, she had put one arm out of the bed and extended her fingers until they ached. She had thought quite consciously that if Alfred was anywhere, he would take that supplicating hand; just brush it with his, breathe on it . . . something. Nothing had happened, nothing whatever. If he were anywhere at all, he would help her now, surely? He would not allow her to be embroiled in a situation so completely distasteful?

A voice behind her spoke. It said, 'The wee girl is enjoying herself, my dear. Come away now and wait for the fuss to die down.'

If it hadn't been for the accent she would have been quite certain Alfred was responding to her need. Even so she wondered if the voice belonged to someone he had sent.

She turned and there was Mr McGovern; Angus McGovern, a voice – a face – from her past. Surely sent by Alfred.

She smiled more warmly than she would normally have done and held out a hand still clutching the crab-smelling handkerchief.

'Mr McGovern! After all this time!'

She let him lead her up the beach to an upturned rowing boat. He took off his linen cap and swiped at the planks before seating her with old-fashioned ceremony. Below them the furore was already dying down. Dear Philip had arrived on the scene and was dealing with it.

'Ten years – I'm sure of it. If not more. Your man had not long . . . how are you keeping, Mrs Bridges?'

'Well. Really very well. And you and Mrs McGovern?' Marie was inexplicably glad she was wearing her pre-war voile with penny-sized spots.

'Brenda died. It was the Blitz. We were in London – my wish. I wanted to photograph some of the work being done by the rescue units. Went out with my camera in the thick of it – completely unscarred. She stayed in our boarding-house.'

'I am so *sorry*!' Marie's distress was genuine and compounded too by guilt of her own vanity. She wished she could be wearing sackcloth. 'I can't believe . . . oh dear, how simply awful. Poor Mrs McGovern! And you too. I really am—'

'You lost husband and son in one year. And your husband's illness – I was spared that. Brenda could have known nothing at all. The house was simply gone.'

'Well. Yes. But . . . it's so sad. All of it.' She looked at him with swimming eyes. He must be in his middle sixties now; his cream linen cap covered thin white hair, his face was beaky and somehow tired and his hands a mass of liver marks. But he retained his Scottish hawk-like look which gave him a passing resemblance to Raymond Massey.

184

He took her hand again. 'We all have to go eventually, Mrs Bridges. We must make the most of the time left to us. That was why I came back to St Ives. I'm looking for contentment, Mrs Bridges. Actively looking for it.'

She wondered exactly what he meant and felt rather too warm. She disengaged her hand gently in order to wipe her eyes with the disgusting handkerchief. If only she hadn't been wearing her voile: it was too young for her, too frivolous.

'I think I can go and collect my granddaughter now, Mr McGovern. Madge's child, you know. Rosemary.'

'Please, my dear. Call me Angus.'

'It's been so pleasant meeting you again after all this time.'

'Fate. Kismet. Weather permitting I am hoping to take some of the cliff walks. Perhaps you would give me the great pleasure of your company?'

'I really can't say, Mr McGovern. I like to help with the children, you see, and—' Marie was already standing and edging away from him.

'There are other children?' He stood up too and moved with her. 'And please – Angus, remember.'

'Er. Yes. Angus. And you must call me Marie, of course.' She looked towards the shore. The *Lancaster* was chugging its way very sedately between the boats; Philip and Rosemary were walking up the slipway towards the cottage. She stopped again. 'Actually, Angus, there was an accident – here – three years ago. Mark, the baby, was terribly – was *terribly* injured.' Even now it was almost unbearable to talk of it. How had they all been there and let it happen? She swallowed. 'His legs are amputated just above the knee. Until he stops growing there will be a lot of . . . pain. He is good – contented and sweet – and very advanced for his age. But obviously Madge and Clem need help.'

She stayed where she was, staring after Rosemary and Philip, conscious of him by her side but deliberately not even glancing at him. He said nothing for a long time, then he gave a long-drawn out sigh.

'A-a-gh. I wondered if there was something . . . more.' He moved so that he was in front of her. 'Look, my dear.

185

It's not just random coincidence that we've met again. Let's take the child out. I've never had much to do with youngsters. Perhaps he could teach me a thing or two.'

Until he spoke she had no idea that he was on any kind of trial. But when he said the right thing, she knew he was vindicated; his presence here was vindicated. Perhaps this was Alfred's way of keeping in touch with her – I can't come myself but . . .

She smiled mistily at the silhouetted face above her.

'Oh Angus. That would be . . . so nice.'

Jan was waiting in the crab rocks at the far end of Porthminster beach as arranged, but there was no sign of Rory. Rosemary was furious. It had been Rory who stipulated Porthminster – 'We'll have to come on the train and I'm not walking right over to Porthmeor just to see you.' It had been difficult for Rosemary to get away from the usual family picnic outside the beach tent, especially when Grandma Bridges and that Scotsman had taken Mark off in the pram. Mummy had kept offering to come crabbing with her as if she didn't want to be left alone with Daddy and eventually she'd had to say she wanted the lavatory which was at the top of the cliff by the well. She ran like the wind but she knew she'd be at least half an hour and either Mummy of Daddy or both of them, would come looking for her. She'd have to say she'd gone to the other end of the beach to talk to Jim Maddern and help him feed the donkeys. After all the fuss about the *Lancaster* last week she hadn't mentioned her assignation. Rosemary liked intrigue.

She panted along Westcott's Quay beneath the church wall and plunged into the Warren with an agonising stitch in her side. A train was pulling out of the station; it must be the one they'd come on. She pumped her legs harder past the putting green and on to the footpath. That was when she saw Jan and realised he was alone.

'Damanblast,' she gasped under her breath. 'Dammit to all hell.' She tried to think of something even worse to say and could not. Her wide blue eyes filled with childish tears and she bent over to touch her toes and get rid of the stitch with a groan of sheer disappointment.

Jan was delighted to see her, however.

'Oh Rosemary. We wondered so much about you. Are you all right? Was there a severe telling-off for you?'

'Course not. Wasn't my fault. Where's Rory?'

Jan gave a Polish shrug. 'There was trouble for us. Mostly for him because he drove.'

'You let him take the blame?'

Jan flushed slightly. 'He is always . . . the ringleader. They know that. Now that there is no school he is grounded.' Jan smiled. 'That is what Mr Trewyn calls it. It means he cannot—'

'I know what it means.' And she also knew that if Rory had really wanted he would have defied all orders and become un-grounded. She did not wonder why or how she knew that; it was simply a fact. And it was like a challenge to her, a gauntlet thrown by the piratical Rory. She had another week in St Ives. In that time she had to get him to travel to St Ives to see her. And if she could somehow make him do that, it would be so much more than the way she'd described it last week: 'a secret meeting'. It would mean he would become hers. For always.

She smiled blissfully up at Jan.

'So long as you could come, that's all that matters,' she took his hand confidingly. 'Mummy says you are a true Polish gentleman.'

His face turned puce. He gripped her hand and said ardently, 'Your mother is so beautiful.'

'Beautiful?' Rosemary could not control her incredulity. 'Mummy?'

'I hardly remember my own mother, but Mrs Briscoe – it is her long hair looped up so . . . just so . . .' he gestured with his free hand. 'I thought we might see her last week, but then your grandfather—'

'That was Philip, not my grandfather.'

'And she is not with you today?'

'Course not. Don't you remember? I said we could have a secret meeting.'

'Yes. But you are so young, Rosemary, I did not think your parents would permit you to go about alone.'

'I'm eight years old,' Rosemary said levelly. She remembered what she had been working out in her head ever since the dancing around Knill's monument. 'When you've finished your National Service thing, I shall be nearly seventeen. You can get married at seventeen you know.'

'Can you?' he asked doubtfully.

'Yes. And I shall get married as soon as I can so that I can have my own house and eat what I like and go where I like.' She gave him another smile. 'P'raps I'll marry you, Jan. And Mummy would be your mother too then.' She hugged his arm. 'We're like a brother and sister now aren't we? Look at our hair. It's zackly the same colour!' She swung one of her plaits over her shoulder and reached up with it into his hair. Then she drew it down his face slowly. 'I'll have to go now, Jan. They don't know I've come right over here.' She looked at him very solemnly. 'Shall we seal out promise with a kiss?'

Jan's high colour receded and he looked bleached white. 'Rosemary . . . you are just a little . . . you are so sweet. If only we were brother and sister. Oh Rosemary.'

'We will be one day. There. I promise.' She planted a kiss on his mouth. Then threw her arms around his neck. 'This is our secret, remember. Don't tell Rory!'

She kissed him again, turned immediately and ran off. The stitch came back before she reached the station but it did not seem to hurt so much this time and she did not stop. When she got to the harbour she slowed to a walk; she was so hot she thought she might explode. But she still smiled.

At eight years old, she was enough of a psychologist to know that Rory would eventually come to her to investigate Jan's attachment. What she had not foreseen was that Jan would not be able to keep away. He saw no need for secrecy, either. The next afternoon he arrived at the beach tent before any of them. He had a picnic and his swimming stuff and was obviously prepared to stay for the afternoon. His manners were exquisite; he could talk to Mark or Angus McGovern with equal ease; with Clem he was perhaps a little too formal. It was obvious to everyone that he worshipped Madge.

Rosemary was piqued. She had not hesitated to use her mother as bait when she 'proposed' to Jan, but that he had risen quite so ardently was affronting. When he appeared the next day – this time at the door of Zion Cottage to help them round with their things – she decided that their groupings should be changed. She loaded him up with beach bags and towels, picked up the bag containing Mark's spare jumpers and drawing things, and announced that they would go ahead and open up. 'We'll get out the deckchairs and hang the wet costumes up, Mummy,' she said, almost shoving Jan down the steps. Madge, who had found Jan's adoration slightly embarrassing, nodded happily. Clem had gone off with Philip in the *Forty-niner* and taken Angus McGovern with him. It promised to be a restful afternoon with her undemanding mother and son.

So Jan spent the afternoon digging sandcastles, searching for crabs in the rock pools beneath the Island, and, in a confused way, coming to believe that he had actually asked Rosemary to marry him. His reward was a swim with Madge at the end of the day. She had a battered three-ply surfboard, and they shared it, three waves each.

'No, really, Mrs Briscoe. You didn't have a good ride on that one. Have another go.'

'Jan, we agreed three waves each whether they were any good or not! Take it, go on! I'm going to swim out to the rocks.'

'It's not safe – please don't.'

'It's not safe to dive from them because of the current underneath. But I'm not going to do any diving.'

But Jan could not let her take any risks and swam behind her just out of her vision, clutching the surfboard and pushing it ahead of him with some difficulty. It was obvious

189

even to him that if there was any rescuing to be done, she would have to do it. When she pulled herself on to the rocks and saw him, he was thankful for her out-stretched hand.

'Jan!' She was panting as she pulled him up beside her but all he knew was that she was next to him, water flowing from her hair and shoulders. You are a quixotic idiot!'

He drew in a deep breath and wished he could bury his face in her costume; the top half.

'Quixotic? This I do not know,' he gasped.

'Courteous to the point of foolishness.' She scooped her hair back, pressing out the water. 'Like my husband.'

'Your husband is foolish?' Jan was ready to fight him.

'He is quixotic.' She looked at him without smiling. So many English people smiled when they looked at him; as if they saw his Polishness and found it amusing. 'Like you. Very . . . honourable.'

'That is bad?'

'No. That is good. But if it stops him doing what he should do . . . is good at doing . . .' she sighed sharply. 'It doesn't matter.'

'Please. Please, Mrs Briscoe. I would like to understand.'

She looked at him again very seriously. 'Yes. I am being rude. Either I must explain or not say anything at all.' Now she smiled, but not at him, at herself. 'It is silly, Jan. My husband is a clever man. He has been asked to got to America and sit on the committee which is investigating peaceful uses for the atomic bomb. He wishes to go. But he will not leave his family.'

Jan said ardently, 'Neither would I!' then, seeing her smile beginning to become indulgent, he added, 'But it is Mark, yes? He is anxious for Mark.'

She nodded. 'Yes. It is Mark. Always Mark.'

'He is worried for you, because of Mark,' Jan said wisely, 'It could not be that he does not trust you.'

Her eyes went past his and studied the outcrop of the

190

Island with it washing bleaching in the sun. 'No. No. I'm sure you are right,' she said quietly.

Rosemary sat with Mark and her grandmother and watched the swimmers with thin lips. She needed to do something really electrifying to shock Jan, and then Rory. Perhaps Jan actually *had* kept their 'secret' and Rory knew nothing about the marriage pact, so she had to think of something so shocking, Jan would be forced to tell Rory, and he would be forced to come to St Ives and see her. She began to gnaw at her bottom lip.

The next morning, she went round to Porthmeor by herself. It was easily arranged: Grandma and Mr McGovern thought she was with her parents and Mark, and they thought she was with Philip and Etta. Rosemary – unusually – wanted to be by herself. There were two emotions she could not bear: one was guilt, the other was shame. The guilt she felt about Mark sometimes came between them so that she could not meet his happy face nor let her gaze wander to the blanket that covered his stumps. She would get up and walk away from him on the flimsiest excuse. Today she felt shame, and it was just as unbearable to be with any member of her family. She walked across the neck of the Island and knew she was a wicked girl and would never go to heaven. She glanced up at that thought, as if checking on it, and saw without surprise that the cloud layer was getting thicker. Philip had said earlier, 'Don't worry, this sky will clear by 's afternoon,' and she said categorically, 'No it won't, Philip, it will get worse.' She nearly added 'And it's all my fault' but stopped herself in time. Philip would not ask questions but the way he would look at her from beneath the brim of his horrible old hat, would make the shame even worse.

She surveyed the beach from the tumble of rocks at the town end, and for the first time in her life saw it as a place of desolation. The sea was flat calm and the colour of Grandma Briscoe's kitchen spoons, the beach tents had their canvas rolled halfway up the frames anticipating a very high

191

tide later, and looked like a row of tired herons. Not a soul in sight, not even Jim Maddern and his donkeys. Well . . . just one. Someone slicing the wet sand methodically with the long hooked knife that pulled up sand eels for bait.

Rosemary had excellent eyesight but she made funnels with her hands and applied them to her eyes like binoculars in an effort to focus the one figure away from the enormous expanse of sea and sand.

It was Rory Trewyn.

She lowered her hands and stayed where she was. Triumph writhed inside her but could not emerge as a shout of recognition or a crazy run across the beach. Her ploy – her shameful ploy – had brought him to her just as she had hoped, but now he was here the shame was no longer so private. Before, Jan had known and she had known, and that was all. Now Rory knew. She began to climb down the rock-fall slowly and carefully; she jumped the last three feet, landed badly in a patch of very wet sand which splashed her socks and shorts, and began to walk towards him. After a few yards she stopped, took off sandals and rolled her socks into them, and left them where they were. The sea was iron cold that morning and she shivered as she entered it. But it stiffened her spine and gave her some sort of courage. And it meant she could approach Rory from the seaward side. What possible difference that made she could not say, but it did make a difference.

He was wearing thigh-high waders and an oiled-wool sweater and with the wicked, slashing knife, looked more like a young pirate than ever. He could hear her splashing in the shallows ahead of him, but he did not look up. She refused to speak first. She bent down and started to flick the water in the air. There was no sun and it did not sparkle as usual. She flicked it higher and further. It rose and fell like molten lead. She scooped a double handful and hurled it. Rory looked up, his black hair dripping.

'You little . . . *bitch!*'

The word shocked and startled her, it hung in the air between them; fishwife talk.

192

She stammered, 'I – I didn't mean to! I was just . . . you were in the way—'

'Not that!' He advanced towards her, the knife held like a dagger. 'Christ, not that!' He took a deep breath and almost shouted – '*Jan!*'

She felt colour flood her face. So he did know. She had hoped – hoped so much – that he had come to see her simply because he wanted to come. But she had succeeded in shocking Jan out of his vow of secrecy. He knew.

She tried to brazen it out. 'Jan? Where is he? Are you going fishing? I don't know how you can bear to cut the sand for bait like that. You slice the eels in half most of the time, poor things.'

He stared at her for another furious moment then suddenly leaned over and slashed vigorously at the flooded sand until the bright silver of an eel came up on his knife.

'Like this, d'you mean?' The creature wriggled in his fingers. He used the knife and severed it completely. The two halves continued to wriggle. Rosemary screamed and put her hands over her face. Rory splashed towards her, caught hold of one wrist and pulled it down. 'Like this?' he repeated, shoving his palm in front of her. 'Like you're doing with Jan?'

She stopped struggling abruptly. The smell of fish was sickening. She knew it came from his jersey but it was as if it all emanated from the tiny creature on his hand, now, mercifully, still.

'What do you mean?' she asked in a small voice.

He was so angry he shook her by the wrist. She fell to her knees and he lugged her up, threw away the fish and seized her in both hands.

'Making him think you'll marry him and hand over your whole family on a bloody plate!' She had never heard so many dreadful words uttered aloud before and she quailed before him. 'Your mother will be his mother! Your father will be his father! Your grandmothers will be his grandmothers! Your brother will be his brother!'

It had the rhythm of a liturgy, each phrase accompanied

by a single spine-clicking shake to give it emphasis. She felt tears somewhere and concentrated on not letting them rise to the surface. She would not cry in front on him. She would not.

'And now . . . this!' He spat the word almost in her face.

She panted the truth. 'I did it to shock you. I did it to make you come to see me. Really.'

'Christ – d'you think I don't know that? That day – Knill's monument – I knew what you were thinking! I knew we could be friends even if you are just a kid! I pinched the *Lancaster*, didn't I? Just to come to see you and show off!'

His honesty matched and surpassed hers. The tears were at the top of her nose.

She gasped, 'And you promised you'd come with Jan to Porthminster beach. And you didn't!'

'Dammit, Jan told you I was grounded. Anywhere outside the perimeter fence was out of bounds!'

'You could have sneaked out—'

He shook her again, this time with a violence that was colder than his previous temper.

'I'm adopted – d'you know what that means, little girl?' He almost sneered the words. 'It means I'm no better off than Jan. I've got no real mother. I've got no real father. I've got no real grandmothers. I've got no—'

'Shut up!' She screamed. 'Shut up! I'm sorry – I'll see Jan and explain and say I'm sorry and—'

'No you won't. Because that'll make you into some kind of bloody plaster saint as far as Jan is concerned. I know. Because I'm like Jan. I want someone to look up to, to – to – *belong* to—' the words were savage, blurted out against his will. He shook her again as if it was all her fault. 'No. I know exactly what will convince Jan. I know what will put him off you for life, little girl.'

He released one of her hands, turned and pulled her up the beach after him. His knife lay where he had discarded it, already covered in a layer of sand and water. He picked it up and threw it into the pail of sand eels and continued

194

along the shoreline. It was a struggle because Rosemary pulled back at every other step. Occasionally his iron grip would tighten and he would jerk her to his side so that she wondered her arm did not come out of its socket. But at least the pain stopped her tears.

They came to the small cove only uncovered at low tide. Above them towered the dark rocks, culminating in Old Man's Head. Rory shoved her ahead of him now and again she stumbled to her knees.

'Take off your shorts,' he ordered curtly.

'Take off my—?' She turned and looked at him, her eyes very wide and blue and uncomprehending.

He explained in a voice that reminded her of Dr Barnes back home.

'You showed Jan your knickers. You're going to show me what is underneath your knickers. Then I'm going to tell Jan what you did. And he'll know that you are no better than Rose Care.'

She'd heard that name. She had no idea what it signified, but she knew she did not wish to be associated with it.

She said on a frightened sob, 'I'll do no such thing! I think you're a horrid rude boy, Rory Trewyn! I never want to see you again!'

'Don't worry, you won't. And you won't see Jan either.' He stood above her. In his waders he looked like a giant. 'Now do as I say. Or d'you want me to do it for you?'

She tried to run before she was properly on her feet and he leaned down, put one hand on her heel and brought her smacking into the sand again. A pebble bulleted into her cheek. She squeezed her eyes shut.

The elastic on her shorts was not tight and he pulled them off her legs without difficulty. Her knickers were a different matter. She clutched at them desperately and kicked at him with her sandy feet. But he was twice her size and she was lying prone, quite unable to use her fists or teeth. When it was too late she rolled on to her back. Immediately the bunched-up knickers slid to her knees and she lay there, exposed.

195

He was shocked. She saw his black eyes widen with a kind of appalled disbelief at what he was seeing. And she knew only too well what he was seeing. One of the big ten-year-olds at school had told her that she would bleed from there when she was older and she had borrowed her mother's gold-edged hand mirror that very night and examined herself most carefully. The girl must have been right. It was like an open wound. She wondered if some ladies healed over eventually. She had put the mirror back on her mother's dressing table and gone to play dominoes with Mark who had a nice neat healed-over place through which he passed his water.

She could not bear Rory Trewyn, of all the people in the whole world, to see that open wound. She scissored her legs to her chest and grabbed at her knickers. And he stared even harder.

From high above them came a shout.

'Rosemary! Rosemary – what on *earth* are you doing?'

Her shorts were flung over a rock somewhere, but she pulled up her knickers, got to her feet and turned to face the voice in one fluid movement.

It was Grandma Bridges with Mr McGovern. They must have gone for one of their walks again; they were always going off for cliff walks.

'Nothing, Grandma!' she called.

'You . . . you're . . . undressed!' Grandma Bridges shouted back in horrified tones.

'I was just . . . just splashing in the water.' Rosemary stood squarely in front of Rory. She scoured her brain frantically and added, 'I was being a mermaid.' She recalled how keen Mr McGovern was on Cornish legends. 'I was the Mermaid of Zennor!'

Grandma Bridges was silently nonplussed. Mr McGovern saved the day by emitting a hearty laugh and calling down jovially, 'See you at the beach tent, Rosemary. First there buys the icecreams!'

The icecream shop was shut anyway but Rosemary laughed too, waved and turned casually for her shorts. Rory was standing like a statue, head bent.

196

'Go away,' she said in a low voice.

'I . . . sorry.' He looked like a beaten dog.

'Go *away* I said!'

'I can't I must come with you and – and—'

She turned on him. 'If you don't go away I'll tell them what you did! I'll get you into trouble! I hate you! Just go away from me! *Now*!'

She watched him go, the tears pouring down her face at last. He did not straighten; he looked cowed, whipped. She imagined how sickened he must feel, seeing what he had seen. Shame was like a weight across her chest and shoulders.

She waited until he had picked up his pail of sand eels and begun to lope towards the Island, then she dragged on her wet shorts, buttoned them and began to make her way across the rocks towards the tents. Grandma Bridges and Mr McGovern were already there and he was bemoaning humorously that he was unable to buy icecreams 'all round'. She knew he was really pleased about it because he hated what he called throwing his money around.

Grandma Bridges said sharply, 'Where are your sandals and socks, Rosemary?'

'I left them in the sand up there,' she gestured vaguely towards the Island. For two pins she would have told them the truth and hoped that her punishment would clean the slate somehow.

'We'll walk home that way then.' Grandma Bridges was stiff and unhappy. She would have been devastated if she knew what had really happened. Rosemary squeezed her soggy nails into her equally soggy palms.

'Getting in the water like that—' Grandma Bridges ignored Mr McGovern's attempts to normalise things. 'Your shorts are soaking too. You deserve to catch a nasty cold.'

A tear fell down Rosemary's nose and plopped onto her blouse. 'I think I've got one, Grandma. I don't feel very well,' she whimpered.'

It worked like a charm, but it did not make her feel any better. Grandma encircled her with one arm and clucked

197

her sympathy and helped her on with her socks. Rosemary felt worse and worse.

'It's all the fault of that Trewyn boy,' Grandma snapped eventually. 'He's old enough to know better!'

'Oh it wasn't Rory, Grandma,' Rosemary said innocently, her eyes as wide as she could force them. 'It was Jan. And he's Polish. He doesn't understand, you see . . .'

Both Grandma and Mr McGovern seemed strangely reassured by this. They nodded and said something about Continentals and the romanticism of an orphaned boy so far from home.

'Don't worry about it any more, darling,' Grandma said in quite a different voice. 'And don't say anything to your parents either. We'll say you caught the sniffles coming for a walk with us. All right?'

Rosemary nodded vigorously. And just at that moment a watery sun broke through the cloud.

CHAPTER NINE

1951

It was Festival of Britain year and Mark, who loved the sound of words, drove everyone mad by singing 'Fest-i-val of Bri – tain' at intervals from dawn to dusk. It was also the year his father was made the Chief Designer at the Aircraft Corporation, but try as he would Mark could not make a satisfying cadence of those words. However, when Jan Grodno called to 'pay his respects' as he always did, he said, 'If the United Nations Atomic Energy Commission ask for your advice, sir, it seems to me you are much more than a designer. I'd call you a boffin extraordinaire!'

That pleased Mark much more. He set the words to waltz time and sat on the harbour beach with his drawing things, waiting for the arrival of Jem Gurnard junior and trying out the new jingle.

'He's a boffin, he's a boffin, he really is a boffin, a boffin extraordinaire! He's a boffin, a boffin, he really is—'

His sister jumped from the harbour wall and landed with a dull thud by his side.

'What are you singing now?' she asked, squatting on her haunches to look over his shoulder at his drawing. Clem had made him a table which would fit over his wheelchair or stand on the floor in front of him, and adapt for almost any purpose. At the moment it was an easel.

'Didn't you hear what Jan called Dad? Jan says Dad is very clever and very important.'

'We already knew that,' Rosemary said tersely.

'Yes but I'm glad Jan knew it too.' Mark glanced at his

sister. She was wearing her flaxen hair in one of the new pony tails; Clem called it her skinned-rabbit look. 'Jan's nearly seventeen now, Ro. Grown-up.'

'Huh.'

'You can get married when you're seventeen, so you must be grown-up to get married.'

'Did he tell you that?'

'He might have done. I knew already.'

'Huh,' she said again.

Mark added two strokes of his HB pencil to the drawing, then licked his fingers and smudged them into greyness.

'Why don't you like Jan any more, Ro?'

'I do. It's just that . . . he's always *around*.'

'He's comes to see you. I think -- when *you're* seventeen, he'll want to get married to you.'

'Rubbish. He comes to see Mother, you know that. He hasn't got a family and he likes to pretend he's related to us, or something. But he isn't. And sometimes he seems so foreign. And he looks at you as if he knows all your thoughts. And I just wish he wouldn't keep coming over.'

'Grandma Bridges doesn't like him either.'

'I know.'

'D'you think Grandma Bridges will get married to Uncle Angus? I heard him say to her yesterday that it was their anniversary. What did he mean by that?'

Rosemary said glumly, 'It's three years since they met. Down here. When Rory drove the Trewyns' speedboat over and got into trouble.' She sighed. 'Yes. I suppose they will get married.'

'You don't like Uncle Angus, do you?'

'Not much.'

Mark licked his finger again and smudged. 'Nor me,' he said. Rosemary was amazed.

'That's the first time I've ever heard you say you don't like anyone. You even like that woman doctor who keeps hurting you!'

'Old Fizzy?' Mark grinned. 'That's what Denver Richards

200

calls her.' He looked earnestly at his sister. 'Fizzy. Short for physiotherapist, see?'

She rolled her eyes. 'Yeh-yeh-yeh. And Denver Richards' father comes from Denver Colorado wherever that is—'

He began to sing excrucitatingly, 'He comes from Denver Colorado so they call him Joe—'

She began to get up. 'I'm going.'

'Oh don't go, Sis. Please. Jem will be ages yet. I promise I won't sing any more! Sit there. I'll draw you if you like. With your new hair.'

She subsided, giggling in spite of herself. He discarded the drawing of Mount Zion and fitted more paper on to his easel.

She picked up the drawing.

'How do you make it look as if you could go right into that little street there?' she asked.

'Shading. You can shade really well with these very soft lead pencils Dad gets me.' His eyes flicked from her face to the paper and back again. His voice went up a semitone as it always did when he was anxious. 'Will it make any difference when Uncle Angus marries Gran, Sis?'

She shrugged. 'I s'ppose so. She'll go away and live with him in Todmorden.' She saw his face and said quickly, 'Or he'll come and live with her in Bristol maybe.'

He said nothing and after a while she added, 'But they might not get married. They seem quite happy to visit each other and have their holidays down here.' She leaned forward and caught a glimpse of someone waving from Westcott's Quay. 'Oh damn,' she said crossly. 'It's Jan again. I thought he said he was going to revise for exams or something today.'

'Be nice to him, Ro.' Mark put his pencil down and passed her the portrait. It showed her with eyes and mouth pulled slightly upwards, looking like a waif. She studied it, frowning. Mark went on, 'He doesn't mind when you're horrid to him, but it's just . . . horrid.'

She looked up and met his bright brown gaze. She said slowly, 'Do I really look like this?'

201

'Yes. Your hair is pulled right up, you see, and it takes the edges of your face with it.'

'I didn't mean that. You've made me look sort of . . . lost.'

'Have I?' He too stared at the cartoon. 'Well, that's how you look, Sis.' He smiled suddenly. 'Why don't you write a letter to Rory and give it to Jan to deliver or something? Ask him to come to tea.'

She sprang back as if he'd attacked her.

'No!' I'd never do such a thing!' She looked at him sharply. 'What made you say that? You can't even remember Rory Trewyn! You were only three years old when . . . what made you *think* of something like that?'

'I don't know. You've told me about the speedboat often enough. And you say you never want to see him again in your whole life. That's what you say when you quarrel with Sheila Patten at school. And the very next day—'

A voice hailed them from above. It was young Jem Gurnard, the same age as Mark and his holiday companion for the past two summers.

'That Polish bloke's a-comin' along the quay, Rosemary Briscoe. 'E tole you about wrecking the Trewyn boat yet?' He read their silence correctly. 'Naw. I reckoned 'e wouldn't.' He chortled. 'S'prised Philup Nolla en't said nuthin' though. My dad do know all about it. Fine ole do it were. Las' winter when it all 'appened and the insurance en't paid up yet. Reckon 'tisn't their li'bility cos the boys shouldna bin driving of it.' He jumped down and squatted by Mark. ''Ow you doin' then? I go to the big school now an' we dun't break up till bank 'oliday—'

Rosemary said, 'Who was actually driving? Was it the *Lancaster*? Was anyone hurt? How did they *do* it?'

But Jem had already lost interest. He wanted to tell Mark about being in the cricket team and going out crabbing with his father in the *Forty-niner*.

Rosemary ran to meet Jan with an eagerness she had never shown before. She had long ago discovered that Rory had

202

never mentioned the terrible incident in Porthmeor Cove beneath Old Man's Head but she still felt ashamed of herself for showing her knickers to Jan; indeed the whole awful business was something she could hardly bear to remember. Rory had been right, she had been completely selfish to suggest to Jan that by marrying her he could become a member of her family. She had tried to show him her true feelings by cold-shouldering him ever since, but it had little effect. In fact Grandma Bridges was the only one who did not think of him as part of their annual holiday. And she would usually relax by the end of the fortnight and say to Mr McGovern, 'Well, I suppose he is foreign, and they are different.'

So all Rosemary's ploys had been unnecessary; even at eleven years old she could see the irony of that. Jan had a place among the Bridges without any kind of favours from her, and the only effect those 'favours' had had, was to cause an unbridgeable chasm between herself and Rory. After what had happened she never wanted to see him again – that was obvious. Even so, she knew there was a connection between them; she did not know what it was, but she knew it would never be broken.

She almost pounced on Jan as he hung over the harbour rail talking to Philip below.

'Why didn't you tell me? Were you hurt? Was Rory hurt? What *happened*?'

Jan pretended to cower, putting his hands over his head protectively. Philip called up, 'I'll go and get the lugger ready then. 'Bout two o'clock? The tide'll be right then.' He trundled down to the shoreline and the *Forty-niner*'s dinghy. He was walking badly, rolling from hip to hip.

Jan lowered his hands, laughing.

'We're going to have a cricket match, did you know? Philip is going to take us all over to the Towans and we're going to have a cook-fire. Your father is going to resurrect an old custom apparently.'

'Cricket match? Don't be silly. Mark can't play cricket. Daddy would never suggest such a thing.' Rosemary shook her head impatiently. 'Never mind that. Why didn't you tell me about you and Rory and the *Lancaster* and the insurance? Were you hurt? Was Rory hurt?'

Jan's fair skin blushed the unbecoming red it always did when he was embarrassed.

'Did Philip tell you?'

'No. Jem Gurnard. Just. What *happened*?'

'I . . . nothing really. But the consequences were bad. I cannot tell you, Rosemary. Please do not ask.'

She was so angry she almost struck him. She clenched her hands into fists and her arms into rigid poles by her side.

'I've got to know. Everyone else must know. I can ask Philip.'

'He won't tell you.'

'Then I'll ask Etta. She will tell me.'

'She does not know.'

'If Jem Gurnard knows—'

'Oh, they all know that Rory and I took the motor boat without permission . . . we'd done it three or four times. We got into trouble of course but Rory said it was worth it. It *was* worth it. Rory can handle it better than Mr Trewyn and it's the most splendid feeling—'

'Then how did he manage to wreck it?' she asked succinctly.

'I . . . don't know. Exactly. I mean, I can't explain.' He began to walk towards the slipway. 'Shall we join Mark? Your mother will be down soon I expect.'

She caught him up and walked by his side without a word until they were outside the Sloop. He gabbled on about the weather being ideal for cricket and the Towans the ideal spot for it and the sea ideal for sailing across to the Towans. And eventually she put a hand on his arm and pulled him up.

'Who was driving the *Lancaster* that day?' she asked.

He looked across at the cottage but no-one was emerging from the front door.

'Rory,' he replied at last.

'That is what Jem Gurnard knows. And Etta knows. But not what Philip knows?'

Jan looked at her at last with a kind of despair.

'I had to tell Philip the truth. I had to tell someone. Besides, he was like you. He knew Rory wouldn't have wrecked the *Lancaster*.' He took her hand. 'I'm sorry, Ro. I should have insisted on taking the blame. But Rory wouldn't let me and you know what he's like when he gets a – a – how do you say? A bee in his hat.'

Rosemary knew only too well.

'But why? It doesn't make sense.'

'I do not do very well at school. The Trewyns were displeased with me. Rory – for him it is different. Everything is easy. He thinks they will not be so angry.'

'But they were.'

'Yes. Also he grieves for the boat. There is no scrap of it left, you see. Nothing. Not even a plank.'

Rosemary was horrified.

'Did it explode?'

'Ah no. The vortex at the mouth of the river, it was very bad. A storm came up and the boat was caught in it and turned round and round. We jumped clear. We had cork jackets and we managed to swim to the sandbank. The boat . . .' Jan made a very Continental gesture indicating that the boat had gone straight down.

Rosemary shivered. 'You could have both been drowned.'

'The Trewyns said this to Rory when they stopped being angry. But it is no good. Some wrecked boats are beached many weeks later over at Lelant, and he keeps going there to search, but nothing turns up.' Jan's colour was normal but he looked worse than before. His pale skin did not tan and against Rosemary's honey colour he looked sickly. 'You see, Ro . . . it is my fault. And I am not happy for some time. That is why it is so good to see all of you again. I have tried to persuade Rory to come over with me, but he will not.'

Rosemary's shoulders slumped. 'No. No, of course not.' She turned towards the cottage. 'Come on then. You'll want to say hello to Mother.'

He followed a pace behind.

'I thought you would be . . . I don't know . . . angry. I thought you would despise me. I am a coward.'

It had not occurred to her that if Rory was a hero – or sort of hero – then Jan must be a sort of coward. She looked round at him. He was the same as ever, taller and his ears much bigger than they'd been last year; but just as pale and anxious and diffident. She had always known he would do anything for Rory. She had not known that Rory would do so much for Jan.

She pushed her sandy hand into the crook of his arm.

'Of course you're not a coward. You're an idiot. Just like Rory. Two idiots.' She grinned. 'Listen. If we're really going over to Hayle Towans for a picnic this afternoon, why don't we look for signs of the *Lancaster* that side?'

'I don't know. It's something to do with the current in the estuary. Wreckage is thrown up on the Lelant side. Always.'

'But if nothing's turned up there, surely it's worth looking somewhere else?' She ran up the steps ahead of him. 'If you could take something back for Rory tonight, wouldn't that cheer him up?' She turned and looked down on him. He had three pimples on his chin.

'Oh yes. Most certainly,' he agreed fervently.

'Then we'll look.' She went on staring at him. His eyes were very blue. For the first time she considered seriously whether she could marry him. She smiled with genuine affection. 'Mark has just drawn my portrait. It makes me look more of a skinned rabbit than usual. But would you like it?'

'Oh . . . yes!'

'Okey-doke. I'll get it in a minute.'

'I like your hair up, Ro. You look like a ballerina.'

'Do I?' She was delighted. She leaned down and pecked his cheek, taking care not to let her face touch the pimples. 'You are nice, Jan. You really are nice. All the boys at home are horrid. They shout or they laugh at you – they're really awful. You are a gentleman. Daddy always says that.'

'Does he?' Jan was bright red again. It gave ground cover

for the spots. 'I value your father's good opinion most highly.'

It was a pity he talked like a pompous politician. But she knew he couldn't help it. After all, as Grandma Bridges said, he was foreign.

Madge was of the same opinion as Rosemary about the cricket match.

'It will make Mark feel so out of it, Clem,' she said when he came out of the butcher's with half a dozen pounds of sausages. 'And really darling, how many are you catering for?'

Well, there'll be your mother and her Angus. Mark and Jem Gurnard. Ro and Jan. Philip and Etta – and you and me, Madge. That's . . .' he counted under his breath. 'Ten altogether. And if there are an average of eight sausages in each pound that's forty-eight sausages, which means—'

'Clem—' Madge was laughing '—you're not doing mathematical calculations for picnics now, are you?'

'It was how your father organised his cricket matches. I well remember that day at Porthkidney Sands – he delegated jobs like an army captain—'

'He *was* an army captain, darling. And he didn't have to bribe the butcher to let him have six pounds of sausages either! How did you do it?'

'Charm.' He smiled blandly at her and took her arm. 'As for Mark. He'll enjoy himself whatever we do. You know that.' He pressed the inside of her arm. 'I thought if we went over to Hayle in the *Forty-niner* it wouldn't be too much like history repeating itself. For your mother, I mean.'

She didn't look round at him.

'No. We never went there. Philip was often away in the *Forty-niner*. We used to go on the train because of Father's privilege tickets.'

'Yes. I remember.' He guided her down Court Cocking. 'Let's go into the milk bar and have a coffee.'

'Such extravagance!'

'We're well off now. We'll be able to afford the very best for Mark.'

'And Ro,' Madge said quickly.

'Swiss finishing school if she fancies it!'

Clem held one of the high stools steady while she perched on it. Further along the harbour Jan was leaning over the rail, talking to someone on the sand below.

Madge said, 'That's what Ro will be doing. Never mind finishing schools. She's only eleven and she's got that boy exactly and precisely under her thumb.'

'Jan?' Clem handed her a frothy, almost white coffee. 'He's in love with you, Madge, not with Ro.' He ignored her protests. 'Besides, that wouldn't do for Ro. She doesn't really care for people who allow themselves to be put under thumbs.'

'I don't know about that.' They both watched almost guiltily as Rosemary arrived and cast herself on Jan. When the two of them had walked past, Madge sipped her coffee and said in a low voice, 'She needs someone . . . special. It would be Mark – she adores Mark – except of course . . . it can't be Mark.'

Clem also sipped. 'She's over all that guilt business now, Madge. If that's what you're thinking of. I told her at the time it was my fault. And we've talked since, too. She realises that a five-year-old child cannot be held responsible for that kind of accident.'

'But—' Madge flicked him a sideways glance. 'It wasn't your fault, Clem. How can she accept that? She must realise you're just trying to comfort her.'

'I don't think so. I was in charge of both children. I simply didn't move fast enough.' He swigged the last of his coffee. 'Don't let's talk about it again, Madge, it does no good. Mark – Mark copes with it somehow. And at least I'm in a position to make sure he will never lack for anything material—'

She caught his arm. 'Clem, wait. It wasn't *your* fault. I've always thought you took it upon yourself for Ro's sake. Of course it wasn't your fault. As for Mark – perhaps he wouldn't have been the boy he is if it hadn't happened. How can we know? And once he's stopped growing and can have

208

artificial legs, he'll be able to do so much more – become independent of us—'

'Is that what you want?'

She hesitated fractionally. Then nodded fiercely. 'Of course. Of course I want Mark to be independent.'

Clem got off his stool and pecked her forehead. He had accepted a long time ago that without the unknown Ned Nicholls his wife might never have been able to express physical love. He had also accepted that without Mark she might well have left him. Mark anchored Madge to him.

He said gently, 'I know. It's just that he does bind us so closely as a family. The other night I listened to his prayers. He listed all of us, then said, "Have I forgotten anyone, God? If I have, can you put them in. And don't tell them I've forgotten in case they feel hurt!" '

She laughed, though he could tell she was moved nearly to tears. He looked at Jan Grodno and worked out his age: sixteen. He had been sixteen when he first noticed Madge as a separate feminine person, not just Neville's sister. And now Jan Grodno loved her. And Ned Nicholls had loved her. He wondered what he could do to make certain that even if Mark ever did become 'independent' she would not leave him.

He said heartily, 'It will be like turning the clock back this afternoon, Madge. It will be like that other time. When I was sixteen and you were twelve and everything was so simple and so sweet.'

They walked slowly back to the cottage and he wondered how he could have considered living without her. And it never occurred to him that he was just as trapped in this marriage as Madge was.

The engine had been fitted into the *Forty-niner* in 1939, just in time for Old Jem and Philip to take her over to Dunkirk the following year. Clem had overhauled it two years ago, but it still burnt too much oil, and they were glad to anchor it off the Towans and take it in turns to row ashore in the dinghy. The sands appeared completely empty and they felt they were staking a claim in an unexplored continent. There were summer bungalows, asbestos, corrugated iron, wood all built into the dunes, but the beach was so vast and undulating they knew they would probably see no-one else all day. They toiled up a dune and Clem looked down on a gigantic bowl of sand.

'This will do nicely,' he announced. 'It's a natural sun-trap.' He cleared his throat self-consciously and deepened his voice. 'I claim this sand-saucer in the names of Nolla, McGovern, Bridges, Grodno and Briscoe! May God bless all who make fires in her!'

Rosemary whooped with joy and Philip looked up from beneath his hat brim with one of his quizzical smiles. Etta said, 'My good Lord. You d'sound so zaccly like old Mr Bridges it fair turns me 'eart.'

For a moment Marie looked startled, then she smiled and moved down into the saucer and away from Angus McGovern. He and Clem held Mark's sling-chair between them; they followed more sedately. Everyone else, even Philip and Etta, went crazy, and either ran about their new territory or announced plans in loud voices.

'We kin build the fireplace here – the smoke'll be took away from us then–' so said Etta, arms akimbo across a black dress which might well have been the same one she wore to the Porthkidney cricket match nearly twenty years before.

Jem bawled, 'Plenty o' wood over yonder–' and Rosemary shouted, 'Where? Is it a wreck? Could it be – ? Oh that's old stuff. Driftwood.' 'Burns better, dunnit?' 'Yes, I know but–'

Jan called, 'Will this do for the cricket pitch, sir? Wickets here. Crease here–'

Rosemary spoke to him in slightly lower tones. 'Don't bother with all that. I thought we were going to look for some sign of the *Lancaster*?'

Jem yelled, 'Bring Mark over 'ere, Mr Briscoe – quick – quick – look, there's a kind o' slide in the sand! 'E'll be able to shoot right down there into the bloody sea!'

Etta shrieked, 'Language! I'll 'ave your 'ide for that,

210

young Jem Gurnard! If your father coulda 'eard that—'

Philip said, 'I'll sit up top. We should need a lookout.' And trudged off on his own.

But Jem was right. A funnel of smooth sand led into deep water and Mark was a natural swimmer and stronger than most. They watched him tumble down it, laughing hysterically and closely followed by Jem and Rosemary. Madge smiled. 'You were right,' she said softly to Clem. 'He'll always enjoy himself.'

The adults left the younger generation to it, and began to collect wood for the fire.

The cricket match lasted most of the afternoon and, like others before it, left plenty of opportunity for conviviality among the waiting batsmen. Mark sat in his chair, folding table across the arms, and did a series of lightning sketches. They were more graphic than anything produced by Madge's old box camera. Jim's expression was caught absolutely as he knocked off his own bails; Philip's fifth run revealed that his legs were as bowed as a cowboy's; the best catch of the match was the one 'held' by Etta's spread skirt; Clem, arm upraised, shouting 'Owzat?' was indeed beginning to look like old Mr Bridges, though young Mark knew his grandfather from only faded sepia photographs. And Madge, jumping for a ball, hair coming down her bare freckled back, looked no more than seventeen.

'May I have that one please Mark?' Jan asked hoarsely, looking over the boy's shoulder.

'If you want to.' Mark was too young to value his own work, he drew by instinct, his hand often discovering things his eye did not see. 'And Ro said you wanted a sketch of her too. I've got it here somewhere.'

Jan put the drawing of Madge carefully inside his shirt. 'Thank you, old man. Don't worry about the other if you can't find it.'

'No, here it is.' He frowned at it. Rosemary did look sort of lost; it must be the skinned-rabbit hair after all. He said, 'Jan. D'you think you might marry Ro one day?'

211

Jan laughed and shifted about in the sand. 'Perhaps. I should be honoured, of course. If she would have me.'

Mark's frown deepened. 'I don't know whether she would or not. But it might be a good thing.' He handed the drawing over. 'Anyway. She says you love Mother, not her.'

Jan laughed again, rather more loudly.

'I love all of you, Mark. As if you were my own family.' He shoved the second drawing into the other side of his shirt. 'I have to go now. I am in next.'

Rosemary stood by Philip's supine figure on the lip of the saucer. Philip had hoped to have forty winks before their side went in to field and he opened one eye and surveyed her menacing length without pleasure.

'Well, miss?'

Rosemary was aggrieved. 'You only call me miss when I've done something naughty. And I've been an angel all day. Even Etta said that.'

'Etta called you an angel?'

'She didn't say I wasn't when Mummy called me it.'

He sighed and closed the eye. There came panting, thudding sounds from just by his ear. He opened it again and saw that Rosemary was doing handstands. It was very hot; not only that but if she misjudged the effort she put into each push, she might collapse on his body.

Philip groaned. 'Dun't keep doing that, my 'ansome. All the blood do rush to your face and you look fit to burst.'

Rosemary sat on her heels, breathing deeply.

'All right. Can I talk to you then? Ask you something?' He groaned again and she hurried on, 'Listen. Philip. Please listen. Jan's told me about the *Lancaster* and everything and I've been thinking and thinking. I mean the whirly pool at the mouth of the estuary isn't there today, is it? We came right across there and it was as calm as glass.'

'Certain times it isn't. When there's storms brewin' up or when ole Neptune pulls the plug out.'

'Pulls the plug out?'

'Nex' time you 'as a bath in that posh washroom you got

212

at 'ome, jest look and watch when you pulls out the plug. You'll get a whirly pool all of you own then.'

'Oh *Philip*. I'm not a little girl! There's no plug and there's no Neptune.' She stood up and did a furious handstand. Philip watched her legs, wondering which way they would fall. When she righted herself, so did he.

'There's allus a vortex there when the weather is bad,' he said. 'An' if you want to know how it happened, I cain't tell you. The boat was pulled down and the boys jumped clear. That's all I know an' all I'm saying.'

She was aggrieved again.

'I don't know why you're cross with me. I wasn't going to ask you about that. I was going to ask you something quite different. Something you might know because you've been a seaman all your life and you know the sea. That was all.'

He eyed her suspiciously. 'Well?'

'Well. It was just . . . where has the wreckage of the *Lancaster gone*? It hasn't come up along the Lelant side because Rory keeps looking for it. And we know there's no Neptune and no plug, so it can't have disappeared down that!' She looked at him sardonically. 'So where is it?'

He had to grin. With her hair scraped back from her face, she had a look of Etta as a young girl. Lonely. In need of an ally. And aggressively sarcastic to hide that need.

He said, 'Well now my maid, that's a question no-one can answer, not me, not no-one. Prob'ly 'tis all churned up down under the sea and won't never be seen again.'

She gave him one of her special smiles.

'Just supposing it had been washed-up this side of the river. Just *supposing*. Where d'you think it might land up?' She put a hand up to shield her eyes and gazed over the featureless dunes. 'It could be anywhere. But someone who knows about the currents and things — like you, Philip — might know where it would be . . . *if* it was.'

He said dryly, 'This sand keeps a lot of secrets, my maid. You could search for a year and not find a thing. Or you could put your hand under the surface and come up with

213

anything. A precious di'mond. Old coins . . . all sorts are found on these 'ere beaches.'

'Yes, but that's all luck.' Rosemary took his arm and pulled him along the lip of sand until they could see the mouth of the Hayle river. 'That's where the whirlypool was, Philip. Now can't you tell where a wreck might have landed? Allowing for . . . the wind . . . and the currents.'

'The sand moves too, you know. But I reckon if 'twere this side, and if there were anything to throw out, it might be worth looking t' other side o' that flat rock down there.'

'Come on then, Philip.'

'I reckon 'tis almost my turn to face the bowling.'

'No, not yet. Jan's next and he'll be ages.'

When the cricket match was over, they lit the fire and laid half the sausages on the old footscraper. It would not be dark for another two hours, yet the afternoon was well and truly over and they gathered round the pale flames with a sense of coming together for the night. Rosemary had lugged Philip off for yet another 'walk', but the others kept close in spite of the smoke − or perhaps because of it. Angus McGovern announced it kept off the gnats and as Etta said, it was better to be kippered than eaten alive.

Madge felt wonderfully at peace. The terrible guilt she had felt for so long was often eased by the day to day business of her happy life. And today had been very special. Clem had turned back the clock for her, made her young and innocent again. She remembered another cricket match and, for the first time, let herself recall its sequel: that awful attack her father had suffered which had put a stop to his sexual advances on her mother that night. She stared into the fire unsmilingly and knew that if it hadn't been for Ned, that experience might have made her frigid for always. Was it sufficient justification for everything that had happened since? She would probably have never understood Clem, and his brief affair with the Canadian girl might well have poisoned their difficult relationship in the end. But . . .

214

Mark would not have been born; and therefore Mark would not have been injured.

She looked at him now. He was eating sausages with his fingers, grinning at Jem who was drunk with sunshine and cricket and food. The two of them had swum before tea and would swim again later. In the water they were equal; if anything Mark was faster. But out of the water . . . Madge looked across at Clem who was laying out the next batch of sausages. How much did he know? Did he feel trapped by Mark's complete dependence? She shivered suddenly.

Her mother said, 'Cold, darling? There's a spare cardigan in the bag.'

'No. Not really. Just one of those moments.'

Marie smiled. 'A goose walked over a grave, perhaps. Most of our memories are happy ones, Madge. We're very lucky.' She glanced at Mark. 'He might not have been the person he is if . . . it . . . hadn't happened.'

If anyone else had said it, Madge might have felt angry. But she smiled at her mother and nodded slightly.

Clem called, 'Anyone for more sausages?'

And Rosemary came running down the dune, a piece of planking clutched to her chest.

'Look what we've found! Jan – look!' She held out the plank. It looked like any piece of flotsam, except that the letters A.S.T.E in scoured black paint appeared on its length.

Everyone stared incomprehension.

Rosemary said impatiently, 'It's the nameboard from the *Lancaster*! Jan – surely you can see—'

Jan took the board and moved into the direct sunlight with it. He looked at the others.

'She is right! That's what it is – see how the S curls back under the A? Rory's father painted that himself!'

Madge said quickly, 'Never mind, Jan. Let's give it a Viking's farewell – throw it on the fire!'

But Jan was delighted. 'We have wondered so much – the *Lancaster* was like a friend. Rosemary, how can I thank you!'

'It was Philip really.'

Philip himself came lumbering down the sandhill. He pulled his hat on more firmly.

'She kep' on an' on. I gave 'er some idea where it might be an' she dug like a terrier!'

The mood of the party soared again. Rosemary and Philip were fed sausages as if they were returning heroes. The women made more tea. Jem and Mark began to pester for another swim.

'You must wait another half an hour at least!' all the adults said in unison.

'Stink-bombs!' Mark said loudly.

Jem screamed with laughter. Mark pulled his mouth down with one hand and pushed his nose up with the other and made retching noises. Jem collapsed on the sand.

'Really Mark. Behave yourself,' Madge admonished automatically. But Clem was laughing too and Jan and Rosemary were capering about like lunatics and her mother was looking at her with raised brows as if to say 'What did I tell you?'

The following day it was as if they had a hangover. None of them could face Etta's midday meal and she removed the untouched plates in thunderous silence. Philip was taking some visitors around the bay in the lugger and after an interval while they waited for the pudding which did not arrive. Etta's voice bawled up from the cellar – 'Just off to Bright Hour!'

'Thank goodness for that,' Rosemary said.

'Now dear,' said her grandmother.

'I meant as it's such a horrible day it will do Etta good to go to Bright Hour!'

Not even Mark smiled at that.

Madge said, 'I'll make some tea and you take a pill, Mark. Then you can lie down for an hour.' She saw rebellion on his face. 'Dad and I are going upstairs for a rest and Grandma and Ro said they were going for a walk.' She looked meaningly at her mother who nodded immediately.

216

Rosemary said, 'I'll bring you back some of that funny seaweed you wanted, Mark.'

Clem groaned. Mark had a large collection of dried seaweed, but the drying process was smelly to say the least.

Mark grinned, accepting the inevitable with good grace as usual. Besides, the window seat was not like going to bed properly. He had a framed view of the harbour and when Jem arrived back on the *Forty-niner*, he would be able to raise the sash and talk to him face to face. Philip had been as good as his word and the window seat had the cosiness of a ship's bunk with the freedom of the out-of-doors. He took his pill, settled back and listened to his parents creaking about above him. The next instant, he was asleep.

Angus McGovern was sitting on his usual seat above Porthmeor. He too looked the worse for wear, especially as he was in yesterday's clothes – shirt and trousers and no jacket. He looked at Rosemary without enthusiasm.

'Shall we go back into the town, find a teashop and have some tea?' he suggested hopefully.

'We could do that. Or we could have a brisk walk to Five Points and back along the lane – that would warm us up.' Marie smiled at him. 'I think it would also help to blow away the cobwebs,' she added.

Rosemary said, 'May I play on the beach until you get back, Grandma? I want to look for some seaweed for Mark, remember. And I could help Jim Maddern with the donkeys. I'd much rather do that.'

'That's a good idea,' Angus said, remembering Rosemary's lagging steps on other walks. 'Then I'll buy you an icecream in the beach shop before you go home. How's that?'

Marie agreed with some reluctance. She had never quite got over the shock of seeing her granddaughter cavorting with that boy three years ago. Rosemary had said it was Jan Grodno, and Marie had forgiven him because, being Polish, he knew no better; but Jan was fair and she was almost sure that the boy on the beach had been dark. It was all most mysterious.

'If it starts to rain, go straight home, darling,' she cautioned. And she said to Angus, 'She's only twelve, after all.'

'Quite.' Angus was of the school that thought children should be seen and heard as seldom as possible.

They walked single file along the cliff top. Angus went ahead, swinging his arms fiercely in an effort to get warm. When he turned round Marie was a hundred yards behind and breathing audibly. He would have waited but she gestured to him to go on, and he did so, accelerating his pace so that he could wait for her in the lee of Old Man's Head.

Marie watched him with an over-objective eye. Every year since they had re-met he had proposed to her, and every year she had asked for more time. It was so stupid; at the beginning of each holiday she was delighted to see him and quite certain she would accept him this year. By the end of the fortnight she had these silly doubts. What did it matter that he was looking so idiotic at this precise moment? So was she probably, panting along like an old woman. He was older than her but he had more energy than she'd ever had. Wasn't that what she needed? And when she was with him she never felt that awful alone-ness that had swept over her so forcibly that day on the Island long ago. She might feel slightly irritated occasionally, but she never felt alone.

She caught him up under the enormous hanging rock and leaned against it, getting her breath back. He swung his arms, smacking his shoulder blades rhythmically, then ran on the spot.

'I'd like to show you some of the mountain walks back home,' he said at last, blessedly ceasing his flailing. 'Cornwall is very beautiful, but Scotland leaves it standing.'

'I can imagine,' she murmured. 'Very hilly though?'

'Hilly?' He laughed boisterously. 'Mountainous, not hilly.' He looked at her seriously. 'If you liked it, Marie, I'd give up the Todmorden home and we could live there. We could live anywhere, in fact. Another country—'

'I wouldn't want to be too far from Madge and Clem, Angus.'

'Bristol?' She knew he didn't like what he called the 'middle-lands'. Then he smiled and reached for her hand. 'Anywhere with you would be paradise.'

She was suddenly and inordinately touched. He had talked of companionship and shared interests, but never in a romantic vein. Perhaps he hadn't noticed her laboured breathing and pepper-and-salt hair. One thing, she didn't wear curlers. But what about her teeth? She had a vision of them magnified a thousand times in their tumbler of water.

He said, suddenly ardent, 'Marry me, my dear. Say you will. Now. We're not getting any younger. Let's have our last years together.'

'Oh Angus . . .' She was only just sixty, but he was probably ten years older than that. How would she feel if he died this winter and she'd kept him hanging on for so long?

He put his arms around her and made the ultimate declaration. 'I love you, Marie. I love you. Don't make me wait any longer.'

He smelled so wonderfully masculine. No man had held her like this since Alfred's death. Clem might give her a quick hug, but it was wonderful to be able to lay her head on a man's shirt and feel his warmth through it.

She murmured, 'It would be lovely to be married on Sundays.'

'You mean get married on a Sunday?'

'No. I meant . . . Sundays are such lonely days.'

He held her more tightly. 'They are. Oh they are, Marie. Everyone involved with their families.' He kissed the top of her head. 'Does that mean yes? Does that mean you will?'

She closed her eyes. After all, why not. There would be adjustments on both sides, but if he was willing to make them, so could she. She moved her head up and down.

'Oh Marie. I'm the happiest man on earth!'

He also sounded surprised. After a moment he loosened his hold enough to kiss her mouth. It was a chaste kiss, for which Marie was thankful. She knew from novel-reading that kissing these days was quite different from how it had been with Alfred. She wasn't quite sure how her teeth would fare with anything even slightly 'probing'.

Rosemary was so bored she thought she might actually start to cry. Her best friend Sheila had a favourite phrase, 'I could weep with sheer boredom,' and until now Rosemary had thought it just an affected remark. But even the smell of the donkeys' coats was depressing and as she set off under the lowering sky to search for the seaweed which reminded Mark of his therapist's alligator handbag, she could hardly drag one foot after the other. She deliberately recalled the complete euphoria of yesterday, but it had gone, and the discovery of the *Lancaster*'s nameboard now seemed pointless.

She left her sandals and socks above the tidemark and crossed the firm damp sand to where it became sloppy. The water was no colder than it had been yesterday, but it seemed to eat into her feet; the blister on her little toe shrieked for a moment then settled into an ache. She stood still, her knees knocking, and gazed out to sea. 'I hate you,' she whimpered and squeezed a single tear on to her cheek. 'I hate you,' she said again, then noticed a fishing boat off Bamaluz Point. 'Not *you*,' she said hastily in case it sank before her very eyes. 'I just hate . . .' But she did not quite know what it was she did hate and when she failed to eject another tear she turned petulantly to walk back to the seaweed rocks; and there, coming down the beach towards her, was Rory Trewyn.

Three years was a big hunk out of her life, and in that hunk Rory had changed. She knew that Jan was five feet nine inches tall and that Rory might be even taller, but Jan was so slight and pale that he never looked big. Rory looked big. His shoulders were wide and powerful and his head was leonine. His features were large too; eyes, nose, mouth and ears all declared themselves vividly. His hair was as black and copious as ever. She knew before he left the cliff path that this was Rory. And she knew too – he made it so obvious – that he had come to find her. Her boredom went as if it had never been; her feet tingled and she felt her face come alive. She forgot the terrible shame of their last meeting. Quite untypically, she went up the beach to meet him. They halted with a yard of no-man's-sand between them.

He said, 'Jan told me how you pestered Philip to find something that was left of the *Lancaster*. I want to thank you.'

His voice was so deep it was hoarse. She felt a flutter of panic. He was grown-up. He'd left her behind in the realms of childhood and gone on to something deep and mysterious. Yet he was the same age as Jan; and as rude as ever.

'I didn't pester. I asked his advice and . . .' She couldn't be bothered to go on justifying herself. Even though she tried to hold it back she felt a grin lifting her eyes to her hairline. She said directly, 'I'm glad you're pleased.'

'Who said I was pleased?' He tried to sound truculent but he was grinning too.

'No-one. I just knew you would be.' Then she remembered that this time she must be absolutely truthful. 'Jan said you were grieving for the boat. I would have too. Not to have anything of her at all must have been awful.'

There was a pause while he seemed to weigh up her new openness. Then he shrugged.

'It was. That's why I wanted to thank you.' He didn't move but it seemed the end of the exchange and she felt another twinge of panic in case he turned and left. Then he said flatly, 'You've changed.'

'Yes.' The smile disappeared and she swallowed painfully. 'I was only eight . . . then.'

'Yes. I know. I've thought of that often. Rosemary . . . Ro . . . I'm sorry. I shouldn't have . . . I can't think why . . . I was so damned angry—'

'You were trying to protect Jan,' she said swiftly in case he actually mentioned *seeing* her.

But he snorted a sort of laugh. 'I wish I could think that. It was only part of it.' His black eyes went past her and stared at the indeterminate horizon. 'I'd just found out

221

about my adoption. I was angry. I took it out on you. And you were eight years old.' He made another snorting sound. 'I'm sorry. It's all I can say. I could have mucked up your whole damned life and that's all I can say. I'm sorry.'

She was grinning again. 'You didn't muck up my whole damned life.'

'I shouldn't swear in front of you either. You're still only twelve.'

'I'm quite old for my years. I know lots of worse words than damn.'

There was another pause. She wondered whether to prove her maturity by voicing some of the words she knew. The awful thing was she couldn't remember them just for the moment.

He said tentatively, 'What were you doing? I saw Etta outside the chapel and she thought you'd gone for a walk with your grandmother. I couldn't believe it when I saw you down here all by yourself.'

'Oh . . . Grandma and Mr McGovern were going all round Five Points and it's so boring. I came down to look for some seaweed for Mark. He collects it.'

'Jan has told me about him. He sounds a great kid.'

'He is. You should see some of his drawings.'

'Jan had a couple. One of you. With your hair up. It made you look much older.'

'Oh. Really?' She felt herself blushing. 'Daddy calls it my skinned-rabbit look.'

'Yes. That too.'

She didn't mind his bluntness. He had been like that before; it was his form of honesty.

She said, 'D'you want to help me look for Mark's seaweed? It's flat and about a foot wide and it looks like crocodile skin.' She turned and moved again towards the rocks, talking over her shoulder. It gave him the opportunity to leave immediately without embarrassment. Or to join her.

He joined her.

'I know the stuff. It'll stink while it's drying.'

'Oh it does. All of it. Last year on the way home Daddy

said the car was so full of fumes it was a wonder it didn't take off like a hot-air balloon!'

He laughed. It was another of his harsh sounds and somehow made her feel very protective towards him; as if he were the young one and she was the elder.

He had lost none of his expertise among the rocks. He kicked off ancient, lace-less plimsolls, and walked easily across the sharpest ridges and spongiest weed-beds without losing his footing once. Rosemary used her hands as well as feet, her hair hanging in rats' tails on either side of her face and making conversation very difficult.

His physical strength was no surprise; she recalled only too vividly how helpless she had been in his grip that awful day three years ago. When she tugged hopelessly at the trunk-like roots of a sea kale, he leapt over to remove it with one enormous heave.

She said, 'I thought you might have a knife.'

'I never carry one now.'

'What about . . . don't you cut for sand eels any more?'

'No. Couldn't stand seeing them . . . you know.'

'Oh.' That was a surprise. She herself had long learned to accept this culling of bait.

He shrugged and said frankly, 'You don't know how I felt afterwards. To tell you the truth, I didn't think I'd ever be able to face you again.'

She looked at him directly. And understood.

'That's how I feel about Mark sometimes. I can't bear it. And I have to.'

He frowned. 'It's not your fault the poor kid is crippled.'

'But it is. Surely you know? Everyone in St Ives must know. I feel they look at me – point me out–' She swallowed and turned to stare out to sea. The fishing boat was still there. At least that hadn't sunk.

'All I know is there was an accident. He fell from the railway bridge on to the line. At Carbis Bay.'

She breathed deeply. 'Yes. That's what happened.' She wouldn't say any more. She couldn't. Not even to her father had she spoken the actual words. 'But you see I lifted him out of his pram and propped him on the rail to look at the view. And then . . .' her voice shook. 'I dropped him.'

There was a moment of sheer astonishment at herself for speaking out at last, then a kind of enormous relief. Her body began to shake with her voice. She stammered, 'I didn't mean to. Daddy says it was his responsibility . . . but I *did* it! Whatever anyone says, I did it! And Mark – he's so good. I mean *good*! A good person. Not good like Etta. A bit like Philip. He's more like Philip than any one of us. He doesn't seem to *mind*! I mean even when the pain is bad he never grumbles – not really – not like me. And his physio woman – she's horrible, but I think he really loves her!'

She was weeping. Rory said uncomfortably, 'Look here, steady on old girl.'

She dashed the tears away, pushed her hair behind her ears and mumbled, 'Sorry.'

'I didn't mean that, you idiot. I meant, it's not much good going overboard with the sackcloth and ashes, is it? It would be different if you'd been mad jealous of the kid and tried to do him in. But it *was* an accident – just like everyone says. And Jan says you're good friends – better than we are. Maybe you wouldn't have been such friends if Mark was . . . well, you know . . .' His voice petered out. He was red from the effort of thinking everything out, couching it in terms he thought a twelve-year-old might grasp.

She took a deep breath, hiccoughing on a sob like a baby. She said, 'So . . . if I . . . if I give my whole life – a bit like a nun – to Mark – if I sort of implicate myself—'

'D'you mean dedicate?'

'Yes. Dedicate myself to my brother. Then it might be all right?'

He said doubtfully, 'I suppose it might.'

'That would be the right thing to do, wouldn't it Rory?'

'Ummm, well, yes. I suppose it would.'

She took another shuddering breath and looked again at the fishing boat. It was making towards Cape Cornwall and looked as safe as anything could on that wide sea.

She smiled suddenly and turned to Rory confidingly.

'I've never told anyone that before,' she said. 'Sheila Patten who is my best friend, is a Roman Catholic and she goes to Confession and says she feels it's like putting down a bag of potatoes.' She laughed. 'It is.'

Rory, not displeased with being cast in the role of father confessor, held up the sea-kale like a banner.

'Onward Christian soldiers . . . looking for a croc!'

Rosemary couldn't stop laughing now she'd started. 'Oh I must tell Mark that one – he'll love it!' she said as she scrambled after Rory towards yet another bed of seaweed.

Marie Bridges undressed in the dark as usual and slid into bed beside her granddaughter. One of the few snags about staying with the Nollas was that she did not have her own room, yet had to retire early so that Mark could be settled for the night downtairs. She supposed rather glumly that all that would change next year when she was married to Angus. He stayed at one of the big hotels at the top of the cliff and never retired before midnight. That would suit her all right, but then she wondered what would happen at night; would he expect anything of her? Her mouth turned down with distaste. She might like the smell of his shirt and the warmth of his arms around her, but that was as far as she could possibly go. Well . . . she had told him that they would talk about it properly before they made any announcements, and that must be one of the things she must bring up.

She sighed deeply and put one arm behind her head in an effort to ease the tension in her neck. Alfred had frequently massaged her neck; would Angus do the same? Did she want him to? And what about undressing in front of him? But of course that was as nothing compared with the enormous problem of her teeth. Surely she couldn't change her mind about marrying him for such a frivolous reason? But then, to her it was no frivolity; to her it was a matter of enormous seriousness. Every time she thought of her teeth the word 'enormous' cropped up. Strange, inside her mouth they fitted comfortably and she never thought about them. Outside, in the glass which she could just see on the bed-table, they looked . . . enormous. It must be the water acting as a magnifier. Although when she simply held them in order to scrub them, they still looked . . . enormous.

Her head was about to drop off. She removed the arm and flung it over the edge of the bed. Rosemary felt like a furnace, yet it hadn't been all that warm today so the child couldn't possibly have sunstroke. Of course yesterday she'd been out in it all day looking for that silly piece of wood. As if Marie's concern had communicated itself, the child rolled towards her and snuggled into her side.

'Gramma . . .' she slurred. 'I'm so h . . . appy.'

'Oh darling.' Marie accepted the small warm body as best she could and tears filled her eys. She knew – quite sharply – how Rosemary felt; the ecstasy that had nothing to do with content, the breathless anticipation for the morrow, and when that came for the next minute – the next second. That was how it had been with Alfred. And that was how it could never be with Angus.

She was telling herself that she must be sensible and accept the companionship and security that Angus undoubtedly had to offer, when the palm of her outflung hand tickled. She brought it over to the other one which was imprisoned under Rosemary's head and managed to scratch it. Then she cast it wide again in an effort to release the mounting heat, and immediately it tickled.

She lay very still in the bed, suddenly rigid with concentration. This was how she had imagined it; she would reach out her hand and Alfred would find a way to touch it. Her palm was being caressed, perhaps . . . perhaps kissed! She clenched it suddenly to try to hold it in. But it had gone. The tears spilled over and down her face, warm and salty, and her body relaxed creakingly, telling her it was old. Even if Alfred were here, alive and vital, they were both past the years of ecstasy. She was a silly old woman, a silly toothless old woman, still expecting too much from life.

She turned her head on the pillow and her eyes, accustomed to the darkness now, saw that her teeth were grinning at her in their glass. She blinked the tears away and grinned back. After all, everything had its funny side. She remembered her wedding night when the gas in the boarding-house bedroom had unaccountably flared up, revealing her in her stays and Alfred in his combinations. She nearly chuckled aloud at the recollection, and as she closed her lips tightly over her gums, the ends of her fingers tingled sharply. She did not tense herself again. She left her fingers where they were, drooping almost to the floor, and felt the weight of her head now quite comfortable on the pillow.

After a while her fingers tingled no more, and she put her hand on the outside of the covers.

Rosemary murmured out of the blue, 'I do love you. So much.'

And Marie whispered, 'I know, darling. Oh I do know that.'

Then she slept.

CHAPTER TEN

1957

That year they arrived in St Ives as many pilgrims arrive in Lourdes. Mark's first pair of aluminium and wire legs had proved useless; worse than useless because his stumps had been damaged by his perseverance and had to be dressed daily. He had a lightweight folding chair with an electric motor, designed by his father, but he had to be carried up the steps into the parlour of the cottage, and he was well aware that at twelve years old *he* was no light weight.

And there was the death of Grandma Briscoe last winter, which felt like a corporate wound shared by all four of them. It had been so different when Grandma Bridges died. She had actually told them she was excited at the prospect, and half convinced them too. And, strangely, her death had been kind; no pain, simply an inability to eat anything. Even her thinness had been ethereal and at the end, when she had hallucinated, she had been smiling all the time. In the four years since, they had come down to St Ives half expecting to find her there.

Grandma Briscoe had become senile and vicious. One night she had appeared outside the house, hair streaming down her back, shouting that her son was a coward and a deserter just like his father. She called Madge a whore and Mark a bastard cripple, then collapsed and was taken to hospital where she kept muttering about 'the sins of the fathers'.

It was unbearably distressing. They did not know how to cope with it and felt guilty and inadequate. That same winter they took in a refugee couple from Hungary, but the language barrier and the anxiety about Mrs Briscoe made that a short-term business. Madge, who was in the house with the Dravas all the time, became ill herself and though Mrs Drava tried to look after her, she must have realised herself that it was hopeless. They applied for emigration papers to Australia and left Britain in June.

And then Mark's left stump had become infected, and he had run a fever . . .

Etta said, 'Let 'im stay with us till the winter really sets in. Jem Gurnard and 'is lad will 'elp fetch 'im in an' out.'

For a moment Mark's face lit up, then he shook his head. 'No, Etta. I'm almost better now. And I want to go back to school in September and let Fizzy work on me a bit more.' He grinned. 'One day I'm going to walk along the harbour with you and Philip. Walk.'

Meanwhile the weather was not good that year and he was glad of his new chair. It was a bumpy ride over the cobbles and he was bounced around like a dummy each day as he manoeuvred up Fore Street and around by the war memorial, but it kept him warm and gave him new pictures to draw. He was still a cheerful soul, but he knew he needed something good to happen this holiday. It couldn't be anything for himself because all he needed personally was St Ives and Ro and his parents and the Nollas. Perhaps he needed something to happen for Ro? He thought about it as he worked on a packed sketch of boats in the harbour.

Ro was going to training college in October to learn how to be a teacher. Of all things. Jan said he'd like her to have a proper profession all of her own, though it seemed he didn't want her actually to work. Jan was a strange chap really. All these years he'd maintained the illusion that he and Ro would get married one day and he talked about their future life together as if it were all settled. As if by talking about it often enough he could make it happen. Yet surely he could see – surely everyone could see – that Rory was the one for Ro?

Mark frowned at his sketch. He had obeyed water-colour

rules and started with the foreground. But he saw now that he should have broken that rule and started way back where the jumble of beached boats became a forest of masts. Sometimes the foreground just didn't make any sense without the background.

Jan said solemnly, 'I am very sorry to hear you have been ill, Mrs Briscoe. Rosemary said nothing about it in her letters. I would have sent flowers.'

'Oh . . . really Jan . . . no need . . . weakness . . .'

Clem said firmly, 'Mrs Briscoe is anaemic, Jan. She needs plenty of rest and good food.'

'Then I could have sent some – some fresh fish perhaps,' Jan suggested doggedly. 'Or some grapes. We grow our own grapes at Mennion House.'

'Actually Mrs Trewyn did send me some wine which she had made from the grapes,' Madge said almost apologetically.

'You wrote to the Trewyns? They said nothing.'

'It *was* nothing! Please Jan, don't mention it again. I want to forget it this holiday.'

Clem said, 'Why don't you go and find Rosemary, old man?' He saw hesitation in the pale face and added, 'You could take her mack if you would. She's gone out without it of course, and it's going to tip down at any moment.'

They watched from the window as Jan departed reluctantly along the wharf, holding the mackintosh carefully over one arm.

Madge said, 'Darling, that was cunningly underhand of you. Is that how you get your way when you go to those awful conference things in America?'

'I don't get my way there, I'm afraid, my love.' He turned down his mouth, then adroitly swung her on to the window seat which was already made up as Mark's bed. 'There. Now lie still like a good girl while I make some tea. Be like Mark. Watch the world go by and relax.'

'What if Etta comes back and finds you in her kitchen?'

'I can wrap Etta around my little finger,' he assured her airily. He grinned wickedly. 'I never told you she came into my bedroom many years ago, sat on the edge of the bed, talked to me for a good half an hour, did I?'

'What did she *say*?'

'A-ah. I think she blessed me. Told me I'd be safe. Something. She was always on my side.'

He disappeared into the kitchen and Madge lay and listened to the sound of kettle and cups, letting her mind drift into an idle neutral. This was where Mark slept; or lay awake in pain. This at any rate was where he drew on the deep well of acceptance that he had inherited – from Ned? She had known so little of Ned except that schoolboy happiness. But there had been something else; she had sensed it. And he had wanted to be an artist. She'd hardly thought of Ned for years until that ghastly night when Mrs Briscoe called her a whore and Mark a . . . Madge turned her head, unable to think the word. Poor Ned, forgotten, somewhere in Holland. Yet living on in Mark. And poor Mark. Poor, poor Mark, with only half a life to lead. And Mother. Darling Mother, sending Angus McGovern away so calmly with the words, 'I'm still married, you see. Actually married. I've never been unmarried.' Poor Mother.

Clem came into the room carrying a tray which he put on the round table beneath the chandelier. He glanced at Madge as he poured tea.

'Do you do everything in life because you're sorry for someone, darling?' he said lightly, as he passed her a cup. 'No – I shouldn't have said that.' He tried to make her smile, bringing his face close to hers and putting on a woebegone expression. 'After all, if you hadn't been sorry for me we'd have never got to the altar!'

She still did not speak and the cup was unsafe in its saucer. He held her wrists lightly; her pulse fluttered beneath his thumb.

He said quietly, 'When I came back home, after the war, you were no longer sorry for me. That's what I remember. That is what makes me so thankful.'

'Thankful?'

'Yes, darling. Thankful. Just as I am thankful that Mark

lived. Thankful that your mother's cancer was so . . . gentle. Thankful that my own mother did not live to remember her cruelty. Thankful that we still have each other.' He grinned. 'You never imagined Clem Briscoe could talk like that character in Ro's old book, did you?'

'Pollyanna.' She began to smile at last. 'No, I never imagined that.'

He looked at her for a long moment. Then he stood up and went back to the tray to pour his own tea.

Ro and Rory walked the length of Porthmeor beach from Island to Old Man's Head without saying more than half a dozen words each.

At eighteen, Rosemary had not quite fulfilled the beauty that had promised at eleven. Her hair was pale rather than blonde, her eyes too light a blue to be noticed, her lips invisible without makeup. Her mother's individual features were imperfect, yet their total became beautiful. Rosemary was the opposite; each individual feature was exquisite; together they added up to a kind of perfect plainness. Perhaps that fact explained her stubborn determination.

Rory Trewyn, at twenty-two, was so good-looking he literally made her heart ache. It ached now as she looked up at him; the pain across her chest made her breathing shallow. But her voice when she spoke was hard and firm.

'I've never heard anything quite so stupid in my whole life! Sacrifice yourself if you must. But not me. Certainly not me!'

He turned from her wearily.

'Look. We went into all this last year when you informed me you were seventeen and intended to marry me. I am not sacrificing anyone, Rosemary—'

Suddenly her iron calm disappeared. The pain across her ribcage intensified to bursting-point, and she caught hold of his arm and pulled him round.

'Don't look away from me, Rory Trewyn! Are you afraid to meet my eyes? It's not just what you said last year by any means! You've written to me since – have you forgotten? I've got it in writing, Rory! You want me to marry Jan. You've told me often enough that you love me – and heaven knows I love you – yet you can't marry me because it's always been understood—'

'That's it exactly, Ro!' His anger rose to meet hers. 'I can't marry you. Leave it at that. Please!'

Her nails dug into his arm.

'No. I won't leave it at that. I want to know why you can't marry me! Don't you love me any more? Why can't you be honest? Have you met someone else?'

'For Christ's sake, Ro! You're eighteen! You'll meet other men when you go to college – like I met other girls when I did my National Service! It doesn't mean much, but it's all part of – of—'

'Go on, say it. Growing up. You think I'm still a kid! I'm not! I haven't been a kid where you're concerned for years! And I know you love me – I *know!*'

She released his arm and threw herself on him. Her mouth found his more by accident than design, and she clung to him desperately. He tried to remain icily still, to repel her with sheer indifference, but after a while his hands went around her waist and he held her to him for an instant before thrusting her away.

'Dammit, Rosy. That's not fair!'

'Anything is fair to me.' She looked at him with her soul in her pale eyes. 'Rory. Please marry me. It's all I've wanted, all I've lived for. It's not just this—' she touched his lips with butterfly fingers '—it's more. We should be together, Rory. Always.'

He said miserably. 'I can't, Ro. Jan and me – we're more than brothers. And he has believed all these years that you would marry him.'

'Oh God. We're back to that. The sacrifice. Just like.I said. You want me to sacrifice myself—'

'No. I just don't want to be the one to muck up Jan's life. You must do what you have to do, Ro. But I cannot be part of it. Don't you see?'

'No,' she replied flatly. 'No. No. No. I don't.'

'Darling. It's so straightforward. If I marry you – tomorrow. Or ten years' time. Jan will always know that it was me who came between him and his family – yes, he calls you his family!'

'And you called me darling. You do love me.'

'I don't know. I don't even know. There's something between us, but is it love? I don't know – and whatever you say now, you certainly don't.'

'I know I don't love Jan.'

'You get on well. He says you kiss him.'

'I let him kiss me sometimes. I want to find out what it's like. So that I can do it properly.'

She was speaking for effect, watching him for signs of jealousy. That kiss years ago on the steps of the cottage had been the first of many such greetings; Jan had made sure of that. But on the other hand she had never put a stop to it.

She was not prepared for his anger.

'You haven't changed, Ro, have you? Not really. You're still using Jan. Still leading him up the garden path.' He shrugged coldly. 'I can't stop you any more. I can't even shame you any more, can I?' He turned and began to walk back along the shoreline. 'He loves you. Perhaps you could learn to love him? Why don't you try?' His voice was tossed over his shoulder at her on a squall of wind and rain. She ran after him, hating herself yet unable to give him up.

'Rory, I didn't mean . . . I'm *fond* of Jan! You know that!'

He kept walking fast so that she had to skip along like a child to keep up with him.

'In that case it should be easy to grow fonder. Until one day he becomes the knight in shining armour you obviously need—'

'Oh shut *up*!'

She stopped but he went on walking. Down the steps from the Island appeared a figure clutching a mackintosh.

She said fiercely, 'Here he is now. I'm going to tell him. Right here and now. Tell him I don't love him, I love you.'

He slowed, waved to the distant Jan, turned and walked back to her.

'Do what you like, Ro. Say what you like. It's entirely up to you. I'm going away at the end of the month. I've got a job crewing on a charter boat. I meet up with it at Rhodes. That's a Greek island—'

'I know where Rhodes is. And you're running away.'

He shrugged. 'Call it what you like. I prefer to think I'm leaving a clear field.' He looked at her levelly. 'By all means send Jan packing, Ro. But is that what you really want? Honestly? Jan's doing very nicely in the family auctioneering business. You could end up living down here. Maybe with Mark. Think about it carefully. Before you burn your boats.'

She stared at him. 'You haven't got a very high opinion of me, have you, Rory?'

'If I didn't have a high opinion of you, I'd never want you to get hitched to Jan, would I?' He smiled almost affectionately. 'Ro . . . you can be devious to the point of dishonesty. But I have a very high opinion of you.'

She wanted to wake up and find it was a bad dream. His last words convinced her as all the previous arguments had not. Yet they were so close; like peas in a pod. Certainly, more often than not, Jan was with them, but she had assumed always that Rory knew just how the triangle was balanced.

Jan arrived at a gallop and came straight to her. He wrapped the mackintosh around her shoulders before pecking her cheek and putting a friendly arm around her shoulders.

'You two! I suppose you haven't noticed the rain?'

Rory grinned across at him. 'This isn't rain, it's a sea fret.'

Both of them laughed at what was obviously an old joke, and Rosemary felt the balance of the triangle shift. She was way out on the apex and the two of them were either end of the solid base. She tried to look up to check on Jan's expression and caught what seemed like a wink. For the first time it occurred to her that the two of them might be manipulating her instead of the other way round. Her father had teased her for so long about having both boys 'on a string', she had come to believe it. Supposing they were playing some macabre game with her?

235

She said, 'Isn't this exciting about Rory going off to Greece? I always told you he looked like a pirate, didn't I, Jan?'

She knew that would annoy Rory; it made the whole expedition sound melodramatic and pretentious.

Sure enough he said, 'It's a job, Ro. Just a job. I tried to join the family firm like Jan, and mucked that up. I didn't go to university after the Navy and that disappointed the parents. I've got to get out − I've got to get away from Cornwall before she smothers me!'

He was deadly serious. She said in a small voice, 'But you love Cornwall. You *are* Cornwall.'

'No. I'm not. I'm me. I'm going to prove it!'

Jan squeezed her shoulders. 'He has to go. He has to cut the strings, then come home and tie them up again himself! Is that not so?'

'That is so,' Rory mimicked solemnly.

Jan laughed but Ro persevered. 'You went away before. When you did your National Service in the Navy.'

Rory sighed theatrically. 'Tell her, Jan. I'm off. I'm going to catch the train to Lelant and walk from there. See you tonight, old man. Cheerio Ro-Ro.'

She did not reply but it didn't matter because he was off across the beach like a cheetah and wouldn't have heard her anyway. She felt terrible; almost as bad as she had before when he'd pulled off her knickers. This time she had stripped away her own pride; she had begged and pleaded and argued; and he had still gone away.

Jan said, 'National Service was the opposite to being free, Ro. If Rory thinks Cornwall is a prison, then National Service was a dungeon.'

'But you don't feel in prison, surely?'

'Ah. It is different for me. My father is dead, but I knew him. I know who I am and what I am. I choose to stay here.'

Ro watched Rory disappear over the Island, then turned to look at the sea. Everything was so grey. It was hard to find the horizon. She could almost hate it herself.

Jan said rallyingly, 'You will be coming over to Mennion

House to supper one night as usual. You will see Rory then. He is not leaving for another week.'

'A week? I thought . . .' She swallowed fiercely. 'Surely if he tried to find his real parents, it would help?'

'Ah. We have talked about this. Often.' Jan gently pressed her towards the cliff path. 'Come on, we shall get our shoes wet, the tide is coming in.' He drew a breath. 'It is perhaps embarrassing to speak of this. You are still so young. But you will understand the delicacy—' he hurried on at her explosion of impatience '—Rory considers it likely that his father – Matthew Trewyn, you understand – was disloyal to his mother – Mary Trewyn. And therefore he is not able to enquire about the matter for fear of hurting his mother.'

Ro stopped to dig her arms into her mackintosh. The rain was coming in with the tide in swathes of heavy mist. She glanced at Jan's face. It was puce.

'You mean Matt Trewyn had an affair with someone else? So he is Rory's real father, but Mrs Trewyn is not his real mother?'

'It is conjecture of course. But it seems possible.'

Ro said thoughtfully, 'I heard Etta telling Mummy once that Mrs Trewyn had miscarriage after miscarriage. That was why they adopted Rory.'

'Gossip,' commented Jan distastefully. 'She is not a popular woman – we are aware of this. But gossip is unpleasant.'

'Yes. I suppose so.' She smiled ruefully. 'You have high standards, Jan. If you knew me properly I don't think you would want to marry me.'

'Aah. That is not so. I accept you as you are.'

For a moment she was tempted; terribly tempted to do what Rory expected of her and slide into an easy marriage with Jan Grodna. It would be second best certainly, but plenty of marriages were, and it would mean she could live down here always and surely see Rory sometimes.

She felt her smile die.

'Thank you, Jan. But you must know . . . I love Rory.

237

It's Rory I want to marry. I'm sorry, Jan. I must be honest with you.'

The colour drained from his face.

'I think I knew already.' The Adam's apple moved in his throat. 'It makes no difference. I still love you. More than ever because you have said this so frankly.'

'But you must see, surely, that I cannot marry you?'

'I do not see that. No. I think, one day, you will accept me.'

'Oh Jan . . .' she literally clasped her hands and wrung them desperately. 'I'm so miserable.'

He went to her and held her tightly. It was what she needed. She pressed the side of her head against his shoulder and felt the thump of his heart.

He said in a low voice, 'I too am not happy. But together we will be happy. Have patience, little Ro. It will be all right.' He tried to lighten his voice. 'We do not need to run away to sea like poor Rory. We know who we are and we shall be happy here.'

He held her for a few moments more, then said bracingly, 'Come. We must go back and see the others. Your mother will be worried.'

She walked ahead of him up the path. He was always anxious to get back to her mother. If she did not marry him she would be depriving him of that too. She began to feel trapped, just as Rory must feel trapped.

She said, 'Have you and Rory had a miserable time of it with the Trewyns? You never talk about it much.'

'Miserable? Oh no. They have been good to us. Very good. Just. And kind.' He caught up with her and they walked past the well beneath the cemetery. 'And we have had each other since the war. I came to live with Rory in 1941 – we were both six. We do not remember much before that. We are closer than brothers.'

Ro hunched into her mackintosh. Whatever she did it seemed she would make Jan and Rory unhappy. Either by coming between them, or by depriving Jan of his 'family'. She wondered, fleetingly, whether she had the strength to

238

sever herself from both boys and look for something else. But she did not let the thought linger.

Supper at Mennion House was stiffly formal as usual. For the last three years the Briscoes had been invited there in acknowledgement of the hospitality they extended to Rory and Jan. Matthew Trewyn had been a bomber pilot during the war so he and Clem got on fairly well by talking exclusively of aircraft. But Mary Trewyn barely hid her boredom, and the boys were never natural in front of her. It was Mark who had saved the evenings before with his insouciant chatter of films and books and fishing. After the meal he had done lightning sketches of them all, unconsciously caricaturing them and making them laugh in spite of themselves. This evening he was strangely lethargic. Madge wondered whether he was incubating a cold. It was more likely that his stumps were hurting him. She bit her lip and tried not to think of the future.

Rory, on the other hand, was unusually bright, helping himself to his father's whisky with a liberal hand and cajoling his mother to play the piano once the meal was over.

'Don't be ridiculous, Rory,' she said dismissively. 'This is 1957. Shall we have the news on the television? Have you got a television, Mrs Briscoe?'

'Er – yes. Just a small one.'

'Really? It makes world events so vivid, don't you think? I was particularly interested in all that business on the Gold Coast. My family have a great deal of property out there.'

'Ghana, Mother.' Rory knelt down to plug in the television set. It was an enormous thing, with doors across the screen to make it look like a cocktail cabinet. 'And surely now that it is Ghana, foreigners can't own great chunks of it?'

'We're not foreigners, Rory! And it will always be the Gold Coast to me.'

The screen began to come to life and showed a picture of Mr Anthony Eden tending a garden somewhere.

Matthew Trewyn looked at the whisky bottle with a frown, then back to the television without pleasure.

239

'Macmillan's all right, I suppose. But Eden shouldn't have let that Nasser force him to retire like he did. The whole Suez thing was a disgrace. We should have told the United Nations to clear off and let us sort out our own problems. We bought the Canal fair and square—'

'Ha!' Rory did not try to soften the scorn in the single guffaw.

'Kindly keep your left-wing views to yourself for this evening, Rory,' Matthew Trewyn requested. 'Jan, d'you want some of this? Apparently Rory's fair-shares-for-all policy doesn't extend to his family and friends.'

Madge said quickly, 'I understood Mr Eden had retired because of ill health?'

'And what caused the ill health, dear lady?'

'Well, I—'

'Mr Briscoe, I was hoping you would talk about your visit to Nevada.' Jan accepted a small glass of whisky and sat next to Madge on the sofa.

Clem smiled. 'You will have seen more than I did, actually. The television crews zoom in where angels fear to tread, quite literally.'

'State secret, eh?' Matthew Trewyn suggested.

'It's no secret that we are working on rocket launchers now.' Clem shrugged. 'Plans and designs are another thing, of course. We – I mean America – won't be putting anything up until next year at the earliest. It matters terribly to them that the Russians have beaten them in that particular race.'

'Not to you?'

'There's a long way to go. A lot of time.'

Rory said, 'Anyway, surely the most important race is the human one?'

'Very clever, old man.'

Mrs Trewyn said, 'If you're going to talk all through it, shall we have the volume slightly higher?'

Everyone fell silent.

Jan said, 'May I show Mrs Briscoe the vines, Uncle

240

Matthew? She was saying you sent her a bottle of the wine when she was ill.'

'Certainly. Allow me to—' Matthew offered an arm and Jan's face fell.

Rory intervened. 'Actually Dad, I wanted to show off the new boat to Mr Briscoe. Any chance of me taking him up the river and back?'

'What – after last time? No fear! Come on Briscoe, I'll take you out myself. This weather is enough to give anyone claustrophobia. Anyone else for a spin?'

Rosemary stood up unobtrusively and moved alongside Rory. But Matthew Trewyn had other ideas.

'Not you, old man. Stay and keep young Mark company. Rosemary, did you ever hear about *Lancaster I*? I expect the whole of St Ives was buzzing about it. That great oaf back there took it into the middle of the vortex – you know, the whirlpool at the mouth of the estuary.'

'I do vaguely remember . . . it was six or seven years ago, surely?'

'Seems like yesterday to me.'

Rosemary fumed. Matthew had hold of her arm and her father was practically treading on her heels. She wanted to snap that it was Jan who had had the wheel that day, not Rory at all. But why should she care?

Madge said, 'What a lovely old-fashioned word. The vinery. And it's so pleasant too.'

Jan said, 'May I call you Madge?' He tried to laugh. 'After all, if I am to marry Ro one day, I suppose I ought to drop the Mrs Briscoe as soon as possible?'

Madge took a step towards the house and was confronted by a huge stone basin.

She said, 'I wish . . . you are both very young, Jan. And Rosemary could meet someone at college . . . I don't want you to be hurt.'

She turned from the basin and walked out of the vinery into the wild, rock-strewn garden high above the Hayle estuary. Below she could see Rosemary running down one of the sand burrows towards the Trewyns' jetty. She was reminded of a cricket match on the Towans years ago, when Mark had found a similar burrow and used it as a water chute.

Jan said from her shoulder, 'D'you remember that day we made a fire on the dunes? The day Rosemary found the old nameboard from the *Lancaster*?'

She smiled round at him. 'I was just thinking of that same day. How strange.'

'No. I have noticed often this thought-link between us. It is the reason I am so certain that one day Rosemary and I will marry. I have been part of the Briscoes for a long time.' He laughed, but she had no doubt of his seriousness.

She said quietly, 'That is hardly fair to the Trewyns, Jan. They took you in and treated you as their own. You see us each summer, that is all.'

'Ah . . . Madge . . . there, I have spoken it!' He laughed again and she wondered whether the whisky had gone to his head. 'Madge. My father left all that he had to me in Matthew Trewyn's trust. That is all. I stay now because of Rory. They are good people, we – we – rub along well enough – that is how Rory says it. We rub along very well. But you are my family. I wait for the summer. And then I am happy.'

Madge could have wept at his transparency. Nobody took him seriously. Certainly Ro did not. And Clem teased her about her Polish admirer; he actually teased her.

Instead she said in the most matter-of-fact voice she could muster, 'Then you are independent financially. I am glad.'

'Ah yes. Of course. And though my work is with the auctioneering company, actually I work with the partner. Jeremy Stockton. Yes, I am thoroughly independent, Madge. I can promise that.'

He had misunderstood her, but it did not matter. His mind, his heart, was so set on its course that whatever anyone said would make no difference. She stiffened her spine consciously and refused to feel sorry for him.

She walked along a footpath between samphire-cushioned rocks, to the side of the house.

'Now I can understand why the Trewyns built their house here.' She stopped, confronted with the enormous view of dunes and sea. 'It – it's magnificent.'

'Yes.' He was right behind her, cutting her off again from Clem and safety. 'Yes, but actually it was built here to be close to the rope factory down on the estuary. Also to bring up the brandy from the contraband boats.' He laughed again. 'The Trewyns do not want views. One needs special eyes to see views. Briscoe eyes.' He urged her on. 'See? Down there somewhere is where we played cricket that day. The weather was perfect. Do you remember?'

'Of course I remember.'

There was another narrow path to her right. It must lead back to the vinery and the house.

'I knew you would. I knew that day was special for you too.' Another laugh, then he suddenly started to unbutton his shirt. Madge was horrified and he saw that and quietened down to the seriousness of before. 'I carry this everywhere with me. Inside my shirt. Always.'

He withdrew some paper. It looked like old parchment, yellow and veined. Then she saw it had been varnished and the varnish had cracked.

'I photographed it and have it in my room. But this – the original – goes with me to my grave.' With enormous care he began to open it and smooth it down. 'I had one of Rosemary also, but that was lost. This one is safe.'

Madge stared at it with incomprehension. It seemed to be the figure of a woman leaping into the air.

'One of Mark's sketches?' She leaned closer.

'Yes.'

'It – is it – me?'

'Of course.'

She looked up at him, shocked out of her careful facade. And as he met her eyes the shock transmitted itself to him. He stared at her, horrified, realising at last that he was in love with her.

He said hoarsely, 'Madge – oh Madge – I thought – I didn't *know*—'

243

She straightened abruptly. She could not afford to be honest.

'I'd throw that old sketch away if I were you,' she said. 'It must be horribly scratchy inside your vest all the time. And not hygienic.' She was amazed to hear her voice emerge steadily and with a hard edge to it.

He said, 'Madge. My God. What shall I do?'

She folded the paper in new lines and it crackled ominously. 'I'll take it. I'll burn it. You'll . . . forget.'

She turned and took the path to her right. She thought she heard him sob, but she did not look back.

The weather improved slightly, and with it the pain in Mark's stumps. He would not permit anyone to lift him more than necessary, but the small stone slipway at the end of the wharf could take his chair right down on the sand and he made sure that he was there most afternoons at the end of the school day. Jem never kept him waiting. He lay prone now alongside the chair, incurious about Mark's painting. Other painters worked on the harbour beach and down Smeaton's Pier. They were taken for granted even when they sat in a wheelchair.

Jem said, 'The *Forty-niner* will come in with the tide and unload straightaway. No reason why we cain't take it out. Just for an hour. Christ, I kin manage that engine. Any kid could. You can take the wheel.'

'Don't be daft, Jem.' Mark was experimenting with a touch of bright cobalt in the green of the sea. He wasn't sure. He tried another, then another. It was too much, he'd have to whiten it out. That was the best of oils. He said, 'Your father would go crazy. As for Philip . . . it would be stealing, Jem.' This was how Rory and Jan must have argued when Rory planned their escapade in the *Lancaster*. Mark half smiled. If he had legs he'd do it, stealing or no stealing. It must be terrific to take control; make things happen.

Jem, already giggling at the thought of his father going crazy, spluttered, 'Rowlocks!' Then rolled over in the sand, convulsed. He knelt up, spluttering and spitting.

Mark said laconically, 'Serves you right.'

'All I said was rowlocks. The things you put the oars in! That's all.'

Mark imitated the slippery Cornish accent.

'Oh ah.'

'I'd kill you if you could fight. D'you know that?'

'You'd try.'

'Everyone in the town's scared o' me.' Jem wiped the sand off his face with the back of his hand, grinning boastfully. Then he looked at his friend who came to St Ives once or twice a year, yet seemed so much part of it. ''Cept you,' he added. 'An' you're only not scared cos you know I *cain't* fight someone 'oo cain't even stand up!'

Mark took his eyes off his painting for a moment and grinned at Jem Gurnard who was his best friend.

'Rowlocks!' he said.

Jem fell backwards laughing, squirming like a sand eel, unable to keep still for longer than a few minutes. It made his friendship with an immobile companion even stranger.

When he recovered he went on with the conversation which was also unusual. Jem wasn't much for conversation.

'No, but 'ow could I? I'd 'ave to kneel down to get at you. Then you'd prob'ly run me down with your bloody wheelchair.'

'Good idea.' Mark went back to his painting, still thinking of fighting Jem. Thinking longingly of fighting Jem. He shrugged. 'You wouldn't fight me anyway. We've got nothing to fight about.'

'We 'ave now. I want to go out in the *Forty-niner*. Just you an' me. It'd be the greatest adventure. Like pirates.'

Mark moved the easel to one side, suddenly losing interest in how much cobalt there was in the greys, greens, whites and blacks of his static sea. That was the trouble with Jem. Every now and then he was just plain stupid. Perhaps he only really understood fighting.

He said with exaggerated patience, 'How could we? How could I?'

245

Jem lookd at him wide-eyed. 'You come out in the *Forty-niner* often enough. What you on about?'

'Your father carries me. Or my father carries me.'

'I'm talking about when the tide is full. You can swim better 'n me. You can get yourself over the gunn'l. You got arms like a bloody gorilla!'

'Oh shut up, Jem!'

But after a moment of glaring futilely at each other, both boys started to laugh. They did not know why. Maybe it was Jem's description of Mark's arms. Maybe it was the thought of boarding the boat illegally and actually taking it to sea. Whatever it was, they couldn't stop. Jem rolled and squirmed and Mark put his head in his hands and made noises like a foghorn.

Madge, shaking an eiderdown from the bedroom window at the cottage, paused and watched. It was an unlikely friendship between Mark and Jem Gurnard. The town's tough boy. But it worked. She smiled as she listened to their cracked, animal sounds. Mark seemed better. And that awful business with Jan Grodna had come to a head and burst. He had gone with Rory to the Aegean; he would heal. Everything would be all right again.

Rosemary was not so sure. She wished now she hadn't been quite so honest with Jan. She had lost both of them; at least Jan would have kept a link with Rory. She felt a strange physical emptiness just between chest and abdomen as if she needed a nourishing hot drink or one of Etta's sandwiches. She tried both and neither helped. She was glad she was going to college. She'd show both of them that she didn't care. Meanwhile, as the weather got better, she spent all her time on the beach or in the sea. Mark was a comfort, his acceptance of the situation held none of the anxiety she sensed in her parents. He did not understand, of course, but he was a comfort nonetheless.

They were swimming together one afternoon. She had wheeled him along to the end of Smeaton's at high tide and tipped him out into the full harbour as if he were a sack of coal. It was his usual method of entry, though he could in fact manage an undignified crawl into the shallow water. The harbour suited him best: he could not manage the surf on Porthmeor beach, he needed deep water, still water.

There was usually an audience and today was no exception. It was an amazing sight, more spectacular than watching the local boys dive for pennies. At first, strangers were horrified to see the truncated body plummeting into the sea. And then they stood in admiration as Mark's powerful arms sliced him through the water without apparent effort. He and Rosemary used the deep clear water like dolphins, turning and twisting side by side then weaving around each other and breaking the surface gaspingly to laugh and take more air.

Rosemary said, 'I'm going to swim under the *Forty-niner*. I'll bring you a barnacle!'

She upended herself, her legs kicked the air and she was gone. Mark followed.

The next time, he led the way and she clung to his waist. His arms shouldered the water; he turned and saw Rosemary's face slightly flattened by pressure, her hair out of its pony tail streaming behind her like his stumps. He would paint her like that. It was glorious . . . he felt drunk on sea water.

They came up on the other side of the old lugger and hung on to its mooring rope, getting their breath.

A female voice said, 'I heard what you were saying the other day. When are you going to do it?'

Mark and Rosemary looked round in surprise. One hand on the rudder of the boat, the other sluicing water from her face, was a girl; though apart from the voice there was very little to support that claim. Her hair was shorter than Mark's and rather bristly. Her voice had a twang that was deeper than the Cornish. From hair and accent they deduced she was American.

'Well?' She sounded impatient. 'I've got to get back. When are you going to do it?'

Rosemary said, 'Do what, for goodness' sake?'

247

The girl flicked dark blue eyes past Rosemary without much interest. She was talking to Mark.

'When are you going to pinch this boat? It is this one, isn't it? I've kept watch on it all week and you've not been near it. But I heard you say—'

Mark chipped in quickly, 'No-one is pinching any boat. You heard Jem Gurnard talking rot. That's all. He does it often.'

The girl looked disappointed. 'Oh. I thought . . . I might have guessed. This place is so *dull*.'

Rosemary swam a little way off and floated on her back.

Mark said, 'It's not dull at all. And I wish you'd keep quiet in front of my sister.'

'Oh, is she your sister?'

'Who did you think she was, my wife?'

The girl giggled. 'Well now, maybe she could be at that.' She stopped giggling and stared at Mark. 'I've watched you. You're paraplegic, aren't you?'

Mark opened his round eyes very wide. It was a medical term which most people had not heard.

He said, 'No. My legs were amputated above the knee.'

She blew her nose inelegantly into her hand.

'Same difference I reckon.'

'I don't. I'll be walking one day. Paraplegics can't.'

'Say. I like your spirit. How will you walk for Godssakes?'

He ignored the question. 'Are you a Yank?'

'Not by birth. I go over there a lot.'

'That might explain it. Though my father says most Americans have perfect manners.'

He turned casually on to his side and disappeared beneath the surface without a ripple. He surfaced next to Rosemary and they swam off together without a word.

The girl shouted coarsely, 'What's your name?' And when he didn't reply, 'It's all right, I'll find out from Jem whatever-you-said. Gurnard.'

When Jem arrived that afternoon after school, Mark swore him to secrecy, but he knew it wouldn't do any good. The

248

girl had appeared to be the same age as they were, but she had the tough assurance of a forty-year-old woman.

When Jem said thoughtfully, 'D'you think she could be trusted to take the wheel?' Mark felt only deep resignation.

'What does it matter if you're never going to speak to her?' he asked.

'Oh. Ah. Yes. Anyway girls are no good on boats.'

Mark said unguardedly, '*She* would be. She's tougher than most boys.' He looked grimly at Jem. 'If you try anything with the *Forty-niner*, I'll half-murder you, d'you hear me?'

'How d'you think you'd do that, big-bonce?'

'Don't bother to find out. That's Philip's boat. It's all he's got.'

'It's my father's boat as well.'

'And it's all *he's* got too. Don't you dam-well forget it.'

Jem said no more. It was so unusual to hear Mark Briscoe say even a small swear-word like damn, that he was shocked into silence.

But obviously not for long.

The day before they went back home, with Mark's stumps well and truly healed, Madge looking pink in spite of the absence of sun, and Rosemary already planning strategies for her time at training college, the awful Yank girl with the crewcut jumped off the harbour wall and landed with a thud next to Mark's easel.

'Hi Mark.' Her grin of triumph nearly split her face in half. She got up, rubbed at her knees and sobered enough to say in robot tones, 'Mark Briscoe. Born 1945. Home town Bristol, England. Ambition, to live here and paint pictures every day.' She grinned again, flumped down by his side and surveyed his current work. 'Not bad,' she decreed. 'Where is it?'

'Hayle Towans,' he told her reluctantly. 'From Mennion House.' He should have told her to clear off straightaway, but he was proud of this painting. It had a Turner look about it. A huge sky, a vast land and sea mass and two tiny, distant figures.

'Who are the people?'

'I don't know. Anyone you want them to be.'

'I like that.' She turned her toothpaste grin on him again. 'Make the viewer work. That's what my father says.'

She wanted him to ask if her father was an artist and he wasn't going to. He began to clean his brushes and put everything away.

She said at last in slightly less confident tones, 'I'm Zannah. That's short for Susannah. I could have been Susie or Anna, but no-one can remember those sort of names. You can't forget Zannah. Can you?'

He rolled the brushes in rag.

'Did Jem tell you my name?'

'Yes.' She glanced at his face. 'I had to buy him six icecreams.'

'*Six*?'

'Choc ices. When he felt sick he had to tell me so that I'd go away.'

Mark would have liked to laugh. After all, right at the beginning of the month, he'd wanted something to happen.

'Did you talk about the *Forty-niner*?'

'His plan? Yeh. Not much of a plan. Just sneak on board, hoist the skull and crossbones and chug around the bay.'

'You've got a better plan, I suppose?'

She said crisply, 'Do it at night. Leave a thank-you note and a couple of dollars for the gas used. Keep everyone guessing.'

'Look. It's dangerous. I'm not bothered about you or Jem. It's the lugger. Philip Nolla is part-owner of it. Has been for about a hundred years.'

'We'll be okay. But if not, the insurance will buy something better. It's an old tub.'

Mark was furious. 'It's his *life*! You don't know anything about the Nollas! Etta is almost a witch – a good witch – and Philip went to Dunkirk in the *Forty-niner* and before that when he was about our age he went out on a rocket line to help with a shipwreck . . . you don't understand!'

She was impressed. 'You're real mad, aren't you? Your

hair looks redder than it did before. Listen, Jam Pilchard or whatever his name is, won't do it without you. So what's the ruckus about?'

She had the knack of killing his anger and making him want to laugh. Jam Pilchard. He must remember that one.

But he still said, 'Maybe not now. But if you work on him enough—'

'Listen, I can't *afford* any more choc ices! I'm broke now till Dad turns up again!'

He said grudgingly, 'You don't need choc ices.'

She was silent, wondering whether he'd given her a compliment or not. He followed up his advantage.

'I might have a go at it next summer.'

'Oh.' Sudden desolation was in her voice. 'I won't be here next summer. I have only ever other summer with Dad.'

Amazingly, he felt his spirits descend a little too. But then he rallied.

'All right. Not next summer then. We'll make a pact. We won't let Jem do anything about it unless we're both here. How's that?'

'Great.' She looked at him with her purple eyes. 'I've seen you before. When I was just a kid. I wanted to look at your painting. And ask you what it was like to have to sit still each day. I didn't have the nerve.'

'Oh.' There was nothing else to say to that, except that he was amazed to hear she ever lacked nerve.

She waited for a long time, staring at him, then she shrugged. 'Okay. So it's a pact.' She stood up. She was already taller than Ro and her arms had visible muscles. She wore boys' shorts and her legs were scarred. She wasn't a bit pretty but he still wanted to draw her.

'Well. So long then. See you in two years. I'll be fourteen then.'

'Same here.'

She began to walk up the slipway and then stopped and looked down on his painting.

'Y'know, that's real good. It's a bit like a Turner. I like it.'

And she went.

251

CHAPTER ELEVEN

1959

By the time the Briscoes arrived at the beginning of July, the work planned and organised by Clem and Madge the year before was complete. The Nollas showed off the tiny bathroom with some trepidation. It took a big piece off the end of the passage and they couldn't imagine why anyone except Mark would need a water-closet, a basin and one of the new-fangled shower things, right next to the kitchen.

'We 'ad all this – the old bath were better 'n this drippin' thing – down in the fish cellar. You 'ad no need to spend all your 'ard-earned money on such nonsense!'

Clem knew Etta wasn't ungrateful. He nodded his satisfaction. 'Very nice. They've made a good job of it.' He put a hand on the shawled shoulder. 'Save the sand going all over the house. You know how that's always got on your nerves.'

'Be an excuse for that Rosemary not to swill her feet down at the tap! That's what you really mean!' But she grinned up at him toothlessly. He seemed to get better-looking each year in spite of his hair thinning. She knew he was an important man too and though that mattered little to her, she was still proud that he chose to bring his family to her home year after year.

His hand tightened on her shoulder.

'Of course. That was the whole reason for having it done.' He grinned right back at her. 'Was it much of a nuisance? The workmen and so forth?'

'Went out and left 'em to it!'

'Said a prayer for them at Bright Hour, I hope?'

'Said a prayer for you more like! Throwing your money about like a lunatic.'

He was suddenly serious. 'Look here Etta, there's enough of that these days. If you ever need anything – *anything* – you're to let me know. Understand?'

She was well into her seventies, and was surprised and delighted that she could still quiver beneath the touch of a man. Her grin widened, and in the darkness of the passage her gums gleamed.

That evening they walked around the town, rediscovering it yet again with their usual deep satisfaction. They went through the Warren, skirted Porthminster beach and took the footpath as far as the 'crooked bridge' across the railway line. Then they turned back and went in the other direction; over the Island where the laundry was no longer put out to bleach because the summer visitors so often stole it, along the road which overlooked the wilds of Porthmeor beach, and finally up the footpath to Old Man's Head.

Mark's chair bumped ahead of all of them most of the way, as if he were trying to show off his – or its – prowess. Madge knew that was not the reason. Mark's innate sensitivity was still there; she wondered whether he was deliberately and consciously pushing Clem and herself together. Certainly he must know that it would be Rosemary who tore after his chair and Clem and she who brought up the rear. She glanced sideways at Clem and he met her eyes with his usual quick smile.

'Penny for 'em!' he demanded rallyingly, as her father would have done.

'Oh . . . I was thinking of Mark,' she nodded to where he was bouncing up the stony track towards St Nicholas' chapel on the summit of the Island.

Clem looked away again. 'Yes,' he said. Then added, 'Of course.'

She said quickly, 'What were you thinking?'

He gave her another quick smile, this time a wry one. 'I was looking at the gulls. Wondering whether their use

253

of the wind wouldn't be a better bet than our use of rocket fuel.' He shook his head. 'Trouble is, we tend to run out of wind after a few miles up.'

She had thought, when he started making his annual trips to the States, that it meant a new phase of their marriage. They were so close in many ways; a perfect partnership. Yet always there was Mark. She thought of Mark, and – perhaps as an escape from thinking about Mark – he thought about space travel.

He caught her hand and drew it through his arm.

'Sorry, darling. What were you thinking about Mark?'

'Oh, nothing much.' She wished she knew more about Clem's work. He couldn't talk about it, so much of it was 'top secret', but she wished she could make an intelligent comment now and then. 'Just his future. What it will be.'

'There will always be a place for him in the drawing office. You know that. His talent could be very commercial.'

'Yes,' she said doubtfully. 'It's not quite what he wants.' she knew what Mark wanted. It was to live away from them. And how could he do that? She thought with a terrible pang: if he stays with us, working for Clem, dependent on Clem at work and me at home, he will eventually dislike us both. And Clem too . . . Clem will always be burdened by a child that is not his . . .

'I know, Madge. But the training and the discipline will be good for him. And if he wants to work on his own stuff, we can make a studio for him . . . perhaps in the garden . . . How would that be?'

It was as if he were discussing a birthday treat for her. She swallowed.

'Yes. Marvellous. You're so good, Clem.'

'Rubbish.' But before he could add something like 'It's our son we're talking about' they rounded a rock and were face to face with a couple sitting on a bench enjoying the view. Madge's automatic smile of greeting widened almost immediately into recognition. It was Rose Care. And the man sitting by her could not possibly be one of her clients, either. It was old Martin Foster, the basket weaver who lived alone in Bunkers Hill since his wife died last year. How he managed no-one knew. He was blind and crippled with arthritis and as Etta said, 'We takes 'im meals, but there's more to life than eatin' and someone must be a-goin' in to 'elp 'im dress and undress and keep the 'ouse clean.'

Madge said, 'Rose. It's ages since . . .' She held out her hand. 'How are you?' She realised she hadn't seen Rose Care since that evening in the boathouse, the year of Mark's accident.

There was a moment of hesitation. Rose's dark eyes flicked from Madge to Clem and back again. She was still unsuitably dressed; her black two-piece and high heels would have been unremarked in Bristol's city streets; here they were merely an older version of her red dress. But she had lost her wanton look. Her hair was confined in a snood and she looked well-corseted.

She took Madge's hand. 'Well. This is a surprise.' Then, perhaps for Martin Foster's benefit, she said, 'Madge Bridges, isn't it? I remember you when you were just a little girl. We used to chat sometimes when I was minding Jim Maddern's donkeys.'

'Er . . . yes.' Madge swallowed again. 'It's Madge Briscoe now. This is my husband Clem.'

Rose said, 'Pleased to meet you I'm sure.' But Clem held out his hand, shook hers firmly and said. 'We've met before, Miss Care. You've forgotten. It was a long time ago, before Madge and I were married.'

'Really?' Rose tossed the information away from her with a flick of her gloved hand, and turned to her companion still seated on the bench. 'Do you know Mr Foster?'

The old man turned his dark glasses from one to the other and nodded solemnly. 'Any friend of Rose's . . . she's a good girl. A wonderful girl. I don't know what I'd have done without her this past year.'

Madge smiled again. Philip often said quietly in the face of Etta's condemnation, 'Rose Care 'as got 'er good side, and dun't you fergit it.' It was now obvious who was looking after Martin Foster.

255

Rose misinterpreted the smile.

'Nuthin' like that, Madge,' she said defensively. 'I'm just doin' a spot o' charring as you might say. Till Mr Foster can get 'imself fixed up with an 'ousekeeper.'

But Martin Foster had something to say about that. He stood up with difficulty and supported himself on Rose's shoulder. 'Charring indeed! Oh, she might do that as well. But she's more than that. She's made 'erself my eyes. And my ears too!' he chuckled. 'She's brought all the news o' the town inside my little place in Bunkers' Hill, so's I'm part o' the place agin!' He turned his glasses on Rose who was actually blushing. 'You might as well be the first to know. She's agreed to become my wife. An' I'm honoured. An' I'm proud.'

It was indeed touching. Madge felt tears in her throat and had to swallow yet again. There was a flurry of congratulatory chat. Clem pumped the old man's hand and told him how lucky he was. Madge found her voice and said it was marvellous, and wondered suddenly how Jim Maddern would feel about it.

'It's good that you will be back in St Ives too, Rose,' she said. 'May I call on you in Bunkers Hill?'

Rose, unusually silent through all this, shrugged with assumed carelessness.

'Up to you. I warn you, if you do, you'll be the only one!'

'Now, Rose,' cautioned old Martin.

'You don't know them like I do m'dear,' she said, patting his arm fondly. 'Like I said to you before, they'll all say I'm after your money.'

'My pension dies with me,' he came back promptly. 'An' whether you marries me or no, I'm still goin' to leave you the 'ouse! So you might as well make me an 'appy man in the time we got left!'

Rose gave Madge a resigned look. 'You see 'ow it is? 'E's wore me down!' And she threw back her head and gave one of her full-throated laughs.

It was the end of the exchange. In any case Rosemary was hallooing from the chapel steps and they had to move on.

Halfway up the steep incline, they stopped and watched as Rose led Martin Foster carefully through the jumble of rocks.

Clem said with a kind of thankfulness, 'So. Rose Care is going to be all right. Respectability at last. Who would have thought it?'

Madge said carefully, 'I didn't realise you knew Rose. Was that when you and Neville were boys?'

'No.' His eyes went from Rose to the soaring gulls, and she knew he wasn't thinking of space travel this time. 'It was after Neville's death. The summer we got engaged. Neville asked me to find her . . . if anything happened to him. Find her and tell her that he had really loved her.'

Madge remembered Rose saying with pride that Neville had been the only man who had asked her to marry him. And now there was Martin Foster.

She took Clem's arm and followed his gaze.

'D'you know,' she said, 'I should think one day we shall run out of rocket fuel. Then we shall have to come back to using the wind.'

He looked at her blankly for a moment, then gave a shout of sudden laughter. 'Madge, you're right! Trust you to see it so clearly! We've no choice really – absolutely no choice!'

They went on their way and began to discuss windmills.

The following Monday they made their obligatory visit to Mennion House. 'Let's get it over quickly,' Mark suggested. 'Then we can enjoy ourselves.' Rosemary said nothing, but she never missed these visits, boring though they were. Rory and Jan sent postcards but never any real news.

It was easier to deal with the Trewyns in the absence of the two boys. Without them Matthew and Mary Trewyn led pleasant, rather aimless lives, going their separate ways each day and coming together as infrequently as possible. Matthew was beginning to run to fat and he had less hair than Clem. Rosemary watched him covertly and thought he probably was Rory's father and hoped Rory wouldn't go the same way.

He caught her eye and smiled gallantly.

'More sherry, Ro? You could do with some colour in your cheeks! How is the teaching going?'

'I don't begin actually until September.' She avoided her mother's eye and accepted more sherry. 'I'm applying for posts in South Gloucestershire. Something with a house.'

'Where you can do your own entertaining, eh?'

'Well . . .' She had made friends of both sexes at college but nobody special. She had found Jan's desertion harder to bear than Rory's. Rory had always been as unpredictable as quicksilver; Jan just the opposite. Sipping her sherry now and simpering at Matthew Trewyn, she thought suddenly that if Jan returned and asked her to marry him, she would accept immediately.

She glanced at Mark and he responded as he always did. 'Any news of Rory and Jan, Mr Trewyn? Last we heard they were taking tourists around the Everglades in one of those boats with a propeller above the stern.'

'They've been everywhere, those lads. Done all the things most men talk about doing.' He went to the windows and looked out over the estuary. 'Don't suppose we shall see them here again. Too small for them. Too dull.'

'That's where you're wrong, my darling,' Mary Trewyn spoke up unexpectedly, a touch of acid in the endearment. 'They're coming home this summer, as a matter of fact. There was a letter at the beginning of the week which I left on your desk for you to read. Obviously you have been too busy.'

'Underneath all the bills I suppose? You put it underneath all the bills!'

'No. The bills have arrived since.'

Rosemary said in a high voice, 'Both of them?' Mrs Trewyn stared at her blankly. Rosemary amplified, 'Are they both coming home? Together?'

Mrs Trewyn relaxed slightly. 'Ah. Yes. Yes, apparently they are flying back with a friend of theirs who has chartered a plane. They will be together. They've always been inseparable.'

Rosemary looked again at Mark.

'Great,' he said enthusiastically. 'Shall we see them? I mean when are they arriving?'

'Oh yes, you'll see them. They're coming to see you actually. I can't quite remember what Rory said in the letter - Matthew, why don't you fetch it?'

He did so with the best grace he could muster and read it half aloud, half inaudibly, until Rosemary wanted to snatch it from him.

'Funny sort of place hm . . . hm . . . hm . . . like the creek at Lelant ten times over and twenty times hotter bla . . . bla . . . Thought we'd time our visit to coincide with the Briscoes' holiday so that we can catch up on all the news.' He looked up triumphantly. 'There. So we can expect them some time during the next three and a half weeks.' He skimmed the rest of the letter and folded it back into its envelope. 'Doesn't say why. Nor for how long. They've got another charter job in the autumn. Mediterranean.' He exploded suddenly. 'Why the hell don't they come home and settle down!'

'You just said what a great time they're having seeing the world, darling,' Mary Trewyn reminded him.

'I didn't say that exactly, my dear. I said—'

'I really think it's time we were going.' Madge stood up. 'Etta is expecting us back for lunch. Perhaps you'd care to come over with the boys when they're here? We could dine at the Tregenna perhaps?'

Rosemary got behind Mark's chair and for once he did not slap her hands away. She wheeled him out to the car and fussed about getting him inside as if he'd never done it before. Her mind seethed with questions, the main one being: why were they coming home together? Did that make it entirely casual, or just the opposite? Was it a holiday, or were they going to tell her something? Like goodbye.

Mark said gently. 'I'm all right now, Sis.'

She stopped tucking his rug around his waist and gave him a rueful smile.

259

'It will be so nice to see the boys again,' she confessed while her parents made their farewells.

'Both of them?' he asked.

'Yes. Oh yes. I've missed Jan more than I would have believed possible.'

He smiled back at her. 'Then you're going to have a good holiday, Ro.' He glanced back at the Trewyns standing well apart on the driveway. 'I hope,' he added.

They arrived a week later, presenting themselves at the door of Zion Cottage with a diffidence they'd never shown before. Then they had belonged to the place and it belonged to them; now they had the same status as the summer visitors. And they looked alike too; Rory had fined down slightly and Jan had filled out. Incredibly there was a smattering of grey in Rory's hair which lightened it; Jan's paleness had weathered, his spots had gone, his formal manner had relaxed. But he would not look at Madge directly, not even when he shook her hand.

There was no room in the parlour so they trickled down on to the harbour beach, Rosemary still behind the wheelchair. She had deliberately set herself to acquiring a tan over the past few days, and her eyes and hair were startling in comparison. It was the time of pale lip gloss too – fashion was conspiring in her favour. She looked stunning and did not even know it. In fact, faced with the two strangers who were Jan and Rory, she was terrified. She looked back and realised that at eighteen when she had ranted and raved and begged Rory to marry her, she had been just a child. She still felt a child; small and insignificant. She was educated just enough to know how little she knew, which was a good and humbling thing to recognise. Now, suddenly, it was demoralising as well as humbling. While she had been learning and theorising, these two men had been living and forging links between them which she knew nothing about, and might well never understand. It was as if they had fought a war together, side by side.

She trembled inside as she watched them. The quality

260

in Rory which had always wanted to protect Jan, was more pronounced. When her father said, 'Well, what do you think of the States?' Rory started to answer, then stopped himself. 'Go on. Tell Mr Briscoe what we thought of the States, Jan,' he said, grinning encouragement. And Jan, who had always been able to carry a conversation with his oddly foreign formality, mumbled some reply incoherently, then said, 'I haven't stopped feeling homesick yet.'

Rosemary knelt by Mark's chair so that their shoulders were touching. She knew that Jan had gone with Rory after he had talked to her, and her heart bled for him. To be constantly homesick for two years was ghastly. And it was her fault. She wished she could call back those two years and tell him she would marry him.

Rory turned to her directly. 'And what about you, Ro? Have you had a good time at college?'

Her heart began pounding away double-time.

Mark guffawed. 'She's found out what the word work means, Rory! I can vouch for that!'

'You lived at home?' He seemed surprised. Had he imagined her living the life of Riley in hall or something?

'Yes.' She cleared her throat. 'Fishponds is so near home it's not worth living in.'

'And you're qualified now? Or is it a three-year thing?'

'No. Two-year.' She shrugged. 'I don't know about qualified. I've got my certificate.'

Mark said, 'With a distinction in her principal subject too!'

'Well done!' Rory looked sincerely pleased. 'Many congratulations, Ro. I didn't think you had it in you!'

She knew his opinion of her only too well and her face warmed ashamedly. But Mark's biceps tightened with annoyance at the implied slight.

'She did one of her practices at my place,' he said in the same boastful voice. 'You should have seen her with the little ones. Drama. They made a Chinese dragon from parachute silk – dyed it and all themselves – then draped it over the wheelchairs – wow!'

261

Ro said, 'Come off it, Mark!' She made a face and tried to laugh. 'It wasn't that much of a success! Remember little Chrissie Williams?'

Mark laughed too and Rory said, intrigued, 'Tell me. What happened?'

Mark explained. 'He got carried away – thought it was a real dragon. He's only six.'

Rory grinned. 'I should have thought that reaction was a measure of your success, Ro.'

'Not *my* success. Theirs. They were terrific.'

'Will you try to get a job there?'

'Fat chance. I've not got any experience yet. I did a practice there solely on the strength of being related to Mark.'

'Useful having someone on the inside,' agreed Mark. He looked from Rory to his sister. 'There's Jem. Mind if I push off and see how he is, Sis?' He didn't wait for a reply. His motor hummed and he reversed up the slipway and along the wharf to where Jem capered and swung his satchel over his head. Ro and Rory faced each other.

'Well,' Rory said. 'It's certainly nice to see all of you again.'

'Yes. I'm glad you . . .' Ro brushed at the skirt of her sun dress. 'And your father says you're off to the Mediterranean next?'

'Just me. At the end of this month.'

'Jan's staying?'

'Yes. One way or another. He's staying.'

'One way or another?'

Rory looked at her consideringly for a moment, then took a quick breath. 'Whether he gets a job back in the firm or not, he's still staying here. He hasn't enjoyed it.'

'I gathered . . . I'm sorry.'

'Yes.' He seemed to make up his mind about something and said quickly in a low voice, 'Ro, be kind to Jan. He's in a helluva state.'

'Of course.' She too made a decision. 'Rory, I'm sorry. I didn't mean to send him away before. I didn't mean to hurt him. I promise I won't do that again.'

He shook his head. 'It wasn't that.' He looked at her. His eyes were black and unfathomable. 'Oh God. Ro. I can't tell you.' He shook his head again as if to clear it. She knew quite suddenly that there was still that indefinable something between them; and he knew it. Her heart jumped and started to pound again.

He said, 'It's the same situation, Ro. It's up to you. I can't make anyone else's decisions for them. Forgive me, my dear. It's up to you.'

It didn't make much sense then. She stored the disjointed words away for later examination and looked over at her father who had spoken her name.

'We were wondering about a picnic over at Porthmeor, Ro. How about it?'

She nodded with feigned enthusiasm. And noticed that Jan appeared to be studying her mother's ankles while Philip sat by her side as if guarding her.

Mark did not go with them. The sand was too soft for his chair at Porthmeor and the weather not warm enough for a long afternoon of sunbathing. He made a point of being by himself for part of each day, not only to achieve coveted independence, but to give his parents a break from the incessant burden of responsibility. Besides, he wanted to talk to Jem.

They sat in their usual place almost within the arm of Smeaton's Pier, on the old disused slipway. Behind them one of the many Porter boys was tarring the bottom of a rowing boat and the smell was heady and exciting. Mark watched Philip and Jem senior row themselves out to the *Forty-niner* in the dinghy, Philip standing in the stern with the single oar swaying rhythmically from side to side, while Jem leaned over to grab the mooring lines and pull them alongside. The way the rope emerged from the sea, dripping and weed-laden, was something Mark consciously tucked away for future paintings. There was a sound that went with it; a slapping, watery sound. But then, you couldn't paint sound.

Jem said sulkily, 'I don't see why you couldn't. I've watched you elbow your way down to the bloody sea often enough when you want to.'

For a moment Mark was confused, thinking of his picture. Then he tuned in to Jem's constant beef these days: the 'capture' of the *Forty-niner*.

'There's no point in it,' he said more curtly than usual. He remembered the plan the girl had; there was much more point to that, much more thrill. 'If it's a beating from your father you want, why don't you just go up and punch him on the nose?'

'Don't be crazy. I said it would be *worth* a beating! I don't *want* a bloody beating! It would be *worth* it!'

'What? Worth piling the *Forty-niner* on the rocks? Worth watching her go down? After all the work Philip and your old man have put into her?'

'She wouldn't go down – nor on the rocks. You an' me can manage 'er. We've done it often enough.'

'When Philip's around, yes.' He wished they weren't so near that tar. The smell made him want to jump out of his chair and run down to the sea and take the first boat he came to. Then he wondered how he knew what it would be like to run.

Jem said, 'You scared or summat?'

That was another thing; he'd like to do it just to show he could. Show himself. He couldn't master the tin legs, but you didn't need tin legs to swim out to a boat and haul yourself over the side.

He said shortly, 'Shut up Jem. Just shut up, will you?'

'Please yourself,' Jem came back sulkily.

They sat together in a lowering silence, staring at the *Forty-niner*, as she got under way, with a longing that verged on sheer lust. Mark wished he'd gone with the others now – this whole argument with Jem had gone past a joke and threatened their friendship. The silence was like a dead weight between them. It was pushing them apart and they couldn't seem to dispel it with the usual laughter or stupid remark. The old lugger swung out of sight around Smeaton's

264

Pier and Jem turned on his elbow away from the wheelchair and sifted sand through his fingers. Mark wondered how he could get away. Jem knew everyone was round at Porthmeor so it was no good saying he had to get back to them at the cottage. If only he had some money on him he could offer Jem an icecream, or a Cydrax at the Shell Cafe. Then, like an answer to a prayer, a voice broke into the simmering silence.

'Hi!' They looked behind them. Standing on the harbour wall was a girl in white shorts and yellow sun top. Her caramel-coloured hair was done in the fashionable urchin cut, and her glorious tan was set off to perfection by a number of silver chains: one round each ankle and wrist and half a dozen around her neck. She wore a lot of lipstick and eyeshadow and her finger and toe nails were painted crimson lake. They stared up at her goggle-eyed.

'Hi,' she said again. 'Have you forgotten me? I'm Zannah.'

'Christ,' commented Jem solemnly. And again, 'Christ.'

She jumped off the wall as agilely as she had done two years before. Her chains jangled as she landed between the boys. Mark winced, never able to understand why people used their legs so profligately. He said 'Hello,' and felt very young.

Jem said, 'I thought you were the same age as me?'

'I am. Fourteen. Well, almost fourteen.' She spoke to Jem but she turned and smiled widely at Mark. 'Thanks for waiting,' she said.

'Thirteen?' Jem was incredulous. 'Bloody hell. You look about thirty.'

'Thanks,' she said again, beaming on him too. 'Girls are always older than boys. Our psychology tutor told us that.'

Mark swallowed. Ro had had a psychology tutor; they were definitely for grown-ups.

He said to Jem, 'She's half American, don't forget.'

'Oh. Ah.' Jem looked across the girl's fantastic legs and met Mark's eyes. He signalled a truce. 'Does that mean they wear out quicker?' He tried to control his appreciation of his own wit and failed; he sounded like bath water running down a drain.

The girl said calmly, 'I'd rather wear out quickly and feel I'm doing something with my life than live to be a hundred and eight because I'm mostly vegetable!'

Mark wondered if she was referring to his static existence and felt his neck grow hot beneath the collar of his shirt. Jem, insensitive though he might be, drew her fire.

'You calling me a vegetable? You got a cheek turning up here like a field of dandelions and calling me a vegetable!'

'I thought I heard you discussing the same problem you were discussing two whole years ago,' the girl said coolly, ignoring Jem's allusion to her yellow sun top. 'So I have to assume you still haven't made a plan.'

It was the way she spoke as much as the long words. It made both boys feel gauche and ridiculous. Neither of them could think of a thing to say in return; she had assumed quite correctly. However, Mark thought that she certainly wouldn't want to participate in any schoolboy adventure now; she was far beyond juvenile piracy.

She waited, looking first at one, then the other, with the shadow of a smile on her long mouth. When nothing happened she sat forward in a businesslike way.

'Right,' she said. 'Okay. So we forget the joy-ride. And I think we'd better forget the thing I had in mind – we'd surely wreck the boat if we tried it at night.' But she sounded regretful. 'I think . . .' she paused until they both leaned forward in an attitude of attention. 'I think we wait for a storm. Or rather, just before a storm,' she added as Mark drew in his breath sharply. 'It'll be dead calm then for one thing. And for another it'll be almost dark. You'll take the wheel – ' she put her crimson-lake fingers on the arm of the chair – 'and we'll start up the engine and cast off. It'll be up to you to take us around the harbour buoy and back in again. During which time you can run up your skull and crossbones if that's what turns you on. I shall write a note and leave some money like I said.' She looked serious. 'The trick is, to get away without being seen. We can chuck you over the side before we drop anchor and you can swim around Smeaton's Pier and into the steps by the rocks. No-one will be around there if there's a storm brewing. We can hide the chair in the rocks and join you later.'

'Where do we go?' Jem asked.

'We split up. It's always best to split up when you're on the run. I'll go over to Porthminster. You can creep up the drain under the church. I've been through it just today. There's a manhole in the market place.'

Both boys were still dumb. She grinned her triumph.

'You see the beauty of it, don't you? You two will disappear immediately. Anyway no-one will suspect Mark – and you'll be behind enemy lines, Jem. If anyone's seen it will be me. And by the time they run round to Porthminster, I shall be a girl again and no-one will recognise me.'

Mark said, 'You're going to disguise yourself as a boy.' His confidence returned. 'I saw that film too. Wasn't it Joan Fontaine?'

She flushed angrily. 'Never mind that.' She turned to Jem, sensing where her allegiance would come from. 'What do you think?'

He stared and swallowed. 'Well . . .' He was reluctant to admit that she had taken over so completely. 'What do you think, Mark?'

'Same as I've always thought. Why d'you want to pinch the *Forty-niner* in the first place?'

'Because it's sort of *your* boat, so it's not really stealing,' the girl explained with exaggerated patience. 'If we're caught, no-one's going to prosecute us are they?'

Jem said, 'There'll be one helluva row. I think I'd rather go to gaol.'

'Shit,' commented the girl. And both boys gawped at her. 'Listen,' she went on reasonably. 'Do you want to live. Or do you want to exist,' They weren't questions but she waited for answers. When none came, she said, 'Talk it over. See you soon.' And she got up as gracefully as a deer and strolled off on her long slim legs with all the assurance of a woman of the world.

Jem said, 'Look at that. Did you hear what she said?'

'I've been here all the time, or hadn't you noticed?' Mark felt irritable still, but exhilarated as well.

'She said shit. She actually said—'

'I heard.'

'And that plan! She's got it worked out to the last detail! I don't fancy that drain.'

'Why not? It's big enough. And the cover is hinged.'

'All right for you. Get your backside up the steps and into the chair and who's going to suspect you?'

'No-one. Cos I'm not going to do it.'

'You'll do it. If she says so, you'll do it.'

Mark did not reply. He found he was imagining a dark, storm-filled sky and himself swimming for the steps just below Bamaluz Point. The escape would be the good part, the exciting part. The escape was what made the whole thing worthwhile.

Jem said, 'Reckon I'll go and have a look at that drain tonight. D'you think there's any rats up there?'

'Dunno.' When he was back in his chair he'd take time to look for the girl. She should have reached the sands by then. He must remember to put his father's binoculars in the pocket of the chair . . . He held on to his thoughts and looked down at Jem. 'We can't do it, Jem. Like she said, it's sort of our boat. We can't do that – risk the boat for a lark.'

'It's no risk. You're at the bloody wheel. You won't *take* any risks! Once round the buoys and that'll be it!'

'I'm not sure . . . I've always had Philip standing next to me. Besides if you don't moor her properly and there's a storm coming up—'

'You heard what she said! D'you want to *live*?'

'Yes. And I want to be able to look Philip in the eye too.'

Jem stood up.

'Listen mate. I'm going to do it. She an' me – we can manage it together if you won't come. In fac'—' he paused as if already regretting what he was about to say. 'In fac' we'll prob'ly manage it a damned sight better without you!' He looked away quickly from Mark's face. 'It'd be better if you came o' course — so's you know I ain't lying when I tell you all about it. But . . . you'd better agree to it tomorrow when she turns up. You'd just better.'

He turned and made off before Mark could reply; not that Mark could think of a thing to say. Jem had said it all: they would be better off without him.

For a long moment he wallowed in self-pity. Then he thought of how the girl had smiled at him and said, 'Thanks for waiting ' That was their secret; the pact they'd made two years before when they'd been kids, that was theirs. Mark grinned. He didn't know why he grinned, but he couldn't stop himself.

Rosemary was happier than she'd been in her life before. She was in the place she loved best in the world, and with the people she loved most. As she swam in the surf that afternoon, she looked from Madge to Clem, from Rory to Jan, and loved them all equally. Her long hair darkened in the water and streamed out behind her like seaweed. Back on the beach outside the tent, Etta laid out the picnic, the last representative of her grandmothers' generation. And then the *Forty-niner* chugged around the Island and pulled in as close to the swell as it could, so that they could all swim out to it and be pulled up on to its old-fashioned poop to sunbathe and dive in safety under Philip's cautious eye.

It was a glorious time. In spite of Rory's veiled hints, Jan made no special attempt to be alone with her; she had to make no choices, no decisions. But by the end of the day she had in fact made a big decision. She would no longer try to force events and she would let Rory go without any regrets. And if Jan still wanted to marry her, then so be it. He knew how she felt and if he was willing to accept the fact that she loved Rory first and him second, then it must be all right.

That night in the bed she had so often shared with one of her grandmothers, she thought about it more deeply and discovered something strange. Even if Rory begged her to marry him now, she could not. The realisation was so forceful that she sat bolt upright in bed to consider it. It was true. Rory was strong and self-sufficient; he could go away and make another life for himself somehow. But Jan . . . Jan was different. She understood now why Rory had been unable to claim her two years ago; Jan was intensely vulnerable. She lay back down slowly. It would make Rory happy if she married Jan; and it would make Jan happy too; and . . . yes, it would make her happy! She smiled at the dark ceiling and wondered why on earth she had been so against it all the time.

Having come to such a selfless conclusion, it was deflating when Jan continued to enjoy her company only when Rory and the others were around. He made no attempt to seek her out exclusively, and when Rory deliberately dropped out of a threesome, he said quickly, 'Let's look for Mark shall we, Ro? I haven't had a chance to really *talk* to Mark. He's so different now. Serious. Adult.'

'He's only just fourteen.' Rosemary was reluctant to lose her small brother and had not yet got used to the idea of him as a young man. So long as he was a child his terrible disability could be dealt with by a kind of indulgence; he could still be hugged and pampered with treats; his artistic talent was enough for him; his electric chair was almost a toy. As he grew older he would feel he had to try again with those rotten tin legs; and unless you were some kind of genius how could you earn a living with charcoal and paint?

They walked along to his usual place by Smeaton's Pier, but he wasn't there. Rosemary began to realise that Jan needed to find him so that he would not have to talk to her. The knowledge made her feel peculiar: rejected all over again.

She said, 'He might have gone to Lanham's for some new brushes. He said something about it at breakfast.'

They went on down Fore Street. People spoke to them, asked Jan how he was. A wizened seaman who knew them because of Philip, said they made 'A pretty enough couple', and Jan laughed. 'That is good for you, Rosemary, but not for me, I think.' Rosemary flushed and hurried on.

270

Humiliation followed rejection. She thought of all the girls the two boys must have met on their two-year old adventure. She muttered aloud, 'Oh God,' and Jan said, 'What did you say, Ro?'

'Nothing.'

They found Mark in the market place just by the war memorial. He seemed to be studying the ground.

'What on earth are you doing?' Rosemary's voice was sharper than she had intended. Drooping over the arm of his chair like that, he looked utterly dejected, not like the contented boy he had always been. She tried not to imagine what adulthood must look like from his level.

He was startled out of a deep reverie.

'I . . . nothing, Ro. Absolutely nothing.' He switched on his chair and glided away from a large manhole cover. 'Where are you two going? May I join you?'

'Let's find a cafe without a step and have some coffee,' Jan said practically. They went on up the High Street like a royal procession and were welcomed into the Snuggerie in Gabriel Street with easy familiarity. There weren't that many eating places in St Ives which could admit a wheelchair. Mark felt in the breast pocket of his jacket, extracted three separate shillings and lined them up on the polished oak table.

'I'm paying,' he said expansively. 'Baps and cream all round.'

Jan grinned, relaxed now. 'You have come into money?'

'I bet Jem something. And I won.' Mark shoved forward one shilling. 'My stake.' He touched another coin, 'My winnings. And – ' he picked up the last coin – 'my meagre earnings.'

'Earnings?'

'You haven't heard? A man came up to me on the harbour when I was painting. Offered me this bob for doing a sketch of his kid.'

'That is good, Mark.' Jan smiled congratulations. 'But you must let me pay for this treat. Rory and I are rich after Florida, you know.'

271

Mark ignored this. 'The joke of it was,' he went on, 'The bloke would never have asked me to do it if I'd been standing up at an easel. Or if I'd been ten years older. So let's make the most of it while we've got it.'

Jan looked at Rosemary and she in turn looked at Mark. Bitterness was foreign to him, but there was no mistaking his tone.

She said softly, 'If you really thought he was giving money to a cripple, why did you take it?'

'Why not?'

She realised that since they had met him in the market place his whole attitude had been slightly aggressive.

She said, 'You've had a row with Jem.'

Jan, unused to their mental shorthand, was completely bewildered. He caught the eye of the waitress and ordered coffee and baps while an incipient quarrel brewed at his elbow.

'None of your business, Sis.'

'Yes it is. You're my brother.'

'What's that got to do with it?'

'And I'm five years older than you.'

'Also I'm a cripple. That's what you really mean, isn't it?' The word 'cripple' had stuck in his throat; he knew she had used it to snap him out of any self-pity, but it lay between them like something obscene.

Jan made room on the table. 'Here we are. Baps, cream, jam . . .' the bill fluttered across the polished surface and Mark snatched it up. 'And coffee.' Jan looked helplessly at the two of them. Mark was red-faced with anger; it was a rare sight. Jan wondered what could have happened. Something obviously had.

Rosemary said pacifically, 'You know I didn't mean that. What I mean is – I'm concerned about you—'

He didn't hear. 'I don't interfere in your life, do I? So why the hell do you imagine you can interfere in mine? Just because you can walk and run doesn't mean you're much good at *people*, Sis! Does it? You've only got to look at Jan to see how much good you are at *people*!'

The whole silly argument was nonsense, but Rosemary still did not relish public examples of her ineptness with relationships.

She said, 'Shut up Mark. Just shut up, will you?'

'You see? You don't like it! You're dithering away between Jan and Rory – can't see the wood for the trees – and all the time you've got no choice! Jan's been in love with Mother since he was my age – he doesn't want to marry you! And Rory—'

Rosemary stood up with a small gasping scream.

'Mark! I said shut up! How dare you – how *dare* you—'

Jan too got to his feet.

'Rosemary, that is not true. There was an attraction – schoolboy attraction – but in the last two years—'

'I'm going. No, I don't want you to come with me, Jan. And I certainly don't want you, Mark! Stay here and eat the baps! And I hope they choke you!'

She left hurriedly. Her chair collapsed on its side as she pushed past; by the time Jan had righted it and shaken his head at the waitress then smiled apologies at the other customers, she had disappeared. He sat down again.

'Mark. You should not have spoken those words. They are words to be thought, never spoken.' He looked seriously at the round young face opposite him. Mark was as white now as he had been red before; even his wiry auburn hair looked flattened.

He said in a small voice, 'I'm sorry, Jan.'

Jan did not reply. After a while he poured coffee, and by the time he had stirred sugar into his, the normal hum of conversation offered a spurious privacy.

He said heavily, 'I have wanted to die. Often in the last two years . . . I have tried to die. Rory would not permit it.'

Mark looked sick. 'I didn't know. Didn't realise . . .'

'Rory thinks it will be all right if I come back and marry Ro. I will be . . . settled. Ro and your mother will be able to give me new life. You must know that I have always loved your mother – even as a small boy. She gives life – never takes it away. And Ro is charming and happy. We have been close – we had *rapport* since we were small children.'

Mark ventured a question. 'Do you love Ro?'

'Ah. Love. It is more than love. It is a need. Perhaps one day you will understand, Mark.'

'And Ro? How does Ro feel about you, Jan?'

To Mark the whole thing was so obvious: Ro loved Rory and Rory was trying to force her on to Jan.

'That I will discover,' Jan said in his ponderous way. 'Rory has a plan. It is like a child's game. Harmless and innocent. But it will help Ro to make up her mind.' He smiled bleakly. 'It will help me also. I am to be the champion knight, claiming the hand of the fair maiden!'

Mark leaned across the table until his head almost touched Jan's.

'For Pete's sake. What has Rory cooked up now?'

'Oh, it is nothing. Nonsense. Ro will climb to Old Man's Head and the one who reaches her first . . . Rory has told me the proper way to climb so therefore I shall be first there. You see, Mark, Rory is very fond of your sister. He wishes her to marry someone who will care for her properly. We shall marry and we shall be happy.'

Mark drew back his head and surveyed Jan incredulously.

'I think Rory is a shitbag!' he said, as much to shock Jan out of his fatalistic attitude as anything. It was a word beloved by Zannah and it certainly had impact. Jan looked up, startled. Mark said, 'He doesn't want to marry Rosemary himself, but he doesn't want anyone else to have her except you. Christ. It's as if he's trying to put her in cold storage!'

Jan stared in horror. 'It is not like that at all, Mark. You do not understand. Rory wants only what is best for everyone. When I said he would not permit me to die, I should have told you that once he saved my life. The Everglades are the natural home of the alligator. We had taken a party off the beaten track and—'

Mark said, 'I don't want to hear about how marvellous Rory is. He knows it – you've told him often enough, I expect.' Mark visibly simmered. 'The thing is, Ro isn't going to get much out of his great plan, is she? And neither is poor old Mum.' He leaned forward again. 'I reckon the best thing you two can do is clear off to your alligator-infested swamp again! Play at being pirates or whatever Rory thinks he is! Leave us to get on with real life!'

Mark switched on his motor and backed out of the Snuggerie with much bumping and manoeuvring. Jan made no move to help him. After Mark had gone and the cafe had once more settled down, he picked up the bill and the three separate shillings and signalled to the waitress.

'Oh dear. Was something the matter with the baps, sir?' she asked.

'No. We were not hungry after all,' Jan replied.

The waitress gathered the things on to a tray and said sympathetically, 'Don't worry sir, it's the weather. There's a real big storm brewing up. Gets everyone on edge, doesn't it?'

'That must be it.' Jan felt a certain relief at her mundane explanation for the unprecedented furore of the morning. 'Yes, of course. That must be it.' He stood up, anxious now to get back to Mennion House and find Rory. The sooner they left the better. Mark was right, it was the only thing to do; if they stayed they were going to mess up a lot of lives.

Ro did not put in an appearance for Etta's midday offering of boiled mutton and dumplings.

Etta said, 'What can I do with her dinner? I cain't a-bear waste!'

'Warm it up for her tea?' Mark felt guilty now; the emotional mess he had uncovered boded ill for Rosemary.

'No-one on God's earth kin warm up dumplin's!' Etta snapped. 'They'd end up bullets, they would.'

Clem said, 'She'll be glad of them even so, Etta. There's going to be a storm and a half this afternoon and if she's gone for a walk she'll come in soaking wet, you see.'

Thunderclouds were piling up on the edge of the sea, sure enough, and the light was poor. Mark glanced nervously through the window.

'Aye.' Etta was mollified as always by Clem. 'I'll leave 'n in the saucepan then and you can warm it all up when you've a mind to. It's Bright Hour's afternoon and after that I'm taking tea with the minister and 'is wife.'

Clem waggled his eyebrows and he and Madge laughed while Etta pulled her mouth in. Mark concentrated on spooning up all his swimming gravy.

Philip put his head round the door.

'Jem and me's going to get the *Forty-niner* in the lee of Wheal Dream,' he announced. 'She's too far out with this storm a-comin' up and there's not enough water in the harbour to float her in there.'

'Wheal Dream?' Mark lifted his head. 'You won't be able to see her from there.' Wheal Dream was behind Smeaton's Pier, within easy reach of the steps in the rocks.

'They'll see 'er from the seaman's mission 'all,' Philip grinned reassuringly. 'Any'ow, the way we shall anchor 'er she wun't pull herself away, never fear.' He peered through the window. 'Flat calm now too. Will be for a coupla hours.'

Mark looked at his plate and wondered whether Jem and Zannah were capable of anchoring her solidly again when they got back. He had a momentary vision of the *Forty-niner* smashing herself up on the rocks around the Island. Not that Jem would do it. If he didn't have the nerve to enter the drain this morning, he wouldn't risk being caught by his father.

When they were alone Madge said worriedly, 'I wonder just where Ro has gone? She never misses popping in at midday even if she can't manage to eat anything. Did she put her watch on this morning?'

Mark tried to visualise Rosemary's wrist but all he could see was a mass of silver chains.

'I don't think she did,' he said. 'But don't worry, Ma. We had coffee and baps in the Snuggerie not long ago. Probably just the thought of dumplings was too much for her.'

'Did she have baps?' Madge looked surprised and pleased. 'I wish you'd get her to do that every morning, darling. She's much too thin.'

'Not as thin as you are!' Clem protested. 'You haven't changed since the day you agreed to marry me!'

'Oh I have.'

Madge gave her gentle smile and Mark tried to look at her objectively. Whatever his father said, she did not look young. She looked sort of ageless; like the paintings they'd been to see in the National Gallery by Rembrandt. She had a way of looking at something no-one else could see.

He said abruptly, 'Would you mind if Ro got married to Jan?'

They turned to him, surprised, perhaps even shocked. He had a momentary twinge of sheer embarrassment in case Jan's crush on his mother was what his father called 'an issue'. Then his father laughed and said, 'Well, we've always thought Jan and your mother might make a match of it one day!'

And his mother said more seriously, 'Oh, don't laugh at the boy, Clem! But Rosemary and he . . . they're not right for each other. Not really. It's a sort of pretend-thing with both of them.'

'I agree.' Clem stopped laughing. 'Have they said anything to you, old man?'

'No. At least I don't think so. I rather got the idea – in the Snuggerie – that something was in the wind. I wondered how you'd take it.'

'Ro's too young,' Clem declared. 'I know she's older than you were, Madge, but that was too young anyway. And Ro . . . Ro wants too much from life.'

Madge said nothing; she looked down at her hands and twisted her wedding ring round her finger.

Mark persisted. 'But wouldn't you mind? I mean, if it happened, would you mind?'

Clem said slowly, 'I don't think so. They've known each other for years. I used to think that Ro's attraction for Jan was that she'd come with a ready-made family!' He smiled. 'But since the American trip with Rory, he seems very much more . . . detached. What do you think, Madge?'

She did not look up. 'Yes. He is detached. Certainly.'

277

But she did not say more, and Mark knew that she minded very much whether Jan and Ro were married or not.

They wanted an afternoon nap and he got them to lift him down to the courtyard before they went upstairs. He insisted that he would go into the fish cellar when the rain started, and at last they gave in. The sky was lurid purple and yellow ochre; he could smell danger. They seemed oblivious to it.

He made straight for the old ruined pier at the side of Wheal Dream. His chair whined louder as he took it down the long ramp. The *Forty-niner* was already close beneath the coastguard's lookout, anchored fore and aft and moored to a buoy as well; there was no sign of Philip or Jem senior, but the dinghy was well up on the shingle so they had gone long since. The water was still calm, but there was a glassiness to its surface, and now and then it lifted on an uneven swell as if shifting position uncomfortably. There was a breathless, waiting quality to the ominous, early darkness; even the air seemed to be thickening.

He stopped the chair and the silence was complete; not even the gulls called that afternoon, no-one was about. It could be all right; Jem had been scared by the prospect of the drain; Zannah had been recalled to Penzance and her careless father. Mark was ready to laugh with sheer relief, when they stood up from the tumble of rocks by the steps and waved at him. His heart sank. Zannah had greased her hair flat and scraped off every trace of makeup. The silver chains were gone and she wore long khaki shorts and a dirty vest. She looked like any of the local boys; she looked like Jem's younger brother.

When she left the Snuggerie, Rosemary's instinct was to hide. She ran down to the High Street, then along Fore Street and left into the Digey. She had no idea where she was going, but the town was packed with holidaymakers and she needed emptiness. The only place she would get that was along the stretches of Porthmeor.

The tide was out as far as it could go and the sun was

almost covered by massed thunderclouds. Where there were gaps it beamed through like a searchlight, hitting the sea angrily and adding to the menace of the coming storm. Rosemary surveyed the beach almost frantically. People were packing up their towels and deckchairs and moving off; she could go into one of the beach tents and cry to her heart's content. It wasn't quite what she had in mind; she remembered the scene in the Snuggerie and wanted to die. It would serve Mark and Jan and Rory right if she died here and now. She could run out to the tideline and keep running . . . except that she was such an excellent swimmer. But presumably that was the bliss of drowning, you swam until you were exhausted then sort of floated into death like going to sleep.

She tore down the sands at full pelt, her sandals squelching in the pools, her pony tail bouncing hard on her neck. Halfway down she was forced to stop and touch her toes in an effort to get rid of a chronic stitch in her side. Then on she went again and full tilt into the water. It was difficult swimming in her clothes but that was good because it would tire her out all the sooner. In fact she was tired already. There was no surf and she rolled on to her back to float over the swell and get her breath, only to find her water-logged clothes pulling her under. She fought her way to the surface and sucked in an enormous gulp of air; there was a horrid pain in her chest. She struck out for the shore and felt only deep thankfulness when her sandals touched bottom. Drowning was obviously a much more difficult business than she'd realised, and she waded out of the water and lay on the sand face down until the pain went. And then she walked slowly up the beach to their tent, undid the strings, went inside and started to cry.

She was still there, gazing bleakly out at the lurid sky and seascape, when Rory arrived an hour later. She had not seen or heard him coming and she gave a little scream when his face appeared around the edge of the fly sheet.

'It's okay – okay—'

'Is Jan with you?'

279

'No.'

'Oh God . . .' She put her face in her hands and wept again.

He took in the state of her, from tangled damp hair to soggy sand-filled shoes, and got himself inside the tent to put an arm around her shoulders. Immediately, with a wail of despair she turned into him and the next moment he had her properly in his arms, her wet, salty, clothes soaking his shirt, her hair in his mouth and nostrils.

'I can't bear it – I can't *bear* it!'

'It's all right, Ro. All right.'

'You don't understand! You don't know what happened!'

'Jan told me. I came straightaway on the next train. I thought you'd go to the cove. You know, where I . . . you know. Then I heard a sound from the tent.'

'I never thought of the cove! Even then you treated me like dirt! That's what I feel like – dirt! I tried to drown myself—'

'Ro!'

'I did! But I couldn't! I feel like dirt – I had to clean myself, but even now . . . I felt like dirt *that* day too! You've always treated me like—'

He kissed her to shut her up at first, and then he couldn't stop because he'd always wanted her and tried to stop wanting her and now he was practically honour-bound to prove to her that he wanted her. And then he stopped thinking and Rosemary stopped wailing. There was a desperation about their love-making: Rosemary was quite certain she would regain a sense of her own worth: Rory knew that Jan was waiting at the top of the cliff path. The shorts and knickers came off as easily as they had done more than ten years ago. Both of them were panting and clutching at each other frantically; the whole thing was over in less than two minutes. For Rosemary it was a promise, a contract, an engagement. She held him to her, murmuring endearments.

He said, 'You've done that before, haven't you?'

She did not stop murmuring immediately; it took a second for his question to register. And then she remembered the finals dance at college: the girls she admired for their assurance and confidence, looking at her in amazement – 'You mean you're a virgin? You actually haven't? My dear, what on earth is a teaching certificate worth if you haven't learned about *that*!'

She opened her eyes and looked at Rory. He hadn't been transported as she had; she had thought they'd gone somewhere together but apparently not.

She whispered, 'How can you ask that at a time like this?'

'Tell me the truth.'

'I haven't done *that* before. No.'

'But something pretty close to it.'

She felt so tired she almost didn't reply, then he got to his knees and pulled her up.

She said, 'Oh Rory. There was someone's brother at the college dance . . . it was nothing. And if you can ask me that, then you've obviously done it before and know. Don't let's spoil it for each other.'

'No. I'm sorry.'

He smiled and began to help her to dress. He was tender and gentle and she almost cried. Something was wrong somewhere and she didn't know what it was.

They went outside to a darkening day that should have been exciting. The beach looked abandoned; half-finished sandcastles ringed the tent, a paper flag on top of a mound was beginning to flap.

'Let's run down to the sea!' Rosemary remembered one time when she and her father had immersed themselves fully clothed; it had had a wonderful, renewing effect.

'We'd better get back, Ro. It's going to empty down in an hour.'

'That gives us time . . . Rory, we need to do something to celebrate! Come on!'

She would have run but he held her back.

'Ro, I'm sorry. I shouldn't. Even if you have done it before, that's no excuse. I'm sorry.'

'It was nothing. What they called heavy petting at college. You were the first.' She looked up at him and saw dismay in his black eyes. 'Rory, it's all *right*. Honestly.'

'No, it's not. You see, Ro . . . oh God . . . Jan is waiting for us at the top of the cliff. We're going to walk along to Old Man's Head. He's going to—'

There was a loud halloo from behind them and there was Jan coming down the path, smiling and waving theatrically.

Zannah said steadily, 'We're going without you if we have to, Mark. It's up to you.'

'I shall go straight back to the cottage and tell Philip.'

'No you won't,' she replied confidently.

'You can't do it,' he repeated for the ninth time.

'Of course we can. Ideal conditions. They've even put the lugger in a more convenient place.'

'You'll never tie her up securely again when you get back. You can see it's going to be a helluva storm.'

Jem said, 'Oh let's get on for Chrissake. By the time we get back it's going to be as black as pitch, and I don't fancy that bloody drain in the dark.'

'If you couldn't go along it in broad daylight this morning with me sitting on top of the manhole cover the other end, how d'you think you'll do it now?' Mark snapped.

'I did do it this morning, clever dick. When I lifted up the bloody cover you weren't bloody there!' He snorted. 'It'll be easier now if anything. There's no-one about for a start so I'll be able to get out without any trouble. And don't forget you owe me a bob!' he added.

Zannah suddenly leaned over Mark's chair.

'You were keen on the idea this morning,' she said. 'What happened?'

He couldn't explain about the awfulness of Jan and Rosemary and how it made their escapade seem stupid and dangerous and downright selfish. He remembered years ago how Rory had treasured a piece of a boat he'd wrecked; would it come to that? The dear old *Forty-niner* reduced to driftwood?

Zannah gave up waiting for a reply and straightened with

282

a sigh. She looked marvellous dressed as a boy; more feminine if anything.

'Come on Jem. Let's get cracking!' She ran down the rocks without pausing to look back again. Her legs were strong and brown, her bare feet so assured and confident. Jem followed just as agilely, but Mark had seen him bound around for years. His envy, his damp eyes, were for Zannah, not Jem.

They dived off the end of the little headland and sported around in the dark sea for a few minutes like porpoises. Mark switched on and went as far as he could along the broken pier. Jem surfaced and made rude signs at him, then swam after Zannah. The plan was for them to fool any watchers by swimming towards the harbour, then diving and making for Wheal Dream under water as far as they could. They got as far as one of the red buoys and clung to it, looking back towards the land, then Zannah nodded her seal-like head at Jem and released the buoy. He grabbed at her and pulled him to her. Mark watched with open mouth. He was kissing her. She was laughing and letting him. It had happened before. God . . . that was why she'd got him so completely under her thumb. Oh God . . .

They dived and were gone. He threw off the rug that covered his stumps, tore at his shirt buttons. He hated Jem with an intensity that gave him enormous energy. He left his vest tucked into his pants; it would give him protection if he scraped the rocks. He took his chair back fifty yards, then went into forward gear and steered for the end of the the pier. They came up for air, saw him, waved and went under again. And then the chair, with him in it, was sailing through the air.

There were no rocks and he'd done this sort of thing often before with Ro pushing him. His chair would be gone for ever but he didn't care about that. He needed to be intact himself; that was all. Once in the water he was Jem's equal. And he and Jem had been spoiling for a fight for years.

He caught them as Zannah was clambering on to the old tyres that served as fenders along the lugger's sides. Jem was gulping in the air, waiting his turn to scramble aboard, when something grabbed his ankle and dragged him down. He shouted and there was a quick flurry of water before he disappeared. Zannah crouched where she was, staring in horror. She had not long to wait before discovering what had taken her confederate. Both boys broke water fighting fiercely, Jem flailing punches anywhere, Mark's head under Jem's chin, driving his fists into Jem's chest with the dull rhythm of a machine. Jem used his knee to thrust away and his hand caught Mark's ear. The two of them went under.

Zannah screamed, then raised herself sufficiently to look over the lugger at the land. Nobody seemed to have noticed anything. She got one leg over the side and tumbled after it, crouching low and listening for a hail of enquiry. Nothing. Unexpectedly the boat lifted on a big swell and she felt the first of the rain. She raised her head and saw the swell pile into a wave which crashed on to the shingle. The boat rolled the other way against its mooring line and she had to hang on to the side to avoid being tipped out. The boys came up within arm's reach. Jem had his hands in Mark's hair but it seemed to make little difference to Mark's butting power. His forehead went into Jem's chest with the monotony of a pile-driver. For a split second she looked into Jem's up-tipped face and shouted, 'Give up!' then the old lugger yawed back again and she went crashing against the engine casing as the boys submerged.

Twice more it happened. Each time they surfaced, Jem shrieked, 'Pax! For Chrissake – pax!' But Mark had gone beyond words. All the frustration of today – of a lifetime – went into that fight. He thought he might drown them both, but he wanted to know, when they got to the pearly gates, that Jem had drowned before he had.

By the third roll, Zannah was desperate. She had shrieked herself hoarse and nothing had happened. It was obvious that all their careful ploys to ensure secrecy were a waste of time; everyone had gone indoors to await the storm and the coastguard was probably drinking tea and thinking his busy time wouldn't be for another hour. She saw that Mark did not care any more and that Jem was at his last gasp. So on the third roll she was ready with the boat hook. It was possible she would fetch blood on one of the boys, but the hospital could deal with that and there wasn't much they could do for drowning.

But luck was with Jem at last. He saw the hook and let go Mark's hair to grab it. He couldn't have held on for long, but the sea was an unexpected ally: the boat rolled back on the swell which pushed the boys up its side. For a moment they were suspended, Mark's head thumping a little less vigorously into Jem's chest, Zannah crouched by the engine casing pulling frantically and Jem getting air into his starved lungs in time with Mark's head movements. The boat hovered and began to roll them back into the sea. Zannah leapt forward and seized Jem's arm, leaned over and got his leg. He rolled into the boat holding Mark to him like a lover.

They walked to Old Man's Head because that was the way Jan went, and Rory followed him so Rosemary came after, unable to walk away from Rory now. She knew the boys had cooked up some plan between them and that it must be pretty awful and pretty serious because of Rory's panic down on the beach. But whether he felt guilty or not, he couldn't blot out those two minutes of heaven in the beach tent. It was still awful about Jan, but it had to be all right now, it just had to be.

Jan was talking practically all the time, pausing on the path by the putting green to throw back at them some gem about the purple sky. Once he started to say something about Mark painting a storm sky, then stopped abruptly. When they got out on the cliff top proper, they walked abreast and Rory joined in the unnatural

285

conversation and tried to include Rosemary.

'D'you remember we used to clamber all round these rocks, the three of us? We've had some great times. The terrific trio.'

Rosemary smiled and held out her hand, but he did not take it.

'It will always be like that,' Jan said emphatically. 'Whatever happens, wherever we go, we shall meet here again and be happy.'

'Rather! What do you say, Ro?'

She looked sideways at the two of them and noticed to her surprise that Jan was taller than Rory now.

She said, 'You're trying to tell me that you're both going away again. Is this whole act meant to be a farewell scene?'

Rory said urgently, 'I'm going, Jan's staying. You know that, Ro.'

'Yes. But I thought after—'

'After what Mark said in the Snuggerie this morning? You surely didn't take that seriously? For goodness' sake, Ro – we both adore your parents, that goes without saying. You've met my adopted ma and pa so you can imagine how we feel about . . .' He wouldn't look at her, wouldn't let her speak in case she said something about their love-making in the tent just now. The familiar pain began in her chest again. And the familiar anger too.

She said tightly, 'Let's forget it, shall we?' and hoped he would read the double meaning in her words. He'd probably forgotten it already. She never would. It was true that she had been 'dithering about', as Mark so elegantly put it, before, but not any more. She knew again what she had known two years before. She loved Rory and he loved her.

He said, 'Right. That's fine. Okay, Jan?'

'Okay. Fine. I apologise Ro, if there has been any embarrassment—'

'No need for apologies, old man! You heard what

she said. We forget it. Back to where we were before. Okay?'

'Okay.' But it seemed he had run out of words and would have turned back for home except that Rory kept walking.

They came to the Head, balanced precariously on a bed of rocks, looking apparently into the eye of the coming storm.

'This is one we never did. Philip showed you how to climb it, didn't he Ro?'

She looked at him and forced him to look back at her. His eyes were narrowed as if in pain.

She said directly, 'When are you going on the next job?'

'Tomorrow.' He took a short breath. 'That's . . . if I go.' Her heart leapt, but he turned away and grabbed Jan's arm. 'I've got an idea. Seriously. Ro – climb up on to the Head. Go on – do it now!' He looked back at her and said urgently, 'Please!'

She didn't want to. She knew she should turn and walk back home with dignity and show them that she needed neither of them. But there was that urgent 'please' . . . and before that there had been the tent.

She said, 'It's ridiculous. Anyone can climb it. I'll show you and you can do it if you're so keen.'

'No. We're not going to watch you. Just do it.'

Jan said nothing. He was staring at the ground. Rory's eyes were black holes looking at her.

She kicked at a stone with her sandy damp sandal. 'Oh . . . all right. This is all nonsense. I'll climb it, then I'm going home. I'm hungry.'

They kept their backs to her as if it were a game of hide-and-seek and she went further along the cliff and clambered over the strewn rocks until she found the ledge with her feet. She remembered her mother telling her of the first time she'd done the climb, the excitement of it, the challenge which, once met, was not there any more. Philip was wise; he knew that until it was done it was

287

a danger, once it was done it was safe. She smiled as her hands found the finger rocks; Philip had sworn her to secrecy and she had kept that particular promise. It was surprising that Rory and Jan, being 'local', did not know the smugglers' way, but she was glad she'd never told them. They'd look till the storm came and never find it.

It took five or six minutes to crawl along the top and look over, and she was surprised to see Rory and Jan in exactly the same positions as when she had left; Jan had not lifted his head an inch. She hallooed and they turned in unison like puppets and stared up at her.

'Okay? Satisfied?' She was still on her knees and even so the height made her dizzy. 'I'm coming down now.'

'Wait!'

Rory held up a hand and came closer to the base of the rock. After a quick glance up at her, Jan looked back to the ground. Rory stood directly beneath her and tilted his head right back to look at her.

'Ro. Please wait there. Please. You won't like this – we knew you wouldn't like it, but we couldn't think of another way. Try to understand. We both love you – you must know that. We both want to marry you, Ro. It's always been like we said – the three of us. And it can't be any more, can it?' She made to speak and he held up his hand again. 'Ro, listen. We didn't know what to do – not so long ago we could have fought a duel, couldn't we?' He tried to laugh. 'But there had to be some way to decide.'

Rosemary interrupted fiercely. 'Isn't that up to me? And haven't I made it quite clear anyway? What about just now – in the tent—'

Jan's head did not move but Rory said quickly, 'Of course it's up to you, Ro. We know that. But we also know that you can't make a decision because you love both of us. If you choose me, what happens to Jan?' His eyes held hers commandingly. He did not follow through with a query about his fate if she chose Jan. She swallowed, half convinced in spite of herself. At least some of the humiliation was assuaged; they both loved her.

She said, 'Well?'

She saw his Adam's apple move convulsively.

'We know there's a way up there, but we don't know where it is. The first one to join you . . .' his words petered out. He didn't have the nerve to say, 'The first one to join you, gets you,' but that was what he meant. She did not know whether to laugh or cry. It was so typical of Rory's sense of the dramatic. It was funny and it was sad and it was insulting. But if it was his way of 'claiming' her, then none of that mattered. He was more ingenious and much more athletic than Jan was. He had been born among these rocks; he would find the way. Poor Jan. But even poorer Rory. He could not find a way to tell Jan the truth, that he and Rosemary already belonged to each other. He had to do it like this; make a game of it.

He held her gaze for one more agonising moment, then took her silence for consent.

'Come on then, old man! Who's going to win the princess?'

He spoke rallyingly and indulgently as if to a child. Jan seemed to be trapped in a world of his own and apparently did not hear him. Rory went to him and took his arm and said something in a low voice that Rosemary could not hear. And at last he looked up and after a while reluctantly nodded. Rory gave him a little shove. Rosemary leaned over the edge to see better; Rory's shove was in the direction of the cliff. Away from the rock. The way she had come herself.

It need not mean anything significant; it could simply mean that they had decided to reconnoitre for an easy way up. But when Rory ripped off his pullover, waved it over his head and charged straight for the smooth and unclimbable inland face, she was almost certain. He had seen other people atop the Head, he must know they never tackled it this way.

While he scrabbled among the tumble of supporting rocks

289

beneath, she looked at the top of his head and remembered the feel of his hair beneath her hands not an hour ago. She remembered how they had clung together, devoured each other, as if they were about to be parted for ever. She remembered Rory's guilt immediately afterwards and the way he had tried to make the whole thing cheap by asking her if she'd done it before.

He had reached the Head itself now and he stood there, pressed against its smoothness, searching with his fingers for a hand hold. She sat back on her heels and looked no more. If Jan had found the smugglers' way, she could be certain.

She took her time crawling across the bald crown of the Head. She was feeling sick and remembered she'd had nothing to eat since breakfast. And she did not want to see what she knew she would see. She looked over the seaward edge. Jan was at the bottom of the ledge, his hands already gripping the finger rocks automatically. He must have done the climb a dozen times before; they had both done it dozens of times before. She was – as usual – a dupe.

How long she crouched there she did not know; it seemed an age. Jan did not appear. There were small scrabbling sounds everywhere but the wind had increased now and there could have been a dozen people climbing up to join her, she would not know. Eventually she uncurled herself and looked over at Jan again. He was halfway up, leaning against the rock as Philip had shown her, spread-eagled there safely enough, but unmoving. Another two footholds and he would be with her; yet still he didn't move. She stretched her legs until she was prone above him and reached over with her arms. She was about to call him and tell him to hang on to her, when there was a shout directly behind her. It made her jump but she knew instantly who it was and what had happened. Somehow, Rory had scaled that sheer face; somehow he had forgotten the grand stupid plan he had worked out with Jan. He loved her and he had climbed Old Man's Head to prove it.

His shout went into the wind and, by some trick of acoustics, was flung back again. Jan looked up at last. She stared into his eyes and saw nothing; no expression; complete and desolate emptiness. And then his foot slipped. He would still have been all right; all he had to do was to keep himself pressed to the rock and he would have slithered back down to the ledge with no more than a pair of skinned hands to show for it. But he pushed himself upright as if to see properly what was happening above him and his body kept going. She felt Rory's hand on her back as he joined her. They both looked in horror as Jan lay back into the wind and plummeted down into the sea. Rory was after him before he had hit the water. With a screamed 'Get someone – get Philip—' he was scrambling down, taking terrible risks himself but never putting a foot wrong. And Rosemary was scuffling along the ledge, over the finger rocks, running . . . running . . . like someone in a nightmare who never gets anywhere.

It took Mark and Jem almost half an hour to recover and begin to grin sheepishly. There was no question of them going on with the escapade. They had no more energy and their appetite for adventure was sated anyway. Besides, the swell was escalating powerfully; the danger was obvious even to Jen and Zannah.

'You were great,' she said simply, looking at Mark. 'You'd have killed him, wouldn't you?'

'No.'

'He couldn't. He tried and he couldn't.'

'He could,' she said soberly. 'But he'd have gone himself too. I rescued you both. You owe your lives to me. And don't you forget it!'

They grinned again, united under their oppressor.

She said, 'Are we going to take our medicine together, or what?' She looked dispassionately at Mark. 'One of your leg bits is bleeding so you'll have to have proper treatment.'

He shrugged. 'I'd have to own up anyway. I ditched my chair.'

'You what?' They were agog with admiration.

'No need for you two to say a word. Zannah, you can disappear. Jem, you can pretend to find me and go and tell Dad or Philip or someone. I'll say I lost control of the chair and went off the end.' He sniggered. 'Which is true anyway.'

'Is that cowardice?' she asked.

'It's called living to fight another day,' Mark told her.

She sparkled immediately. 'What can we do next? Something really terrible!'

The boys groaned aloud and Mark said, 'Look, chuck me in and let's get back. If we wait much longer we won't be able to swim against this sea.'

It was raining in squalls by the time he'd got himself up the steps on his bottom. They found his sodden blanket and shirt and bundled him up in the lee of a rock; they were all shivering convulsively.

Zannah said, 'Git – go on Jem – git. I'm staying with him till you get back. Go *on*!'

Mark was thankful; without his chair he felt completely helpless. Zannah sat close to him and put her arms around him so that their two shivers became one.

He said close to her ear, 'You let him kiss you.'

She managed a stuttering laugh. 'Is that what bugged you?' She turned her face into his and kissed his eyes, nose and mouth. 'There. Does that make it even?'

He said nothing but he let go of his blanket and got his arms around her too.

It was only five minutes until Jem returned with Clem and Jem senior, but each one of those minutes was expanded into an hour of sheer happiness.

And then Jem was babbling something about Jan and a terrible tragedy. And Mark was being lifted between the two men, and his father was saying, 'We'll tell you later, old chap. Lean back now. We'll soon have you warm and looked after.'

And he knew that Jan was dead, and he, Mark, had

walked out on him only this morning when he had still been able to use his chair. He tried to tell his father about his chair but no-one was listening. Zannah was trailing behind, mistaken by everyone for a boy. And now, when it was too late, he knew how Jan had felt about love.

CHAPTER TWELVE

1963

Etta put her head through the car window and looked around its interior very carefully before she greeted them.

'So you 'aven't brought 'er again this year?'

They all began to speak at once, telling her in almost identical words and tones that one day Rosemary would come back to St Ives, but not just yet.

Clem laughed. 'Did you get that, Etta? She's fine and sends her love.'

'Ah.' Etta removed her head and straightened her back with difficulty. 'Come on then. Let's get you indoors. I got the kettle on and Philip's waiting for you.'

'He's here?' Madge got out and pecked Etta's cheek, which was all the salutation the old lady would permit. 'He's in the house, d'you mean?'

'Ah,' Etta said again, then answered the unspoken question. ''E's not quite so spry on 'is feet no more, so 'e'll wait till you gets the stuff out of the car.'

Madge hovered by Mark's side while he hoisted himself on to his tin legs; she did not make the mistake of trying to help him. He reached behind him for his stick and thrust himself forward with a kind of fierce aggression. Etta said approvingly, 'Well now . . . you en't got fed up with us yet then, young man?'

He grinned. It was four years since Rosemary had come with them and each year Etta asked the same questions and made the same imputations.

'Not pygmalion likely, Etta,' he said. 'And neither has

294

Ro.' He too pecked the withered cheek. 'Any news of Rory?' he asked directly.

'Naw. An' you won't 'ave to put us with 'avin' tea over at Mennion 'Ouse, neither,' she said dourly, walking just ahead of him. 'There's bin an almighty bust-up there and she's gone orf to Lunnon.'

'Surprise, surprise,' commented Mark, and Madge said, 'Oh dear.' Then with one accord they all stopped and looked across the harbour towards Hayle. The sea glittered in the late afternoon sunshine and the beach was littered with the new breed of visitors called hippies. The tide was halfway in and the boats swung gently at their moorings. Godrevy looked as if you could swim out to it in five minutes.

'It's too clear,' Etta pronounced. 'It's going to rain before long.'

And Clem said quietly, 'It hasn't changed. It never changes.'

But Philip and Etta had changed. The shock of Jan's death and Mark's near miss had taken its toll; Philip could no longer climb the iron ladder to Smeaton's Pier, and Etta was at last glad to use the bathroom at the end of the passage. She could cook fish and potatoes and make tea, but she let Madge take over the kitchen for anything else. And if she thought she was quite alone she would talk aloud; not to herself, but to people who were not there any more. One day Madge heard her addressing Jan.

'You shouldn't 'uv done it. You were allus a headstrong lad – I know that – but you shouldn't 'uv left that girl all on 'er own like that. An' now 'e's gone off the Lord knows where.'

Madge felt her eyes fill. Then Etta said inexplicably, 'Your son. Your flesh an' blood. An' you left 'im.' And Madge turned away, knowing that not even Etta's illusions were logical. She closed her eyes momentarily, praying that Etta would not become like Clem's mother and live in a nightmare world of filth and evil. And then Etta came out of the parlour and saw Madge gathering up the swimming things from the passage clothes line.

'What's it to be today then, hot or cold?' she asked, as she had asked Marie Bridges so often.

'Er . . . I'm not sure . . . we'll have a picnic, Etta.' Madge wondered whether Etta was speaking to her or one of her private people.

'Right then.' The old woman gathered up her apron front and rubbed her hands on it. She gave Madge a lizard-glance and said firmly, 'You might 'ear something you dun't want to, 'anging about in the passage like that, my girl!' And went into the kitchen.

Madge smiled, reassured. Etta knew full well what she was doing after all.

She missed Rosemary more than she would have believed possible. For years it had been Rosemary who injected energy into their holidays down here, instigating outings, swimming parties, fishing trips. And now, Rosemary would be sitting with her on the harbour beach, making the empty hour into something positive: 'Come on Mummy, stretch out, we've got sixty minutes to get *brown*!' Madge smiled again, closing her eyes and tipping her head back to feel the full impact of the sun. She did not mind her own company and was always glad when Mark and Clem went off together, but there was no doubt about it, Rosemary had been the bit of grit inside the oyster shell.

The heat was glowing red against her closed eyelids, warming all the passages behind her face. She wished it were quieter; her ears did not enjoy the constant chatter of the crowds who thronged the beaches now and she remembered the time when the harbour had belonged exclusively to the local children. But Mark loved all the newcomers. He had already started to sketch them; a hundred or more faces on a piece of card two by one-and-a-half, flowers, head bands, long hair, beads . . . Clem said it was a social document and Mark said it was 'freedom'.

Madge's sentimental smile died; Mark used that word 'freedom' often now, yet never in connection with his own progress on his tin legs. He used it longingly, as if he had had it and lost it. And Clem couldn't understand. Clem thought that by taking him into the drawing and design office, he had given Mark a measure of independence. His own salary and his own work.

Madge took a deep breath and opened her eyes. Clem had taken Mark along to the Clipper for a pre-lunch drink and she knew he would be talking shop right now. She could imagine Mark, perched on one of the tall stools which were exactly the right height for him, looking into his beer instead of the scene around him, nodding and saying, 'Gosh, yes Dad, I can see what you mean,' and trying desperately to match his father's enthusiasm. He thought such a lot of Clem; as well as respecting and loving him, he admired him. He'd never do anything to hurt his father.

Madge pressed her lips together and swallowed another sigh. Neither Ro nor Mark were completely happy at the moment, but as Philip had said once, there was more to life than just being happy. Live a day at a time . . . pile them up until they made some kind of structure that was strong and worthwhile . . . let dreams have a separate place of their own perhaps. Again she smiled, this time self-mockingly. Sometimes she wondered what her mother was making of it all, now that she knew everything.

The tide was coming in and Maddern's pony and trap waited patiently on the shore for the first of the boats to bring in its catch. Madge made herself think about tea and whether mackerel would be acceptable to the others. It would mean that Etta could cope with it, which she would enjoy in her grim fashion. She would pickle them in vinegar and they could have salad and a mountain of bread and butter. Then, if the weather held, they could drive to Marazion and watch the sun go down behind the Mount. Etta and Philip would enjoy that too.

She noticed Philip signalling to her from the Fisherman's

Lodge. She got to her feet with some difficulty, gathering up handbag and book and shuffling through the sand barefoot to meet him. He opened the gate for her and they sat outside, backs to the wooden shack with its leaning chimney, the milling crowds shut away behind them.

'Here they come,' Philip said quietly. And around Smeaton's Pier came the first of the diminished fishing fleet, a big tub-like boat, broad in beam, with a wide stern, like a child's toy bobbing down a bath of water.

'Good catch by the looks of 'en.'

A boat put off from the harbour beach and the business of unloading began. There was an oil painting by Sargent in one of the galleries that was an exact representation of what was happening now; painted a hundred years ago, bridging past and present.

Philip said, 'Broodin' over young Mark, are you, woman?'

'No. Thinking of time. And how some things never change.' She smiled down on the ancient trilby. 'I don't think of Mark all the time, Philip.'

'But most of it, I reckon.'

She was silent, remembering the terrible heartache for Rosemary not long ago.

Philip did not look at her. 'I think o' young Mark as my own son. You know that, dun't you?'

She said nothing. Philip must know . . . he must. Was he trying to take on some of her guilt?

He sighed audibly. 'No need to worry, woman. No need . . .'

His voice petered out. Madge felt a pang of concern. He was only a year or so younger than Etta. They were both . . . old. They sat there together and watched Jim Maddern pole his dinghy back to the waiting cart. And Madge clung fiercely to her feeling of timelessness where surely guilt had no meaning at all.

Mark had not seen Zannah since that ghastly evening four years ago, and neither had Jem. The public story of their escapade, that day of the storm, had become apocryphal; their own real version no less so. Jem saw it still as an heroic venture and a wizard wheeze. Mark saw it in lurid colours of tragedy. Even his love for Zannah could not redeem it; there were doubtless reasons for Jan's terrible end; one of them might well have been to reveal to Mark his own impotence.

He looked at his latest sketch, narrowing his eyes so that each individual figure became blurred into the whole. Even so he knew that Zannah's face with its long aggressive chin and short hair was there, as were Jan's and Rory's and Rosemary's. Very carefully he turned the picture on to its face and focused again on the real thing.

Because of the terrible winter, this summer seemed the best for aeons and people were everywhere, no room any more for the artists. There was the usual crowd of families, mostly local, lining the harbour wall, but right down to the tideline the hippies had taken over. Etta was disgusted by them; they slept in the tents or under the arches or under the stars even; they never washed; they threw their rubbish everywhere, and – if reasons and excuses were offered for all of these offences – they were simply a disgrace. Mark was fascinated by them. Their philosophy of freedom – doing their own thing – appealed to him because he saw it as unattainable for himself. He longed to lie full length on the hot sand, eating fruit and buns and letting tomorrow take care of itself. But if he managed to get himself sitting at floor level, he'd never get up again. And their drowsy contentment relied a great deal on smoking 'pot' besides the hot weather. Mark knew from personal experience that drugs had their drawbacks; and of course, the sun was not going to go on shining like this.

So he looked, and envied, and tried not to remember that at the end of this short two weeks he had to return to the drawing office and the discipline of the slide rules.

Meanwhile he waited for Zannah.

She hadn't appeared for two years previously and he had

told himself every day since that if she did not turn up this year, he would give her up for good. And they were already five days into the holiday.

The trouble was, Jem and his father had taken the *Forty-niner* up north, so Mark had no-one with whom to share and restructure again and again those four-year old memories. And no-one to act as scout for him when his legs couldn't keep up with what was happening. It was Jem who discovered that Rory had left home in the widest possible sense; no forwarding address, no correspondence, nothing. It was Jem who would have found out all about the latest scandal from Mennion House; why Mrs Trewyn had gone to London and for how long. And when Zannah did not keep her biennial tryst, Jem would have gone looking for her. Although how he would have started when neither of them knew her full name or where her father lived, was a mystery.

Mark tightened his mouth against his own irritation and turned his sketch right side up again. He fished in his jacket pocket and broke off a lump of charcoal from the stick there. In front of him, no more that twenty yards away, a man and girl were entwined and asleep. She wore a leather headband into which were tucked bunches of daisies and buttercups, already wilting in the scorching sun. The hair which flowed from beneath the band was the same colour as his own, rust-red. It was unbelievably tangled and matted so that it looked like an unravelled piece of knitting, and it fell across her face and his, veiling their clinging mouths and surely half-stifling them. Beneath the shawl of hair, his hand appeared to be cupping her breast. It was an erotic pose, made innocent by their unconscious state.

Mark began to draw.

The three of them swam from the end of the pier at high tide. Neither Clem nor Madge were as strong as Mark in the water, and after ten minutes they clung to one of the mooring ropes and watched their son use his whole body

300

like a dolphin as he knifed through the water with a kind of ecstatic energy.

Clem said, 'D'you remember two or three years ago you were talking of Mark's independence? You were right. See how he gets away from us as soon as he possibly can.'

There was an unfamiliar note in his voice; Madge wondered if it was sadness.

She said, 'He always did. When he had his electric chair, he would get down on the beach with his painting things . . .'

'Yes. But he wasn't a loner then. Now he is. Of course he had Ro then. And other years Jem Gurnard was at home in the summer.'

The thought of Mark being a loner was awful. Madge blinked sea water from her eyes and said, 'Is it the work at the office? Can he cope with it all right, Clem?'

'He's marvellous. Especially at the mock-ups. I was going into technical details with a VIP layman the other week, and Mark did a lightning sketch which showed it all without any words. But—' he hauled himself high on the rope to check on Mark. 'He's not keen on the maths side.'

Madge swallowed. 'He'll get used to it.' She wished she could thank Clem for what he had done. 'He likes working with you. You get on so well. So well.'

She met his eyes in a moment of sudden awareness, then quickly looked away. And, with shocking suddenness, something grabbed at her legs. It was Mark of course. He pulled her under and when they surfaced, laughing, the moment had passed.

He said into her spluttering face, 'I was diving again by the old pier. Looking for the chair.'

Clem said, 'Again? The sea had that a long time ago.' Then he added, 'We thought you were leaving home.'

Mark laughed but Madge knew it was the wrong thing to say to him. And she wondered: did Clem sometimes wish he could be free of the terrible responsibility of Mark?

* * *

301

The drawing had gone. He had left it on the harbour in the box which slid beneath his old easel like a drawer. He went through the other things, though he knew he had left it on top. The old water-colours were there and some sketches of Ro as she bent over the desk of one of her pupils, but there was no sign of the hippie drawing. Yet no-one knew about the drawer, and nothing else had been touched. He had some decent brushes and a bag full of tubes of oil paint which were intact. He couldn't understand it. He folded everything up and struggled back to the cottage and the fish cellar where he left what Etta proudly called his 'mess'. He knew he hadn't left the drawing there, but he searched through old paintings anyway, without success. Then went upstairs and questioned his parents and the Nollas. Then stood at the window and looked out, as if he expected to see the drawing floating on the very high tide.

'It's like being grilled by the Secrets people,' Clem commented humorously, raising his brows at Mark's hunched and predatory pose. 'It'll turn up, old chap. You should have left your stuff there. Probably someone looking at it and will bring it back—'

'Bring it back!' scoffed Etta. 'It's they 'ippies what's took it! An' they never bring nothin' back!'

'It was in the drawer,' Mark said stubbornly. 'And no-one knows about the drawer except you and me. And Jem.' He gnawed his lip. And one other. She had to be out there somewhere. He rested his hands on the window and stared through the glass for the crop-haired figure hung with silver chains.

Philip said, 'Why dun't you go an' sit in your usual place and get on with some more work, m'boy? Take your pasty with you and make the most of the sunshine.'

'I'd nearly finished the whole damned picture!'

'Then start again.'

'Oh . . . I can't!'

'Course you can. Everyone can.'

So he went out again, took the steps one at a time,

collected his easel from the fish cellar and, using it like a second walking stick, made his way along the harbour. And waited.

When she materialised beside him, it was the same shock as before. He had looked for an eighteen-year-old sophisticate, sleek and sharp to the point of being abrasive. He had expected that the silver chains would be no more, but had been certain that their glinting sparkle would still be in evidence somehow. And the short, beige-coloured hair, the long belligerent chin, would always mark her out.

The girl who suddenly arrived, holding the drawing carefully and reverently between her hands, was certainly familiar. Her rusty, tangled hair, blowing across the lower half of her face like a yashmak, identified her immediately as the female half of the erotic twosome who had been the latest addition to his multi-figured sketch. Her leather, flower-bedecked head band of this after-noon had gone, but the metal rim she now wore like a tiara was looped with a fresh daisy chain, and on top of her shawl of hair was draped a liana of small, reddish flowers. Beneath all that she appeared to be wearing a grey-white muslin dress; no shoes or socks and, apparently, no underwear.

She stood before him, the picture in front of her like an offering, saying nothing, simply looking at him. And then he knew. She could do nothing about her eyes, they were still purple. This creature, a definitive flower person if ever there was one, was Zannah.

He took the picture numbly and went on staring, waiting for that vibrant personality to show through. She lifted one hand and moved the hair away from her mouth; her chin was still prominent, but the mouth was different, not so firm, the lips fuller and tremulous. He continued to wait; her voice would be the same, hard and American and very real.

She said softly, 'You were hurt. You didn't come to me. You didn't wake me. But you still drew me although you were hurt.' The accent was the same but the register was much lower and there were no cadences: she spoke in a monotone. He wanted to shake her physically as if he could empty her of all this rubbish and find the old Zannah behind it.

He tried to smile. 'I didn't realise it was you. Sorry. It was just . . . archetypal.'

'You mean I'm a symbol of the whole peace movement? That's nice.'

He hadn't meant that exactly, but he let it go, and went on smiling politely.

She tucked her hair beneath her chin and leaned back against the wall. She was taller than he was. His tin legs had been cut down as far as aesthetically possible to make movement easier.

She said in her gentle, middle-C voice, 'I looked everywhere for you, but I was looking for another chair.'

'I never had another one. I wanted to get something positive out of . . . all that.'

'You're a wonderful person, d'you know that?'

'Oh God . . . et tu, Brute.'

'No, I mean it.'

'That makes it worse. Look . . . thanks for returning the drawing, though you shouldn't have pinched it in the first place. And goodbye.'

'You *are* hurt. And angry. I guess I should be flattered, but to inflict pain on another human being is—'

'Oh for Christ's sake Zannah – shut *up*!'

It was the first time he had spoken her name and as he did so he knew she was right; he was hurt. He thought of the unknown man, legs twined around her, hand cupping her breast, and he wanted to yell aloud his pain.

She said with a touch of urgency in the sibilant murmur, 'We believe in free love, Mark. Morals – ethics – they're just rules to make the old society work. We don't have to have them. We can make our society work with love. Just love. So it has to be free. Surely you – you of all people in the world – can understand that? Mark—' She

304

picked up the edge of the drawing and pointed to the sleeping couple; he noticed with horror that her finger-nail was filthy. 'Listen Mark – I don't even know the name of this man. We ate together yesterday around a fire at Sennen. We walked here together. There were a lot of us. Bound by love. Human beings on the edge of eternity in a beautiful world created just for us. We slept together on the sand. For an instant in time we were bound. That is all.'

He said dryly, 'But apparently that is everything too. The whole bloody credo. Free love? It's free sex, that's all. It's cannabis so that you don't have to exercise self-discipline. It's weakness. In the end it's cowardice.'

She flinched. 'You've changed. You are totally reactionary. I used to admire your free spirit—'

'In a fettered body? And I used to admire the fact that you never thought or spoke clichés!'

She said with a suddenly hard edge to her voice, 'I've always been looking for freedom. Ever since I was born. That was the whole point of the business with the *Forty-niner* – to do something against everyone and get away with it.' She flipped the drawing back to him contemptuously. 'You had it. Freedom. Inside your head you were free and when you chucked yourself into the sea and swam out to stop Jem that night, you proved you were free *outside* your head too! I thought you could do anything – anything you wanted to! And you've changed. You're bitter and condemning of things you don't understand – won't understand! You've closed your mind in some way . . . you're just . . . different.'

He put his head back against the wall. He wished she would leave. He did not want to turn and struggle back up the slipway with his stick, but he wanted her away. He closed his eyes and hoped she would take that as dismissal. She did not. He knew she had moved closer because he could smell her. She smelled of Indian hair oil, the awful scent the hippies used, joss sticks, and – faintly – some-thing else. Something which took him back to that evening

305

four years ago when she had held him close until Jem fetched help.

She started whispering, practically into his ear. He could have sidestepped away from her without difficulty with the wall as support, but he did not.'

'I dived and dived off the end of the old pier, Mark. And I scoured all the beaches hoping something would be washed up. And when it was, I took the wheel and got Daddy to cut out the spokes and I wore it everywhere – long before I went to San Francisco – when I was only fifteen. It's one of the small front wheels – the ones that steered the chair, you know? I've got the other one too. I shall never lose them, Mark. I shall never forget that time when we were kids. Everything seemed so . . . possible.'

He pressed himself hard against the rough granite of the wall. The underlying smell from her tawdry, anointed body was pure Zannah.

She whispered, 'Why do you think I dyed my hair red? To be like you of course. Why do you think I joined the Frisco people? To find your – your completeness – your one-ness with the world. You can scoff now, but you had it, Mark. You had contentment – acceptance – Christ, I don't know what it was. But you had it.'

There was a very long silence. She withdrew slightly, but she did not leave, and he no longer wanted her to.

He said at last, wearily, 'I was happy because I was a kid and I was spoiled and everybody made a fuss of me. No mystery. That's all it was.'

'No it wasn't. It was more than that. There was a tale going round St Ives – Jem told me about it. You should have been killed when you fell off that railway bridge. And you weren't. It was a miracle. You're a special person. You belong to fate.'

'Shut up. Claptrap. Superstition. Etta was going to be ducked for a witch when she was a girl and Philip rescued her and married her. Some people still thing she's a witch – she thinks so herself sometimes. Superstition.' He

306

opened his eyes and turned his head. 'I think that's what I react against, Zannah. Your people – the flower people or whatever they call themselves – let them preach peace and wander around penniless pleasing themselves. Marvellous. But when they start going into the realms of fantasy and illusion—'

'It was the *local* people who said you were a miracle. Nothing to do with—'

'It's the same sort of scare-mongering but yours is brought on by cannabis.'

It's not as harmful as cigarette tobacco!'

'I'm an expert on drugs.'

She stared at him for some seconds, then drew in her breath. 'I haven't argued like this since . . . for ages. We don't argue. It's one of the wonderful things about being one of them. There is never discord.'

He grinned suddenly.

'We always argued. You. Me. Jem.'

'Yes. We did, didn't we?'

A voice from the beach yelled, 'Hey! Everyone! Food! Come and get it if you want it!'

Zannah said, 'I must go.'

'Where will you sleep tonight?'

'Anywhere. I've got a sleeping bag.'

'Will you sleep with him?' Mark jabbed a finger at his drawing.

'No.' She smiled. 'I'm so glad about the legs, Mark. You and Jem – you must have such fun now that you can walk.'

'Jem's a seaman. I haven't seen much of him for the past couple of years.'

'Well, your sister then.'

'Ro?' He was going to tell her, then changed his mind. 'Yes. It's good to walk with Ro.'

He watched her join the others. Smoke curled up from their midst as they lit a cooking fire. He wondered why he had condemned them so wholeheartedly to Zannah when until today he had envied them their carefree attitude.

She turned and waved to him, holding her aluminium crown with her free hand. After a second's hesitation, he waved back.

He did not want to be seen along the harbour the next day. He lurked in the fish cellar until he saw his parents leave for Porthmeor beach with the picnic hamper, then he went back up to the parlour intending to sit in the window and watch the hippies. He knew the parents would be hurt if they thought he was avoiding them, but he had swum with them twice and had a drink with his father at the Clipper, and sometimes their anxiety for him was hard to bear. He reached for his father's binoculars so that he could see if Zannah was amongst the heaving crowd on the beach, and swore quietly when he discovered Clem had taken them with him.

'Langwidge!'

It was Philip, head round the door, smiling slightly. He came into the room settling his hat firmly on his ears.

'Sorry, m'boy. Looking for Etta.'

'She went with Mother and Dad. Porthmeor.' Mark saw the surprise in Philip's blue stare and said defensively, 'I wanted to be by myself for a bit.'

'Fancy a row? The Gurnards left the dinghy. We could go over Porthminster and trail a mack'rel line if you felt like it.'

Mark considered. Unless she came up the court, there was no chance of him spotting Zannah in the crowds and it was hot in the tiny parlour. He nodded and levered himself to his feet.

He was expert at getting into the dinghy, sitting himself on the gunnel and manhandling his legs over one by one, and he was a good oarsman too. He rowed slowly across the bay while Philip fitted spinners on to a pair of lines and let them go off the stern. Then he rested the oars and they drifted lazily towards Porthminster with the tide.

It was another glorious day. Philip was no conversationalist unless it was with his mother, but the silence was never awkward. Mark half closed his eyes and did not think about Zannah; then he did not think about the hippies and his sudden and inexplicable turn against them; then he didn't think about the office and the effort of subduing imagination to inches and angles. It was exhausting. He opened his eyes to find Philip looking at him from beneath the brim of his trilby with unprecedented intensity. He sat up self-consciously and grinned.

'All right, Philip? Anything on the lines?'

'Naw.' The old man turned and pulled experimentally. 'Naw,' he confirmed. He stared at the spinner glinting beneath the water. 'Your mother says you're not so 'appy these days, boy?'

Mark shrugged, then realised he couldn't be seen.

'You know how it is. I suppose when you're a kid you think everything will be rosy when you grow up. And then . . . you grow up.' He laughed. Philip did not join in. The water lifted the boat gently and gave Mark a momentary view of the old pier and the cove at Wheal Dream.

Philip said pensively, 'Sometimes the Lord is cruel, or so it do seem. But gen'lly 'E do leave us some way we kin manage . . . gen'lly 'E does that.'

Mark said, 'You mean my legs? Yes, I am managing very well with them now, Philip.' He wished people weren't afraid of mentioning his tin legs. In a way he'd prefer them to know that he was using artificial legs rather than think that he was naturally five foot five and walked like a drunk.

'Aye, you are that. But I wasn't thinking o' your legs zacktly.' Philip turned and glinted a quick grin, then went back to watching the spinners. 'I were thinking of Etta. Wund'rin' 'ow Etta 'as bin able to manage.'

Mark concentrated on the wizened profile in the stern.

'Etta? I should think Etta has managed very well, Philip.'

Another look. 'You've 'eard the tales then? They thought she were a witch and I kem along on a white charger and

309

saved 'er?' He cackled a laugh. 'I dearly wish it 'ad bin like that, my boy.'

'It's how she sees it, Philip.' Mark leaned forward. For some reason he wanted to touch Philip reassuringly. 'I think it was what she told my grandmother. Ages ago.'

'I don't doubt it.' Philip must have seen Mark's outstretched hand, but he ignored it. 'The truth doesn't sound quite so good you see, boy. Oh, I stopped 'em from stonin' 'er. Aye, that's what they was doin' – an' it were this century too. Nineteen nought four it were. Nigh on sixty year ago.'

Mark frowned, wondering how old Philip actually was and what he was getting at. Was this some kind of allegory? He put his hand on the gunnel and shifted position slightly and the dinghy rocked.

'Then I ast 'er to marry me.' Philip pulled on his hat brim so that there was no chance of him catching Mark's eye inadvertently. He said quickly, 'I worked it out with 'er that it weren't too bad a bargain. She wouldn't want to bring children into the world if they was going to be tainted with any kind o' wizardry. An' she wanted to get out o' that part o' the country. Be respeckable. Go to chapel like other people and 'ave a man to proteck 'er. To keep 'er. Keep 'er safe from talk an' that.'

Suddenly one of the mackerel lines began to jerk. Philip ignored it as he had ignored Mark's hand. Mark found he was holding his breath. He had heard stories of Philip's past before; the old man respected and admired by everyone who knew him. But this story was . . . different.

'Aye. She would 'ave quite a catch in Philip Nolla. Quite a catch. 'Cept for one thing. There couldn't be no children – not never. And no-one knew that save Philip Nolla 'imself. An' if 'e brought 'ome a wife then no-one would ever know it. So that were the bargain. She'd protect 'im. An' in return 'e'd protect 'er.'

Mark thought of Etta, grim and loving, yet never loved as much as Philip. He thought of Etta, letting herself be seen as a barren woman, taken on by a good man. And then he thought of Zannah.

He said hoarsely, 'Why are you telling me this?'

Philip began to pull in the mackerel.

'Because we bin 'appy. We've shared everything, troubles and joys and we bin 'appy. Whatever people says, Mark, it's not everything.'

Mark wanted to hurt him; he wanted to hurt someone, anyone. He said deliberately, 'Obviously for you it's nothing.'

Philip ducked his head lower, gripped the mackerel in one hand, removed the hook, tapped the head against the side of the boat; the fish lay where he threw it, quite dead.

Mark asked angrily, 'What about Etta?'

Philip said something inaudible, cleared his throat and repeated, 'I dun't know, boy. I cain't answer for Etta.'

'Do you *care*?'

The head came up at last and the blue eyes were unexpectedly hard. 'I care. Every day . . . every time I look at 'er . . . I care. You got to look further 'n that, boy. You got to think what else would 'ave 'appened if we 'adn't linked up our lives.'

'She could have gone away somewhere else. She didn't have to marry you. You were the one who needed respectability – in a place like this where you'd lived all your life—'

Philip interrupted fiercely. 'She said she loved me! Don't you understand, boy, what I'm tryin' to tell you? She wanted to be with me. Whatever . . .' He shook his head as if to clear it. 'Mark . . . that girl . . . if she says later on that she wants to be with you, you must believe her. If you send her away because you're crippled, she might never be 'appy again! An' neither will you!'

Mark felt his face stretch wide. Philip held his gaze relentlessly for a long time, then he turned and began to wind in the other line.

'Let's go back, boy. There's nuthin' more to be said or

311

done out 'ere. You're too young for what I sed to you this day. But there might not be another time. Keep it in your 'eart for now.'

Mark said stubbornly, 'I don't know what you mean. There's no *girl*. How could there be a *girl*? I'm practically handcuffed to one of you all the time!'

Philip said, 'You gunna row back? Or d'you want me—'

'Are you trying to say we're in the same boat?' Mark realised what he'd said and sobbed a laugh. There were indeed tears at the back of his nose. 'You had legs, Philip! You could have gone away – somewhere else – yourself! You didn't have to stay here where you'd got this reputation for being so bloody marvellous! You could have started somewhere else where no-one expected you to be virile!' He paused, half expecting Philip to say 'Langwidge' at him. But nothing happened. The small man, the man he'd been brought up to admire and even revere, sat in the stern of the boat in an attitude of abject surrender. It was as if, with his bowed head and shoulders, he expected Mark to rain blows on him. Yet Mark – even though he consciously tried – could not summon contempt for him. He looked at him and told himself he was sorry for him. But that was not true either. Strangely, there was still admiration and respect beneath the undeniable anger.

He said curtly, 'I'll row then.' And fitted the oars carefully into the rowlocks. Philip's 'confession' had had one result: Mark knew that he must not see Zannah again.

But he could not stay indoors all the time and when he set one of his tin legs outside the door, he was immediately obvious to anyone who might be watching. He left the house early the next morning to buy the Sunday papers and catch the branch train to Lelant where he would feel safe from the hippies. He left a note for Clem and Madge telling them he would be out all day. He knew they'd accept it all right, but Etta would bemoan the fact that he'd taken no sandwiches; and Philip would think it was all his fault. Mark couldn't be bothered with all that; he felt suddenly as if he'd spent his whole life worrying about other people's feelings and now he simply didn't care. The weather wasn't so good, but he didn't care about that either. He'd find a warm spot among the dunes at Lelant and read the *Sunday Pictorial*, then he'd go to a restaurant and have a slap-up lunch. He wasn't used to eating out alone, it would be something achieved.

It was seven thirty when he passed the parish church and the early communicants were just filing out. He remembered going to services there with his grandmothers; Grandma Bridges had sat smilingly and commented at the end, 'It's like being in an upturned boat with the sea swishing away just outside.' And Grandma Briscoe had said they were all shipwrecked sailors with doom just over the horizon. He had been there since but never to a service, and he wondered if he might return home that evening in time for Evensong. It would spin out his absence for another hour at least.

The last worshipper emerged; a hiker already shouldering into a large back-pack. He paused for a word with the vicar who obligingly gave him a hand with one of his straps: it was probably that gesture which made Mark realise it wasn't a man hiker, it was a girl. The next moment she turned away, smiling, and he could see beneath her cap a wodge of red hair.

He sidestepped into the doorway of Prynne's. Always before, she had seen him first and been able to make her appearance when she chose. Now he had that advantage and was thankful for it. He could choose to stay where he was until she went away. If it meant missing the early train, too bad. There were other trains.

She took her time, still chatting to the vicar though she was moving away. He got the impression they were friends. As the man gathered his cassock against a draught from the harbour, he called, 'Good luck then – and be careful for goodness' sake!' Which was an informal farewell from minister to flock member, surely? Mark realised how little he knew of Zannah. Not even her full name.

She began to lumber down towards the Warren, bent almost double beneath her load. Mark waited until she had disappeared before striking up the High Street and into Tregenna Place. Was she going to make camp along the cliff somewhere? It was more civilised this side of St Ives, and people would surely move her on. But at least she was out of her hippie gear, so she would receive civil treatment.

He paused at the top of the station approach to get his breath and there she was again, her head bobbing up from the Warren Steps in slow motion after the steep climb. He watched her hang on to the rail and stare out across Porthminster. He knew she was making her farewell; she was catching the train like he was, she was going right away.

The pang he felt then was physical. He didn't want to see her, yet the thought of her absence was awful. Last year he had known she wouldn't be here and that had been bearable, but the year before when she should have made one of her unexpected appearances, he had waited for her and had been miserable.

He watched her as she resettled the weight on her shoulders and marched across to the booking office without looking to left or right. He knew how she felt. The sinking misery of departure infected him too. There was no point any more in his day out; he nearly turned and went back to Zion Cottage. It would be the sane sensible thing to do; but even as he thought the thought he was swinging into motion again, passing the booking office and making straight for the waiting train. He could buy a ticket from the guard, and he wanted to keep the element of surprise on his side for once.

She climbed into the long open carriage and began to get out of her pack. He pulled himself up and came up behind her. He braced himself against a seat and took the weight of the rucksack in his hands. She gasped a 'Thanks' and struggled to some avail. When she turned to take the load from him she still did not immediately realise it was him. Then the metal frame slid to the floor between them.

'Mark!' The eyes were almost navy blue this early in the morning and unexpectedly – shockingly – they filled with tears. 'Oh Mark!' She tried to laugh and added inanely, 'It's you!'

'Yes. It's me.'

He smiled up at her, then reached behind for his stick and sat down. She stayed where she was, staring down at him, her eyes drowning. He smiled slightly and patted the seat next to him and she sat down.

'I thought . . . I kinda thought . . . we'd said goodbye,' she stammered.

'Did you? Did we?' He had wanted to say goodbye two days ago, but he had not realised she felt the same way. She had been so bloody persistent when they were kids.

'I tried to find you. To explain some more. But no-one answered at the cottage and Mr Nolla had gone out in a boat. So I kept watch on the others, thinking you'd join them when they ate their picnic. But you didn't.'

'You kept watch?'

'Yes. From the cliffs.'

'All day?'

'Sure. Almost. And when you didn't show up I knew it was goodbye. And I couldn't stand that. So I figured I'd go back today. And here you are.' She too smiled. 'How did you know? Did you follow me?'

'No. I saw you come out of church. Then I followed you.'

'Oh Mark.' She swallowed and smeared at her eyes with the palm of one hand. She was wearing corduroy trousers with a lot of pockets but she did not seem to possess a handkerchief. Mark passed her his and she used it vigorously. Then she crushed it between her hands and looked at him earnestly. 'You see, it's not like it seems. I know you must think I'm some kind of whore, sleeping around on the beaches with anyone who comes along. But when

315

it happened it wasn't like that because I was looking through *their* eyes. Now I'm looking through *your* eyes and I've stopped. Honest to God. I'm going back to London and I'm going to work my fingernails off and—'

He said stiffly, 'You mustn't change your way of life because of me, Zannah. I've absolutely no right to—'

'Oh don't be such a pious *idiot*!' The eyes became purple and blazed at him. 'You sound just like you did when you were preaching to Jem and me back in '59! It wasn't a way of life – it was an experiment! Okay. I tried it and it wasn't for me!' She had a corner of his handkerchief round her little finger like a tourniquet. 'I made a mistake. Isn't a person allowed to make a mistake in your book?'

He did not immediately reply and then the guard arrived and he had to explain there had been no time to buy a ticket. By this time they both realised that the train was moving and they were nearly at Carbis Bay.

She said urgently, 'You bought a ticket to Lelant. That's only another three minutes.'

And he said at the same time, 'I only meant that I can't interfere with your . . .' He stopped and looked at her and then said, 'Zannah, d'you have to go on the early train? Get off at Lelant with me. Just for an hour. Please.'

It was as if she unloaded another rucksack. She leaned back in her seat and a smile spread from one side of her face to the other.

'I can go back to London at any time,' she said after a long pause, during which he thought he might have held his breath. Then the smile became a giggle and she leaned forward and put her hand on his knee, felt the metal of his leg and moved up to his thigh. 'And thanks for interfering, Mark Briscoe. I honestly began to think you never would!'

And they both laughed.

There was a cafe open on a Sunday right among the dunes. It was a wooden shack, almost derelict, and the wooden sign announcing 'Teas' swung in the wind with a rusty squeak. The proprietor warmed two pasties in an old Calor gas oven and cut bread and butter. He told them he had served in 'the first lot' and lived here since 1920 on his pension and what he got in the summer from serving teas. Mark said, 'I'm not a victim of the last war actually. I was dropped when I was a baby.'

'Then you're a victim anyway,' the man said gloomily.

'Oh no he's not.' Zannah bit hugely into the bread. 'He's a miracle. He should be dead and he's not. He went off the railway bridge at Carbis Bay.'

'I've heard of you,' said the man less gloomily. 'She's right. I reckon you are a miracle.' He poked Zannah's shoulder with a yellow finger. 'Good job for you, eh miss?'

Mark wanted to cringe with embarrassment, but it did not worry Zannah at all. She smiled sunnily.

'A jolly good job,' she agreed.

As soon as the man had delivered the pasties on thick earthenware plates and plonked a bottle of tomato sauce between them, Mark said in a low voice, 'Let's get out of here.'

Zannah shot him a look then said, 'No problem,' and gathered the pasties into the tear-stained and crumpled handkerchief. 'We'll be back for tea,' she called. 'Going to eat out in the sunshine.' There was not a glimpse of sun and the unoiled sign seemed to squawk a protest, but the man nodded with unwanted and unwelcome understanding and Mark stumbled thankfully into the dunes and threw himself down among the sharp grasses with a kind of groan. Zannah gave him another look, noted the red face and spread the handkerchief busily.

'Just as well to get out of there,' she said, passing him a pasty and immediately starting on hers. 'I've got loads to tell you. Private stuff y'know. And walls have ears.'

'Zannah, d'you mind if we don't talk any more? You see, there's no real future for me. Not your kind of future. And—'

317

'Not that kind of private stuff!' She deliberately blew some crumbs at him. 'You've been listening to too many dirty old men in crummy caffs, Briscoe! That's what is good about the Peace People. They're never dirty.' She pretended to sniff under her arm and made a face. 'Not in *that* way!'

She forced him to laugh. He'd never met anyone like her. Most of the women he knew would think she was vulgar. It was as if she knew what Philip had said to him and was trying to knock it all down in the only way she could.

He relaxed and took a bite of pasty. 'Go on then,' he invited.

'W-a-a-l . . .' She chewed exaggeratedly and he wondered whether, beneath the bravado, she was nervous, 'You might not like it. I mean, it might seem like me being nosey.'

'That would make a change.' He looked at her humorously. 'I don't know a thing about you, Zannah. Not even your other name. And you know practically everything about me. Wouldn't that indicate that you are a little . . . inquisitive?'

She flipped some sand at him.

'Okay, okay. 'I'm *curious* about things I like. I'm very curious about painting and sculpture. I find out everything I can about them.' She swallowed. 'And I have tried to find out everything about you.'

The compliment was obvious. He wished he could lower his temperature somehow.

She spread her hands. 'Listen. I'll tell you about me first. Shall I? It'll stop you feeling all embarrassed about yourself and put me in the hot seat for a spell.' She sighed. 'I've wanted to tell you anyway. Right from the beginning when we were kids. But you were never interested.'

She paused as if for permission to continue. He realised he had a mouth full of unchewed meat. He said through it, 'I'm interested. I'm really interested. Why d'you think I got on that train?'

She was reassured and gave him a flash of a smile.

'Yeah. You gave yourself away there, didn't you? Oh lordy, I don't know where to begin. Ask me a question.'

He tried to think of something sensible and all he could say was, 'Where were you two years ago?'

It seemed like the key question. She stopped fidgeting and went very quiet. Then she looked down at the sand between her legs.

She said softly, 'I was in Penzance. My father . . . died. We were all there. For the funeral. Then I went back to the States with Aunt Di.'

Something hit the sand by her left ankle. It could have been the remains of her pasty or it could have been a tear.

He said, 'Zannah. I'm sorry. I shouldn't have . . . Please don't say any more.'

She looked up. It had been a tear. But now she was angry. 'Why not? Is that what your family do -- bottle everything up so that they can keep the stiff upper lip, the closed family ranks? I *want* to talk about Daddy! I want to talk about him to *you*!'

He wished he could get to his knees and hold her, but it was an impossibility. He said, 'It's okay. I'm here. Talk.'

The tears suddenly spouted from her eyes and on to her pasty. 'Oh Mark. You didn't know him. That is what is so *awful* – you didn't *know* him!' She sniffed furiously. 'You would have liked him so *much*! And he would have liked – he would have *adored* you! The way you know things without having them explained . . . the way you draw your thoughts . . . oh God. He was great, Mark. He was . . . what's the word? Irreverent. He was so damned *irreverent*! He drove Aunt Di almost out of her mind! And he was such fun! He made everything such fun!

He wanted to tell her that she had inherited all those qualities, but all he could say was, 'I'm sorry.'

She said in her old fierce way, 'I'm not! I'm glad! He was always talking about Mummy. And painting her. Trying to make her real. He wanted me to know her. But all I knew was that he was unhappy without her. All the time. And now . . .' she broke down completely, crouching

319

over the pasty and sobbing out the words. 'And now they're together.'

'Oh Zannah.'

The best he could do was remove the pasty from her hand and shake out the handkerchief for her. She cried helplessly for a long time, then she took it and scrubbed at her face.

Then she looked at him. All the trace of the peace brigade had gone. Her face was streaked and dirty, just as it had been that night four years ago when she had held him to her tightly to control his shivering body.

She drew a trembling breath.

'You see, Mummy was dying anyway. She had something ghastly growing on her brain and they operated and then it grew again. So she thought she'd have me to be company for Daddy.'

This simplistic explanation had obviously been rote-learned as a child. Zannah gave a watery smile.

'It didn't work out quite like that. He had his work and he had to go all over the world. I went to school in the States so I lived most of the time with Aunt Di. He would join us when he could. And every two years without fail, we'd open up the Penzance studio and spend all summer here. You know about that. They were marvellous times. I can't believe they're over. He never . . . shut me out of anything. When other artists came – or when he met them – I was always there. I expect they hated me and thought I was precocious and horrible. But he didn't. He believed in me . . . he sort of . . . respected me. D'you know what I mean?'

'Of course.'

'Yes. You would. Aunt Di thinks I joined the Peace People as a sort of reaction thing. Grief. Bereavement. But she's wrong. I'd have done it anyway. And he'd have understood. And now it's over he wouldn't crow or anything. He'd say it was another experience under my belt. I want to be like him. Experience things. Get *back* to him.'

He said, 'You don't have to go anywhere to find people once they're dead. They are with you all the time then. They *become* you.' He stared at her. 'You say you wish I had known him. Maybe I do. Maybe I'm looking at him now.'

The tears flowed again.

'Oh Mark. How do you know that?'

'I don't. But it's common sense, isn't it?'

She said eagerly, 'And there's his work. You probably know that, too.'

'What was his name?' Mark held his breath, prepared to lie. But when she said, 'Gerald Scaife,' he let it go in a gasp of surprise. 'Gerald *Scaife*? Yes, of course I know him. We've got a rather bad copy of something of his at home. An abstract. My God. You are his daughter.'

She looked slightly more cheerful. 'Ah. A little respect at last!' She stretched out her legs. 'Oh, I'm so glad you know his stuff. There's a retrospective exhibition of it at the Tate starting next week. That's why I have to be in London.'

'The Tate *Gallery*?'

'Sure.'

'Gosh. He must be really good.'

'One of the best,' she said unboastfully. 'That's how I know you're good. I've got an eye trained by one of the best.

'Oh Zannah.' He did not know what to say. 'Thanks. Really. Thanks.'

'I'm at art school too. I mean, I'm not just a gut critic.'

'Tell me about *your* work.' He realised he had known all the time that she was an artist.

'I'm going to sculpt.' She glanced at him with defiance. 'I like techniques. And materials. You know. I like to find out what bronze can do. And how wood looks inside. And the way you can polish stone.' She wriggled her backside into the sand. 'I'm not wonderful actually. I have to work. And work. And then work some more.' She laughed. 'I don't mind.'

321

'I should think not. You're damned lucky.' He gave her the pasty and she took it and tried to eat.

'Yes. I am lucky. But so are you. I know you must sometimes think you're not. But that's not true. You see, you are able to experience things without actually doing them. You've got some wavelength . . . I don't know what it is . . . that puts you in touch with other people and how they feel and react. It's all there in your paintings. I have to go places, do things, make a damn fool of myself. And you're there already. Do you understand what I'm saying?'

'No.'

'Maybe that's as well. If you did it might go.' She bit a lump of gristle and made a face. 'Shall we ask for our money back?' She removed it and began to take the pasty to bits like a monkey looking for fleas.

'Actually, it was your picture that made me start feeling curious again.'

'Curious?' He tried to grin for her. 'You mean nosey?'

'Well, yes. I think I mean nosey.' She grinned back. Then she began to flick the insides of her pasty to a gull. In an instant hordes of them were screaming and squabbling. It gave him a moment to think about her background and how she had explained it. So much was now clear about this girl: her surface brashness and her inner uncertainties. A child of one parent; an artist; a broken-hearted artist; finally, an orphan. There was something so damned brave about her. He thought that whatever happened to her she would manage to beat some kind of a drum and fly some kind of a flag.

The gulls finished the pasty and wailed disconsolately for a few moments while she laughed at them. Then they were gone and the dunes were grey and quiet again.

He said, 'Go on. Being nosey is a kind of therapy for you. Like my physio. Tell me.'

She shifted sand from one palm to another.

'It was that picture of yours. The one I stole so that I could look and look at it. It revealed your subconscious to me.'

'Listen, Zannah. I didn't know it was you. I told you that already.'

'No. And probably you didn't know that most of the people there had faces I recognised. Your sister for one.'

'Oh come off it. You don't know my sister that well.'

'Yes I do. And your mother. I've seen her lots of times talking to old Mr Nolla.'

'Rubbish.'

'And the boy who died in that fall from Old Man's Head. And his friend, Rory Trewyn.'

'Zannah. You're into all this stupid psychology thing. And you'd been smoking dope. I could smell it on you.'

'They were *there*. In your picture. I've seen photographs of Rory and Jan.'

'Newspaper photographs. They're never any good.'

'Daddy and I – we've called at Mennion House in the past. Daddy knew Mr Trewyn quite well. The boys were always at school, but Mrs Trewyn gave me a photograph album to look at. They haven't changed much since they were at school. And they were in your picture.'

He surrendered without grace. 'All right. So what?'

'Well. It showed what was on your mind. Then I heard about the split at Mennion House. And I wondered if it was anything to do with that accident four years ago.'

'Possibly,' he said gloomily. He hated talking about Jan and Rory. It was like walking around a maze with no exit. He tried to change the subject. 'I can't get over you going to Mennion House. We always went, each holiday. It was awful.'

'Yes. It was a sort of armed truce between them. It's better really that it all blew up in the end. And nothing to do with Rory or that Polish boy. Did you hear about it?'

'No,' he said cautiously.

'Jeremy Stockton – the partner at the auctioneering firm – turned out to be Matthew Trewyn's son!' Her eyes were wide; in spite of the Peace People and her penchant for shocking people, he realised that Zannah Scaife still had some pre-war morals.

'How on earth did you discover that?'

'Everyone – all Daddy's old friends – is talking about it. Actually they think that Matthew did the decent thing really. He fostered the boy out till he was fourteen, then took him into the business and eventually made him a partner. If only it hadn't come out it would have been all right I suppose. But Mrs Trewyn couldn't stand everyone knowing. At the golf club and things.'

'Yes. I can imagine. Poor woman. And poor Mr Trewyn too. How did it come out? Or couldn't you quite discover that?' He couldn't take it too seriously. It was like one of Ro's magazine stories.

'That was easy. This guy Stockton, he wanted to find out about his real parents. Do you know Mrs Foster who lives in Bunkers Hill? She's a widow now, but her husband used to make baskets. He was blind.'

'Martin Foster. He married Rose Care and Etta went on and on about it. Rose had a reputation . . . oh no, not Rose *Care*?' It became more and more like a story and drew him in almost against his will.

Zannah nodded. 'He found that out from the parish records. And he kept asking her about his father. And at last she told him and someone heard—'

'Mrs Trevorrow! I bet you anything it was Mrs Trevorrow!'

'I don't know. But Mrs Trewyn heard about it the next day. And she packed up straightaway and left.'

They stared at each other, amazed that adults could weave such tangled lives.

'But that's not what I wanted to tell you.' Zannah sat forward now, confident in her interest. 'I thought if Matthew and this Mrs Foster were in *love* . . . you know, like your parents and mine . . . then they probably had *more* children. Rory. He's dark and Mrs Foster is dark. So I went to see her.'

'You . . . *what*?'

She sat back again. 'You're mad? Maybe it was kind of nosey, huh?'

'Nosey? It was impertinent! Oh God – it was insulting! What did she say? What did she do? You absolute idiot, Zannah!'

'Well, she took it better than you're taking it. She sort of smiled all the time. Like she knew something I didn't. And she called me mettlesome! That's one of Daddy's words – he had old-fashioned kind of words. He used to say all my adventures were "scrapes"! Anyway, Mrs Foster thinks I'm mettlesome.' Her smile was different, begging a response.

He shook his head resignedly. 'All right. But she didn't tell you anything.'

'No. I think if she was tortured she'd never grass on anyone.' She dug her hands deep into the sand. 'But she went to make me a cup of coffee. It was like cough medicine, but I drank it nicely and thanked her. Because while she was outside I flipped through her photograph album and found an old snap of Rory and your sister. Rosemary looked about ten, and Rory no more than fourteen.'

He said, 'That doesn't prove a thing, Zannah. Anyway, it's none of our business who Rory's real parents are. What difference does it make?'

'Surely you can see?' She arched her brows impatiently. 'Once he's over this Jan thing, he'll come back. He's a Cornishman. His roots are right here. And your sister will come down on holiday and it will be all right!'

'Zannah . . .' He lowered his head, faced with the impossibility of conveying to her the strange emotional ties between Rory, Jan and Rosemary. He began to scrape sand into walls between his tin legs. 'Zannah. I know the verdict of the inquest was accidental death. But . . . it wasn't quite like that. Ro and Rory both know . . . *I* know . . . Jan deliberately pushed himself off that rock.'

He heard her swift, indrawn breath, but did not look up.

His left leg was almost covered in sand. He began on the other one. And he started to tell her.

At the end she said angrily, 'It certainly wasn't your fault! You – you – bird brain! Just because you spoke your mind in that damned cafe place . . . my God, when I think of that day! And we expected you to join in that stupid *game*!' She took a deep and shuddering breath, then went on, 'And you know it wasn't your sister's fault! Or Rory's!' She leaned forward and put her hand on the pile of sand which now completely buried his tin legs. 'Oh Mark, don't you see – it makes it better! He chose to die! Not like my mother who had no choice in the matter! He'd had a good, normal life with the Trewyns. And he chose to end it. It was probably something to do with his *genes* dammitall! If he told you he'd tried it before, then how on earth your sister can imagine it was anything to do with her . . .' She stopped speaking quite suddenly but went on looking at him with total concentration. Then she said on an indrawn breath, 'Oh Mark. I do love you.'

Thoughts of Jan disappeared on the instant. He too was caught in that look. Gulls wheeled and cried and the waves broke beyond the dunes, but they were trapped and held in a timeless moment.

He whispered desperately, 'You mustn't. You mustn't.'

And she whispered back, 'You can't stop me.'

He knew that, and a terrible thrill wrung his heart.

He said, 'You're still a kid.'

'So are you. But you love me too.'

His voice rose, 'I . . . *can't*!'

There was a long silence. Her hand had worked through the sand, and his thigh told him it was pressing on his tin leg. He felt tears behind his eyes.

She said, 'Would you like to come and see Daddy's work in the Tate?'

He couldn't reply. The tears gathered in his eyes.

She said, 'Fine. Two weeks tomorrow. I'll meet you at Paddington and we'll have a taxi.'

He found his voice and said hoarsely, 'I shall be at work.'

'Take a day off. You need to see my father's stuff.'

She started to get up and when she was on her knees she touched his leg again. Much higher up. And she smiled right into his face with blazing triumph.

'Oh Mark. Oh darling. I think you can. I think you can.'

CHAPTER THIRTEEN

1964

Etta and Mark sat over the drawings until a large orange moon hung over the harbour, making the whole area look like a film set. The chandelier tinkled gently as Etta stood up to fetch the teapot from the sideboard again. It took her a long time; she used her arms on the table to lever herself straight. Philip's death had taken its toll.

'Had enough, Etta?' Mark asked, taking his cup from her. The two of them had long dispensed with niceties; they left the saucers stacked on the dresser and ate their fish with their fingers. 'It's late. We can go on tomorrow.'

'Naw. I like to 'ear your plans, boy. Though why you wants to move down into that ole fish cellar I don't know.'

He said for the umpteenth time, 'Less effort for the tin legs. Anyway it's been my special place for a long time now. I might as well do it out properly.' He looked into her face. 'You're sure you don't mind, Etta? Legally I've got no right to be here at all, you know.'

'What 'ave we got to do with all that legal nonsense, eh? If it's cos o' that, you'll stay right 'ere in the parlour where you've allus bin!' She returned his look through the steam from his cup and her face softened. 'I know you didn't come down 'ere to claim your legacy, my boy – I know that. You came to be with Etta Nolla. That I do know. An' that's what matters.'

'Other people might think differently,' he said gloomily. 'Jem hasn't been near me since I got here.' He looked back at his sketches. 'That's another reason for making a flat downstairs, Etta. No-one can think I've come to oust you out of the house, and no-one will tell you you've reverted to being a nursemaid!' They had both been told that Mrs Trevorrow's heart went out to Etta Nolla who was expected to nurse a cripple.

Etta cackled. Mark had arrived at the beginning of March, just as soon as he had worked out his notice and packed his bags. He had found Etta sitting in the kitchen, staring at the empty range, her lungs audibly creaking. He had ordered coal, made up a bed for her on the ancient horsehair sofa, and fed her beef tea for a week before she pushed it away and demanded ordinary tea, hot and very strong. She had not so much wanted to die, as been unable to find anything to live for. Suddenly, on the verge of pneumonia, she had Mark.

She said now, 'I dun't know as I'll be able to manage on my own.'

'Which is just as well, as you've got a permanent lodger.' Mark looked again at the massive windows he had drawn into his plans and wondered whether a single girder would be able to take the load of the house above them. He had to have the front wall made of glass, there was nowhere else for light. Clem would know. He'd write to him tomorrow.

Etta said, 'It might be too much for you, my boy. I en't getting no younger nor no spryer.'

Mark put his hand over hers; he could feel every tiny bone in it.

'Etta. I've never been much help to anyone. The boot's been on the other foot. The sort of thing I'm doing here – no-one else could stand it. Tea. Fish. Spuds. Bread. It suits you and it suits me. And it makes me feel . . . good.'

'I know. But it still might git too much.' She sucked in her lips. 'Ah well. We'll wait and see. Eh?'

Mark nodded. He was certain it would never be too much for him. He had thought St Ives would be unbearable without Philip, without Zannah, without his parents. It was nothing of the sort. He felt amazingly fit; there had been no warning ache from his stumps, yet the weather had been damp and cold until today. His mother had been tight with anxiety about the whole thing; she had finally wailed, 'Darling, you'll never *cope*!' And he was coping.

The next day he went to see Pearce the builder with his sketches between the pages of the *Cornishman*. Nathaniel Pearce had been responsible for the grim rows of council houses above Ayr, but he had been merely taking orders and they were solid enough. He was an old man now, but his married son had taken on the business and shared the bungalow in Orange Lane. Mark was fagged out by the time he'd climbed Porthmeor Hill. He paused on one of the rough unmade roads that terraced the cliff, and looked out across the bay. The sun shone again but the wind was cutting; the horizon was bumpy with white horses and the few fishing boats were keeping close to the shore.

Mark stood still, letting the icy wind cool him down, and revelling in the leaping joy which had possessed him ever since his mother had arrived back home from Philip's funeral. He was going to *live* here. For always. It was what he'd always wanted; not a schoolboy's dream because he had not dared let himself dream of such bliss. It was a need in his very bones. As if he'd grown here at some time and been uprooted against his will. He smiled, permitting himself a whimsical fantasy of his small baby feet rammed into the railway ballast at Carbis Bay station. Maybe that was when he had been 'planted' here. If only he could sell that rubbish to Ro, she might be persuaded into realising she'd done him a favour that day!

He went on up the hill and found Pearce's spanking new bungalow without difficulty. Nat himself opened the door to his knock and stood there narrow-eyed, unfriendly.

'Saw you coming up the lane. What do *you* want?'

Mark was rocked back on his heels. He had noted Jem's absence without too much surprise; Jem and his father had a large slice of the *Forty-niner* and had expected to get Philip's. Or at any rate to get it through Etta in a few years. And Jem would come round, he was incapable of harbouring resentment longer than a few weeks. But that other people, who had always been so friendly and who were completely unaffected by Philip's strange bequest, should cold-shoulder him, was a definite shock.

He said, 'I've got some conversion plans here.' He waved the folded newspaper, suddenly conscious that to Nat Pearce an eighteen-year-old was still a child. He began to stammer slightly; a trait he must have inherited from his father. 'I thought of converting Etta's cellar into a flat. W-w-well, a sort of bed-sit actually—'

'She's got the run o' Philip Nolla's 'ouse in 'er lifetime, young man! An' I ain't noticed she's dead yet!'

Mark nearly told him that was no fault of Etta's neighbours; then he decided on diplomacy.

'Look, Mr Pearce, I'm there as a friend. A visitor—'

''Ten't the season yet. She 'as you in the season an' not before. You're presooming, young man. Philip Nolla treated you like a son, but you en't no son of anyone in St Ives, an' it's no good thinkin' you are!'

Mark felt as if he had been struck physically. No-one had spoken to him so unkindly in his life. And so unjustly.

He said, 'Perhaps I could have a word with your son?'

'No, you cain't. If 'e were 'ere 'e wouldn't want any work from you. But 'e ain't 'ere. So good day to you.'

Mark leaned heavily on his stick, waiting for the door to close in his face. Nat Pearce had another thought and stuck his head through the gap.

'Let me give you a bit of advice, lad. Go back 'ome till feelings cool down some. You came down too soon—'

Mark said, 'Etta would be dead now if I hadn't come down. I didn't come to claim anything! I wanted to be with her—' He wanted to tell this man how Etta had loved her husband; enough to sublimate all her own maternal instincts to protect him. He looked at him helplessly. 'She was completely alone and ill.'

331

Nat Pearce said stubbornly, 'Someone would've gone in and found 'er and got 'er off to Camborne General.'

'She would have hated that!'

''Tis not your con*cam*, lad!' But Nat's lined face was softer. 'Look. You go back now. You won't get any builder in the town or out of it, to start knocking Philip Nolla's house about. An' even if you could, the planning folks at Penzance 'ud turn it all down! So just go 'ome like a good boy and wait till the summer. You're a summer visitor, that's what you are.'

He did close the door this time, and after a few, fuming seconds, Mark turned himself and began to trudge back. He knew a sense of defeat waited for him at the edge of his mind and refused to let it come further. He took the top road to the cemetery gates and went in to find Philip's grave. It was too soon for a headstone to have been affixed, but he had no difficulty in finding it because the heaped oblong of earth was smothered in flowers. The blooms in Etta's anchor had long withered but the dark laurel and the berries and the florist's ribbons made it presentable. The Christmas roses which his mother had told him she'd bought, had died and been discarded. Beneath the anchor was an array of flowers. Early daffodils and anemones from the Scillies in jam jars; bunches of snowdrops in fishpaste pots; tiny, flagging crocuses transplanted straight into the soil. Mark stood above them, staring down, actually counting them. Etta had not been here since the funeral, and this was the first time he had visited the grave.

He said aloud, 'Well, you kept your reputation. Just like you wanted. And . . . somehow . . . I don't know why . . . you've taken mine.' He stopped counting. There were over one hundred blooms fluttering on Philip's grave, brought by people who loved and admired him. He remembered his mother saying, 'Don't go down, Mark. Please. You don't understand how it is. They won't welcome you.'

Again he spoke aloud. 'I don't care. I've a right here.

You gave me that right, Philip. I'm not going back. I'm going to fight for that right.'

A thought wormed itself between the determination and defeat. It was, quite simply: Etta will make it all right.

He began to stump back between the tombstones. Of course Etta would bring some of her cynical common sense to the problem. He would tell her about Nat Pearce and she'd cackle a laugh and tell him to take no notice. Next time she got along to Bright Hour, she'd make it quite clear that young Mark saved her life . . . he could practically hear her saying it. But the thought had been more definite than that. Of course, Philip had relied on Etta to make things all right. And by sticking to her role of barren wife, she had done that. Had Philip sent the thought into his head? Did thoughts live on . . . have a life of their own . . . dart into somebody else's consciousness?

Mark came out of the bottom gate and closed it thankfully. What he needed was a swim in the icy Atlantic. Then mackerel and tea with Etta. Then his precious phone call to Zannah.

Before that he spent the afternoon trudging the streets of St Ives, trying to find a builder to look at his plans.

'It's incredible,' he protested to Zannah over a crackling connection to her hostel. 'It's as if they knew I was coming and ganged up on me!'

'You need an older man,' she said. 'Everyone is against us because we're young. I told Aunt Di about us, and she was all for it when she thought you were some kind of war hero. But when I said you'd lost your legs in an accident and you were eighteen, it was a different ball game. Oh.' She started to giggle. 'D'you get that, Briscoe? A different ball game!'

'For Pete's sake, Zannah. What am I going to do? Come up with some answers like you always do!'

'Oh Mark. Darling Mark. What does it matter? Look, when this trustee business finishes, I'll have enough cash for both of us. We can go to Frisco and just . . . live! Darling, we love one another. Let everyone else – everything else – go hang!'

'It's because I love you that it's got to be this way, Zannah. Before, there was just no chance for us realistically. But when Philip gave me an actual *place* here – it's more than the house and the boat, Zannah, can't you see that – then it all became possible. Oh I know I'm still living on the allowance from home, but I'm going to be a working artist, my darling! Soon I'll sell my stuff, and with the income from the boat I'll be really independent! Then I'm going to ask you to marry me. It'll be up to you then. You might change your mind, or—'

'Shut up, bird brain. I know that's how it's going to be. You're as good as Daddy, if not better. It's in your blood and bones, nothing to do with your brain, which is just as well as you're not hot in that department! And I'm going to be a sculptor and we'll be so happy everyone will come and look at us!'

He leaned his forehead against the glass of the telephone box and closed his eyes.

'Will you come down for Easter, Zannah? I want to swim with you. In the cove at Wheal Dream.'

She said, 'Are you unhappy down there, my honey?'

'No. I'm angry right now. But it's good here, Zannah. It's right for me.'

Her sigh rattled his eardrum. 'Put the phone outside and let me hear the waves. A-a-a-ah. Oh Mark.'

'I know.'

'I just wish Daddy were here. I mean I wanted you to know him. That's why it was so marvellous you seeing the Tate thing. But I want him to know you too. He would help you, darling. Practical help. He'd find a builder and he'd get the plans passed. And he'd understand. He wouldn't say we were too young. He'd love you like I love you.'

He could hear her weeping so he said, 'I do hope not, baby.' And after a second she began to giggle again. He said, 'Darling, I could ask my own father. He's wonderful. And he'd do it like a shot. But I want to do this on my own. I mean, I don't mind using people with influence, but I want to find them and talk to them and persuade them. And I don't know anyone!'

There was a pause; he could almost hear her thinking.

She said, 'It's so illogical. I mean if they're putting flowers on Philip's grave, why can't they respect his wishes? He wanted you to live there. In his house. I don't get it.'

'It's nothing to do with logic.' He tried to ease her frustration. 'Look. I'll go and see Jem. I can win him round. Don't worry.'

'But he's young too. No-one will take any notice of Jem. What about Dudley?'

'Dudley?'

'The Reverend Dudley. The vicar. He thought the world of Daddy.'

'Darling. Philip was chapel. Nearly everyone is.'

'I've got it. Really. Matthew Trewyn. He knows everyone in that end of Cornwall. He'll fix it for you.'

He hated to squash her. After Jan's death and Rory's desertion, how could he ask anything of the Trewyns?

He said doubtfully, 'They say he just sits around in Mennion House, sozzled most of the time. I don't know whether—'

'He needs something to do! You'll be his salvation, darling! Get him going – stimulate him – motivate him—'

'Like you did me? Was that what the Act of Piracy was all about?'

'Could be.'

'You're cunning. And underhand. And completely devious.'

'And you love me.'

'And I love you.'

He came out of the kiosk and propped himself against the glass for a few moments, savouring the wind and the sound of the waves. Last night there had been that

335

huge red, frost-moon; now there were silver-edged clouds moving fast across the night sky. He wondered what tomorrow would bring. The weather was all-important down here; a constantly changing character. He watched Godrevy lighthouse winking in the darkness and knew to the right of it was Mennion House sitting in the marram grass and wild thyme of Hayle dunes, ugly and very lonely. And inside, solitary and disgraced, was Matthew Trewyn.

How on earth could Matthew Trewyn help anyone now? He was the one needing help. And Mark was the last person to give that help.

But as he pushed himself off the glass and on to his stick, Mark made up his mind. He would go and see Matthew Trewyn.

Etta thought he should take a taxi.

'A *taxi*?'

Mark was incredulous. Etta would rather walk all day than pay any man for transport.

'You'm looking tired, boy.'

'Am I?' He took the trouble to stand up and study his reflection in the glass above the sideboard. His face certainly looked thinner but it had been too round before. 'Nonsense, Etta. You should see me after I've done a day at the drawing board.'

'You're not 'ankering for your folks then?'

'No.' He felt guilty about that. He loved them more than ever, but sometimes their constant presence was a burden. He said soberly, 'I've never been free before, Etta. Probably – after a few months – I shall take it for granted. Not now.'

'Free? With me 'anging like a millstone round your neck?'

He laughed. 'Lifebuoy more like. You're keeping me afloat.'

She sucked her lips in against a smile, then she pointed a gnarled finger. 'That's it. By sea. You kin go over in the dinghy, if go you must.'

He sat down again. The dinghy would be by far the easier way for him to go over to Hayle. There was a landing stage at the foot of the dunes, then steps right up to the house with a hand rail all the way.

'They wouldn't let me have it,' he said slowly. He would like to row the *Forty-niner*'s dinghy. He went swimming most days but the water was icy and the effort of unstrapping and restrapping his legs was gigantic. To row was another way of using the water; just as energetic but more appropriate to the weather.

'Don't ask 'em, then.' Etta stuck out her jaw belligerently. He'd heard those words, or similar, and seen that expression on Zannah's face. Etta poked again with her finger. 'You got a share in the boat. You got a right to the dinghy.'

So the next calm and windless day, he went down the harbour beach, sat on the gunnel of the dinghy, lifted his legs inside, unhitched the mooring rope and fitted the oars into the rowlocks. No-one saw him leave and no-one evinced the slightest curiosity as he rowed out of the harbour and across Porthminster and Carbis Bay. It was a marvellous feeling. He'd rowed the dinghy often before, but always with someone else aboard. He took long, slow strokes, resting on every twentieth for a few moments to gaze around him and relish the shouldering swell beneath the boat. The silence then was wonderful; not silence at all, just absence of every human sound. Then came the intense physical effort again when he was conscious of loud breathing and even a grunting groan occasionally. Then more silence.

As he tied up at the Mennion House landing stage, another of his clear, concise thoughts arrowed into him. It was that Ro would find the answers to all her questions and fears down here. He did not shrug that one away as he had done the previous one; it was completely logical and inevitable. He saw that she had been running as in a nightmare through cloying mud, away from the very place which could offer solace. He began to search for

337

words to use in a letter to her. Tranquillity. Simple solutions. Clarity of water moving on the face of the . . . He was at the top of the steps and the conservatory door was open.

He walked through it and into a dark passage cluttered with coats, tennis racquets, golf clubs, old plimsolls. He had never been this way before, his chair would not have got through. He opened a door at the end and was in the kitchen. A loaf and wedge of cheese were on the deal table which took up the centre of the room; the bread was shrinking with staleness and the cheese smelled sharply of its own rind. Under the window the deep white sink was jammed full of crockery and the tap ran gently over the lot; the window itself was slashed with gull-droppings and most of the cupboard doors swung open. Oddly, the floor showed signs of some attention; the coconut matting was rolled neatly and stood on its end in a corner, a broom leaned beside it and beneath the table was a full dustpan. Mark edged carefully around it and opened another door.

He was on familiar ground now. The hall stretched ahead, shabby and untidy but still beautiful in its wide proportions. The stairs curved out of it elegantly; hanging on the banisters was a pile of clothing topped by a dressing gown and a clutter of shoes lay on the bottom two steps. He paused, frowning. Then he cleared his throat self-consciously and called diffidently, 'I say! Is anyone around?'

There was just a second of waiting silence, then the sitting-room door opened with a jerk, and a woman emerged and closed it behind her. Mark's frown deepened. He recognised the woman: it was Rose Foster, the woman Zannah supposed was Rory's mother. And he could see suddenly that it was very likely. Her hair and eyes were more than dark, they were black; she had the wild, almost piratical air that Rory carried with him. Mark was rigid with concentration. She was here, in Mennion House, and Mrs Trewyn was not.

She came towards him and said in a low but aggressive

338

voice, 'What do you want?' And there was a faint emphasis on the 'you'.

'I – I've come to see Mr Trewyn,' He wished to God he could cut out the stammer, it made him sound a schoolboy still.

She said, 'Why?'

He wondered if he should tell her to mind her own business, but it went against his nature and besides it might *be* her business. All the stuff Zannah had worked out had sounded pretty thin at the time, but it was very probable that Matthew Trewyn's business was also Rose Foster's.

'Er . . . actually . . . I needed some advice. On builders and planning permission and things.'

'I heard.'

She surveyed him a moment longer then brushed past him. 'Come on into the kitchen. I'm clearing up, and we can talk as I work.' She jerked her head at the sitting-room door.

'Mr Trewyn is asleep at the moment.'

Mr Trewyn? It didn't sound as if she'd moved in as his . . . whatever. He followed her back into the kitchen and when she pushed a chair at him, he lowered himself into it.

She gathered up the dustpan and tipped it into a paper sack. Then she did the same with the bread and cheese. Then she went to the sink.

'I put these to soak while I saw to him. I heard yest'y that his daily help hasn't been for over a month, so I guessed he'd be in a pickle. Never could look after himself. When I was here nearly forty years ago, he had to be looked after hand, foot and finger, and men don't improve. They just gets worse.' She glanced at Mark. 'Pull that chair closer and you can dry the crocks and put them on the table.' She rummaged in a drawer and came up with a tea towel, then spread clean newspaper over the table. 'I'll scrub that later. It's not deep dirt. I'll give 'er that. She weren't much of a wife to 'im, but she kept everything nice, and trained 'er staff to do the same.'

So Mrs Foster had worked here years ago. Perhaps that was when . . . but no, she'd said forty years ago and Rory wouldn't be thirty yet. He looked at her back as she tackled the washing-up, and tried to imagine her as young and passionate. It wasn't easy. She'd come down from Zennor way about five or six years ago, married old Mr Foster when he was on his last legs, and inherited his house in Bunkers Hill. Etta said she had 'gobbled up' the old man. But his mother liked her. In fact she had stayed at Mrs Foster's house for Philip's funeral.

'Come on,' she said, already up to her elbows in suds. 'Get on with it. You've got arms like a gorilla – let's see you use them!'

She grinned at him suddenly to take the sting out of the words, and he found himself grinning back. She did have a certain attraction: an enormous energy and drive. Matt Trewyn would be all right if she was going to take him over.

She waited until he'd polished half a dozen glasses, then she said, 'Mr Trewyn is asleep because he is drunk. I don't think he'll be able to help you. But he'd like to see you – he thinks everyone has deserted him, not just his wife.'

He cleared his throat to get rid of any stammer and said brilliantly, 'Oh.'

She stacked half a dozen plates neatly against a tea-cup; her hands were so capable and her bare arms were still round and firm.

'I wouldn't want you to think my visit here is on a regular basis.' She grinned at him. 'I haven't seen Mr Trewyn face to face since I left his . . . service—' she laughed at the unexpected innuendo, then sobered. 'But I know what it's like to be an outcast.' She lifted her shoulders to her ears. 'Funny you an' me choosing the same day to come calling.'

'Um . . . yes. A coincidence.'

She rinsed the sink, seized another towel and began on the piled crocks on the draining board. They diminished rapidly.

She said, 'I'll make some tea and you can take it in to him and wake him up. I'll finish here.' She filled a kettle at the tap and moved strongly to the gas stove. 'It's only surface dirt. I'll go into Hayle and get a'old of Mrs Vissick and put the fear o' God into 'er. She'll be up tomorrow and at least the 'ouse will be back to normal. As for 'im—' she adjusted the gas flame and sighed.

'Aren't you . . . I mean, don't you . . . what I mean is won't you stay to look after him?' Mark brought out at last, blushing to the roots of his hair.

'Me?' She laughed again; she did a lot of laughing. 'Gawdlemighty boy, 'e'd soon drink himself to death if I stayed 'ere.' She looked at him. 'You're as green as your mum, aren't you, young man?' She put cups and saucers on a tray. 'Listen, Mark Briscoe. If you cain't get no 'elp from poor Mr Trewyn – and I doubt if you will – come 'an see me. A week from today. Eight o'clock of the evening.' She chuckled. 'That's if Etta Nolla will allow it!' She made the tea and placed the pot on the tray. Then she made a wry face. 'Pity poor old Etta couldn't let the rumours stand, my boy. Then you wouldn't be 'aving all this difficulty!'

'Rumours?' He was still admiring her firm, decisive movements from stove to tray and back again. 'What rumours?'

'Surely you 'eard? When Philip left you 'is all, there was folks who thought it was because you was his own kith and kin. But Etta scotched all that by clinging to your ma like a leech all through the funeral, and now taking you in.' She leaned over the table and touched his cheek, quite hard. 'Don't look like that, boy! 'Twas only gossip and it's over now. Everyone know your ma . . . and Philip . . . straight as dies, the pair of 'em. Now if it 'ad bin me—' She laughed uproariously. 'What would you have thought of me as a ma? Eh?'

He was still reeling over her last words. No wonder his mother had arrived back from the funeral white-faced and shaking. No wonder she said she could never come

341

to St Ives again. And Philip! If they knew about Philip!

She said, 'Not much, eh? You wouldn't want Rose Care for a ma!'

He swallowed hard and looked at her. There was a kind of brazen innocence about her that was infinitely touching. He said without a trace of a stammer, 'I should be very honoured, Mrs Foster.'

Her colour darkened and her laughter died. She picked up the tray and marched to the door.

'Come on then. All this talk is getting us nowhere.'

She waited in the hall for him to get himself up and moving. Then she went into the sitting-room and put the tray on a low table. Mark, following behind, was back in the past; the big leather chairs with their built-in ashtrays on the arms were the same as he remembered, the piano in the bay window still wore its Indian shawl. Rose had evidently spent time in here; the whole place smelled of lavender furniture polish, and there was a clear, bright fire in the grate. Matthew Trewyn sprawled in one of the chairs beside it, his arms touching the floor either side, his head lolling loosely, mouth open, snores emerging irregularly. Mark hung back, wishing he'd never come.

Rose went over to the sleeping man and shook him vigorously.

'Come on now, Maister!' Her voice became at once hectoring and servile. 'Wake yourself up! You've got a visitor!'

Matthew came to slowly and grumpily.

'You still here, Rose? What would I do without you?'

He reached for her with one flailing arm and she side-stepped neatly.

'Ah Rose . . . Rose. I should never have sent you packing all those years ago. I knew it would come out in the end – and it did. Oh God . . . it did.'

Rose said loudly, 'You've got a visitor, Mr Trewyn!'

Matthew tried to focus his eyes. 'Visitor, did you say? Who . . . Christ, it's the little Briscoe boy, isn't it?' He made an effort to stand up and failed. 'Haven't seen you

342

since . . .' he couldn't bring himself to speak of the inquest and funeral. He relapsed into the chair. 'I heard you'd got some cork legs but I'd never have thought . . . never . . . well done, lad! Bloody well done!'

This was the Matthew Trewyn Mark remembered, bluff and instantly friendly. He looked up and nodded his thanks.

'Actually they're aluminium, not cork. Very light – as light as cork and a lot stronger.'

'Make you top heavy, do they?'

Mark could cope with what he called the techniclinical approach. He grinned.'

'I have been known to turn turtle! They make them shorter to counteract that. Apparently my natural height should be six two. Not two six.'

Matthew laughed loudly. Rose did not.

'You're a fine figure of a man,' she said with a hint of reproach.

'Let's have some tea, Rose! Eh lad? Eh . . . er . . .'

'It's Mark,' Rose said clearly. 'And the tea is here.' She marched to the door. 'I've got work to do,' she announced, and left.

Mark noticed she had put the tray near a high chair which would do nicely for him. He made some remark about being mother and sat himself by the teapot. Matthew eased himself upright by degrees, talking all the time.

'What *about* your lovely mother – how is she these days? And your father going from strength to strength? It's the quiet ones who get there, my boy – Mark – every time. The quiet ones. And you . . . that Mrs Vissick told me a tale about you. I won't repeat it.' He guffawed. 'So . . . old Philip Nolla left you his all, did he? No wonder the tongues are wagging.' He leaned forward at last and took a cup from Mark's outstretched hand. 'It's like old times this, Mark. Bit more civilised than I'm used to nowadays, I'm afraid. Good job you came the day Rose took pity on me. Things had got rather run-down here. Mrs Vissick – the daily help you know – she was taken on by my wife . . . you've heard about my wife?'

'Yes. I'm very sorry, sir. I hope it will—' Mark sipped his tea and practically scalded the roof of his mouth '—eventually blow over.'

'Don't know. It's not actually finding out about my lurid past you see, lad. She always knew about that. It's the disgrace. Golf club. That sort of thing.'

'Er . . . yes. Quite.'

'It's worse for a woman, you see. You . . . me . . . we'll soldier on. People accept us again, seven days wonder, all that sort of rubbish. Women . . . they let these things fester inside them.'

Mark sipped again and decided to take the bull by the horns.

'Actually, it was about that kind of thing. Indirectly. I mean . . . I came to see you because . . . I want to make a sort of flat out of Etta's fish cellar. The services are down there – a lavatory, sink, gas – lots of people are converting their fish cellars and it's not difficult. But until I can get the corroboration of a builder I can't get any plans together to submit to the Council.' Once he'd started it wasn't too bad. He pulled out some of his sketches and began to talk enthusiastically about his ideas. Matthew became interested and stood up at last to take a sketch over to the window.

'Ideal,' he muttered. He looked up. 'You could be independent down there,' he commented. 'No trouble to the old girl – Mrs Nolla – yet within earshot of each other if anything went wrong.'

Mark nodded vigorously, surprised that this insensitive man could see immediately the advantages of the plan.

'And it might help to scotch all this talk of me ousting Etta,' he added. 'I don't want to do that of course, but she needs someone.' He smiled for the first time and with a certain pride. 'She needs me,' he admitted.

'Yes.' Matthew grinned back. 'Yes. She's damned lucky.' He flapped the sketch. 'I don't know what I can do to help. Lost a lot of my contacts . . . Got a copy of this?'

'Yes. You can keep that if you're interested.'

'I am. I'll see what I can do. Perhaps someone from further afield . . . Truro.' He sucked in his breath consideringly. 'They won't like that. The local men. Could make it very difficult. But I can certainly get you planning permission. No trouble at all.'

'It's very good of you. I mean in the circumstances—'

'Do me good to think about something else. Nothing's gone right since . . . Why the hell Rory had to banish himself like he did, I'll never know. Never understand. That's why Mary was so bitter. Christ, we were cut up about Jan, but we didn't run off to God knows where, did we!' He recalled himself. 'Sorry, old man. I forget your family was involved. Did your sister get over it all right?'

'I . . . yes, I suppose so. In a way. She's just different. I'm going to try to persuade her to come down again. She's never been back since.'

'Why? If she doesn't want to come, won't it just open old wounds? I suppose that is why Rory stays away.'

'I rather think she should face things, sir. *Look* them in the face.' The moment of vision on the surface of the water had gone. He fumbled for the certainty he had had then. 'It's still so beautiful down here, so . . . eternal.'

'Yes.' Matthew Trewyn came back to the table and poured himself another cup of tea. 'Perhaps that's what Rory should do. If I knew where he was, I'd write and tell him so.' He looked at the sketch again, unseeingly. 'You know, Mark, when Philip Nolla asked me to take in another of Rose's children all those years ago, I thought it might be his. Mary lost her child, and it seemed the best thing to do. Any stock of Philip Nolla's would be hard-working and clean-living, and if Rose passed on her energy and laughter . . . well.' He shrugged. 'No doubt about Rose being Rory's mother. But Philip? Philip would never run away from anything like Rory has done.'

Mark said involuntarily, 'Then you're not Rory's father?' He put his cup down with a clatter. 'I'm sorry. I shouldn't . . . none of my business.'

345

'Not at all, old man. My business belongs to the world and his wife now. I'd rather you heard it from me. No. I'm not Rory's father. I did my best. So did Mary. But I think he must have known.'

Mark revised some of his impressions. Perhaps Matthew Trewyn only seemed insensitive.

He stood up and leaned on his stick.

'I'd better go. I've rowed myself across, and the tide will be dropping soon.'

'Good to see you. Good of you to . . . Come again. Any time. I don't go into the office often now, you know. I'm usually somewhere around.' He grinned. 'Jerry keeps things going for the old firm. At least I've done something right.' He seemed to have forgotten his promise to take Mark's plans to the Council. He went to the mantelpiece and pulled a bottle from behind a large carriage clock; it was empty. 'I say old man, tell Rose to bring in some more whisky, would you?'

Mark went back the way he had come, but there was no sign of Rose anywhere. A note on the table said, 'Casserole in oven with rice pudding. Expect Mrs Vissick in the morning.' He smiled, thinking how he would tell Zannah about this visit with all its surprises. And then he stopped smiling. There was too much unhappiness linked to each of the surprises.

He went back to the sitting-room to tell Matthew that Rose had left.

'That's all right. I'll get my own whisky.' The older man straightened away from the mantelpiece. 'Glad you came, Mark. I'll do my best for you.' He sketched a comic salute. 'Everyone used to come to me if they wanted anything done. Who sent you?'

'Er . . . Miss Scaife, actually. You knew her father.'

'Miss Scaife? Susannah Scaife? My God. She must be nearly your age now. And Gerald . . . Gerald was a fine chap. Never the same after his wife died, but a fine artist. Susie Scaife, eh. Imagine that child remembering me.'

Mark felt as if they were talking about someone other

than Zannah. He remembered her saying a long time ago, 'My name is Susannah. I could have been Susie or Anna, but no-one remembers names like that. You'll never forget Zannah.'

All the way home he thought of Zannah Scaife, who had been determined from the moment she met Mark Briscoe, that he would never forget her.

The next day when he came out of Philips' Dairy, Jem fell into step by his side. He was delighted, about to hand over the heavy bag of groceries, then changed his mind. Jem's face was stony.

'If you need the dinghy again, perhaps you would mention it to me or the old man first. You might 'ave part share in the *Forty-niner* but Philip Nolla 'isself wouldn't a' took it without our say-so.'

Mark was suddenly so angry he could taste his own bile. Without a word or a thought, he put his stick neatly between Jem's feet. Jem stumbled to his knees. Mark waited till the furious face was raised to his. Then he said very quietly, 'I should have drowned you when I had the chance. Keep your bloody dinghy. I'll sell my share of the *Forty-niner* to one of the summer visitors and buy my own dinghy!' And he swung himself away with his seaman's roll, leaving Jem staring in sudden consternation.

During Bright Hour Etta sat as close as she could to Mrs Trevorrow, and afterwards asked for her arm to the bottom of the hill. It was an unprecedented request; Mrs Trevorrow did not know whether to be flattered or alarmed.

'Weather's still unkind, Mrs Trevorrow,' Etta said in a voice that still trembled with weakness. 'If it dun't come soon, I reckon I wun't see another spring.'

'It's the wind,' agreed her companion. 'But the sun must come nicely through your passage door and—'

'That boy of my Philip's will need good friends after I'm took. Like the son I never could 'ave, 'e is. So good about the 'ouse too, and a real Cornishman for all that.'

347

'Philip's boy?' asked Mrs Trevorrow faintly, almost holding her breath in anticipation.

'Did I say . . . ah well, you guessed all along, didn't you. An' I kin trust you to keep a secret. After all, the wife of a solister—'

'How can you bear it? Poor Mrs Nolla. All these years. And butter wouldn't melt in her mouth. I don't blame your Philip. He was a good man. It was her. It's always the woman.'

'Do you mean Mrs Briscoe? Oh no, you got the wrong one there. It was Mr and Mrs Briscoe what took the child on and gave it a 'ome. Saved Philip and me from disgrace y'see. But he's allus bin like a son to us. Oh no, the mother were as Cornish as Philip. The boy is a proper Cornishman. That's why I rely on you to befriend 'im after I've passed on. 'Tis your secret, Mrs Trevorrow. But you will know. And you will see that justice is done. I am quite certain of that.'

'But dear Mrs Nolla, how could you stand it? My heart goes out—'

They came to the harbour and Etta took a deep breath.

''Twere partly my fault after all. I couldn't bear my 'usband no kith and kin. 'E were a natural man, Mrs Trevorrow. A natural man. I dun't want to say more. You unnerstand.'

'Oh my dear, I do. Oh I do. And we all thought you were . . . well, unsympathetic perhaps. And all the time . . .'

'And you will keep my secret?' Etta smiled gently at the gulls quarrelling over some fish heads on the wharf.

'. . . Rest assured . . . and the boy will be one of us . . . one of us, my dear . . .'

Etta disengaged her arm. 'I can manage now, thank you Mrs Trevorrow. Excuse me from asking you into the cottage for tea—'

'In any case I am in a hurry. I have to call in to see Mrs Peters. And Miss Lowe. Are you sure you can manage?' But she was already walking back up Fore Street. And as

Etta went up the cobbled court, she said aloud, 'I 'ope you're satisfied now, Philip Nolla!' And she began to laugh.

It was a week since Mark's visit to Mennion House and he had heard nothing from Matthew Trewyn. These things took time, but he wished he knew whether anything was happening. He hardly liked to call again so soon. Even Zannah counselled patience. He hadn't told her of Rose Foster's invitation yet; he did not know why.

That day the strangest thing had happened. He had taken his swim very early to avoid anyone witnessing the business of removing his legs and wriggling into the sea like a sand eel. The church clock was striking eight as he started across the bay to Porthminster and the intense cold of the water was making his stumps ache so that he got no further than the first buoy. As he duck-dived for the return, he saw another swimmer running down the harbour beach, clad in singlet and shorts. Mark paddled with his hands until the swimmer reached him. It was Jem.

'Gawdlemighty!' The small bullet head broke water, spouting like a whale. 'It's bloody cold! D'you do it every morning?'

Mark felt his heart lift in his body. This was the Jem he knew. But he kept his voice sour. 'You probably know the answer to that. I suppose you've spied on me before?'

'Not me.'

'But others have.' Mark began to move towards the shore. 'What are you doing here anyway?'

Jem swam alongside, still gasping convulsively.

'Well . . . I thought . . . mebbe . . . I ought to give you the chance you wanted. To drown me.'

He met Mark's round brown eyes, and suddenly grinned. 'Not that you'd catch me o' course.' And he was gone, arms flailing, legs kicking frantically. Mark could have caught him easily with his dolphin stroke, but he did not. He watched Jem pant his way up the sands, grab a towel and run up Jinty Passage.

349

Now, as he swung himself from side to side along Fore Street on the way to see Rose Foster, he wondered for the umpteenth time if it had been Jem's way of apologising for his words about the dinghy. In which case Mark would have to find some way of acknowledging that he shouldn't have tripped Jem up with his stick. Damned childish anyway. And he could do with Jem's friendship; he *needed* Jem's friendship.

There was a flight of ten steps to Rose's front door and steps were difficult. He hooked his stick over one arm and used both hands on the rail to pull himself up. It was dark; he wondered if that was why Rose had stipulated eight o'clock. No-one to see him struggling.

She didn't made the mistake of opening the door before he reached it, either. She gave him time to regain his breath and composure and knock twice. Then she put on the hall light, opened the door and immediately preceded him so that if he stumbled he'd do it in private.

'Close the door after you, will you?' She pushed at another door further down the passage. 'Go on in. I'll just put the kettle on.' And she exited left.

Mark realised immediately that someone else was in the room as he edged into it, but after the outside darkness the brilliance of Rose's lighting dazzled him and he could not see who it was. He assumed for a second that it was Mr Trewyn again and that Rose had got him over here to sort out the business of Mark's cellar conversion. Then he knew it was too tall, too wide for Matt Trewyn. He blinked and leaned on the back of an armchair. It was Rory.

For a long moment, neither of them spoke. For Mark the initial shock of recognition was repeated several times as he noted the changes in Rory. And Rory had never seen Mark out of a wheelchair.

Rory spoke first.

'Come and sit down, old man. It must be hard going. And Rose's steps are tough enough anyway. Here. Have this high chair. I take it a high chair is easier than an armchair?'

'Thanks. Yes.' Mark sat down carefully.

Rory laughed. 'Sorry. It's your voice. It hadn't broken when I saw you last. I can't get over . . . sorry. I'm being more than rude. Insulting.'

'No. It's almost five years. And you've changed too.'

Rory made a face. 'Old, you mean. I'm thirty now, Mark. And a lot has happened.'

'But you've come back.'

'Not to stay. I gave Rose a forwarding address. She wrote and said my father was in a state and demanded my presence. So here I am.'

Mark's mind churned. So Rory knew Rose Foster was his mother. And still thought Matthew Trewyn was his real father.

He said lamely, 'It's good to see you, Rory.'

Rory did not respond to this. He sat down close to the small electric fire and shivered, which was, perhaps, response enough. Mark noted that his neck and the back of his hands were weathered to a burnt sienna brown so he must have come from somewhere warm. And his hair was sprinkled liberally with grey. He did indeed look very much older.

Rose came in carrying a tray. She put it down on the table and began to pour tea. It occurred to Mark that this was where his mother must have sat for her meals two short months ago.

She said briskly, 'Bit of a shock, Mark? I didn't tell you Rory was on his way home in case it put you off.'

Mark took a cup of tea gratefully. 'It wouldn't have done that, Mrs Foster. I'm very pleased to see Rory again.'

'I wasn't sure. You Briscoes are a funny lot.' She put a cup near Rory and sat down herself. 'This is the one to help you, Mark. He's been building houses for the past four years. Working with construction firms all over the States. What he doesn't know about building isn't worth knowing. Right, Rory?'

Rory looked up. 'Probably.' He picked up his cup and

351

stared into the steam. 'Crewing on charter boats gave me too much time to think, Mark. I started off as a brickie. But I can do a bit of everything. Carpentering, plastering, even electrical work.' He looked through the vapour at Mark. 'Rose has told me your difficulty. I'll stay long enough to do the flat. No longer.'

Mark hardly knew what to say. He stammered delighted thanks and mentioned the planning permission.

'I'm going over to see the old man tomorrow. We'll get something going between us.' He turned his hooded gaze on to Rose. 'Satisfied?' he asked.

'For the moment.' She sipped. 'I want you to stay here for good though. That's what I've got in mind.'

'You're incredible. D'you know that? You had two children by Matt Trewyn. Do you nag the other one like you nag me?'

He was only half joking and Mark glanced apprehensively at Rose, expecting her to flinch away from the implications behind the question.

She said very straightly, 'I had one child by Matt Trewyn, and he is Matt Trewyn's responsibility. Your father is dead, Rory. You are my responsibility. And you'll never solve anything by running. You ran away from Rosemary. Now you're running away from that Jan Grodno. It's so . . . *silly*!'

He was silent, staring at Rose for a long moment, shocked by the news that Matthew Trewyn was not his father. Then he shrugged as if it didn't matter. 'Rosemary obviously feels like I do. She's never been back either.'

Mark said suddenly, 'I think she should. She feels it was her fault. But of course it wasn't. And she needs to come back to believe that.'

Rose said swiftly, 'You see?'

Rory looked from one to the other, then sighed deeply. 'I'll tell you why Jan jumped off that rock, shall I? Then you can tell Ro and perhaps one of us will get some peace. It was because of me. I climbed the rock that day . . . somehow I got to the top of Old Man's Head the wrong way. And Jan knew what that meant.'

'It was a stupid *game!*' Rose said angrily. 'Good God, Rory, if he was such a fool – he must have known that if the girl really loved him she wouldn't have cared if fifty others got to her first!'

'He didn't love Ro.' Rory stared at the single glowing bar of the fire. 'He didn't even love Madge Briscoe, though he longed to have her as a mother.' He sighed deeply. 'He loved me.'

Rose and Mark were shocked into silence for a long minute; then Rose said, 'Oh my God.'

'Exactly. He told me how he felt, begged me to let him stay. I thought the only answer was to push him into a marriage with Ro – as if that could cure him. Give him the family he wanted. I was willing to push Ro into it too, just to get free. It was ghastly. Awful. I loved him too, but not like that. And after a while I began to hate him. And I was the only one he trusted. Oh God. You're right, Rose. It was awful.'

She said strongly, 'You shouldn't be telling us. You should be telling Rosemary Briscoe. My good Lord. 'Tis always the way. The men do fight it out between themselves and the woman is supposed to take what's left. You must tell that girl what you've told us, Rory. And soon, too.'

'I thought of it, Rose. But she couldn't stand it being raked up all over again. You don't know what it's like between us. The link – the ties. She's cut them now. Let them stay cut.'

Rose made an impatient gesture that nearly sent her tea flying. 'You cain't cut blood ties, my boy!' She folded her arms furiously. 'You didn't show much surprise just now when I told you Matt Trewyn weren't your father!' Her voice had slipped into Cornish again. 'You must 'a guessed that there was different blood in you! Well, does it come as a surprise to 'ear that you 'ave got Rosemary Briscoe's blood – Mark's blood – a-coursin' through your veins?' She stood up and went to the sideboard. She picked up a photograph album, flipped it open at a well-worn place and handed it to Rory. 'There's your dad, my boy. Neville Bridges. 'E wanted to marry me. An' I turned 'im down because it wouldna done. An' 'e went off to that Spanish war and got 'isself killed!' She sat back down again. 'An' if I 'adn't done that, 'e might 'ave bin 'ere today!' She shook her head. 'Never mind that. Water under the bridge. But you *are* part of the Briscoe family – something Jan would have been pleased about. You cain't deny it by staying away! All this business about love – what's love in the end? A few hours o' 'eaven, then payment. Marriage and blood-ties – them's what counts. I dunno whether you and Rosemary Briscoe are more than summer lovers. Mebbe you are, mebbe you idn't. But you're linked all right. Whether you like it or not – you're cousins. And the sooner you accept that, the better!'

Rory sat holding the album, looking at Rose then at the faded photograph. Her colour was high, defiance was in every line of her body.

He said, 'I can't really tell . . . it's a sepia snap. But he – he – looks a bit like Madge Briscoe.'

'Philip Nolla gave it to me.' She seemed to relax a little. 'Neville din't know which way to turn. I couldn't look after you, my boy – I din't 'ave no feelings that way – and it 'ad to be a secret. It would 'ave killed old Mr Bridges, and Mrs . . . oh, it would 'a broke 'er 'eart. Things was so diff'rent then. 'Tis 'ard to imagine.' She sighed. 'So Neville told Philip Nolla, and 'e went to see Mr Trewyn. An' when madam lost 'er baby, they talked it over and said they would take you on themselves. It was best. Philip allus said it was best. They gave you the sort of schoolin' . . .' She looked away. 'It was best.'

There was a long silence. Then Mark said quietly, 'I think you're marvellous, Mrs Foster.' It sounded so silly and kiddish. He cleared his throat. 'I'm glad Uncle Neville . . . I mean, Mother and Dad talk about him often to us. I'm glad he knew you. And had Rory.' Rory was still staring at the photograph. Mark tried to sound hearty.

354

'Hope it's not too much of a shock, old man, to learn we're
. . .' His voice died. It was all so tremendous, there were
no words.

Suddenly Rory stood up. He put the album carefully on
to the sideboard and went to the door.

'I'll see you tomorrow, Mark.' He opened the door. 'I
must . . . think. I'll go for a walk.' He glanced at Rose who
was low in her chair, all defiance gone. 'Don't wait up. And
. . . thanks.' He went through the door and just before he
closed it, he added, 'Mother.'

His footsteps went along the passage and then down the
steps. Rose began to weep quietly.

Mark said, 'Let's have another cup of tea.'

She gulped and swallowed. 'You're a good boy. A really
good boy.'

'No I'm not.' He thought of Zannah and smiled. 'I'm
just lucky. You're lucky too.' He laughed suddenly. 'Tell
me about Uncle Neville. Tell me what he was really like.
I'm sure he wasn't the saint and hero Mother and Dad seem
to think.'

She sniffed, took her tea, and after a few sips began
to talk.

CHAPTER FOURTEEN

1965

Etta died quite suddenly and undramatically eighteen months later. She waited until all the gossip was old hat and the Briscoes resumed their pattern of visits, before she called Mark up to her sitting-room to discuss her 'final arrangements'.

'I want you all here,' she announced. 'Nothin' under cover, like at Philip's. You're my fam'ly an' I want everyone to know it. An' that means Rosemary too. An' that young Scaife girl o' yours. An' Rory Trewyn.'

'If Rory comes, Ro won't,' Mark said, trying hard to pretend they were talking about someone other than Etta.

She said grimly, 'That's the only loose end. I've tied the others, an' I depend on you to tie that one.'

'You know very well I've tried, Etta. Be fair.'

Etta nodded sadly. 'She were always a stubborn girl were Rosemary.' She cheered up. 'But she'll 'ave to come down to look after you, my boy. You cain't stay 'ere all on your own an' that's that.'

Mark was silent; he had continued to keep house for the two of them and last winter had nursed Etta through another bout of pleurisy.

She said sharply, 'You do see that you cain't stay 'ere alone, don't you?'

He scraped back his chair. 'I hate talking like this, Etta. We're neither of us alone. We've got each other and we manage very well.' He held on to the sideboard and clumped a single step to the window. It was a beautiful summer's

356

evening and the wharf was packed with strolling people. St Ives had been well and truly discovered.

He said, 'How can you talk of dying on a day like this?'

She replied in the same sharp tone. 'Because on the day I die I'll be in no state to discuss anything!'

He tried to laugh but she would have none of it.

'I want it all done proper-like,' she insisted. 'I want the Old Wooden Cross – that was the first 'ymn your sister learned and she sat in that there window seat when she learned it. An' I want your mother dressed up in that linen thing she wore up to the Knill's monument last time. An' o' course your faither will look a real gent like 'e allus does. An Rosemary will 'ave to walk alongside young Rory Trewyn, an' look 'im in the eye. An' afterwards, when they've all gone back 'ome and she is 'ere seein' to your meals and suchlike . . . then they will 'ave another chance.'

'Neither of them want another chance, Etta. I've told Ro what happened that night at Rose Foster's, even . . . I've told her everything. And it makes no difference. And though she came down last year to see the flat and everything, Rory made no attempt . . . it's obvious he feels the same as she does.'

He had not told Etta that Jan had been 'in love' with Rory. Indeed he knew little about homosexuality himself and could not imagine the awfulness of Rory's experience. But Etta still had her sixth sense and shook her head, dismissing all arguments.

'Rubbish. She will have to make the first move and if she cain't do it, then you must do it for her.' She puffed her lips out in a sigh. 'That Scaife girl would know what I mean without all this argy-ing. She knew you was for 'er long before you did. An' Rosemary knew that Rory Trewyn b'longed to her right from the start.' Suddenly she looked bone-tired. 'I cain't talk about it no more, Mark. But don't let any more time go by . . . 'Tisn't fair to Neville nor to Jan. They might be dead,

357

but they're still important. I cain't do no more, boy.'

Mark came to her clumsily and put his hand on her shoulder. She turned into him with a sigh.

'Eh, boy. You've got an 'ansome pair of arms. Arms is important . . . to 'old folks up.'

She permitted him to hold her for just a moment, then she raised her head.

'We got it all straight then. We got it all straight . . .' She levered herself to her feet. 'I'm going to bed. 'Tis early, but I'm tired.' She went to the door and paused there, hanging on to the jamb. 'I was angry with Philip, my boy. But if 'e 'adn't let your mam 'ave 'er 'ead, you wouldn't be 'ere now. You make folks 'appy, my boy. That's what you do. You make folks 'appy.' And she left him sitting under the chandelier with tears on his face.

He stayed where he was all night in case she called him. In the small hours he went as quietly as he could into the kitchen where she slept on the sofa now that the stairs were too difficult for her. She was breathing gently, her withered cheek pillowed on her hand, her hair wispily about her face. He went back to the parlour and lay down on the window seat where he had slept when he was a summer visitor. He did not unstrap his legs, but she did not call. At six thirty when the road sweeper came round the court, he went in again to boil a kettle for tea. He knew instantly that she was dead; her body was in exactly the same position, but it was no longer inhabited. He sat by it, weeping like a child because she was the last of that old century's generation: a different breed, hard and honed, yet fey and magical too. And now that it was too late, he wanted to ask her questions. What had she meant about Philip letting his mother 'have her head'? And how had Etta borne Philip's celibacy all those years? And what had she done to change the climate of opinion in St Ives so dramatically last year? And why had she adopted them and loved them all so fiercely?

The last question was the only one that had mattered now,

and he knew the answer to that already though he could not put it into words, and could only weep anew with gratitude for the strange, illogical bonds which linked them all like one of Philip's fishing nets.

He knew he should go for the doctor, but first he went about making tea as he always did these days; very strong and very sweet, just as she liked it. He poured two cups and drank them both. By then it was nearly eight o'clock and the town was waking up. He poured water into a bowl and shaved sketchily. And he found he was humming some song. In was incredible. He felt his awful grief subsiding physically. He stopped shaking; a new strength surged through his shoulders and arms. He smiled down at Etta's body and finished the song. It was something his mother had sung to him when he was small and could not sleep: a Bing Crosby number. He knew only a few words: '. . . meets the gold of the day . . . someone waits for me . . .' And he remembered the single word Etta had demanded for the headstone in the cemetery. 'Reunited.'

They all came just as Etta had wished. Zannah and Rosemary stayed with Rose Foster in Bunkers Hill, and Clem and Madge went to Mennion House. Small, black-edged cards were displayed in shop windows all over the town announcing the time of the service, and the florists were busy with wreaths and sprays of the old-fashioned flowers Etta had asked for: clarkia and marigold, zinnia and wild tulip; bedded in cushions of samphire and sea-pinks.

The chapel where she had sat for Bright Hour was as full as it had been for Philip; Clem, Rory, Matthew Trewyn and Mark were her pall-bearers. It was difficult for Mark, he was so much shorter than the others, but Mr Trevorrow, who was an expert in funerals, solved the problem with a special padded shoulder-rest his grandfather had used.

Mrs Trevorrow said, 'We use it for a footstool now, but that is what it was. A pall-rest. Specially made for Mr Trevorrow's grandfather, who happened to be of shorter stature than many others. It can lengthen or shorten with this screw, and the velvet means it won't slip off the shoulder, or mark the suit.'

Madge, remembering that awful winter's day when the Trevorrows had snubbed her so thoroughly, looked anxiously at her son. But he was used to his acceptance now and nodded gratefully.

'Just right . . .' He put it on his shoulder and waited while Mrs Trevorrow buckled the strap. 'It's very comfortable. I'm sure Etta would be tickled pink.'

She wasn't affronted. 'You've been a good boy . . . a good boy,' she said sentimentally. Then suddenly turned to Madge and Clem. 'And you have done more than most families . . . much more. We're glad. Glad you've come.'

Rosemary watched the four men place the coffin carefully on to the rests and take their place in the front pews. She had been to St Ives twice since Mark moved down here, but this third time she felt different. Mark had said urgently, 'You mustn't expect miracles, Sis. Just keep coming each year like you used to, and wait for it to happen.' And she had done that and felt as if she were visiting a ghost town whose ghosts were strangely elusive. The brash, tanned faces of the summer visitors came between her and the people she expected to see. Philip and Marie, poor old Mr McGovern and Grandma Briscoe, and . . . Jan.

She sat like an invalid day after day, looking at the sea, listening to the summer noises all around her and remembering the thin, albino-pale girl who had tried so hard to force events into her own pattern; and failed. Where did accidents stop being accidents and become the logical sequence of cause and effect? What if the accident of her own birth had never happened . . . would Jan be alive now and would Mark have flesh-and-blood legs? But that was a road her mind had travelled often and she knew only too well it was a dead end walked by everyone with 'paranoid

360

tendencies'. The accident of her birth had happened, just as had the accident of Mark's fall and the accident of Jan's death. She tried instead to think of her Uncle Neville and his summer love affair with Rose Foster. And that brought her back to Rory. And why he had made no attempt to see her during either of her visits.

Now, this third time, this third visit, when she should be unhappy because of Etta's death, she felt . . . different. For one thing the sight of Rory in his black suit came as a shock. He was changed almost beyond recognition, his shoulders bowed, his hair grey, his black eyes sunk into a weatherbeaten face. She knew he had converted Etta's fish cellar into a flat for Mark without any help. He had used a pickaxe to hew out the rock and had mixed concrete and mortar by hand. He had used the forge at St Erth and made wrought-iron gates to hang in the wall, giving the flat privacy without taking away the view. He had turned plumber and installed a sink and a shower. The lighting was subtle, directed on the granite walls with their pictures.

She knew too that he had taken his father in hand and rescued the auctioneering business from bankruptcy; that he had installed a new engine in the *Forty-niner*; that he and Mark went fishing most weekends.

When Mark told her these things, it had sounded typical of Rory. Energetic, ebullient even. He had laid his ghosts to rest by the simple expedient of filling every hour of every day with activity. With achievement. She had imagined him laying his head on the pillow each night, wearily but with satisfaction. He had the family Jan had wanted; he could find it in his heart to be magnanimous – generous – to his adoptive father. He had returned to his homeland and found some sort of contentment.

She realised, as she looked at him kneeling in prayer, that she had painted the wrong picture from Mark's words. If Mark had painted Rory, she would have understood. He had always been driven; as a boy he had been driven outwards, to seek the intangible in the big world outside

361

this small town by the sea. Then he had been driven to escape his own guilt and horror at Jan's death. Now he was still driven. In the context of his true parentage – the wild black haired Rose of Zennor, and the equally wild middle-class boy who had wanted adventure – he was driving himself back into his very roots. Working – digging himself into the land almost physically – still seeking the intangible.

He sat just in front of her and next to Mark, getting off his knees with a small involuntary grunt. His body and head were the same size as Mark's so that now they were on a level, and they turned and glanced at each other as the minister's voice announced the first hymn. It was hard to see that they were cousins; Rosemary was often surprised that Mark took after neither of the parents, but in that glance there was a deep kinship. As she turned to the page in the hymn book, she thought: that is one thing Rory has done, he has established his relationship with Mark: I must tell him that. Then she remembered; there was no relationship between herself and Rory so she could not tell him anything.

Madge too watched the quick exchange between Mark and Rory, and tried to remember Neville on that last visit to St Ives when he must have seen Rory for the first and last time. Poor Neville; immature in the worst possible way, with none of youth's strengths and all its weaknesses. How good Rose Care would have been for him. If he'd stayed with her how she would have bullied and protected him, loved him and laughed at him. Yet from what Mark had told them it had been Rose who had sent Neville away. Perhaps she had known him better than any of them.

They stood up to sing the first hymn, 'Abide with me', and there was a rustle as someone crept down the side aisle and moved into the empty seat by Rory. It was Rose. Madge smiled. Rose, who was so cynical about Cornish funerals and had not gone to Philip's, though she knew that he had

362

valued her more than most. She wore a black blouse and skirt that made her look like a barmaid; luckily she was hatless and her abundant hair, darker than Rory's, was wound around her head like a crown. As Madge looked and smiled, Rory reached out, took his mother's hand and tucked it into his arm, then held his hymn book for her to see. Madge's eyes flicked to her own book as if they were intruding on a personal moment. She tried to sing and could not. Beside her Clem's deep voice reverberated strongly. 'Help of the helpless . . .' She bent her head lower still. Etta and Clem had been as close as she and Philip. Etta had known about Mark; she was almost certain that Clem knew too. Now Etta was gone and Mark was as independent as most people. There was still Ro, of course. But if Ro eventually left home, what was there to keep Clem there any longer?

Susannah Scaife saw the arrival of Mrs Foster and Rory's welcoming gesture, and frowned over the tiny print in her hymnal with a sudden impatience. She was so full of love and curiosity and eagerness that she sometimes wondered why she did not physically burst. Just the thought wiped away the frown and made her smile. She had visions of Mark turning round and mopping at her melting body apologetically: 'I always knew she'd burst one day.'

Mark had told Zannah only half of Rory's tale, and she simply could not understand what was keeping him from the girl he so obviously loved. Nothing on earth would keep her and Mark apart: not Aunt Di, not Mark's tin legs, not his fear that he was impotent, not even Etta Nolla with her lipless mouth and constant menacing presence every time Zannah had turned up for a weekend. Zannah glanced at the coffin and gave a little nodding salute. Last Easter when Zannah had spent three weeks at the cottage, the old girl had personally escorted her to her room each evening at nine thirty sharp. Mark had accepted the situation with an amused shrug, and Etta had ignored Zannah's furious protests and literally herded her up the stairs and put out her light too, with the terse comment, 'Philip couldn't afford this new-fangled 'lectricity, and neither can young Mark, so don't put it on again, my girl.'

Zannah had told Mark exactly what she thought about interfering, parsimonious, frigid old biddies; but she hadn't told Etta. And, surprisingly, Mark had said, 'Etta isn't frigid, my love. Etta is as full of love as you are!' She had known in her bones that he was right and she had kissed him sulkily and replied, 'Well . . . yes . . . but if it hadn't been for last year in London, I might well think you *are* impotent!' He hadn't even been put down by that, but his next kiss had been very satisfying and after it he had sighed deeply and said, 'If it weren't for you, Zannah Scaife, I would be.' And, as usual, that had made her cry.

So now she wanted them all to be happy and it was simply maddening that they weren't. She supposed that Clem and Madge Briscoe were okay; though of course they weren't like her parents must have been. But then . . . her parents must have been very special. She lowered her head quickly as she always did when she thought of her father and babbled quickly inside her head: 'Just let them be happy now . . . just let them . . .' Then she blinked hard and looked at her book again. 'Through cloud and sunshine . . .' She breathed deeply and began to sing. That's what it was all about, surely? There had to be cloud as well as sunshine, and though she hadn't known Jan Grodno, she was sure he would want Rory and Rosemary to be together. She stiffened her spine. She'd have to work on it.

Like her mother, Rosemary could not find the voice to sing; she mouthed the words but when she saw Rory take Rose Foster's hand even that automatic lip service trembled to a stop. No wonder Jan had loved Rory more than anyone; no wonder he had leaned back into eternity that

day when Rory had shown him that his love had been
given to a woman. Perhaps he had known – when Rory's
face had appeared at Rosemary's shoulder – that they
had consummated that love only an hour before. It must
have been so obvious, especially to someone as sentient
as Jan was then.

The hymn came to an end and they sat down for the
address. Rosemary, unused to chapel funerals, was as
surprised as her mother had been last year, at the suddenly
popular image of Etta as a sister in God. She heard of
her unflagging work for Christ and realised that it added
up to Etta's regular attendance at Bright Hour. And the
diligent service in God's holy name . . . did that mean
waiting each day for Philip to come home with his catch,
helping him to mend his nets, shaking rugs and sweeping
the court?

The final hymn was announced. She recognised, with a
spasm of her heart, that it was Etta's favourite, 'The
Old Wooden Cross'. Mark turned and looked at her over
his shoulder and gave her a funny lop-sided smile. He
whispered, 'She wanted it for you. It was the first hymn
you learned.'

They stood up. It all came back to her; the window
seat and the piece of driftwood so light and crumbly
between her fingers. The minister like a black crow sitting
at the table with his bible before him. A pot of jam going
the rounds. Her mother, flushed and pretty. Etta . . .
Philip . . . and a man with rusty-red hair in a camouflaged
uniform.

Yes. Probably all Etta's 'diligent service' had been in
God's name. Even to trying to stop her mother going
swimming with Uncle Ned. Rosemary swallowed another
treacherous lump and managed to smile back at Mark who
also had red hair. And quite suddenly it was all right;
quite suddenly God and Uncle Ned, and even Uncle Neville,
seemed to take the burden of her 'accidents' and make them
theirs.

She straightened her shoulders until she was almost

the same height as Zannah Scaife, and she began to sing.
As her voice climbed the crescendo of notes, clearly and
steadily, Rory heard and turned to look at her.

It was a week later and Madge and Clem were returning
to Bristol the next day. They had gone for a walk along
the Zennor footpath at Mark's request. He wanted to
talk to Rosemary.

They sat on the harbour and watched the gulls screaming over some discarded chips. The visitors, anxious
to feed them at first, were half frightened by their frantic
squawking and tearing of the paper, and backed away
in confusion. People laughed and tried to scare the gulls
off with flapping newspapers; the old-timers scowled
and said you should never feed gulls and what damage
they were doing to the marvellous old roofing tiles of
the town.

Rosemary said, 'It's changing. It's not the place we used
to know.'

Mark looked at her, his face set in stubborn lines.

'It is. Underneath . . . there's a kernel . . . Ro, please
listen. You've got to stay. I can't manage on my own –
you've just got to!'

'Of course you can manage on your own – don't give
me that! You've managed for yourself *and* Etta since
you came down to live. You've done absolute marvels and
we're all proud of you, so stop looking like an unmilked
cow!'

He was forced to laugh, but he noted, not for the first
time, that Ro was different. Not so buttoned up.

He played his trump card. 'Etta wanted you to stay and
live upstairs. The night she died she sat me down in the
parlour and told me exactly what she wanted done. And
she wanted you to—'

'You're making that up, Mark!'

'I wouldn't make up anything about Etta. She'd come
back and put a hex on me or something!'

'Yes. She might at that.' Rosemary laughed, then

366

sobered. 'How can I give up everything just like that? I've got a job. And there's Mum and Dad. And anyway . . . St Ives. You know how I feel, Mark. I should hate it. I'm only a summer person.'

He held up one hand with spread fingers and ticked off each of her objections.

'You can get a job down here – there's a special school at Helston. They'd jump at you. And Mum and Dad might be glad to be on their own after all these years. It's obvious that was one of the things Philip had in mind when he left me the cottage. As for you being a summer person – what was I? We belong here, Ro. I don't know why, but we're more than summer people. Maybe Grampa and Grandma Bridges put down roots and we grew from them! Everyone knows it. Oh they were a bit funny at first, but it didn't last long. We're wanted down here, Ro. Dammit – we're needed!'

There was a long pause. Some children crawled from beneath an upturned boat and ran yelling down to the sea. Rosemary could remember doing that.

She said, 'You haven't mentioned Rory.'

'Neither have you.'

'I don't love him any more.'

'Oh. I see.'

'Does he . . . I mean, you see quite a lot of him . . . does he mention me?'

'No.'

'Well. That's all right then. I suppose.'

'Then you'll come?'

'No. I didn't mean that. Oh *Mark*—' she picked up a handful of sand and squeezed it hard. 'Can't you see? If he'd go away again it would be all right – *might* be all right. But if he stays . . . we're cousins. How can I avoid him?'

'You can't. But if he doesn't mean anything special to you now, couldn't you get to know him all over again? As a cousin? He – he's a good person.'

'No. I don't think I could.'

'Then I'll ask him to go away. He'd understand. And he'd go.'

'*No!*' She threw away the sand as if it had stung her palm.

Mark said quietly. 'Quite. For you, St Ives means Rory. If he isn't here then you're waiting for him to come back. If you knew he was never coming back—'

'Mark. Shut up. Please.'

'Okay. I only know because of Zannah. I think I know everything I know because of Zannah.' He laughed. 'But if she went, then I'd still have this place. Where she had been. Where her parents had been.' He took a quick breath. 'Did you know that Mum knew Barbara Scaife? She met her once apparently.'

'No.' She touched Mark's arm. 'Zannah is quite a character, brud. A bit . . . weird at times. And you're both so young.'

'Yes. It's good, isn't it? We don't know about time. It's as well to start as soon as possible.' He looked at her directly. She noticed how very brown and round his eyes were. She felt her own filling with tears.

'Oh Mark,' she said helplessly.

'Yes. We're lucky, aren't we?'

He looked past her and saw Zannah coming across the beach. She wore her aluminium 'crown', this time woven with the reddish flowers she had worn around her neck two years before. She looked very zany and he could have wished, for Ro's sake, that she had conformed for once.

'Hi!'

She was carrying a large flat pebble, white and shot with crystal. She held it towards Ro.

'This is what I meant about the stones. You need to see what is inside them. That is why Hepworth makes those holes in her sculptures – so that you get the inside as well as the outside. It's terribly important.'

Rosemary took the pebble and stared at it as if the answer to everything might be there.

Zannah went on enthusiastically, 'We just don't know how far the crystal goes. Or where it came from. I mean it was part of the stone and it changed. But it's still part of the stone. It's obviously different, yet it's essential – I mean the stone would be nothing without it.'

Ro said, 'Er . . . quite. You mean, dull and uninteresting?'

'No. Just empty. They couldn't exist without each other.' She took the stone back, realising Rosemary did not comprehend. Then she said in the same voice, 'Rory Trewyn is down on the beach. He said he'd probably clear off quite soon.'

'Clear off?'

'Yes. He seems to think he's a bit . . . superfluous. You know, being a bastard cousin.'

'Zannah!'

She ignored Rosemary's reprimand and went on musingly, 'He's looking for something in the rocks. Where I found my pebble. Some special kind of seaweed. Very wide and flat with frilly edges. He says he's looked for it before and never found it.'

Rosemary glanced at Mark and said, 'Oh.'

And Mark said, 'It's for my collection, I expect. He doesn't know what I mean actually. You remember, Sis. The stuff Fizzy used for her handbag.' He grinned at Zannah. 'Fizzy was my physiotherapist and she had this crocodile handbag . . .' He reached over and put a hand on Rosemary's shoulder. 'Why don't you go and help him?'

Rosemary looked from her brother and back to Zannah. Her face was wide open and she felt an engulfing sense of déjà vu.

She said, 'D'you think I should?'

'Yes. He must feel a bit of an outsider after all. And he shouldn't. You could tell him that for a start. Dammitall, Ro, you could try being *friends*!'

She said, 'Yes.' Though she knew that would be difficult.

Zannah said, 'Look. He doesn't like himself. And you're not keen on Rosemary Briscoe. Couldn't you help each other in that way?'

369

Rosemary could take advice from her brother but not from this strange creature with a wheel-rim on her head. She lifted one shoulder irritably and moved off. She went in the general direction of Porthmeor; she could change her mind at any time on the way.

Madge and Clem rested on a rock above the first of the Five Points. Clem had started off wearing a jersey over his shirt. He was now carrying it carelessly by the knotted sleeves. It was very hot.

Madge said, 'If you screw up your eyes, you can practically see each atom of the air. They kind of dance.'

He narrowed his eyes obediently and sure enough the sunshine swirled before them.

He said, 'Interesting that you knew Zannah's parents. You met them during the war, I suppose?'

'Yes. Just once.'

He felt her stillness through their joined shoulders.

'Were they as crazy as she is?' he asked.

She did not laugh. 'She's not crazy. They weren't, either.'

'I was joking. She's the best thing that could happen to Mark. I just hope . . . I mean she's hell-bent on exploring every experience she can. What if something – someone – else crops up that she thinks is more interesting than Mark?'

'She'll explore it in her work.' She sighed. 'Artists are so *lucky*. They can experience everything that way. Like actors.' She straightened. 'In a play,' she added.

'Yes. I understand that.' She moved away and he pushed himself off the rock and joined her. 'So you think Mark and Zannah will be all right?'

'I don't know.' Her head was down, studying the springy turf at her feet. 'I pray about it,' she said in a low voice.

'Yes,' he said again, tacitly acknowledging that he did the same. 'Meanwhile . . . we don't have to feel that frightful pity for Mark any more, do we?' She stumbled

370

and he put a hand under her elbow and held her up. 'Sometimes – at night when you were asleep – you used to call his name. You haven't done that since . . . for some time.'

She leaned on him. 'That's . . . good, isn't it?' He could hear the sense of loss in her voice. She said, 'And you? You said *we* don't have to feel pity. I didn't know – you've never said—'

'But you *must* have known. That is how I understood you. The way you were so often sorry for people – I didn't like that at first. Then – because of Mark – I understood.'

'Oh.' She gave a small laugh that sounded like a sob. 'He didn't like it either, did he? Philip saw that. Philip gave him his freedom, I suppose.'

'It's what we all wanted for Mark. His independence. And now we're missing him.' He squeezed her arm. 'Darling, it's only natural.'

'Yes. Of course.' They came to the narrow gully leading to Old Man's Head and Madge went in front. She looked up at the massive monolith. 'And we've still got Ro,' she said.

He did not reply. They did not pause by the rock; in fact Madge quickened her pace until she was almost jogging. Clem shouldered his jersey and lengthened his stride. When they were above the line of beach tents they both slowed automatically. Far below them on the wet sand in the rocks, Rory and Rosemary were moving carefully as if looking for something.

Madge breathed, 'My God. That's . . . isn't it?'

'Yes.' Clem started to fumble with his binocular case, then stopped. 'She's been different this time. Stronger. And happier. She and Mark have gone into one of their old slanging matches. Like they used to.'

Madge said, 'I feel so sorry for Rory—' she stopped herself, glanced at Clem and started to laugh. 'Well, I do! Everything was against him from the start. I sometimes think that if Neville had had more time – to get all that

371

discontent out of his system – he might have turned out like Rory. Putting everything into every little thing he does . . . you know.'

'There's a lot of Neville in him.' Clem looked as the two tiny figures on the beach moved towards the water. 'He's so damned polite, calling me sir all the time.' He turned and smiled wryly at Madge. 'I've asked him to call me Tagger.'

'Oh Clem. You always wanted to keep Neville alive somehow. But you didn't dream that it would be like this.'

'No.'

They went on past the putting green and into the town. The summer crowds moved slowly and aimlessly around beaches and shops and icecream parlours, like the moving atoms of air on the cliff top. Still and silent amidst the throng, Zannah and Mark sat on the sand waiting for Jem to arrive with the day's mackerel. Zannah was dressed in her hippie gear, her long hair hanging either side of her face like curtains. Mark hailed them enthusiastically and they paused for a moment on their way to the car park.

'Mum! Dad! I think . . . would you mind awfully if Ro stayed? I think she might. I've put it to her that I can't cope alone.'

'You've got me,' Zannah put in.

'That's why I need Ro. As chaperone.' He hugged her. 'Anyway you're back to art school in September.'

'Ro has school then too,' Madge said quickly.

'She'd give that up.' He shielded his eyes from the sun and looked up at his mother. 'Don't look like that, Mum. She's got to face this place some time. It's where it all happened for her.'

'I don't think—'

Clem interrupted. 'I do. It's been a long time. Quite long enough. I'm for it. If you can persuade her, old man.' He looked at Zannah. 'Don't feel you're not appreciated, young lady. But you're going to have to put up with my son for a long time. Have a break while you can.'

Unexpectedly Zannah turned pink. It was the first time the family had publicly acknowledged that she and Mark were a bona fide couple. She smiled mistily.

Clem said, 'Those flowers in your hair . . . wild marjoram, aren't they?'

'I don't know. I just picked them.' She pulled a blossom from her crown and handed it to him. 'They're growing all over the place behind the seamen's mission.' She indicated Bamaluz Point. 'They're just weeds.'

Clem took the purplish flower carefully.

'We'll have to get back to Mennion House. Packing and so forth.' He piloted Madge towards the steps. 'See you this evening for dinner at the Clipper.' He almost carried her up the steps to the wharf. 'We could have rowed across in the dinghy if we hadn't brought the car,' he went on conversationally. 'It would have been much pleasanter than driving through this traffic.'

She said nothing until they reached the car park. Then she said quietly, 'You've always known, haven't you?'

He unlocked the passenger door and she slid into the hot, leather-smelling interior. He walked round the car and got in beside her, winding down the window after closing his door.

'The first time we brought Mark down. I knew then.' His voice was low. 'That was why . . . when I didn't respond immediately to your warning cry about him . . . along the Carbis Bay footpath . . . that was why I felt responsible. It could have been a subconscious wish to annihilate . . . what had happened.'

They sat side by side, not touching, staring through the smeared windscreen at the rank of parked cars opposite.

She said at last, 'But the marjoram. How did you know about the marjoram?'

'Ro. She told me that on the afternoon of that damned children's party, Uncle Ned—' he drew in his breath as he spoke her childish words '—took you to look for marjoram plants. That was when I knew. For certain.' His

373

eye caught the glint of the wing mirror and he saw that she was reflected in it. Tears were rolling down her face. He looked away.

She said, 'He died. At Arnhem.'

'I know that too.' He told her about overhearing the conversation between herself and Gerald Scaife. 'So I met Zannah's father for a moment. Just a moment.' He tried to make his tone lighter.

She said, 'Oh God . . . oh God . . .'

He said nothing, trying to imagine how it had been for her all these years. She had seemed happy, yet underneath, all the time, had been this terrible grief.

She cleared her throat and said strongly, 'And now Mark has gone. And it looks as if Ro is going too. So . . . it's all right, Clem. You're free.'

He did not understand. 'Free?'

'You had to stay. I realise that. But there's no need any longer. You've done your duty – more than—'

'Did you think I stayed from a sense of *duty*?' He was outraged.

'Oh I know . . . we've been close. Good friends. And after . . . after . . . Ned . . . there was more. But you couldn't have liked me very much, surely. There must have been times when you hated me. I understand that.'

He said levelly, 'I have loved you since you were twelve years old, Madge. There was a moment of madness in Canada which I was selfish enough to . . . it was the war. When Mark fell on to that railway line, I knew I loved him. And that meant I loved you.' He put his hands on the steering wheel and gripped hard. 'Has it been pretence with you all these years? Is that what you're telling me?'

'No. Oh God. No. I was so mixed-up. When Father and Mother . . . Father almost died one night making love to her. I thought I would be safe married to you. Then I realised there was something wrong with me. And then . . . Clem, is it really all right? It is, isn't it? I mean neither of us could have put on an act all these years?

374

Clem—' She turned on the seat and took his hands forcibly from the wheel. 'Darling, I love you. And you love me. It's so – simple!'

He too twisted sideways and managed to take her in his arms. They held each other gently with a kind of tender compassion. And then they kissed and held again.

He said into her ear, 'Do you want to go up to Bamaluz and pick some marjoram? I don't mind. Really.'

She pecked his check with infinite gratitude.

'No. That's over now, Clem. The marjoram is for Zannah and Mark. Not for me.'

A red-faced man tapped on the glass. 'You going, mate? Only I bin waiting for your parking space for ten minutes now!'

Madge sat up quickly and started to laugh. And Clem switched on the ignition. They moved forward slowly and the engine stalled. They could not stop laughing.

Rosemary said, 'We looked for this stuff before. D'you remember?'

Rory did not look up. He had rolled his old flannels to his knees and waded through the pools as easily as he'd ever done. But his legs and feet marked him as an older man more than any other feature; his calf muscles were knotted and his toes as gnarled as Philip Nolla's hands had been. Rosemary felt protective and it was a feeling she hadn't experienced for Rory before.

'He said, 'Of course I remember. I remember . . . everything.'

'You came to help me that day. It was your way of patching up our differences.'

He grunted a laugh. 'Differences. That sounds very civilised, Ro. I don't think you and I have differences. We have quarrels. Furious quarrels.'

'But we always made them up.'

He straightened slowly, put his hand in the small of his back, and stared at the horizon.

'Is that what you've come to do today? Make up a quarrel?

But we didn't have a quarrel, Ro, did we? We were wrenched apart. There was no quarrel.'

'Our quarrels were always about Jan. This . . . this separation . . . was about Jan too.'

He turned and studied her. She knew she must look a mess. There hadn't been time to get a tan and she was very pale.

He said, 'Did Mark tell you why Jan killed himself?'

She flinched, closed her eyes, then said, 'Yes.'

'Were you disgusted?'

She whispered, 'How could I be disgusted? I love you too.'

He groaned and she opened her eyes to see him bent as if in pain. She made to clamber towards him and he held up a restraining hand.

'I didn't mean . . . I meant were you disgusted by my behaviour? My treatment . . . of you?'

She stood very still, thinking of all that pain and resentment. And she remembered the moment in the chapel when some of Etta's wisdom had lightened her mind.

'Rory. We were all . . . wounded. Damaged. But it has to end somewhere. Let it end. Now. Please.'

There was another silence and she knew that if he continued with the self-recriminations she would have to go away from him. But after a while he began to move again, squelching over a bed of green weed to a tangle of brown kelp. She did not go with him; she waited.

He bent and pushed at the heavy seaweed; it was a miniature jungle, weighed down with sea water. He felt in the pocket of his trousers and brought out a penknife. He hacked for some time, then he stood up and exhibited a flat piece of weed, the size of Mrs Trevorrow's fox fur, frilled at the edges.

'Is this it?'

'Yes. You've found it at last.'

'Like you found that piece of nameboard from the old *Lancaster*.' He smiled at her. 'Something for my cousin.'

'I'm your cousin too, Rory.'

'Yes. And so much more.'

'Zannah Scaife said that you were intending to leave Cornwall again.'

'I thought it would make it easier for you to stay with Mark if I'm not around.'

She said steadily, 'No. Not any more. In fact it would make it much harder for me if you left.'

He smiled again. 'I don't think I could leave anyway. You said just now that you love me. You spoke in the present tense. I won't try to tell you how sorry I am for . . . things. I'll just say – I love you too, cousin Rosemary. Could we get married, d'you think?'

At last she smiled back at him, then held out her hand. He came to her and took it. Then he waved the enormous piece of seaweed in the air like a banner. And they began to walk towards the sea.

THE END